THE FORBIDDEN TEMPLE

A SEAN WYATT ADVENTURE

ERNEST DEMPSEY

JOIN THE ADVENTURE

Visit ernestdempsey.net to get a free copy of the not-sold-in-stores short story, RED GOLD.

You'll also get access to exclusive content not available anywhere else.

PROLOGUE

KERALA, INDIA - 1908

D r. John Portman couldn't believe his eyes.

It wasn't the first time he'd stood at the gates of the Sree Padmanabhaswamy Temple in Kerala, but the sight of the shimmering golden structure in the waning light of the sun was something that would never get old. The precious metal coating the building seemed to offer a brighter illumination than even the fiery center of the solar system. The golden reliefs of Hindu deities and other important figures sprang to life, covering nearly every square inch of the upper exterior.

Outside the entrance, however, was a stark contrast. Ordinary city streetlights hung over cracked, hard-packed dirt sidewalks. The clay-tiled roofs looming over buildings next to the temple seemed out of place, as did their crumbling and haphazardly painted walls. The entryway into the temple, too, was nothing eye-catching. Ordinary white walls surrounded the darkened archway into the ancient building. The bright white paint seemed a bizarre choice next to the center, where the arched door led beneath a miniaturized golden mountain.

He didn't care about the mismatched exterior decor of the

entrance. Getting in was the point, not standing around outside in the Indian heat, wondering about architectural and design aesthetics.

Portman was one of the foremost experts on ancient Indian mythology and history. His understanding of Indian culture and the old Vedic texts was so vast that he'd been offered multiple jobs to teach at universities and museums in Mumbai and across the region.

John had, of course, turned them down. He much preferred the lifestyle he'd built in Cambridge and had no intentions of moving to a new home. Even when he remotely considered the notion, the sweltering heat here beat the idea back into the shadows.

As an unnecessary reminder, a bead of sweat rolled down his right temple, clung to his jaw for a second, and then dropped to the dry cobblestones at his feet. He unconsciously reached for the white handkerchief in his breast pocket and dabbed at his forehead.

"What is the delay?" he asked the man to his right.

Anik Laghari shrugged. "Security at this site is very tight, sir." Anik was one of John's liaisons on this trip to India—on most of his trips to India. He'd been an extremely useful resource, and John frequently leaned on the younger man for assistance in cultural matters, such as the proper way to order tea. John tried to fit in as best he could wherever he went. Anik had made that simple enough for him. It helped that the younger assistant spoke proper English, even carrying the accent without flaw.

That was more than he could say for the other man standing on his opposite side. Reyansh Anand was also a good assistant—helpful and eager to get things done. He was, however, less the academic and more of a brute-force type. The tall Indian hovered over the shorter Dr. Portman, standing five inches over six feet tall. His bronze, muscle-strewn arms glistened with sweat in the afternoon heat. Reyansh listened to the conversation with his jaw set firm as he stared ahead at the gate.

Something about his gaze might have been unsettling to anyone who didn't know the man, but John and Anik simply assumed it was grumpy Reyansh.

"They are clearing us to go in, sir," Anik answered the professor's next question.

"I'm aware that's what they're doing, Anik. I just don't understand what's taking so long."

"Patience, my good friend." Anik offered a sympathetic smile and patted the older man on the shoulder. It was a gentle gesture, but it still shook the wire-framed glasses on John's nose. "This is an extremely sacred place to us. Even for a world-renowned researcher and historian such as yourself, all protocols must be followed."

John reached up and pressed the glasses back up toward his forehead. "Indeed," he said, though his voice didn't hold an ounce of sincerity or understanding. It wasn't that he believed himself better than most; he simply wanted out of the oppressive heat.

Fortunately, the professor was only required to wait another minute before one of the security guards returned from a building off to the right. John wondered what could have possibly needed to be settled in the little shack to approve his visit when all the necessary channels had already been cleared. He only spent a moment on that thought, knowing it was fruitless and would only exasperate him.

The guard handed John his papers and gave a nod. "Follow me, sir," the security guard ordered.

Finally.

John picked up a small bag lying at his feet. His two colleagues hefted similar bags in each hand and started forward through the entrance.

It wasn't the first time John Portman had entered the ancient temple. He knew what awaited beyond the gates. It was why he was here: to analyze the mysterious vaults within and, perhaps, try to open them.

The temple was a structure dedicated to the worship of Lord Vishnu, one of more than a hundred centers of worship in the area that gave patronage to that particular deity. It had been built in the medieval era of the former Tamil Empire, construction beginning in the early seventh century. The temple was a tremendous source of pride for the people of this region, and the idea that an outsider from

England would be given permission to examine anything within smacked some of the locals with stinging suspicion.

John, of course, didn't care about that. He had one thing in mind: to get into one of those vaults and find out what awaited beyond the mysterious doors.

The Indian government hadn't granted him permission to open the vaults. That was something John figured would require much deliberation, committee approval, and votes from politicians. In the end, they would deny him the opportunity. However, accidents happened from time to time. Who was to say that he didn't "accidentally" open one of the vaults while conducting his research?

His mind was made up. He had to know what was beyond the vault doors. It was a secret that had been kept for hundreds of years, perhaps more. While his tiny fleck of an ego didn't care about fame and accolades, there was something deeply appealing about becoming the first to open the forbidden vault.

The security guard led them around a turn and down a long open-air corridor. White pillars lined the walkway, spaced only a few feet apart atop a reddish-brown wall that came up to John's midsection. Golden beasts perched on top of the columns faced inward, silently roaring at their mirror images on the opposing side. Above them, the ceiling curled into a row of royal-blue tiles that stretched from one end of the passage to the other. In the center of the blue line, circular mosaics filled the space with a splash of color, one after another, all the way to the far end of the corridor.

John gazed up at the spectacular artistry as they walked down the path. He nearly stumbled into the guard at one point and had to brace himself on Anik's shoulder so that he didn't startle the armed man.

The guard didn't notice the moment of clumsiness and abruptly turned into another passage that cut into the center of the temple. He pushed through a heavy door and stepped into the next room.

The guests followed as a gust of cool, musty air wafted over them. The interior chamber of the temple was at least ten degrees cooler than outside, a welcome climate change to each man.

John stuffed the handkerchief into his breast pocket again, realizing he'd been holding it this entire time and wouldn't be needing it until he left the site.

The guard motioned with one arm extended, pointing at a stone stairway that led down into the bowels of the temple.

Torches and candles burned along the sides of the room, casting an eerie orange glow into every corner. The staircase, however, retreated from the light, bathing itself in shadows all the way to the bottom where the vault door awaited, unseen in the darkness.

Another door on the opposite side of the room led to a similar chamber, almost identical in every way to this one. John knew there were six such rooms, each containing a matching staircase to this one.

Almost identical, he thought.

Portman knew that one of the chambers was different, its vault door holding a mystery—and a threat. At least that's what he'd been told. In his previous, albeit short, visits to the temple, John hadn't been permitted to see what was being dubbed Vault B.

He'd stood before the doors of the other five vaults, at the base of the staircases, gazing at the intricately designed barricades that had kept thieves and treasure hunters at bay for thousands of years.

Each door contained multiple keyholes, all requiring a particular method of use with the matching keys so that the vaults would open properly. Rumor had it that if any of the keys were turned out of sequence, something horrific would happen to the person attempting to gain entry.

John had heard these legends and figured them to be part of an ancient oral tradition passed down from the elders of the community to frighten away those who might be tempted to purloin the vast treasures that lay just behind the vault doors.

There was, of course, no way to verify there *were* any treasures within the secret chambers. No one had dared open the vaults since they were closed and sealed during the reign of the Tamils.

Down through the ages, a single soul had kept possession of all the required keys. He was the temple's guardian, its curator, and its keeper of secrets. No temple guardian, it was believed, had ever opened any of the doors, adhering to an ancient code that was passed down from one keeper to another. The men responsible for protecting the keys and the vaults might have had suspicions as to what sat just beyond the heavy metal doors. Some might have even risked a peek sometime in the distant past, but no one would ever know it.

Even members of the government were curious as to the vaults' contents, but up to that point had never been able to clear the way to allow researchers and archaeologists to go in and explore.

John walked through the chamber and to the next doorway. He stopped and turned back to the guard, waiting for him to open the portal into the chamber of Vault B.

The security man glared, his darkly tanned face creased at the corners of his eyes, his forehead wrinkled, and his lips curled down. His head shook once at the professor's unspoken request.

"I was granted permission to analyze the doorway to Vault B," John said. "My permit says my team and I are to be allowed unrestricted access to the entire temple, save for entering the vaults themselves."

The guard swallowed hard. There was something in his eyes. It wasn't sternness or fierce determination. It was fear, the kind a person usually didn't find in a hardened military man or someone accustomed to assuming risk on a daily basis. Was it paranoia—or was that fear based on something real, something genuine that the professor had not yet seen?

Internally, he scoffed at the grown man's superstition.

John had heard the stories, the rumors, the myths. He feared no such thing. He was a man of science, logic, and reason. Superstition had no place in his line of work.

"We have been granted access to the entire temple," John repeated. "You certainly don't have to go in there, but I'd hate to walk all the way back to the front of the building and fetch the keeper."

The guard sensed the threat in the professor's voice and swallowed the lump of air in his throat. Despite the inner sanctum of the temple being several degrees cooler, large droplets of sweat trickled down the guard's cheeks. Some clustered in damp puddles in the worry lines on his forehead.

He nodded and walked across the room. This door was locked with a single key, one of ancient make and design. It looked like something from a castle in a time long forgotten. The iron skeleton key dangled from the guard's nervous fingers up to the point he shoved the thing into the keyhole and twisted his wrist.

Then the guard stepped back and gave a nod. "That chamber is forbidden," he said. "I will go no farther."

His accented English gave away his origin. He must have been a local, by John's account. The man had likely grown up in the shadows of this place and thusly heard all the stories, the legends of what possibly waited within the golden walls.

The guard should have been excited, but John understood. Superstitions, especially localized ones, held a powerful sway on the human mind.

John gave an appreciative nod and grasped the golden ring dangling just below the key. He tugged on it for a moment and then gave up, realizing the thing was stuck.

Reyansh stepped forward and barged between the professor and the door. "Allow me."

He grabbed the handle and yanked it hard. A loud squeak escaped the hinges. Metal ground on metal with a low, grating tone. Then the door was free of its captivity and swung open with a whoosh.

A new smell burst from the chamber beyond, washing over the four men as they stared into the darkness. The room reeked of decay and death, though by all measure nothing of the sort should have been there. No animals or people could access the antechamber of the mysterious Vault B. All ways in and out were sealed tight. Considering there were only two doors, one into this vault and one into the next, keeping things closed off was relatively simple.

John stood on the threshold, staring into the darkness beyond. The light from the torches and candles around him seemed to dim suddenly at the door, daring him not to enter the realm of shadows on the other side. It was almost as if the orange, flickering glow feared the darkness in the next room.

Poppycock.

John reached up to a sconce, wrapped his fingers around a torch's bronze handle, and hefted it from its seat. He felt the warmth from the flame drifting over his skin, prickling the hairs on his hand and wrist with a comforting heat.

The professor blinked rapidly as he gazed ahead into the abyss. Then he turned to his companions and nodded to two more torches. "Better take a few of those, lads."

The men did as instructed, each removing a torch from the wall and returning to the professor's side. The combined light from their flames still didn't seem to pierce the darkness beyond, but that wouldn't stop John Portman. He was here to do one thing and he had no intention of being denied.

He raised his right foot and moved it forward into the shadowy space on the other side of the door, then set it down. As he passed over the stone line separating one chamber from the next, the room suddenly burst to life from the light of his torch.

The rectangular stone chamber was much like the previous: built from smooth stone, hewn from a far away quarry. He'd wondered, in his early days of studying the location, how ancient builders had transported the materials across such vast distances. People like him had pondered the same thing about the pyramids and other mysterious structures from the ancient world.

Now, however, wasn't the time to consider such feats of engineering. He was on a mission, and John intended to see it through.

He took another step forward and gazed down into the stairwell below that led to the antechamber of Vault B. His assistants hesitated before entering the room, almost as if they too were overwhelmed by the superstition of the guard waiting back on the other side.

"Anik? Reyansh? Would you mind giving us a little more light?"

The men nodded and made their way around the room, touching their torches to others and setting the room alight in a dim orange glow. The torches in this room didn't seem to shed as much illumination as the others—or was it simply John's imagination?

He covered his mouth against the stench of rot that permeated the area. What *was* that infernal smell? Something had found a way in, whether the doors were sealed or not. Perhaps it was a dead rat or multiple rats that had snuck in one fateful day as the temple curator was doing a routine check or, perhaps, going somewhere he shouldn't have.

Whatever the case, John wasn't about to be pushed away by a bad smell. His nose, he was certain, would acclimate.

He took a step toward the stone stairs and lingered at the top step. The air was colder in here, even more so than in the previous room, and the chill seemed to be coming up from below.

That made no sense, of course. Cold air fell. Hot air rose. His imagination, it seemed, was taking hold of him.

He shook off the fruitless thoughts and stepped down onto the staircase. Reyansh and Anik followed close behind, perhaps out of fear or simply out of their sense of duty to the man they'd worked so closely with the last year.

John descended the stairs carefully, bracing his hand against the wall as he moved until he reached the bottom, a short landing where another metal door greeted them.

There was something on the door; an engraving of some kind jutted out toward them. He raised his torch and gasped, taking a brief step backward, stopped by the firm hands of Reyansh.

"My apologies, Rey," John said, stiffening his posture to feign bravery.

The big Indian said nothing.

John once more held the torch up to the door and gazed at the intricately carved head of a serpent. It looked more like a dragon's head than a snake, but he knew exactly what it was.

A cobra.

"It's a warning," Anik said. "Death waits for those who enter."

John glanced over his shoulder at the younger man, then to Reyansh, then back to the door. "Poppycock," he said. "There isn't anything on the other side of this door but another door. That's why we're here, yes?"

The men nodded, albeit reluctantly.

"Very well then, open it."

John stepped to the side and allowed Reyansh to move close to the door. The big man grabbed the latch with his hand and twisted, then pulled hard. The door grumbled in protest, but it was no match for Reyansh's power. A loud, rusty squeak echoed through the small space and up into the chamber above, sounding like a banshee giving a howling warning to intruders.

The professor covered one ear for a moment to protect against the piercing sound, and then, when the door was fully open, he removed the hand and held his torch aloft. The dancing tendrils of light lapped at the darkness beyond, giving barely a glimpse of what was on the other side of the threshold.

The smell of rot nearly overwhelmed the three men. Anik gagged for a moment, before collecting himself and shaking off the nausea.

John wouldn't be denied. He'd come this far, toiled through the necessary legal battles, and now stood on the cusp of a discovery that would put him in the history books for all time.

He wasn't there to merely analyze the doorway of Vault B. He was there to open it.

John glanced back up the stairs and confirmed their guard was still nowhere to be seen, likely waiting back in the first chamber, trembling from irrational fear.

"Quickly," the professor said. "We haven't much time."

He stepped into the room and made his way straight across the giant stone tiles to the far wall. As he neared the end of the path, his torchlight danced across something unusual, different than anything they'd seen thus far. The other two men were less daring and moved slowly, cautiously, into the chamber until they were standing just behind the professor. As their torches' light joined his, their eyes fell upon something that was as ghastly as it was beautiful.

Twin serpents twisted and rose up the sides of a golden door. Their metallic, scaly bodies wound up to their dragon-like heads, mouths open, tongues flickering at each other. Positioned against the spines of the two snakes were two large discs, also engraved into the golden door, each displaying what appeared to be a fleur-de-lys surrounded by a series of dots and triangles. Two flowers were imprinted on the door near the cobras' heads.

That wasn't the half of it.

The most fascinating and terrifying part of the doorway was the frame itself.

The gold had been fashioned to look like an overgrown forest of thick vines, snakes, and tree trunks rising up to the top where another cobra head jutted out at each corner.

And in the center, the most frightening visage of all: a massive, snarling cobra head—far larger than the others—jutted out more than a foot above the doorway, giving a final warning to any who would consider entering the forbidden chamber beyond. The serpent's eyes were blank, hollow as death itself. Sharp teeth protruded from the top and bottom of the beast's gaping mouth, surrounding large fangs. A long tongue dangled from the center of the mouth, lapping at the air in a permanently menacing gesture.

The almost whitish eyes glared at the men from the shadows of what appeared to be horns protruding from the sides of its head.

The professor steeled his resolve. He clenched his jaw and leaned closer to the ghastly portal. It was then he realized his initial mistake.

It wasn't vines and branches twisting and rising around the doorframe; it was a collection of miniature sculptures of human beings—some falling, some climbing—each fixed in a terrified pose. But what had caused them such fear?

"Fascinating," John said as he waved his torch around the intricately carved doorway. "I've never seen anything like it."

"It's a warning," Anik said. A tremor muted his tone.

"A warning?" John asked. "You're not talking about that silly legend, are you?"

Anik stared at the massive cobra in the center. His eyes glazed over, and he spoke as a man possessed. "He who opens this door will unleash the wrath of the underworld, and death will follow."

"What are you talking about?" John asked. He turned and gazed at his assistant, who seemed to be locked in a strange trance. "Snap out of it, Anik. I need your help. We must work quickly."

John set down his bag and opened it. He reached in and pulled out a strand of something that looked like putty. It was wrapped in a coil, and he immediately set about unwinding it.

Reyansh did the same, pulling out a similar strand of putty from his bag.

Anik's head flicked to the side, and he looked down at the other two. "What are you doing?"

"The plan, Anik. What's wrong with you?" John's eyes betrayed the concern in his mind. "Come on. We must work quickly. This door is sealed from the other side. There's no keyhole, no way to open it aside from using explosives."

"The guard and the curator won't be happy about this," Reyansh warned.

"They will be when they realize what riches await on the other side. Find me a government official who doesn't like money."

Reyansh shrugged. "I suppose."

Anik still wasn't helping. Instead, he was now focused on a square vent to the left of the door. He took a slow step toward the wall, and when he reached it he bent down at the waist, gazing into the hollowed-out space.

He cocked his head to the side and held out his torch to get a better view. "I...I think I see something in there."

John looked up in an instant, his attention lost on the task at hand. "What is it?" he demanded. "What do you see?"

Anik leaned closer, holding his torch to the hole, almost inserting it into the dark cavity.

"I can't tell. I'm not certain, but it looks almost like something is moving...."

Something shot out from the square hole.

Anik howled in terror, clutching his face as John jumped back. Anik faced the wall for a moment, blocking John's view of whatever had struck his assistant. Then the younger man spun around, still kicking and flailing.

It was then that John saw what had emerged from the hole.

A cobra was latched onto Anik's face; its fangs plunged deep into the young man's flesh. His cheek was already swelling, nearly closing an eye shut.

Reyansh leaped into action, dropping the explosive putty on the ground to help his friend.

Anik lashed out and dropped to his knees, the venom already coursing through his body, wracking his nerves with agonizing pain.

"*Stay still!*" Reyansh shouted, even as Portman backed away.

Anik writhed and grappled at the serpent but couldn't get the animal to unleash its toothy grip.

Reyansh snatched at the tail and wrapped his fingers around it. Then he lifted and snapped it down. The beast's body whipped up and then loosened its fanged bite on its victim, dropping to the ground. It slithered back to the wall and coiled up, raising its head to prepare another attack.

Anik grabbed at his swollen face. Both eyes were nearly swollen shut now. The venom of this deadly creature was, apparently, working extremely fast.

"Come, Anik. We have to get you help."

A moan escaped Anik's lips, and he slumped down onto his backside.

"No, we have to get help." Reyansh turned to the professor, "Dr. Portman, get the security guard. Tell him to call a medic!"

For the first time in as long as he could remember, Portman didn't know what to do. He froze in sheer terror, but his fears were only beginning to be realized. As he stared at the vent the cobra had emerged from, he saw more movement.

Another serpent slithered out of the hole like black liquid pouring out of a vessel. Then another, a third, a fourth, they just kept coming; a dozen snakes had flowed from the vent and onto the chamber floor.

Reyansh followed the professor's terrified gaze and saw what he was looking at. "Anik!" The big man did nothing to cover the fear in his voice. "Come on!"

A stinging burn shot into Reyansh's right calf. Horrified, he looked down and realized his fear. A cobra head was attached to his leg, the fangs buried deep.

Growing up in the area, he had a strong knowledge of serpents, especially of this species. These, however, were unlike any cobras he'd studied. Most snakes would bite quickly and withdraw. Never before had he witnessed a serpent bury its fangs in this way and not let go.

He released Anik's shoulders and swiped at the creature, knocking its head free of his leg on the second try.

Anik toppled over onto his side amid a pooling collection of snakes that snapped at his head, neck, arms, and legs.

Reyansh stood up, his head dizzy and his leg burning with a pain that trickled slowly up toward the knee. "Get out of here, Professor!"

Portman shook his head even as he backed away toward the door. He slashed the torch left and right to ward off any stray serpents, but the waving flames seemed to entice them, and a few broke off from the pack, winding their way toward him.

"Shut the door!" Reyansh yelled. "Don't let them get out!"

John's heel tripped over the door's threshold and he nearly fell, only catching himself at the last second with a desperate hand on the doorframe. He balanced his weight and stared at the nightmarish scene unfolding before him. He grimaced as Reyansh desperately tried to make a break for the door, but he only got one step closer before another snake latched on to his thigh and brought the big man to his knees.

Reyansh reached out with a last-ditch effort, extending his hand toward the professor. Then he shook his head and mouthed a last command. "Seal it! Forever!"

His order was followed by a bone-chilling scream of pain as more snakes sank their dripping fangs into his flesh. He dropped to the floor, prostrate, fingers clawing at the surface. The nails dug in and scratched hard as if that would save him from the venom already pulsing through his veins.

John shot out his hand and grabbed the door to his side. A large cobra, at least eight feet long and several inches wide, slithered rapidly toward him, intent on letting no one escape. The professor shoved the door shut as the snake struck out at his shin.

The door slammed closed, pausing suddenly before it gave way, severing the serpent's head between the frame and the portal's sharp edge. The dead snake's head dropped to the ground, leaving the body behind in midair.

Even detached, the head wiggled and twisted for a moment as if possessed by something from another world.

John's breath came in quick bursts as he stood in disbelief, staring at the cobra head on the floor. The sounds of agony from beyond the door faded to an eerie silence.

John slumped to the floor, still gasping. He looked to the blank ceiling above with forlorn desperation in his eyes. "What...what have I done?"

1

LJUBLJANA, SLOVENIA - PRESENT DAY

The sound wasn't loud, but it didn't take much to rouse Sean Wyatt from his sleep.

Ever since his time in the ultra-covert government agency known as Axis, he'd been a light sleeper. It was times like this he was glad for that involuntary habit.

He rolled over to the edge of his bed, slid open the nightstand drawer, and removed his Springfield XD .40-caliber pistol.

The polymer and metal fit perfectly into his palm, fingers wrapping around it like a glove. Sean sighed. This gun had been a friend in times of need for a long time now. He'd been a fan of Ruger weapons for a good portion of his life, but once he tried the Springfield, he'd become a convert.

Now, though, things were different.

Sean had been through a rough time over the last six months. After events in Nova Scotia, he'd had a bitter revelation, one that had shaken him to his core.

In the years of working for Axis and for his friend's International Archaeological Agency, Sean had taken many lives in self-defense. Unlike many poor souls, he wasn't haunted by the faces of those he killed. No, his epiphany had been much darker.

He realized that he enjoyed the killing.

That realization had rocked him.

Was he a bad person? Was he evil? He certainly felt that way.

He'd gone to therapy, been debriefed in a few instances, and consoled by his friends more than a couple of times in the last six months.

While some of it helped, much of it did nothing to alleviate the guilt that riddled his heart.

Was he a psychopath? A sociopath? Some other kind of "path" he'd never heard of?

His therapist insisted he was none of those things, but in her eyes he'd seen a lack of conviction.

The only thing that got him by was reminding himself that those he'd killed were evil, truly wicked people intent on harming the innocent. Sean constantly told himself he was merely a tool, a precision instrument used to root out the bad in the world.

But was he?

He thought he'd gotten away from that—the killing, the hunting, the running, and hiding—when he left Axis to join Tommy's IAA. Working as head of security for an archaeological agency should have resulted in far less death and at the very least, less intrigue. Now it was starting to feel like the opposite was taking place.

He swung his legs over the bed's edge and planted his feet on the ground. The action didn't make so much as a light whoosh or thud. Years of practice had turned moving silently—even in the supposed safety of his room—into second nature.

Sean reached into the drawer again and removed a different weapon. He stuffed the Springfield into the belt of his pajama pants for a moment as he inspected the new weapon.

The sleek black pistol had no hammer, none of the usual trimmings that most weapons displayed.

Instead, a blue LED on the side indicated the magazine was full and completely charged. Sean sighed and gripped the weapon with resentful fingers. The gun was similar in weight and size to his trusty

.40-cal, but early testing of the weapon and others like it had not gone as hoped.

Tommy had insisted that the entire agency be outfitted with a new line of weapons a friend at DARPA was working on—nonlethal defenses that could render an enemy unconscious or, at the very least, significantly stunned.

Sean winced, full of doubt.

He heard the noise again and moved away from the bed. His left hand unconsciously reached for the gun in his waistband and dragged it out. *Just in case.*

Sean and his team had been sent to Slovenia to assist in the recovery and transportation of an impressive chunk of amber rumored to be one part of an ancient civilization's treasure horde.

The city of Ljubljana was situated directly in the path of the so-called Amber Road, a trade route used in ancient times to connect Saint Petersburg, the North Sea, and the Baltic to the Mediterranean.

The prized gem was little more than tree sap from millennia ago when trees had been leveled and squeezed of their sticky, sweet blood during massive tectonic upheaval. People, however, put incredible value on the gem and paid top price for it. The result was the hardened, yellowish-brown stone that washed up on the shores of Russia and even Poland. Huge veins of the stuff appeared in the earth and sparked mining operations across the continent, the largest of which were situated in the north.

The piece of amber Sean was charged with watching over had, allegedly, been a gift for one of the prominent families in Italy. As the story went, the remarkable specimen nearly made it that far, instead being lost in transit from Saint Petersburg.

Sean didn't mind these guard-and-move jobs. They usually didn't involve much. IAA operations were kept secret—as secret as the civilian world could manage—until the discovery was announced and the artifacts were safely stowed away in a highly secure location.

Occasionally, however, problems arose. Sean's immediate concern upon waking was that this was one of those times.

The artifact in question, the subject of his guardianship, was a piece of amber reportedly created by one of the sculptors from the court of Fredrick William I of Prussia, the very king who'd gifted a chamber of amber to Czar Peter I, to win his favor. According to the story that led Tommy's agency to this city, the czar had sought to open business dealings with a prominent, wealthy family in Venice. The gift of amber was more than a peace offering; it was a symbol of loyalty and one Peter I had hoped would help establish his kingdom across continental divides.

When Tommy's team of archaeologists uncovered the lost artifact, each member of the group gazed wide-eyed at the priceless gem, captivated by its beauty.

It had been sculpted into the shape of a cross, with beveled edges on each arm and grooves cut into the center in an almost Gothic style.

Sean was stationed in Slovenia to watch over the amber cross, and make sure it was safe until its scheduled transport to the nearest lab that specialized in analyzing it. That lab was in Poland, and the train that would take the artifact there was still five hours away from embarking.

Sean padded across the room on the balls of his feet. His footfalls didn't make a sound. He'd even learned the creaks of every plank covering the floor for just such an occurrence. Again, old habits.

He reached the doorway of the small priest's cell and looked around the corner. The church corridor was empty, devoid of life or movement of any kind.

The musty, museumesque smell of the church had evaporated with time, Sean's nose going deaf to the scent of old stone, wood, upholstery, and books. The only smell he detected now was the lingering scent of incense, probably from a single cone left by a monk performing his late-night prayer ritual.

He looked down the length of the hallway again in both directions and then slipped out of his room, wearing nothing but pajama pants and a T-shirt. The corridor's only source of light came from the white candles that burned on black iron sconces every ten feet along the walls. Based on the length of the wax shafts, they'd been replaced by someone during the night, a practice that surely had to annoy that someone. It was two o'clock in the morning, after all. Sean wouldn't want that monk's job, whoever was burdened with it.

There was the sound again. It came from the sanctuary. A thud. Not overwhelmingly loud but enough for his trained ears.

He crouched lower, bending his knees as he made his way down the passage toward a set of double doors that hung open. He reached the next portal and stuck his head through. A dim flickering light emanated from the sanctuary doors to his left. It was the side entrance to the expansive room. He couldn't see inside since the doors' panels were stained glass, as were other windows that lined the wall, but the light from within was still visible through the swirling colors depicting the journey of apostles, battles of Israel's past, and the mission of Christ.

Sean knew that if he went through the side door, he'd have only a few seconds to get the drop on the intruder. The second they realized trouble was there, the thief would take off toward the main entrance and escape out the front door. If Sean worked his way around to the other entrance, he'd have the same problem, only with the side door being the escape as opposed to the front.

He glanced to his left at a closed door and narrowed his eyes. Then he smirked. He opened the closet door and pulled out a broom. It took less than twenty seconds for him to wedge the broomstick through the handles, effectively barricading the door. Now the thief would only have one way out, through the front, where he would be standing.

Sean walked around to the atrium, nothing more than a narrow foyer where parishioners could gather before and after the services every week. There was barely enough room for thirty people. He'd wondered if that was by design: get them in and out as fast as possible.

He reached the two main doors that opened to the two aisles dividing the pews in the sanctuary and stopped. He gripped the brushed bronze handle with the tips of his fingers and gently pulled back, dragging the door open as slowly as possible to prevent any sort of sound that would alert the thief.

As the door cracked open, inch by inch, Sean peeked through the widening gap toward the front of the room.

Someone in a black ski mask and matching long-sleeve shirt, pants, and boots was crouched at the altar.

The altar was a gilded cube with a pyramid on the top that held up, somehow, the platform for the priest's Bible. It was a bizarre piece of furniture, but Sean wasn't one to judge interior design. And at the moment, he simply didn't care.

Sean grinned as he passed through the door like a vapor sifting through a screen. He was as undetectable as any deadly asset in the world. It was one of the things he'd focused on during recent months: retraining, and relearning the ways of stealth to hone his skills back to the razor-sharp edge they'd been in his prime.

He stayed low, creeping down the left aisle toward the front, only occasionally risking a glance to the podium to make sure the thief was still there. Not that he had to look. The burglar was being clumsily loud, desperately trying to figure out why the safe at the base of the altar wouldn't open.

Sean had been doing this gig a long time. He made sure to always have a false lead out there in case their operation had a leak or someone got greedy. Maybe it was one of those two things that happened to lead to this break-in. Maybe it was dumb luck. Either way, Sean had to smile as he rose from behind the pews, pointing his weapon at the criminal.

"If you're looking for the amber cross, you're not going to find it in there." His voice echoed through the sanctuary.

The thief froze in place. To Sean's surprise, they didn't make a break for any of the exits, one of which he knew would do the thief no good.

Sean took a wary step across the floor in front of the foremost church pew. He moved deftly, crossing one foot over the other as he kept the pistol locked on to the target. The thief still wasn't moving, crouching on one knee in front of the safe.

"Decoy," Sean said. "I had a feeling someone might make a play for the cross. Don't worry. It's safe."

He stood in the center of the room now, his sights still trained on the thief. Sean frowned. Something wasn't right. Basic human instinct was fight or flight. Usually, in his experience, most thieves chose the latter. Unless they were scared, which typically meant they weren't professionals. Pros didn't get scared; at least they didn't show it. This thief, however, was frozen stiff. Maybe it was fear.

"Put your hands up where I can see both of them. Nice and high." Sean inched closer toward the altar.

The thief didn't budge.

"Look. Don't make this harder than it has to be. Just put your hands up slowly, and no one has to get hurt."

The thief's covered head twisted slowly to one side until the eyes inside the mask met Sean's. They were dark brown, rimmed by thick brown eyelashes. Italian, perhaps? That would make sense. They weren't far from the Italian border, and given the history of the amber cross it would make sense that a thief from Italy would want to lay claim to it. Or maybe Sean was reaching.

He gave the order again, this time in Italian.

The eyes behind the mask narrowed.

A sickening realization snaked its way through Sean's blood. The thief was stalling.

As if on cue, the thief's eyes stretched out wide, indicating the grin behind the mask covering his mouth.

Sean fired the weapon in his hand. The magnetic propulsion charge within the weapon cracked like the sound of someone snapping their fingers. The round spun through the barrel and shot out of the muzzle at incredible speed, striking the thief just below the neck. Thousands of volts coursed through his body in an instant, and the man dropped over to his side, convulsing violently.

Sean glanced at the weapon and grinned. "Not bad."

He twisted his head around and looked toward the doors with one thought: *the cross.*

He'd always used decoys in situations like this. Now, it seemed like his little plan had backfired. He'd kept the amber cross in his dormitory cell to keep a close watch over it during the night. Safes could be cracked. Doors could be unlocked. But it would be difficult for a thief to steal something out from under his pillow. Unless, of course, he wasn't on the pillow.

Sean had inadvertently made the job extremely easy for these crooks.

He charged up the slightly slanted floor, running for the doors to the foyer. He didn't give a second thought to the stunned thief next to the altar. That guy would still be there when Sean finished with the other one. If he caught the other one.

He slammed into the doors at the back of the church with a thud. A sharp pain shot through his shoulder as his entire body's weight scrunched into a compact form and then bounced off the doors, sending Sean stumbling backward a few feet. He grimaced at the fresh pain.

"What the—" He quickly stepped back to the doors and shoved the one on the right. It only moved an inch before he realized what the problem was. The other thief had used his idea, blockading the door with the same broom Sean had chosen for the side door.

"Clever."

He jolted for the next doors, hoping the thief had only taken the time to find one broomstick. He reached the other entrance and shoved the metal plate attached to the wood. The door swung free, and he pushed it harder so it would swing wide. Then he ducked low and leaned out into the foyer. The second thief was sprinting out the main door to the street outside.

Sean let out an aggravated "of course" and sprang from his crouching position. He pumped his legs as hard as he could, bare feet pounding the clay tiles in the foyer. He reached the front door and nudged it open. It had only cracked the space between the other door and itself when six heavy knocks slammed against the thick wooden portal.

Sean ducked down out of instinct and pulled his weapons close to his face. The other thief was shooting.

He sighed. Thieves were one thing. Armed thieves were quite another. Most he'd dealt with in the past were scavengers, trying to get a piece of a lost treasure from antiquity and turn a fast fortune on the black market. These guys, however, were ready to kill for the prized amber cross.

He didn't have time to ponder who knew about it and who had access to talented thieves with a penchant for firearms. Sean stepped back and kicked the door open, ducking to the other door for cover as the first swung wide.

A burst of cool air blew into the foyer, but no more shots rang out, no bullets thumped into the door or blasted through the building into the walls within.

Sean twisted and looked out into the chilly night. He instantly spotted the figure dressed in black, sprinting away from the church toward an alley. Sean raised the magnetic weapon and squeezed the trigger.

The light on the side turned red. He squeezed again. Same result. This time with a repetitive warning beep. "Ah! Stupid piece of junk." He threw the gun against the rock wall to the side with a clack and raised his Springfield in time to see the right leg of the thief disappear behind the corner of the alley.

He started down the stairs in pursuit when he heard a loud bang. Then another. Sean frowned. The sound had come from the alley. It wasn't a gunshot. It was something else, like the sound of metal hitting something solid.

His senses heightened, his mind on full alert, Sean reached the sidewalk, checked both directions, and trotted across the street, keeping his weapon low but ready.

Sean reached the corner and slowed his pace, keeping on his toes even though his bare feet didn't make much noise on the cold, damp asphalt and concrete. He paused for a second and listened, eyes narrowing as if that would elevate his sense of hearing. He eased his head toward the edge of the brick building and twisted enough to take in the alley. He ducked back for a second and then emerged again with weapon raised.

"Stop right there," he said. Old feelings rushed into his mind. The thrill of the kill filled his thoughts. For a moment, he almost hoped this new thief would make a move. He could almost feel the recoil of the pistol in his hand as it discharged, sending a deadly hollow point into the chest of the target.

The thief didn't move. On the ground at the stranger's feet, a metal trash can lay across the body of the person Sean had been pursuing. Now there were two of them?

Something long and yellow dangled from the newcomer's left hand, the gold shimmering in the dim light. Sean's eyes narrowed and he looked closer, realizing the thief was a woman. She had a dark gray hood over her face, casting much of it in shadow, but the figure was lithe, athletic, in tight black pants and a snug fitting zip-up hoodie. Sean frowned. The lips, they looked familiar, barely visible in the dull glow of streetlights behind him.

"You certainly have a strange way of thanking a girl," the woman said. She raised the golden cross a few inches to show it to him.

Sean swallowed hard. His eyes blinked, full of fear, thinking he was seeing a ghost. Then the woman slowly raised her free hand and flipped back the hoodie, revealing her porcelain face, the dark chocolate hair pulled back into a tight ponytail, the matching eyes.

She smiled at him.

Sean lowered the weapon, suddenly terrified at the thought he'd almost shot her. Then he rushed to her. She started to move toward him, but he was faster, driven by a longing he'd felt for months. They collided hard, wrapping arms around each other as their lips met in a viselike kiss.

The downed man on the ground next to them groaned and started to roll over, but Adriana snapped her heel backward, striking him in the back of the head, rendering him unconscious once more.

Sean snorted and pulled his head away for a moment, taking in this beautiful woman in his arms.

"Thank you for the assist," he said.

She shrugged. "I figured you might need some help."

Sean shook his head, still taking in the apparition before him. "How did you find me?"

She scrunched her face; eyes narrow in disbelief. "Really? You know finding people and stuff is sort of my thing, right?"

Sean grinned wider than he had in a long time. Then he nodded. "Fair enough."

He kissed her again, harder this time, longer. When they released once more, he stared into her eyes. "I missed you."

Adriana Villa gazed back into his icy blues. "And I you."

2

LOS ANGELES

Brock Carson sat quietly, legs crossed, fingers curled up to the ceiling. His eyes were closed. His chest rising and falling in rhythm would have been almost undetectable by a visitor. The open door to the deck allowed a gentle breeze to roll into his home, wash over him, and tickle the stick of incense sitting to his left propped up in a golden censer and sending the tendrils of gray smoke into several directions.

He finished his daily twenty-minute meditation with a deep exhale and then gradually opened his eyes.

The Los Angeles morning sun cast a warm glow over the entirety of the city. He rose from his meditation pose and padded over to the door. His white linen pants shimmered in the breeze. Brock stood there for a moment, taking in the view from his mansion looking out over the valley below. The sun struck his bronze skin and warmed it instantly against the breeze. His dirty blond hair wafted now and then as the wind picked up and then died down again. It brushed against his ears, but he didn't care, didn't even notice much. His attention was on something else, something disturbing.

Brock gazed down at the city he loved, the city that had made him who he was, a landscape shaped by concrete, metal, and glass. It wasn't love that filled his heart, though. It was bitterness.

A thick haze of smog hung around the center of Downtown Los Angeles. It was nearing the end of that time of year when the smog would blow away and clear skies would once more return to the City of Angels. At the moment, however, it lingered like a dirty mist that seemed more a permanent resident than a seasonal annoyance.

He sighed and turned away from the sight, closing the door shut in the process.

Brock Carson had moved to Los Angeles several years before, desperate to carve out a name for himself in Hollywood and become a famous actor. He knew millions of other people wished for the same thing, but he always knew he'd make it. He had the look, the talent, and the drive that pushed him to do anything—almost anything—to become a star.

And rise he did.

Part of why he always figured he'd be wealthy and famous was due to the fact he had nowhere to go but up.

He'd grown up in a poverty-stricken home in a poverty-stricken neighborhood near Mobile, Alabama. Brock had watched his father beat up his mom more times than he could count, usually after a day on the fishing boats in the Gulf of Mexico, but sometimes when the Seminoles would lose on the weekends during football season. Those were the most violent, after a day of lubricating his mind with booze and testosterone. Brock had fought his dad off a few times, once he'd matured and grown big enough. There were many times, though, when he'd lost that battle.

One such time had pushed Brock to leave for good. He'd felt guilty about leaving his mother in that situation, but he also felt like there was no other option.

It hadn't always been that way. Prior to the oil rig disaster that flooded the beaches and fishing lanes with sludge, they'd been a pretty normal family. Dad had a drink now and then, but nothing crazy. After the accident, they'd received a small settlement from the oil company, but by then the damage was done. His father had spiraled into depression after nearly a year of being out of work. Fishing was all he'd known. So was the Gulf Coast. He couldn't just up and move to some other fishing town. It was his life. So, the drinking began, and so did the abuse. Brock never forgot the cause, even after he left.

His meteoric climb to stardom came faster than anyone he'd ever heard of. Like most actors, he was working in coffee shops and restaurants, trying to eke out a living while taking every casting call he could.

When a chance came along for a small role in a new sci-fi feature, he'd jumped at it. He poured everything into that audition, trained for weeks, hundreds of hours, just for a few simple lines.

He got the part. After that, it took only a few more months before he was called again, this time for a bigger role.

Brock slipped on a beige button-up short-sleeve shirt and looked at the wall. He had a copy of every movie poster for every film he'd ever been in as the lead. At the moment, there were eleven, and each one had brought him millions. His net worth at the time was over fifty-five million dollars, and going up every day thanks to savvy investing strategies and constantly looking for more roles.

He'd made his name, built his fortune, and established his legacy. Well, almost.

There was one thing left for him to do.

His thoughts drifted through the clear skies in his head like leaves fluttering in a gentle fall breeze. He snatched one from long ago when he was just getting started in Hollywood. Back then he was nobody, sharing a tiny apartment with another actor roughly the same age as him. Neither of them had much, certainly nothing to spare at the end of every month. They were scraping by on a razor's edge.

Then something had happened.

Brock received an invitation to a seminar being conducted by a well-known actor, Richard Farrow. He'd jumped at the chance, hoping with every fiber of his being that he could meet the man, someone he'd revered and emulated his entire life.

He never got the chance to shake hands with Farrow. There were too many people desperate for a photo and a quick handshake, or even just the chance to get within a few feet of the famous actor.

While Brock certainly felt disappointed not being able to meet someone he idolized, the keynote Farrow had given inspired Brock to his core. He'd certainly had selfish dreams of becoming famous and wealthy as a star in Hollywood. Those goals had still driven him in the early days, even after the speech by Farrow.

But Brock had another reason for achieving stratospheric success.

Farrow had used his fame, his platform, to drive home an exceedingly powerful point during his talk: humans were destroying the planet.

Brock had heard all about climate change, the arguments between sides as to what was really causing it. He'd come to his own conclusion that climate change was a natural event, a constant in an ever-changing planet, solar system, galaxy, and universe. People, however, had accelerated the process.

Farrow suggested that there was still time, that people could make a difference if everyone focused their efforts on coming up with real ideas and policies that could begin to reverse the negative effects the population had on the planet.

Brock immediately recognized Farrow as a dreamer, a speaker, and an action-taker. The man had spent considerable amounts of money on projects to clean up beaches and seas and to save forests from overharvesting. He'd organized a movement called Clean Planet, but despite all his efforts and the enormous sums of money he'd thrown at it, the project had little effect. Sure, he'd saved a few thousand acres of rainforest in Brazil, removed a few tons of plastic from the world's water supply, but the dent he made was insignificant.

Brock watched Clean Planet flounder. It was so much like some of the other nonprofits he'd seen rise from nowhere. Occasionally, teams would make the news. One of the anti-whaling organizations became the focus of a reality television show, though after a while it became evident to the population that those people were nothing more than a nuisance to the whalers, using nonlethal weapons to attack massive ships with little to no effect. Usually, it was the latter.

Others had tried similar tactics to prevent the slaughter of baby harp seals or to keep certain mega-corporations from polluting rivers, oceans, or natural habitats.

The law, it seemed, always worked in favor of the big companies.

It wasn't just the giant entities, though, who constantly wreaked havoc on the world's ecosystem.

Ordinary people did more than their part.

Brock saw it on an almost daily basis. People driving down the interstate would toss a burger wrapper, a drink cup, a napkin out their window and onto the grass next to the road. He cringed every time he saw it happen.

It was a strange thing, Brock recounted, taking on this mission. Before Farrow's speech, he'd known that people should do better when it came to taking care of our home planet, but what difference could someone like him make? He was, after all, a nobody.

Now, however, that wasn't the case.

He'd considered doing something like what Farrow had done; dump tens of millions into new projects to help drive back the polluting offenders. He could even get behind Farrow's movement, effectively doubling their influence and spending power.

That, Brock knew, wouldn't work. It wasn't good enough. It would be a waste of time and resources.

Those methods had been tried over and over again with feeble results if any. It was like tossing a water balloon into a volcano.

The more Brock saw on the news, the stronger his resolve grew.

He turned his head and glanced at the statue on a shelf over his gas fireplace. It was one of several he possessed. The golden deity's four arms curled out into different directions. One hand held a lotus flower, another a seashell, a third spun a golden disc on a finger, and the fourth gripped a long golden mace.

Brock had been raised an atheist, but after coming to Hollywood, he'd studied several eastern religions, Hinduism and Buddhism chief among them. While he didn't narrow his beliefs to a single dogmatic theology, he did consider a few to be more important for his life's path than others. Buddhism had a profound influence on him and had taught him the value of meditation and bringing one's mind to a stillness that could connect it to the surrounding world. Hinduism brought its own benefits as well, especially in regard to the balance of nature.

He incorporated beliefs from other religions, too, as a person might pick various kinds of food from a buffet. It worked for him, giving him a higher sense of purpose and elevating his desire to effect real change in the world. Unlike what had been accomplished by Internet-fundraising campaigns and empty promises.

Brock admired Farrow and the work he and others had done. It was the only way they knew. Or so they would have had the public believe.

He nodded at the idol in a silent show of respect and then turned away, walking to a black staircase. The stairs split off, one side leading up to the second floor, the other going downstairs. He veered left and made his way down the steps, walking softly out of habit rather than necessity to stay quiet. It was his home, after all. Although he did have one guest waiting for him below.

Brock reached the landing at the bottom and turned 90 degrees into a cavernous finished basement. The ceiling was ten feet tall, and the room stretched sixty feet in one direction, forty feet across. A fireplace crackled in the corner, more for effect than a need for warmth. A 72-inch flat screen television hung from the center of the wall. His favorite feature was the bar in the opposing corner to the fireplace. The cherry wood finish of the counter, façade, and shelves behind the bar gave the room a touch of Old-World class amid the backdrop of modern contemporary conveniences and design.

In the far corner, his workspace bloomed like an oasis of technology. Three high-definition computer monitors were propped on an L-shaped desk. The glass top of the workstation was cleaned to a shine, the only items cluttering it being the keyboard, mouse, and a notepad with pen.

None of those things were the reason for his descent to the bottom floor.

He strode across the room, twisting his head to glance out the massive windows displaying the view of the mountains and valley beyond. In the distance, he was again reminded of the air pollution as the downtown skyline remained partially shrouded.

The last corner to the left had a smaller window, one that was closed and covered with blinds and black curtains. While Brock Carson's property was secure, surrounded by tall fences and walls on three sides and a sheer cliff in the front, one could never be too careful.

Especially considering what he was about to do.

3

LJUBLJANA

Sean stared across the table at her as she sipped her coffee. Adriana's dark brown hair shimmered in the sunlight, an iridescent ripple amid a smooth brunette sea.

They'd requested a table on the street to sip their coffee and have breakfast. The cool morning air gave necessity for light jackets, but the bright morning sun bathed them in a comforting warmth as they ate their breakfast of quiche pockets, cheeses, fruit, Nutella, and bread.

The Ljubljana Castle towered over the city in the distance, high above the rooftops of the multicolored homes and shops that lined the streets. Pedestrians strolled by, some with shopping bags, others with travel backpacks, and still more simply walking along the sidewalk with their hands in their pockets as they discussed the topics of the day.

Sean had never really spent much time in Slovenia and certainly not in this particular city. The need had never come up. Now, he regretted that fact. The beautiful countryside, the architecture, the food, the people, had all grown on him in the short span of three days since he'd arrived. Unfortunately, it was time to go home.

He and Adriana had delivered the amber cross to the Italian government officials for safekeeping. They would ultimately determine what happened to the artifact. More than likely, it would wind up in a museum somewhere, which is what Sean hoped would be the case. A spectacular work of art like that should be available for all the world to take in and appreciate.

Adriana caught him daydreaming about the cross as he gazed up at the castle to his right.

"You want to go visit the fortress before we leave, or you just thinking about something?" She flashed a playful grin as she spoke.

His eyes blinked wearily, not from fatigue, simply from being happier than he'd been in a long time. For the first time in forever, Sean was completely relaxed. He'd dreamed of feeling content like this. Now he had it. The woman he loved was sitting across from him. He was eating amazing food. Things had been quiet for the last several months—the thieves at the church notwithstanding.

The feelings of comfort and appreciation waned as he thought about the two criminals. They'd been international thieves, wanted by Interpol.

Sean figured they weren't no-names, locals who just happened to learn about the priceless treasure he was protecting. It was almost never that simple. Since the times of the American stagecoaches, the Pony Express, and beyond when barons fought off thieves from their carriages, most heists were carried out by experts. The ones that no one heard of were the masses of fools who thought they could walk into a bank with a pistol and get away with no trouble.

The experts, however, always had plans on top of plans. The two who tried to take the amber cross had been clever. Without Adriana's help, Sean wasn't sure if he could have caught the second thief. He'd been lucky she'd turned up when she did, although he learned it wasn't luck at all.

She'd tracked him down to the cathedral through a series of connections, one being his best friend, Tommy Schultz, who also happened to be his boss.

Tommy, affectionately known as Schultzie, was able to tell her where she could find Sean in regard to what city and country, but he'd been kept in the dark as to where, specifically, Sean was hiding out.

It was an old habit Sean picked up from his days in Axis, back when he worked as a field agent for the ultra-covert group that reported straight to the president.

He'd intentionally not told Tommy where he was staying in case someone was eavesdropping on their conversations. That sort of thing didn't happen often, but it did happen from time to time and in much more secure organizations than theirs. While the International Archaeological Agency was pretty tight, they did experience issues with hackers now and then.

These two criminals in Ljubljana couldn't have learned where he was from skimming emails or text messages. They found out some other way, which was almost more troubling.

For the moment, however, they were safely behind bars and wouldn't present a problem in the immediate future. The Slovenian police had been more than cooperative in bringing in the criminals. It didn't help that they'd committed the crime in a historically significant church.

"No," Sean said, finally answering her question. He'd been in a daze since they'd sat down. "I'm good. Besides, we have to...I have to get back to Atlanta."

"I know. And yes, you can say we. I'm definitely coming with you." She raised her cup of coffee and held it in front of her lips to hide the grin her eyes betrayed.

"So...you don't have some lost piece of Nazi art to go find? I figured you'd be hot on the trail of something like that."

She shook her head. "No." Her tone was dismissive, and she took a long sip of coffee. "I haven't done that in a while, though I've been meaning to."

They'd caught up over the last thirty-six hours, but Adriana had remained coy as to what she'd been up to.

It had been so long. Was it a year? More than that?

Neither one of them wanted to think about it.

Adriana had dropped off the map. Sean had been busy.

It wasn't that he hadn't tried to get in touch with her, but she didn't return his calls, texts, anything. She'd simply said, "I love you. This is not over, but there's something I have to do."

That was it.

As the months drained by like water swirling in a sink, he'd waited to hear from her, to see her, to hold her once more.

Now she was back, seemingly all of a sudden. He wanted to pick up where they'd left off, but she was keeping something from him. It wasn't anything sinister—that much he knew—but Sean felt like it had carved a divide between them, a trench that he couldn't bridge, not unless he figured out what had happened.

He wasn't going to ask again. She'd fill him in on her own time.

"So, you're coming back to the States with me then? For sure? Nothing has come up?"

She laughed and set down her coffee. "No, silly. What would come up?"

He rolled his shoulders and leaned his head to the side. "I don't know. Whatever came up before."

Her grin faded, eyes glazing over with a fog. "That won't come up again. I promise. And like I said the other night, I'll tell you about it when I'm ready. And when I feel it's appropriate."

He didn't know what that meant. He tried not to care. Sean was an easygoing kind of guy. He didn't like to be tied to too many commitments when it came to his professional life, which was why working for Tommy turned out to be a great match. It combined his love of history with his passion for travel. The biggest thing it played to, however, was his passion for relaxation. He'd had a stressful life for a while, and the last thing Sean wanted was to add more to it. Being able to sort of work at his own pace, his own schedule, and have plenty of time between projects was a good thing for his mind and body.

Adriana had mentioned he seemed stronger than before, more energetic. He'd explained it away that he had more free time to work out and focus on nutrition. Deep down, she figured there was more to it than that, but she didn't push the issue.

"Does Tommy have another job for you already?" She made the transition to another subject swift and painless.

He smirked. *This woman gets me, unlike anyone I've ever met.*

"He said he needed to meet with me about something, so I guess maybe he does. That's not the norm. Usually, I have weeks, sometimes months, between projects. I help out in the lab and with other parts of research in the meantime, but he doesn't keep tabs on me, and he certainly doesn't request a meeting unless there's something going on."

"Perhaps he needs your world-class expertise." She scooted closer to him and placed her palm on his knee.

The move sent a tickling sensation up through his leg and curled the hairs on the back of his head.

"World-class." He blew it off. "Pfft. Schultzie is just as good with all that stuff as I am."

"And yet he seems to need you."

"I guess."

"You don't give yourself enough credit, my love. Modest to a fault."

A snicker escaped Sean's lips. "It's not modesty if I truly believe it."

She ticked her head to the side and shrugged. "Maybe not." Then she took the last bite of a piece of cheese on her plate, savored the flavor for a moment, then drew another sip of coffee. "When do we leave?"

"Four hours."

"That soon? Must be important, whatever he has for you."

"For us," Sean corrected. "You're coming with me this time, and I won't take no for an answer."

Adriana blushed. "So commanding. Do I look like the woman who can be bossed around?" She used her flirtiest, most playful, tone.

He reached across the table and grabbed her hand. His smile was gone, replaced by a thin straight line across his lips and an intense gaze in his eyes. "No, you don't, which is one of the reasons I love you." He let go and leaned back, lacing his fingers behind his dirty blond hair. "That said, you're coming with me, and there won't be another word about it. Whatever Tommy wants me to do can be done with you by my side."

Her smile widened. "Relax, cowboy. I'll come along for the ride."

4

LOS ANGELES

"Hello, Richard," Brock said, slowing his stride across the floor. His toes squished into the thick shag carpet with every step. He let the long strands of fabric seep between them as he always did as if the guest in the corner chair wasn't even there.

The man in the corner couldn't speak. The gag in his mouth only allowed muted protests of garbled words and moans. The prisoner twisted and shook, but he couldn't get free of the ropes binding him to the metal chair—a relic from the 1960s or '70s by the looks of it.

Brock's head of security, an athletic, ambitious woman named Heather Marlow, was a dedicated servant, unquestioningly resolute and loyal, both to the cause and to Brock Carson. At the moment, Heather wasn't in the room—per Brock's wishes.

It was just the host and the prisoner.

Brock slowed his pace to an even more deliberate gait until he was only a few feet in front of his guest and then stopped short, leaning forward to hover over the bound and gagged man.

The prisoner looked up at him with wide, angry eyes.

"I suppose you're wondering why you're here, hmm, Richard?"

More muffled squeals escaped the rag stuffed in his mouth. His eyes bulged out of his red face. The man's thin brown hair was normally styled to a perfect spike to the right. He was in his late fifties but still tried to keep up with the trends of twenty-somethings in pop culture.

Richard Farrow stared up at Brock as he loomed over him. His eyes searched his warden for answers. As Brock's lips trembled, cracking into a smile, he knew he would soon have what he sought.

"I'm going to take that rag out of your mouth, Richard." Brock spoke to him as though he were a child being punished for a tantrum. "When I do, it won't help for you to scream. Understand?"

The man nodded.

Brock pointed around the room without looking, showing off the walls around him. "There's no one here to hear you. And these walls are insulated, so even if someone was right outside, they likely wouldn't hear you. So, don't bother. Got it?"

Richard considered the statement, this time with greater sincerity. Then he nodded slowly.

"Good." Brock flashed a bright white smile that had been seen by millions on the red carpet and on silver screens across the planet.

He reached out and violently yanked the gag out of his captive's mouth.

Richard breathed heavily, gasping for air in huge gulps. He let out a string of obscenities, some directed at Brock's familial ties. When he was done swearing, his face still burned red. If he was a cartoon character, Brock imagined, smoke would have been pouring out of the man's ears.

Brock shook his head when Richard stopped to catch his breath again. "Richard, such a foul mouth you have. And to think I actually revered you."

"What do you think you're doing, you little punk?"

Brock rose up onto his tiptoes and then lowered himself back to his heels. He laced his fingers behind his back and twisted to the side as if about to give a PowerPoint presentation to a seminar.

"I'm so glad you didn't ask the obvious question: 'Do you have any idea who I am?' I mean, duh. Of course, I know you. I worshipped you, Richard. I wanted to be you. Well, almost you." He flipped his shaggy hair back behind one ear. "Obviously, my hair is better than yours."

Richard raged against his bonds, but the chair barely moved and didn't even creak under his weight. "Good news, moron. You're going to jail. And you'll never work in this town again. What is this, some kind of publicity stunt?"

Brock shook his head, clicking his tongue as he did so. He leveled his eyes to the prisoners. "Really, Richard? Publicity? You think I need the publicity? I'm an award-winning actor, man! I have wealth beyond what I could have ever imagined. Cars. Women. Mansions in three countries and two additional states. Do you really think that's what this is about?"

Richard frowned. "What do you want, then? It sounds like you have everything."

The host nodded, though from his expression he let on that he was keeping something back, a huge but that would come after the response. "True. Very true. I do have everything I could ever want. Except for one thing."

The prisoner shook his head, his eyes full of confusion. "What's that? Because I gotta be honest. The second you untie these ropes, I'm going to kick your squirmy little—"

"Now, now, Richard. I don't think so. First of all, I'm not going to untie anything. Second, you will give me exactly what I want."

Richard frowned. "What's that?"

Another wicked smile cracked across Brock's face. "Justice, of course."

The frown deepened. Hard lines creased Farrow's forehead. "What?"

Brock spun on his heel and retraced his steps; pacing. "You see, I respected you for so long, Richard. The first time I saw you speak was at an event for your charity. You know the one, right? The one for your Clean Planet project?"

"I've done a lot of those events."

"I'm sure you have. This one was special to me. You inspired me.

You made me see that the world needs our help. Before that event, your speech, I was so selfish. Everything I did was just for material gain."

"Doesn't look like you've changed much."

Brock cocked his head to the side and pursed his lips in partial agreement. "There's no law against having nice things, Richard."

"How convenient for you."

He ignored the barb. "There is, however, a law against siphoning money from charities and nonprofits." Brock twisted around and clicked a remote in his hand. One of the computer monitors bloomed to life, displaying a spreadsheet with dozens of entries that featured enormous amounts of money ranging from thousands to tens of millions. "Do you know what that is, Richard?"

The man looked concerned but didn't answer, instead staring at the screen with obvious bewilderment. "No." He didn't sound convincing.

"That's an assessment of the money you've stolen over the last ten years. I could have gone back further, but I figured why bother? That right there is more than enough to indict you on federal charges."

Richard snorted. "Is that what this is? You some kind of cop working for the IRS or something? Undercover actor? I always thought you weren't that good." His voice turned to gravel with the last derisive remark.

Brock shrugged and bobbed his head. "Oh, I'm sure you'd love to say any number of things to get under my skin right now. We both know I'm good at my craft. Maybe even better than you, but I would never say such a thing to my idol."

"You have a weird way of treating those you revere."

"Well, I did revere you."

Richard thought he knew where this was going. "What do you want, Brock? You want some of that money? Fine. It's in offshore accounts around the world. Some are in Swiss banks. I can send you whatever you want. Just let me out of here, and we won't tell anyone about this."

Fear dripped from his lips as he made the offer.

Brock bellowed. When the laughter died down, he grew serious once more. "Oh, Richard. I don't want your money. In fact, all of that money has been transferred to accounts of my choosing. You have nothing left to give except one thing."

The fear on the prisoner's face rapidly swelled to rage-filled disbelief. "You're bluffing."

"Oh, Richard," Brock waved a hand at his captive and chuckled. "So stubborn, even to the end. That money is going to help make a real difference for the environment." He began pacing back and forth once more. "You see, your plans were always well-intentioned but lacked that real punch that could make an actual difference. It was too politically correct. You know?"

Richard said nothing, still wiggling his wrists and contorting his shoulders in an attempt to find freedom.

"I have no idea what you're talking about, Brock. But I promise you this: The second I get out of these ropes, I'm going to give you the beating your parents never did."

Brock scowled at the threat. "You know nothing about my parents," he sneered. Then he took a step to the side, just behind his prisoner. Richard craned his neck to see, but he couldn't turn his head far enough to get a view of what Brock was up to.

"Look, kid, just let me out of here, and I'm sure we can all figure out a way for us to do a lot more good in the world. You know? Maybe you and I can team up. I could use another famous face on the Clean Planet project."

"I'm sure you could use more of my money, as well, Richard, especially considering your little entity is broke, as are you."

Farrow didn't like where this was going. He started talking faster as a desperate truth began to set in: he was a dead man.

"Fine. Okay? You want a confession from me? You got it. I took money from my various charities and moved it into the offshore accounts. You don't know what it's like, Brock. Being famous isn't all it's cracked up to be."

"Oh, I'm sure it's been a trying experience for you, what with your Italian sports cars and million-dollar mansions in various luxurious places around the world. Insurance on a Ferrari is no joke. I learned that firsthand."

Richard cut to the point, hoping that addressing whatever this madman wanted would somehow spare him whatever the guy was doing behind his back. What he hadn't seen was Brock picking up another rope that had been lying on the floor behind the chair.

"Please, Brock. I don't know what you're planning, but you have to let me go. Okay? If this has been a joke, then...good one. Hilarious. Well done, man. Are there cameras around or something? Is that what this—"

His words were cut short as rope looped around his neck and instantly drew tight, cutting off his windpipe.

The man's face radiated bright red once more. His eyes bulged even farther out of their sockets. Richard squirmed frantically, giving one last desperate attempt to free himself from the bonds.

He couldn't swallow, couldn't breathe. His lungs burned for air that he couldn't get. Brock continued to pull the rope hard, twisting it behind his victim's head so that there would be no break in the blocked airway.

Richard tried to say something, anything, but it came out like a mouse's squeak, with a spray of spittle.

"That's it," Brock said. "Let it go. Let it all go. Don't worry. I'll make it look like a suicide. The media will have a field day with all of your misallocated funds. They'll say you couldn't stand the pressure or something like that. I'm certain your fans will make some kind of memorial for you, perhaps outside one of your mansions."

He leaned close as Richard's vision began to blur. He was near the breaking point, his brain, lungs, and heart screaming for air.

Brock whispered into the man's ear. "I've already taken everything you have. Thank you for your donation, by the way. It will make what I'm about to do that much easier."

He gave the rope one last twist. Richard's eyes nearly popped out of their sockets. Then the tension in his muscles suddenly went limp. Brock felt the man's head sag forward and to the side. He kept the rope taught for another twenty seconds in case his victim was faking, but when he reached the two-minute mark, he knew the man was dead.

Brock let go of the rope, and the head slumped forward, the chin resting on the chest.

With a deep breath and a sigh, Brock nodded at his handiwork. Richard Farrow was dead, and now all of his financial assets were in Brock Carson's control.

"Phase one complete," he said, dusting his hands as he'd just done a hard day's work. "I'm hungry. I think I'll get something to eat."

He slapped the dead man on the shoulder and strolled out of the room.

5

ATLANTA

S ean waited for the cool air to finish blowing over him. The mechanical arms ran over his head and to either side of him. The clean room was designed to eliminate contaminants from getting into the lab in the basement of the IAA building in Downtown Atlanta, though Sean wondered how effective the system really was. It reminded him of the big metal-detection machines that airports had implemented a short time after the terrorist attacks of 9/11.

The machine finished its job, and the door on the other side opened automatically. Adriana was already inside, chatting with Tara Watson and Alex Simms, Tommy's faithful lab assistants. Based on their pale complexions, they hadn't been out in the sun much during the summer months. Now that fall was almost here, they likely wouldn't get a chance until next spring—unless Tommy decided to start sending them out on their own field excursions.

As Sean stepped out into the laboratory, the group turned and faced him. Tara and Alex waved and smiled, welcoming him back as they always did. He'd seen them the week before, so it wasn't like he'd been gone for months. Still, it was always nice to come home to friendly faces.

Sean strode across the room and wrapped Tara in a warm hug. Then he let go and embraced Alex, denying the handshake the younger man offered in lieu of a hug.

"Brothers gotta hug," Sean said, slapping him on the back.

The gesture shook Alex's entire body, but he tried to stand firm so he didn't look weak in front of the ladies, especially Tara.

"So, what have you two been up to while I was gone?" Sean asked. He let go of Alex and took a step back.

"We were just telling Adriana all about it," Tara said. "We've equipped your weapons with new laser sights."

Sean frowned. "My weapons?"

Tara grinned. "Yeah, your old ones. We heard about the malfunction with the new stuff. Sometimes, the old ways are best."

She handed him a Springfield pistol. He took it and examined the weapon. The slide was open so he could see into the chamber. The magazine was lying on a desk nearby.

"When are you going to do this one?" he asked.

She grinned with pride. "It's already on there."

Sean frowned. "What?" Then he saw it. The attachment was nothing more than a tiny circle on the front of the muzzle, just below the barrel.

"Nanotechnology," Alex explained. "That little thing can put a red dot on a target up to two hundred yards away."

"Accurately?"

Alex nodded.

"Wow. Where'd you guys get this?"

The two glanced at each other but said nothing.

"Whoa. You made it?"

They rolled their shoulders at the same time. Tara nodded.

"That's...amazing."

"We have our moments."

Sean scowled. "So, you heard about the new gear, huh?"

"We had our suspicions before, but yeah, Tommy told us," Alex explained. "That stuff was still highly prototypical. I know the R&D

guys tested the crap out of it, but we weren't sure it would hold up in the field."

Sean was impressed and let it show. "Well, I'm not going to be using that stuff again anytime soon. As you said, tried and true is good enough for me."

"You're okay, though, you know...with the other stuff?"

Sean nodded. "I'll be fine."

Adriana flashed a puzzled glance but didn't have a chance to push the issue.

"Well, well, well. My prodigal son has returned."

The familiar voice came from a side door into the room. Tommy stood just inside it with a darkly tanned woman at his side. She wore a navy-blue business suit with an expensive-looking gold chain dangling from her neck. Her thick black eyebrows matched the hair on her head that draped halfway down her back.

"Why do we have to go through the whole airlock thing, but you get to just walk right in?" Sean asked, ignoring Tommy's initial greeting.

His friend chuckled. "Perks of the position. Also, I'm pretty sure that thing is useless. I may have it taken out."

Sean rolled his eyes and watched as Schultzie and his guest made their way around the worktables, desks, and litany of display cases containing artifacts from all over the world. Scrolls, tablets, vases, urns, weapons, and jugs filled the glass boxes, pieces from collections that were long thought lost to both civilization and history.

Tommy stopped close to the group, filling the gap in the circle. He motioned to his companion. "Please excuse my friend's rude behavior. Sean isn't usually...okay, he's always like this."

Sean shook his head and snorted. "Sean Wyatt. And you are?"

The woman extended her hand and shook his firmly. "Dr. Priya Chaudhry, Director of Indian Antiquities at the University of Mumbai."

Sean raised both eyebrows. "Well, Doctor, it's a pleasure to meet you, and I must say, the rest of us are out of our league in the presence of someone with your credentials."

She smirked a bashful yet appreciative grin and gave a nod. "I assure you, Sean, you and your team are not out of any league. A piece of paper doesn't convey intelligence or expertise in all things."

Sean let go of her hand, realizing he was still gripping it. He motioned to Adriana. "This is Adriana Villa. Adventurer, historian, and my girlfriend."

Priya's perfect smile remained intact as she shook hands with the Spaniard. "A pleasure, Adriana." She motioned to Tara and Alex, affectionately known as "the kids" to everyone else at IAA. "Have they brought you up to speed on what's going on?"

"Not yet," Tara said quickly. "We were just about to."

"Not a problem," Tommy said, cutting in. "Probably better to do it in the conference room anyway."

Sean's eyebrows tightened over his nose. "What's all this about?"

"You'll see soon enough, buddy. Come on. Tell me about Slovenia. Did you have a good flight?"

The group made their way out of the lab, following Tommy out the side door he'd come through a few minutes before.

A short elevator ride and a quick walk down a corridor led the six people to a long conference room and a glossy mahogany table with twelve chairs set around it. A flatscreen television hung from the wall at one end. Windows lined the exterior wall, giving an uninterrupted view of Centennial Olympic Park below where children played in the ring fountains to the sounds of different songs. Green grass was littered with leaves of yellow, red, and orange, a sign that fall was coming early this year—and that winter wouldn't be far behind.

Once everyone was seated, Tommy moved to the head of the table and stood with his arms folded across his chest. "Dr. Chaudhry has come to us with an interesting case."

Sean's right eyebrow arched. Case?

Occasionally, the IAA would take on a case from a private entity or even a single person, though those were few and far between. Most of what they did was in cooperation with other groups, teams, and governmental agencies. However, from time to time—like any good band—they got requests.

Through the years, fame had followed the exploits of Sean and Tommy, along with those of some of their associates. While they never sought the spotlight, that bright beacon was often too difficult to avoid. With every publicized adventure, every incredible discovery, their legend soared higher and higher, making their profile ever easier for people to find.

For the most part, Tommy didn't field calls from private citizens or entities. He'd built the IAA with money his parents had left him after their deaths—deaths that had turned out to be untrue. They'd been held in North Korea for years, leading the rest of the civilized world to believe they were dead. When they returned to the United States, so much had changed, but one thing they were proud to see was that their son had taken the love of history they'd instilled in him and turned it into something that helped preserve antiquity for generations to come.

The money he'd been left had grown into a massive fortune, thanks to shrewd investments. It allowed a few perks: a private jet, a nice home, and reliable car, and food wherever they wanted a table in some of the most exclusive restaurants in the world. Tommy, however, didn't have expensive tastes.

The jet was for convenience. The home was modest but tasteful, as was his car. Food was the one place where he spared no expense, and even then it was only once a week. Maybe twice.

So, he didn't need anyone else's money. Through the years, he'd turned down more money-hungry, fame-seeking treasure hunters than he could recall. It only seemed to be getting worse. With various networks offering reality shows about treasure hunters looking for shipwrecks, scouring the desert, or chasing new leads, it was no surprise to Tommy. A new breed of amateur history sleuths had been born. Many wanted to piggyback on someone like Tommy.

All of that was why he was so grateful and eager to help Dr. Chaudhry. He jumped at the chance.

"The case," Dr. Chaudhry said, "is a mystery we can't seem to figure out. We were hoping you could help us." She spoke with a distinct British accent.

Sean put his hands out and leaned back, propping one leg over the other knee. "Well, Doc—"

"Please, call me Priya," she corrected him with a sincere grin.

"Okay then. Priya. What do you have for us?"

She clutched a reddish-brown handbag in her right hand. With a quick flick of the left, the zipper was open. She fished out a single envelope sealed in a freezer bag.

Sean cocked his head to the right, eyeing the object as she set it flat on the table and nudged it toward him.

Adriana scooted closer, flashing a sidelong glance at Priya before focusing on the item on the table surface.

The kids and Tommy remained back, telling Sean they'd already seen it. He couldn't help but wonder why they were even meeting in the conference room about it. Why the ruse? He let the thought go and played along.

"So, it's okay to open it?"

"Of course."

Sean pried open the zipper lock and reached in. He plucked the letter out and set it down directly in front of him. There was nothing remarkable about the envelope. It didn't look particularly old, no more than a year, if that. That realization sparked more thoughts. What was so important about this letter? He'd been more deliberate with his thoughts lately, part of a new mental exercise he was trying. Occasionally, it annoyed him, but it was integral in helping him get through the process of feeling better mentally.

"Go ahead," Tommy urged. He was leaning against the wall in the corner with his arms folded.

Sean stood the envelope on its bottom and pulled apart the top. Whoever had opened it did it cleanly, using a letter opener or a sharp knife. He craned his neck and saw the names and addresses on the front. Unsurprisingly, it had been addressed to Dr. Chaudhry. Who it was from, however, seemed a tad odd. It was mailed from her, as well.

Sean frowned. "Um, did you mail this to yourself?"

Tommy shot up from his leaning spot and pumped his fist in the air. Then he pointed around the room at the others. "You guys are buying! I told you he would ask it."

Sean's scowl deepened, crease lines radiating out from the corners of his eyes. "Would ask what?"

"The obvious question." Tommy kept laughing, but the rest of the room clearly didn't think it was as funny as he did.

Sean rolled his eyes and looked back to Priya. "So, someone sent this to you but didn't put their name and address on it. They just put yours in both places?"

"That's correct."

His eyebrows shot up, and he glanced at Adriana. "Odd," she offered.

He snorted. "Yeah. I guess that's right up our alley."

Sean pulled out the letter and unfolded it, spreading it out flat on the table—or as flat as he could get it with three crisp seams across the face.

Instantly, his frown returned, eyes narrow with suspicion then confusion. He looked up at the others, meeting Priya's gaze first. "What is this? A joke?"

She shook her head. "I don't believe so."

Sean crinkled his forehead and brought his eyes back to the paper. "So...what exactly am I looking at? Some kind of scepter?"

"It's not a scepter," Priya corrected. "This is a rendering of the mace held by the Hindu god Vishnu."

"Ah." Sean gave an absentminded nod. His response didn't convince anyone in the room that he knew what she was talking about. Before she could inform him, he chirped up again. "The mace, usually displayed on the right side of the deity, in the lower hand. Yes. I've seen the pictures. I briefly studied Hindu mythology and religion."

She grinned at the revelation. "Yes, the mace is typically carried in the lower right hand by Vishnu. What else do you know about the mace?"

Sean's shoulders lifted an inch and then slumped back down. "Not much. I've studied a lot of ancient theologies as well as current ones. Nowadays, they're all starting to run together a little. I'm not getting any younger." He waved a hand that signaled he didn't mind getting older. The truth was, it bothered him a great deal, but that was something he needn't share with present company. Not with Dr. Chaudhry, at least.

Priya blinked slowly and nodded. "The mace is a weapon of incredible power. It's been known by many names, but one of the more common ones is Gada."

"Gada?"

She acknowledged Sean's question with a single nod. "Yes. The legend suggests that Vishnu created it from the bones of a powerful demon."

"Bones of a demon?" He didn't try to hide the incredulous tone in his voice.

"Yes. When Vishnu created the mace, he designed the weapon to be invincible, indestructible. It is said that nothing can defeat Gada."

Sean pursed his lips. His eyes fixed on a sequence of nonsensical symbols below the mace. They were grouped randomly. Some were bunched together; others stood alone. If he hadn't known better, he'd have thought they were alien letters forming words to a sentence, but there was one problem with that. None of the symbols were identical. In the groupings, there would certainly be repetitive symbols if each one stood for a letter. It could have been a cipher of some kind, though that still would beg the question as to where the repetition was.

A single index finger tapped lightly on the shiny table surface as he considered what she was saying. "Okay, so why did someone send you a drawing of this...weapon, along with all these strange symbols?" He flipped over the envelope to make sure of one other detail he'd noted before. "I see there was a stamp on the front, along with a government stamp. That tells me it was delivered with normal mail, at least by our standards. I'm not sure how the postal service works in India."

Truth was, he did know. Most postal services in the world operated on policies and systems that were nearly identical, with little differences here and there.

"Yes," Priya agreed.

Sean took a deep breath and exhaled. "Okay. I believe you. I mean, you'd have to be pretty nuts to fly all the way here from Mumbai to chase down a lead you sent to yourself, right?"

"Indeed."

Tommy cut in after a long period of silence. "This is where we stopped before you got here, Sean. So, now that everyone is caught up to speed, Priya, what is it you'd like us to do? My first assumption would be you want us to help you find your friend. Then the mace." He gave a nod toward the sheet of paper.

"The mace is only one piece of this puzzle," she said.

Tommy's brow furrowed. "What do you mean, one piece?"

"Yeah," Sean added. "And what puzzle?"

6

LOS ANGELES

The television in Brock Carson's living room displayed a young news anchor. The blonde woman was probably in her mid twenties. Her ruby-red lips nearly matched her V-neck dress perfectly.

It seemed every time Brock turned on the news, it was a different anchor, as if they only had a shelf life of a week these days. He'd grown up in a time when each network had the same talking head for decades. The anchors he'd watched in his youth were staples, linchpins of the industry. Apparently, generations to come would not experience the same.

Brock stretched out his arms across the back of the sofa and eased into a more comfortable position. A woman stood behind him and to the right, with arms folded across her chest. Heather Marlow was in a pair of khaki shorts and a black T-shirt. She looked more like she was ready to go on a camping trip than head of security for a prominent movie star. He knew the appearance had fooled more than a few people.

Her tanned, muscular physique brought out all the clowns. Some men hit on her. Several mistook her for a feeble, dainty princess.

Brock knew better. She was a trained killer, honed in the crucible of the United States military. After two tours of duty with the Rangers, she'd settled into civilian life for a short time, but it never felt right to her. Her skills were too good for a desk job, or any other kind of "normal" job, for that matter. She'd spent time training him in everything she knew as well as in a few skills she was learning. The intensive system she taught had paid immediate dividends in his action-film roles, allowing him to do many of his own stunts and fight scenes that other, less well-trained actors couldn't perform. He'd become a lethal fighter in his own right, though he'd still never bested Heather in a sparring competition. He recalled the last failure in the ring with a twinge of disdain and a good dose of humor.

The story of how Brock discovered her was one that still made him laugh from time to time.

She'd been on a bender, drunk and angry at the world for something for which he'd never gotten a straight answer. Maybe she'd just been hammered for the sake of it.

He'd just left one of the elite Los Angeles nightclubs he frequented and was on his way to his car when two men came out of an alley and tried to mug him. Brock saw the woman out of the corner of his eye as he prepared to defend himself. Apparently, she'd been across the street in a fit of nausea from too much booze. Her momentary evacuation of her stomach must have cleared her head, too, because she shouted at the men from the other sidewalk, threatening them with more swear words than he'd ever heard from a woman that pretty before.

Or any woman. Ever.

She trotted across the street, stepping up to the closest attacker. Two more men emerged from the shadows near a dumpster, one holding a knife, the other a chain.

Brock remembered the surprise in the men's eyes as he and Heather gave them the beating of a lifetime. The one with the knife ended up carrying it to the coroner's office with the blade jutting out of his eye. Of course, the police didn't show up until three of the assailants were unconscious and one dead, and Brock and his new friend long gone.

No one had seen a thing. If they had, no charges were ever pressed. Not that it would matter. Brock had enough money and power to get out of almost anything short of a dozen eyewitness confessions. Not to mention they were simply defending themselves.

That night, he'd brought Heather back to his place in the mountains, given her a clean bed to sleep in, clothes, and anything else she might need.

At first, she was leery that the famous actor was going to take advantage of her, or at least try. He'd shown himself to be useful in a fight, though she was confident she could take him if necessary. True to his word, though, Brock hadn't made a single move, instead giving her privacy and a safe place to sleep for the night.

The next day, he offered her a job as head of security. Then he got the story of her time in the military, the things she'd done, seen, and covered up.

On the television, the anchor shifted her focus to another camera, a universal sign that she was about to change subjects. Right on cue, a box appeared in the top-right corner with a picture of Richard Farrow and the words *Mysterious Suicide* underneath it.

"*This morning, award-winning actor Richard Farrow was found dead in his Beverly Hills home. A maid claimed to find the actor unresponsive. Authorities are reporting there is no suspicion of foul play at this time and are currently treating this as a suicide.*"

"Ha!" Brock clapped his hands together in a dramatic motion. "Sometimes it's too easy, you know?"

"It wasn't easy dragging his corpse in there last night," Heather commented. Her blonde hair shook as she spoke, tickling the bottom of her ears.

"You managed, as I knew you would." He reached up and squeezed her elbow. She jerked the arm away but gave him a reluctant grin.

"Nothing I couldn't handle."

The anchor continued: "*Police are claiming that Farrow took his own life sometime last night after he returned from dinner. Witnesses say he had gone out to eat alone. Many friends have suggested they are surprised by this, while others said Farrow battled depression his entire life.*

"Fans of the actor have taken to social media by the millions, sending out their condolences, positive thoughts, prayers, and well-wishes to family and friends. Richard Farrow is survived by—"

"Blah, blah, blah," Brock said as he pressed a button on the remote and turned off the television. "We know who he's survived by. No one. Just a few distant relatives. The guy was a jerk and pissed off most of the people in his sphere of influence."

"And you idolized him."

Brock snorted. "That's true. I did for a while. Not anymore, though. Not after the lies he lived, the money he stole from people."

"And because he didn't do what you thought needed to be done."

"Precisely." Brock stood up and rubbed his hands together. "Speaking of, are you ready to take a little trip?"

Heather raised a suspicious eyebrow. "Already?"

He nodded.

"The pieces are in place. It's time."

She appeared somewhat thrown off by the suddenness of his plan.

"I didn't realize you wanted to go so soon."

He rolled his shoulders. "You've been working on the security side of things, right?"

She nodded. "Yes. Supplies, weapons; everything is ready."

"Then what's the problem?" He put his hands out wide and flashed a big smile, like he was about to walk into a theme park. Truth was; they were doing anything but that.

"You're talking about going into an ancient Indian temple that has recently been touted as the most valuable building in the world. The five vaults they'd opened brought in tens of billions to the Indian government."

"And where do you think that money went, huh?" Brock crossed his arms.

"The politicians, obviously." Heather mirrored his stance and stuck her head out a little farther to emphasize her point. "I'm just saying, this is basically the Fort Knox of Hindu temples...of all temples. Not only is it a historically important site; it's also a holy site."

"And a bank, apparently."

She forced a laugh, though she still didn't approve of rushing forward with things. "Yes, that, too."

He stepped toward her and stretched out his hands, placing a palm on each of her smooth, taut shoulders. "Look, it's going to be fine. We've done the research. We know what to expect. We've got this."

She gazed into his eyes, her own still full of uncertainty. She'd never fully trusted men, none that came and went in her life. Brock Carson had changed all that. She trusted him almost completely, despite the fact that he was certainly more eccentric than most people she'd met.

"Okay," she said. "I'll get my things."

He nodded. "Good. The flight leaves tonight."

"I still can't believe we're doing this."

"No?"

Brock knew she was on board, fully, with his plan. It was wild, irrational, and driven by a passion she still didn't quite comprehend. That said, she believed in it.

During her time in the military, Heather had seen and done things that some would consider evil. Not her. She'd fought evil, tyrants, and murderers, killing them without reservation, without even a smear of guilt on her conscience.

Brock, however, had shown her something she'd never expected to fight for.

Off the coast of California, near the outlying islands of Hawaii, the Great Pacific Garbage Patch floated menacingly close to American shores. The flotilla of plastic, fishing nets, and general garbage had gained prominence for a few milliseconds in the national media, though it was barely a footnote when compared to political intrigue, the economy, and the current cultural climate.

A few news outlets mentioned it at the end of a show, and then the horrific image was lost to memory, at least to most people.

There were some, the vigilant fighters who kept watch for the planet, who knew about the threat looming ever closer to an American beach. Out of sight and out of mind could change rapidly the second a four-year-old stepped on a needle that had floated over from Bangkok. Then the narrative would change.

Brock had no intention of letting that happen.

It hadn't taken much to convince Heather of the problem. She'd grown up on the Gulf Coast of the Florida Panhandle, right in the wake of the massive oil disaster that had sent black sludge across the coastline for months after a drilling accident spilled millions of gallons into the ocean. She'd seen firsthand what reckless treatment of the planet could do to the human way of life and to the planet itself.

"It's going to be tricky," she said. "I know you think it will be easy and that we have everything covered, but it's never that simple."

"I know," he said. "And you've done a good job of taking my already considerable skills and honing them."

"You're certainly better with a gun than you used to be."

"Thank you," he said with a mock bow. "Go ahead and make the call. Have your team in place. We'll be there tomorrow night at the rendezvous." He shook her by the shoulders as he would a small child, and then let go. "Tomorrow we take a real step in making the world a better place."

Priya reached into the messenger bag she'd been carrying on her shoulder and pulled out a laptop. She flipped it open, and a second later the screen blinked to life. She tapped away on the keys for several seconds, entering a password and login information, and then spun the device around so everyone else in the room could see what was on the display.

Everyone leaned closer to get a better look at the images. The picture on the right was one that everyone recognized. It was the mace of Vishnu, Gada as she'd called it. The rendering was similar to the one on the paper at Sean's fingertips.

The second image was a stark contrast, different in shape to the imposing, bulbous mace. It looked like a sort of trident, but different than ones most of those in attendance had seen through their studies of ancient weapons or mythology. The most frequently seen trident was the one used by Neptune or Poseidon. Many scholars had argued through the centuries that those two deities were one and the same, simply crossing over into other cultures. This weapon on Priya's computer wasn't entirely dissimilar but did possess a few subtle differences. It was, however, just a drawing.

"Looks like a trident," Alex blurted.

"That's precisely what it is," Priya acknowledged. "It is the trident of Shiva. It's called Trishula."

Tommy nodded, recognizing the object and its moniker. "Yeah, I remember reading about that. It's supposed to be an indestructible weapon."

"I thought the Gada was indestructible, too," Sean chimed. "We dealing with a game of rock/paper/scissors where everyone has rock?"

Priya frowned at the analogy but moved on. "Shiva is the destroyer in Hinduism."

"Destroyer of what?"

"Whatever he chooses. He is part of a holy trinity, or Trimurti, with Vishnu and Brahma the creator."

"Wait," Tara jumped in. "If Brahma is the creator and Shiva is the destroyer, what is Vishnu's role again? Sorry. I never studied Hinduism, not in depth, anyway."

Priya passed her a reassuring smile. "It's no problem. Vishnu is the maintainer, the protector of life and balance. Without him, the universe would exist in a perpetual cycle of creation and destruction. He keeps everything safe."

Tara nodded, understanding.

"So, why are you showing us this trident and mace?" Adriana asked, ending her long bout of silence. "And who sent you the letter?"

"These two mythical weapons go hand in hand with one another. Both are, as Sean put it, rock against rock. One neutralizes the other."

Sean stiffened in his seat and leaned forward. He steepled his fingers for a second while resting his elbows on the table. "Why do I have a bad feeling about where this is going?"

When she spoke again, her voice was as heavy as gravy, thick with sadness and concern. "One of my colleagues was working on a project, a dig. It was pretty standard. Nothing crazy. They were searching for artifacts near Bhangarh Fort."

The blank expressions around the room told her they had no idea what she was talking about, or where that place was.

"Bhangarh Fort," she explained, "is a mysterious fortress that was built in the seventeenth century near the city of Jaipur. It's well known for being a haunted attraction for tourists."

Tommy rolled his eyes at the insinuation. "Haunted?"

"Yes, I know. Silly. Nonetheless, there are strange occurrences that have been recorded in that area. People have disappeared." A hint of concern laced her voice. "Now my colleague has gone missing as well. His team has no idea what happened to him."

"And you think he's the one who sent you this letter?" Sean tapped on the paper.

She nodded. "Call it a hunch if you want to, but Ishaan wouldn't simply vanish like that. The fact it happened in a place with a good amount of documentation regarding strange occurrences only makes me feel more worried about his well-being. The only thing I can figure is that he found something, something important."

"And you think someone knew what he found?" Tommy asked.

Priya lowered her head. "Yes."

The group fell silent, both out of respect for their guest and to collect their thoughts.

"Have you contacted local or regional authorities?" Sean asked the first question that popped into his mind. He knew it was an institutional kind of query, one that any officer or agent would ask. Normally, he wouldn't be so by-the-book, but in this instance, he was trying to gather as much information as he could.

"Yes. They're putting together an investigation, but those things take time."

"When did you lose contact with…"

"Ishaan. Dr. Ishaan Patel. Over a week ago."

"A week?" Tommy scoffed at the notion. "Incredible. Here, they won't start a search until after someone is gone a day or two, but a lot can happen in seven days." He couldn't remember the exact time frame, but as a person who'd gone missing once, he'd experienced the lack of immediate concern on the part of certain authorities. Sean had saved his life, tracked him down without so much as a thin lead.

Tommy could see the concern in his guest's eyes. He couldn't tell if this Ishaan fellow and Priya were more than just colleagues or peers, but from that hint of despair she let leak, he figured there was at least a good friendship there. He shook off the thoughts. That was none of his business. Then again, knowing every piece of information in a scenario like this was important. Sean had taught him that over the years.

"No," she said. Though there was a hint of sadness in her voice, she didn't cry. "I know a few detectives have started the process—at my request, but I'm certain you all know how long the process can take. I fear Ishaan won't have that kind of time."

"You believe this letter—the drawing—was sent to you by your friend and perhaps that has something to do with his disappearance?" Adriana asked the question, connecting the dots for the woman's visit. She figured everyone in the room understood what was going on, but Adriana liked to make sure everything was crystal clear.

Priya nodded. "I know it's a stretch, but I think Ishaan must have stumbled on to something, something he wasn't supposed to find. It's odd that he sent this with no other explanation."

Sean still didn't follow a particular line of thought. He motioned to the computer she'd propped up on the table. "Why are you showing us this trident?" he asked. "Do you think your friend's disappearance also has something to do with it? If so, why did he only send you the image of the Gada?"

It was a question Priya had been considering and one for which she didn't have the answer. "That...is why I'm here. Your agency has shown incredible abilities in being able to figure out things like this. I'm here to ask for your help in finding Ishaan."

Tommy held his breath for a moment, staring at the computer screen and the two images on the display. Under ordinary circumstances, he would have simply told the woman that there was nothing they could do, that the Indian authorities would have to be trusted to find her colleague. In this case, however, he felt compelled to help. The cops would have no leads, not any they would understand, anyway.

This sort of thing was right up Tommy and Sean's alley—not the kidnapping-investigation part, but certainly the historical mystery.

"All we have to go on is that piece of paper and your belief that, somehow, the mace and the trident are connected to your friend's disappearance." He stated it as he brought a fist to his chin and scratched the corner of his mouth. Deep contemplation filled his voice.

"I realize it's not much to go on. I wish I had more answers."

"If you did, you wouldn't be here," Tara said in a sympathetic tone.

Priya let out a short laugh. "That's true."

"So," Sean said, sounding like he was ready to wrap up, "your friend was working an ancient dig site near a place that has been rumored to have hauntings and disappearances. What was he looking for again?"

She shook her head. "Standard stuff. I'm sure you all have been on many digs in the past. As far as I know, they didn't discover anything unusual."

"And the rest of his team is okay?"

Priya nodded. "Yes. Other than being concerned for Ishaan, they're fine. Many of the workers have returned to their homes in light of the disappearance. A few have stayed on to take care of things until this is figured out. Our point person in charge is Dr. Lidia Farrington. She's overseeing site security."

"Farrington?" Tommy asked. "Doesn't ring a bell. You, Sean?"

Sean shook his head. "No. Haven't heard of her."

"She's one of our foremost experts in the Tamil dynasties of Chera, Chola, and Pandya. She also has extensive defense and security training. The site will be fine under her watch."

Sean wanted to bring up the fact that her friend Ishaan had disappeared under Farrington's watch, but he left it alone.

He leaned over the paper and stared at the image of the mace once more. "So, this mace and that trident are both indestructible weapons. One protects humanity, and one is capable of destroying it. I guess my big question is; how do they work?"

"Considering these two weapons are mythical in nature, we aren't certain. That's like asking a Jew or Christian how the Ark of the Covenant works."

Tommy and Sean flashed a mischievous sideways glance at each other but said nothing. Adriana caught the gesture but ignored it for the time being.

"Fair point," Sean inserted. "But you believe they're real, right?"

"I am not a religious person, Mr. Wyatt. I do believe, however, that many of the things taught in religion are based on factual events and people. Perhaps the trident and the mace are metaphorical objects. Perhaps they're real. What I know is that Ishaan sending me this makes me think he's found something that has to do with it, and I want to know what that is. If you can figure that out, we might be able to find him."

Sean considered her response. It elicited more questions in his mind, but he kept them quiet for now.

"What do you think, Sean?" Tommy asked. "Can we help out?"

Sean smirked at his friend. "I was going to ask you the same thing, but yeah, I think we might be able to lend assistance. I didn't have anything pressing in the near future." He fired Adriana an apologetic glance.

She blew it off. "When do we begin?"

His sheepish grin turned to a full-blown, toothy smile.

I love this woman.

"Okay then," Sean said. "Fire up the jet. Let's see what we can do to help."

8

THIRUVANANTHAPURAM

The white Cadillac Escalade pulled up to a two-story shack on the edge of town. Another matching SUV stopped just behind the first.

The back-left window rolled down, and Brock Carson poked his head out, taking in the rickety building. He gave an approving nod. "It's perfect."

The window rolled up, and a second later the door swung open.

There were no people around, not that he could tell. This area was in a rough part of the city, where drugs and criminals ran rampant. No one would think to look for him here, not that anyone would think to look for him to begin with. As far as the rest of the world knew, Brock was traveling abroad to clear his head from the loss of an actor he so admired.

The slums of a lesser-known Indian town would be the last place anyone would think someone of his stature would visit.

The building had been abandoned a few years ago, a failed bakery from the looks of it. Brock had used one of his many umbrella entities to make the purchase. It would never be tied to him in any way. One thing he'd learned long ago was always keep the shells moving. The second anyone blinked, the shells would have moved a further three times. His money was untraceable. Well, almost. He'd left a single back door open to all of the money he was using for this project, and it all led to a dead man who'd just hanged himself in Beverly Hills a few days before.

He stepped up onto the cracked sidewalk and put his hands on his hips. Heather joined him a moment later, along with two more guards—one on either side of the two of them.

He gazed at the building as if admiring it, though there was little to find admirable about the structure. Long cracks ran from the top-right corner down through the center, dipping straight toward the ground and a large double window next to the entrance. An old awning, tattered and frayed, clung to an aluminum pole by a thread. How the thing hadn't blown away in a storm was a mystery.

The windows, for the most part, were intact. Only one pane on the left of the big front window was busted out. The two upstairs windows appeared to be fine, save for missing one of the shutters. The plaster exterior walls had been painted a pale red color that had faded almost to pink over the years.

Brock didn't care about any of that. How the building looked wasn't important to him. It was all about location and function.

He stepped to the door and twisted the knob. The thing creaked as he turned it. When he pushed on the door, the hinges screamed their protest as rusted metal ground on more rusted metal.

He crossed the threshold into the old bakery showroom. Glass display cases were covered in dust, as were the shelves, furniture, and a ceiling fan. A few cobwebs dangled from the latter.

"Nice of them to leave it unlocked for us," Brock commented with a cough.

"It sure is dusty in here." Heather moved slowly around the perimeter of the room. She ran a finger along one of the dirty glass screens, picking up a thick layer of dust on her skin.

"We'll get it cleaned up in no time," Brock said. There was a hint of pride in his voice, though she didn't know why.

He rounded the corner that separated the display area and a path into the kitchen and ascended the creaky staircase leading to the second floor.

At the top, he spun around the post and continued forward down the narrow hallway, passing a bathroom on the right, a small office, and then reaching a huge room at the end. It must have been a bedroom in its past life, but now it would be the staging center for his primary objective. He wandered over to the window, ignoring the empty room in favor of the view it provided. He gazed out into the clear night. Something in the distance held his eyes and wouldn't let go. For good reason. What he was staring at was the reason for his being there.

The golden rooftop of the Sree Padmanabhaswamy Temple shimmered in the light of the full moon. A child cried in the night. A cat let out a snarling meow. Other than that, however, the evening remained still as he stared at the impressive sight.

Footsteps on the stairs behind him clunked heavily, a sign the men were bringing the gear upstairs to begin preparations.

He spun around in time to meet Heather's gaze. She had been standing only a few feet behind him.

"You are good," he said with a toothy grin.

"Stealth has kept me alive."

He turned and looked out at the temple once more. "Spectacular, isn't it?"

"It is. I wonder what that roof alone is worth."

He chuckled. "Probably more than I have."

She smirked and folded her arms. "Maybe we should just try to steal the roof?"

Another laugh escaped him. "My dear, money isn't our problem." He glanced over his shoulder at her with a mock-reprimanding glare. "Besides, in a few years, money won't matter if we keep destroying the planet like this. We won't have anywhere to spend it."

She knew he was right, which was one of the reasons she'd so eagerly jumped on board with what many would have called a crazy plan.

The men began setting up tables and chairs. Electrical wires ran out to a generator in the next room where a ventilation tube could send exhaust out of an open window. They stacked equipment on the table surfaces, including radios, computers, and a few other tech gadgets.

It took the men less than five minutes to have everything prepared. There wasn't much. They only needed a single computer with one backup, some communications gear, and a power supply. Everything else was overkill. The less attention they drew, the better, which was why they were in a decrepit building that, by all rights, probably should have been condemned long ago.

Brock moved over to the table with the laptops on it and began typing. He finished his keystrokes and hit the Enter button. A new image appeared on the monitor. It was a zoomed-out view of the temple or a rendering of it.

"This is the target," he said.

The other three paid attention as he spoke.

"The two still in the trucks already know their jobs. They're pickup and delivery only. If something goes wrong at any time during the mission, call for an extraction and get out as fast as you can."

He leaned forward and moved his fingers across the trackpad. The screen's view changed, zooming in until the temple broke down into a schematic blueprint of the different levels and rooms of the structure.

Brock's fingers moved quicker now as he moved the view away from the general scene and to a more detailed depiction of the main level.

"We don't have to worry about upstairs. Nothing for us there," he said.

"No security?" Heather asked.

"There will be some up there, but they'll be occupied with their usual duties. The guards we have to worry about are on the main floor. The toughest part will be getting through the gate. At night, it will be completely locked down with as many as fifty men keeping watch over it at any given moment."

Heather gave a nod and took over. "I was right about the big switch. The commandos that have been in charge of guarding the temple for the last, I don't know, maybe several decades, have been removed and replaced with ordinary cops from the city."

Brock snorted. "Good to hear. We shouldn't have any trouble with them."

"Doubt it."

He went back to his plan, touching the screen. The view began to run smoothly through a corridor of white lines meant to represent the corridor they'd need to take to reach the first vault.

"We go through here. It's a direct offshoot from the entrance. Once we're inside, we'll have to hurry down this passage to get to the first of the six vaults."

The guards and Heather listened with intense focus.

"This is a dangerous spot," Brock added. "Only a few alcoves for cover here. We'll largely be exposed."

"Which means if there are more guards inside, we'll be sitting ducks."

"Correct. So, if that happens, shoot fast and ask questions later. Our weapons will be muted somewhat with the suppressors, but we all know they don't sound like in the movies. They're still loud enough for a trained ear to recognize, so let's be judicious about discharging those guns."

The others nodded.

"We hang a right here," Brock continued, pointing at the screen where the corridor veered around a corner.

The scene changed as the camera view passed through another short corridor before reaching a door.

"We go through this door here," Brock said, "and that will take us to the first vault chamber on the other side."

The camera flew through the closed barricade and into the next room. The ceiling opened up high above, and the walls towered over the floor, where a recess in the center led a set of stairs to a lower level.

"This vault has already been pilfered," Brock noted. "It's one of the ones the government opened and ripped off, with the Supreme Court's approval nonetheless."

The group shared a short laugh.

"Ignore that one," he said, pointing to a set of doors set in the other side of the vault. "This is where we're going."

He zoomed in once more and the camera view flew through the doors, leading into another chamber. He maneuvered the screen down the flight of stairs in the center of the room and stopped when a pair of doors with some kind of serpents glared out at them.

"What in the world?" one of the men uttered.

"I know, right?" Brock grinned, glancing over his shoulder at the guard. "Pretty grotesque, right? Considering Hindu culture reveres snakes, it's interesting that they would make these two so angry and foreboding."

Even the digital replicas of the serpents presented a menacing threat to the viewers. He stopped the animation and stared at the screen, raising a tanned index finger.

"Behind that door is what we're after. Remember to stay focused once we're inside." Brock didn't feel the need to remind Heather of this, but the two guards might have needed a little refresher. The plan was to only take two of them in with Heather, leaving two getaway drivers. The rest of his henchmen were in positions around the country, each holed up in a specific city where the second phase of his plan would begin. There were others on their way to different parts of the continent, stretching as far away as Hong Kong.

"There's no telling what kind of traps lie beyond that door," Brock added.

"And it's sealed from the inside," Heather went on, "which you already know. So, we're going to use a special compound I've concocted to blow the thing open."

One of the guards, a big man standing around six feet, four inches scrunched his face in disapproval. His long black beard made him look like a warrior from ancient times that might have fought against Julius Caesar himself. "Won't using explosives alert the locals?"

"Yeah," the other guard agreed.

Brock's lips creased. "Once we have what's on the other side of that door, you won't ever have to worry about the cops again."

9

JAIPUR, INDIA

Lidia Farrington sat in the front seat of the black SUV, staring straight ahead as her driver navigated his way through traffic.

Jaipur had grown rapidly through the last century, boasting a population of just over three million people. That didn't include some of the outlying areas in the hills and mountains.

The roads and public transit systems had developed at a much slower rate than that of the populace, thus creating congestion on the roads and sidewalks in much of the town.

She hated coming here, preferring the solitude of being out in the middle of nowhere working on a dig site. Lidia had never cared for big cities. She'd heard people say that culture was more abundant there, but she disagreed. Lidia had enough culture in her day job. That was kind of her thing, after all, studying cultures. Sure, they were ancient and usually long forgotten, but they were still cultures and she figured that was enough.

She ran a hand through a few loose strands of her auburn hair and glanced out the window at the huddled masses of people budging their way down the sidewalks. She often wondered where they were going, what they were doing, especially in the middle of the day when most people were working.

It was none of her concern. She didn't know why she had those kinds of thoughts, so she pushed them aside as she'd done so many times before.

She stole a glance over her shoulder into the back of the vehicle and nodded. "I appreciate you all coming on such short notice. Priya was extremely grateful for your willingness to help with this...problem."

Sean had been staring out the window at the people, buildings, and surrounding desert hillsides. Jaigarh Fort, perched high on the mountaintop, loomed above the nearby apartments, houses, and businesses. The famous structure also looked down on Amer Fort, a spectacular piece of engineering, architecture, and design that drew many tourists to the city every year. Jaigarh Fort was also the home to one of the largest cannons ever created, the Jaivana.

On the flight from Atlanta, Sean and the others had gone to great lengths to learn as much as they could about the region, its customs, and its people. Sean had been to India before, but only twice. One of those times had been a layover. The other had been on a mission. He'd never been to Jaipur, though, and was disappointed that he wouldn't have more time to do some of the more touristy things; such as taking in the Pink Palace, an incredible castle made from pink and red sandstone that connected to the opulent City Palace.

The forts had been something he wanted to see as well, although he considered the problem that Jaigarh Fort was situated at a pretty high elevation. Through the years, Sean's interminable fear of heights had kept him from visiting some of the most important historical locations in the world. It was something he'd fought his entire life. The phobia gripped him like a demon, causing his heart rate to quicken and his breathing to shorten. As much as possible, Sean did his best to stay out of those kinds of situations. Still, seeing that huge cannon would have been something to remember.

From what he'd read on the flight, the massive gun was just over twenty feet long. It had only been fired one time in its history, but never in battle. The huge shell traveled over twenty-two miles and took more than two hundred pounds of gunpowder.

He sighed as the towering fort disappeared behind a beige apartment building.

"Happy to help," Sean said in response to Lidia's comment. "We live for this sort of thing." He tried not to sound excited about trying to track down a missing person, but he wasn't thinking about the man who'd disappeared. He was fairly certain the guy had chosen to vanish. Sometimes, people just wanted a little time off, some R and R. Then again, the circumstances surrounding this particular disappearance were rather mysterious.

"How far to the site?" Sean asked quickly. He already knew the answer from checking on his phone upon landing at the airport, but he figured a little small talk couldn't hurt.

"A little under two hours," Lidia said.

She was a striking woman. Her face sported a dozen freckles under emerald-green eyes. She spoke with a distinction that revealed her well-educated background and perhaps a life of luxury during childhood. The English accent was unmistakable though hardly a rarity in that part of the world.

Sean nodded and glanced at Adriana sitting diagonally in front of him. He was a little scrunched in the back of the SUV's third-row seat, but Tommy had insisted that they all ride together despite the fact that Lidia had come with a small caravan of two vehicles. Sean's knees were almost to his chest, but he didn't complain; although two hours in that position will seem like an eternity.

The group of Americans had grabbed a quick breakfast of dal kachoris—a sort of fried bread with grilled onions and garlic inside. They reminded Sean of samosas, and after devouring the first one, he ordered another from the street vendor outside their hotel. The spicy, salty flavors still stuck with him despite chugging a cool chai tea a couple of minutes after.

"I guess you haven't heard any word from investigators," Tommy said.

"Unfortunately, no." Lidia's tone was cold, borderline irritated.

The guests got the distinct impression she was annoyed at the fact she'd had to drop whatever she was doing to drive two hours to pick them up. Maybe she felt like she had a handle on the situation and didn't need them meddling with her affairs. Perhaps she was just having a bad day. Whatever the cause, she'd been less than cordial.

"What can you tell us about what Dr. Patel was working on before he disappeared?"

"I would have thought Dr. Chaudhry filled you in on those details."

Tommy looked back at his friend and then straightened, resting an elbow on the windowsill. "She told us a little about it. Said everything was pretty standard. The usual kind of stuff."

"There you go."

Tommy bit his lower lip.

Sean felt the need to cut into this dance. "Was Dr. Patel acting strangely in the days leading up to his disappearance? Did you notice anything unusual about his behavior? Was it inconsistent with his normal demeanor? Anything at all that would make him do something…irrational?"

Lidia's eyes narrowed as she considered the questions. She didn't take long to respond. "Your background is in psychology, correct, Mr. Wyatt?"

She said the mister part with a hint of derision, almost as if he were beneath her because he didn't tote a Ph.D. with him in his back pocket.

"Yes, ma'am," he said in a weak Southern drawl. "And history."

"I can understand why you would ask those questions, but I can assure you Dr. Patel was in a perfectly normal state of mind before he disappeared. He didn't say or do anything out of the ordinary. He was in a clear mind right up to the day he vanished."

He pursed his lips at the response. "Good to know."

"The next thing you would like to ask is about the time frame of his disappearance, yes?"

"Sure. That would be good to file away."

"We have a small camp set up around the site. The options were to stay in platform tents or somewhere in the nearby town. Since most of the accommodations we could find were…inadequate, we opted for camping, only going into the cities or villages when the need for supplies arose. The night Dr. Patel disappeared, he'd been working very late. Being in charge of security, I often conduct a quick sweep of the camp to make sure everything is safe."

"Do you have issues with safety out there?" Tommy asked.

"We've had run-ins with thieves on occasion. They typically don't take anything critical. Mostly flashlights, lamps, a tablet now and then, but nothing we can't replace. That doesn't mean we should just let them have free access to all our stuff. There's a fence surrounding the camp to keep out intruders, but we are pretty much on our own when it comes to policing the area."

Sean wanted to get back to the night Ishaan Patel went missing. "So, you were out on your patrol, and what happened?"

"Dr. Patel was still awake. Local time was around 11:30, which was quite late for him to be up. He usually goes to bed around ten, if not earlier. Many of us in this field are morning people. When you work in hot, arid regions for weeks at a time, you learn that morning is the best part of the day to get things done. Once the sun comes up over the hills and the buildings, if you're not under some kind of tent shelter, you'll bake in no time."

"Good to know." Sean rolled his eyes. He'd spent more time in hotter places than where they were headed, but she didn't need to know that and he didn't feel like getting into that with her. "So, he was up late working?"

"That's what it looked like. The lamps were on in his tent. I could see his silhouette hunched over his desk. He was working on something. What it was I don't know."

Sean stopped his line of questioning and decided the best way to get more information would be to wait and see for himself when they arrived at the camp. For now, he would enjoy his uncomfortable ride in the third row of the SUV.

Tommy, however, wanted to press the issue. "You didn't hear or see anything out of the ordinary that night?"

"No," Lidia said in a flat voice. "The only thing out of the ordinary was the next morning when we all got together for breakfast in the mess hall and realized Dr. Patel wasn't there. I left the others to their food and went to his tent. When I opened it, I found it empty. There was no sign of a struggle. Nothing appeared to be missing. His computer was sitting out on the workstation, along with several of his notes. If it was a robbery, the thieves would have certainly taken his laptop."

Tommy nodded and turned his gaze out the window. Once more, the SUV's cabin descended into an uncomfortable silence as the passengers pondered the mysterious disappearance of Dr. Ishaan Patel.

10

BHANGARH, INDIA

Rain pelted the SUV, the droplets plunking the metal roof over and over again like tiny weights. Thousands more hit the windshield every minute as the wipers swiped back and forth in a desperate and futile fury. Sheets of water flung from the glass, only to be replaced the next second by more precipitation.

A trip that would normally have taken a few hours had lasted four due to the deluge and a few spots where road construction had slowed travel to a crawl.

"I guess we're here for the rainy season?" Tommy spoke up as the SUV pulled into the camp.

Little rivers of muddy water streamed down the rocky hillsides that surrounded the dig site. White tarps were positioned over the areas where the workers would normally be sweeping, digging, and sifting through centuries of dirt and rock.

The driver, an Indian guy who had yet to reveal his name, wiped his mustache with his forefinger and thumb before throwing the SUV into park and killing the engine.

"We're in the desert. There isn't much of a rainy season here, and this is not it."

Tommy pouted his lips at the remark then nodded. "Okay then. My name is Tommy, by the way."

"I know who you are," the man said and flung open the door. He pulled his shirt over his head and trotted off into the deluge, his boots clopping in the mud as he made his way up to a gate and disappeared beyond it, into the camp.

"Not much of a talker?" Sean asked from the back.

Lidia shook her head. "He doesn't like that you're here."

Adriana frowned at the comment. "Why is that? He doesn't know any of us."

"He thinks he does. And I don't necessarily disagree with him."

She started to open the door.

"Wait. Hold on a second. What are you talking about?"

Lidia paused for a moment and took her hand off the door handle. "Fine, I'll tell you. I've followed your career for a long time, Tommy. I know what happened to your parents and why you founded your agency. I also know that you don't shy away from attention when it comes down to it. You two seem to get into no end of trouble, and personally, I'd like to steer clear of it. Dr. Patel is a good friend. I'd hate for anything to happen to him because you two make things worse than they already are."

"That's fair," Sean said.

Lidia's eyes narrowed. "It is?"

"Sure. We get into all sorts of trouble like you said. But we don't seek attention."

"And we certainly don't try to get into trouble," Tommy added. "In fact, he retired a few years ago and moved to the beach just to get some peace and quiet."

"Really?" She seemed genuinely surprised.

"I go looking for trouble," Adriana added with a cold tone.

Lidia twisted her head a little more and met Adriana's gaze. It was as icy as her comment.

"Okay then." Lidia opened the door and stepped out.

Tommy and Adriana opened their doors, too.

The group exited the SUV and trudged up the hill, with the group from the second vehicle marching close behind, including Priya, who'd opted to ride in the more comfortable and spacious second SUV.

They passed through a makeshift gate that was little more than a pallet with hinges attached to a metal pole. The fence wasn't much better; a few tangled strands of barbed wire wrapped around the commune of a dozen or so tents, including a huge one in the center held up by two tall wooden poles. A couple of long tables were propped up in the center. Four smaller ones were positioned in the corners along with benches. A fire pit full of blackened logs sat just outside the big top, off to the right and surrounded by camping chairs that were getting soaked in the downpour.

The dig site sat off to the back of the camp through another pallet gate. The camp was set up on a sort of plateau surrounded on two sides by fifteen-foot-high rock walls. The walls ran in a U shape to the back of the temporary residential community where it opened up, forming a narrow path. The pallet gate on that side was closed, though that didn't prevent Sean and the others from seeing into the area.

A massive quantity of white tent fabric stretched out over the area. It, too, appeared to be surrounded on all sides by rock walls—around ten feet tall—giving the appearance of a quarry in a strange sort of way.

The tall, brush-covered hills that surrounded them made Sean more uneasy by the moment. He disregarded the rain splashing on his face and head as he twisted around, taking in the area while the others hurried for cover under the Big Top tent and the haven it provided. Sean sighed and caught up with the others. There was nothing he could do about it now, but he got the distinct feeling they had just walked right into a kill box.

It wouldn't take much for a few shooters in elevated positions on the nearby hills, or simply on the rock walls surrounding them, to open fire and slaughter everyone in the camp. He shook off his unease as he stepped into the shelter of the central tent.

A man who looked like he was in his mid-thirties with a thick, black mustache, matching hair and java-brown skin hovered over a large four-burner camping stove. He was busily stirring a giant pot when the newcomers stepped into his mess hall, but he looked up at them with a smile.

The smell of onions, curry, lentils, and fresh bread baking filled the air. In the heightened humidity, steam rolled out of the huge pot, spilling over the kitchen's work area and down to the ground. Although he was using a propane cooking stove, smoke from a brick-and-mud oven off to the other end of the tent poured through the Big Top, giving an even more authentic sense of camping.

"Hello," the cook said. "Welcome to Bhangarh." He waved his hand, the broad—almost silly—grin on his face never faltering. "Dinner will be ready in about an hour. I'm guessing you are the Americans, huh?"

Tommy nodded. "Yes, sir. I'm Tommy; this is Sean and Adriana."

The man waved politely. "Just call me Raj," he said, still keeping the same goofy grin on his face. "Let me know if you need anything, like a snack or something. I have some naan over there if you're hungry from the drive."

He pointed to the end of the table nearest the newcomers. Several baking dishes were stacked one on top of the other. Their Pyrex walls were fogged with steam from the warm, traditional Indian flatbread inside. Raj must have just pulled them out of the oven, which had been fitted with a baking stone on top of a rack, apparently for just such a purpose as making bread.

"Thanks," Tommy said. "We'll wait for dinner if that's okay to you. Probably need to get settled and have a look around."

Raj appeared unaffected by the comment. "Suit yourself, although I doubt you'll be able to do much looking around for another hour or so. This storm looks like it's here for a little while." He gazed out under the lip of the giant tarp as if to get a better glimpse of the sky. Then he went back to stirring his pot. Whatever he was cooking smelled amazing to the hungry visitors. Sean didn't want to correct his friend, but he was starving and the smell of the freshly baked bread, the fire smoke, and the ingredients from the pot were making his stomach growl.

"Over here," Lidia said, motioning to the group.

She'd branched off as they approached the kitchen and had been speaking to a young woman with pale skin and blonde hair. The two had nodded several times, Lidia motioning to the visitors on a few occasions before the younger woman gave a final nod and then trudged away.

"Sarah has taken care of your accommodations," Lidia said. "She will show you to your tents and get you squared away." She eyed each of the visitors. "Unless you'll be needing anything else, I'll leave you here for now. Priya will catch you up to speed on any details I may have missed."

Lidia abruptly spun around and strolled away, walking under a canopy toward a tent on the opposite side of the campground. She met with one of the security men from the other SUV and began talking with him as the two walked through the flaps of her platform tent and disappeared.

"She's not the friendliest person in the world," Priya said from behind the others.

Her sudden appearance startled the visitors, and they whirled around to face her.

"She's just got a lot on her mind, I'm sure," Sean defended. "It's a lot to take care of at a dig this size."

"Yeah, no big deal," Tommy added. "I'd be high strung, too, if I was running this place and the person in charge had disappeared."

"Well, I appreciate your understanding." Priya leaned close as if about to share a deep secret. "But I can assure you: She's always like this. Between us, she could be dropped off at the most private, relaxing beach on the planet and still be uptight."

The guests shared a quiet laugh at Lidia's expense.

"She does manage things well, though, and we're lucky to have her. Just don't expect to be invited over for Christmas dinner anytime soon."

Sarah returned to the group huddled under the big tarp and

grinned eagerly at them. "I have your tents ready if you'd like to put your things away."

"Sure," Tommy said. "Thank you."

The visitors followed the young woman across the camp and into the rain again until they reached one of the white tents. She held the main flap open and motioned them inside.

"You have this one and the one over there to the right," Sarah explained and pointed to the next tent over. "The bathrooms are over there in that tent," she pointed to two at the front end of the camp. "There are solar showers and toilets available."

Sean pursed his lips. "And here I thought we'd be roughing it." He let out a quick laugh. "Pretty much like all the digs we've been on, huh, Tommy?"

"Yep. Pretty much."

"We figured you guys wouldn't have trouble adjusting." Sarah motioned for the SUV drivers to place the travelers' belongings into the tents.

The men did as instructed, setting down their things and disappearing back out into the rain.

"I'll let you all sort out your stuff," Sarah said. "I believe Raj said dinner will be ready in an hour, yes?"

The three nodded.

"Great. I'll see you then." She cast a wary eye at a particularly long black polymer case. "I don't know if I want to know what's in that?" she joked.

"Probably not," Sean quipped.

"Okay then." Sarah smiled and exited through the flaps.

The interior of the tent was more spacious than it looked from the outside. There were two large cots, one on either side, with thin mattresses, blankets, and pillows on top. The floor was set up on a wooden base, much like camps such as this had been for hundreds of years.

Sean had stayed in one in Montana once that had a concrete platform. Those were more permanent fixtures than these, which would be dismantled and transported elsewhere once the long task of investigating the site was completed.

There was a small stove at the back with a chimney that poked out through an insulated ring in the canopy above. A little wooden chair and desk sat in one corner with a lantern on the surface of the workstation.

"You want to take this one, Tommy?" Sean asked. "Adriana and I can take the other."

"Nah, you guys keep this one. I'll go next door." He tightened the backpack on his shoulders and then glanced down at the hard-shell gear case at his feet. "You think we brought enough...stuff?" He said the last word with a hint of humor in his voice.

"I sure hope so," Sean answered. He set his bag on the floor and bent down, unlatching both clasps on the front and sides of the case. Then he flipped open the lid, revealing a small arsenal of weapons.

There were three tan Springfield 9mm pistols. Three matching 5.56 AR-15s were packed tightly in there as well. Sean had built those weapons himself, buying parts from a manufacturer in North Georgia called Dawn of Defense. He'd always thought the name interesting since its initials were the same as the Department of Defense. Clever. Sean's black .40-cal Springfield XD was also in there amid the collection. There were two boxes of flash-bang discs as well as several other electrical devices for communications, security monitoring, and other purposes.

"You don't think the AR-15s are a little overkill?" Tommy asked, eyeing the weapons.

"Not after what I dealt with the other day," Sean said, referring to the faulty equipment he'd been issued with on his last mission. "Besides, this is more like a private security operation than an archaeology job." Sean was careful how he said it. He didn't want IAA to slip into being just another Axis, for him or for his friend. He knew Tommy didn't want that, either. Despite that, Sean was determined to be prepared for anything. There were too many variables.

Tommy rolled his shoulders. "We should get a corporate sponsorship from this company. You know that, right?"

Sean smirked. "Yeah, maybe. What can I say, I like their weapons."

"And I trust your judgment on that."

"I don't mean to butt in, boys, but would it be okay if you put your guns away for a few minutes so we can have a look around before dinner?" Adriana crossed her arms, clearly ready for a change of subject. She had her own weapons packed away in her bags but didn't feel like they needed to be displayed or discussed at the moment.

"Sure." Sean blushed and closed the lid, locking down the clasps again before straightening up.

"I'll catch up," Tommy said. "Gonna put my things in the other tent."

Sean nodded and watched his friend leave through the front. When they were alone, he turned back to face Adriana and found her standing mere inches from him. Their toes nearly touched. He could feel her breath on his neck as she gazed into his eyes.

"So...you weren't wanting to take a tour of the camp?" She put her arms around him and pressed her lips into his.

He soaked in their softness. Even after the flight and long drive, she still managed to smell like Tennessee spring flowers with a mix of evening honeysuckle.

She pulled back after a thirty-second embrace and stared into his eyes, letting her fingers lock around the back of his neck for a second.

"Yes, actually. I do. I just wanted that kiss first."

She sauntered around him, letting her hands fall loose down his shoulder as she stepped to the door.

He watched like a tiger who'd been offered a steak, only to have it pulled away and replaced with a bowl of lima beans.

"Really? That's it?"

She nodded and stepped outside, leaving him alone, shaking his head with eyes still on the doorway.

He took in a deep breath and sighed. "I really do love that woman."

11

The camp turned into a flurry of activity when the cook began ringing the dinner bell.

The old triangular piece of metal reminded Sean and Tommy of the Wild West wagon trains that had a similar method of calling travelers for supper. Many ranches, too, had dinner bells like that, at least those that they'd seen. Apparently, it wasn't just an American West thing.

Mere seconds after Raj began the incessant dinging, people began coming out of the woodwork from all angles.

Some of the dig team were in their tents, probably working on research that couldn't be done in the rain. Others poured in from beyond the site gate. They'd probably been toiling away on their tedious work for the majority of the day under the shelter of huge canopies. The massive stretches of fabric were normally there to give them shade in the sweltering heat, but on this day they had given the dig teams a dry place to work.

None of them appeared soaked as they clamored toward the mess hall and began forming lines at the table where Raj had set out huge bowls and platters filled with various kinds of Indian fare.

The glass baking dishes with naan bread still sat there but were now surrounded by steaming bowlfuls of dal makhani, basmati rice, tandoori chicken, spiced potatoes and onions, and several smaller sauce dishes filled with onion chutney, garlic chutney, and tamarind.

Sean fell into line behind Adriana, while Tommy joined Priya in the second line to his left.

"Looks amazing, doesn't it?" Sarah asked. She was just in front of Adriana.

"It certainly does," Adriana agreed. "I'm amazed what Raj can do in a setting like this, without some of the conveniences of a modern kitchen."

"Right! He's the best."

Sarah scooped a spoonful of rice onto her plate and then topped it with dal makhani.

Sean and Adriana followed her through the line, helping themselves to generous portions of the food on offer, and then continued with Sarah to a table that was still empty.

Some of the site workers in the mess hall stared at the three visitors with wide eyes. A few looked suspicious, but most seemed to be in awe of the famous guests. The last thing Sean and Tommy wanted was for them to become the focus of attention. What mattered was getting to the bottom of Dr. Patel's disappearance. Anything that distracted from that could be a hindrance they didn't need.

Tommy and Priya rejoined the group as they reached the table and helped themselves to the bench seats farthest from the center of the mess hall. Sean and Tommy did their best to keep their heads down and focused on their food, while Adriana and Sarah chatted openly.

"So, do you know Dr. Patel very well?" Adriana asked.

Sara nodded as she took a bite of the chicken. "Yeah," she said and wiped the corner of her mouth with a napkin. "He's a good guy. Chatted with him quite often. You guys think you can find him, right?"

"We'll certainly try."

Sean and Tommy nodded.

Tommy chewed a piece of naan and then turned to her. "Is there anything you can tell us about the day he disappeared? Lidia gave us her side of things, but it might help to speak with anyone else who had the chance to talk with him before he...left."

"Left," Sarah said. "That's an interesting way of putting it. Makes it sound like he did it of his own accord."

"You think he didn't?" Adriana chimed in again.

Sean gnawed on a piece of bread as he listened closely.

"Many of us spoke to him the day before he disappeared, but the day he...left, as you put it, I don't know if anyone talked to him. He was gone when we woke up, vanished in the middle of the night."

"Do you know what he was working on?" Tommy threw the obvious question out there, hoping for a nibble.

"You mean on this site?"

"I mean was there something else, something no one else knew about?"

She shook her head with lips pursed, thinking while she answered. "No, not that I can think of. We're all on the same page here."

"Do you think," Adriana said, "he could have been working on something in secret?" She noted the confusion on Sarah's face and elaborated further. "What I mean is, do you think he might have had an ulterior motive for being here, in this place?"

Sarah's forehead wrinkled, her lips curled down in a frown. "No, I don't think so. I mean, sure, it's possible. The guy kept to himself quite a bit, but that sounds kind of far-fetched, doesn't it? Are you saying he set up this entire dig as a cover for something else he was looking for?"

Sean's ears pricked at the last part, and he stiffened.

Tommy took a bite of chicken and then forked a piece of potato into his mouth.

Sean looked up toward the old fort. He'd ventured up there earlier when the rain dissipated and taken a quick self-guided tour of the grounds. He was impressed at the upkeep of the place: grass mowed, stone pathways perfectly maintained. The fortifications, parapets, and gates all still appeared as they might have a few hundred years before when the fortress was newly constructed. He'd glanced into a few darker alcoves out of curiosity but didn't give much credence to the legends of hauntings surrounding the place. Sean didn't believe in paranormal activities, but that didn't mean there wasn't something fishy going on.

"I wasn't saying that," Tommy said in response to Sarah's question. "But you just did." He winked at her and took another bite.

Sarah blushed, the red color in her cheeks enhanced by the yellowish glow from the lanterns hanging around on the posts. The sun was setting to the west, and darkness fell quickly around that area. Surrounded by the rocky hills, the little camp was quickly enveloped by the shadows of dusk.

"I see what you did there." She made the comment in the midst of chewing her food. She swallowed before continuing. "Truth is, no one knows what he was up to. Is it possible he's been hoping to discover something else while working on the site? Sure. That's kind of the nature of what we do, isn't it?"

Priya shifted in her seat and nodded. "It certainly is. You never know what you're going to find, which is why the notion that Dr. Patel was specifically looking for something is a bit of a stretch."

"Maybe," Tommy said and went back to eating.

They finished their meal in relative silence, occasionally talking about the old fort, the land surrounding them, and some of the interesting pieces of history that took place in that ancient land.

When she was finished with her food, Sarah excused herself with a polite smile and left the table.

Priya waited until she was out of earshot before filling in the others on the situation. She leaned forward and spoke just above a whisper so no one at the other tables could hear.

"I should have mentioned this before, but Sarah and the others don't know about the letter Dr. Patel sent with the picture inside. You three are the only ones here besides me who knows anything about it."

"Understood," Sean said. "Any chance we can take a look inside Patel's tent before we turn in for the night?"

"Certainly. When we finish eating, I'll take you over to it and show you inside. There isn't much to see, and we've already been through it a number of times. Lidia told me that the police came by yesterday and also had a look through his things but found nothing but notes and a few personal belongings."

"Notes?" Tommy asked.

"They claimed it was mostly scribbles, doodles, a few legible words, but not much to go on and certainly nothing that would lead someone to kidnap the man...or worse." There was deep concern in her voice.

Sean and Tommy exchanged a knowing glance that they then shared with Adriana, all eyes darting back and forth.

Sean wiped off the corners of his lips with a napkin and set his fork down on the empty plate. "What do you think, Schultzie? Should we have a look?"

Tommy's lips creased into a devilish grin. "That's why we're here."

The three slipped out the back of the mess hall tent and looped around to their own quarters to grab a few things before following Priya over to Dr. Patel's tent. Even though the rain had ceased, the ground was still soaked and the air damp with humidity. Sean wiped his forehead on the back of his hand like he'd done so many times back in the American South on hot summer days.

There were wooden planks laid out like a giant spiderweb all around the camp that provided narrow paths between tents and the center of the area. Walking on them kept the mud off the travelers' feet, but it was also difficult to keep one's balance. Luckily, most of the planks were wide enough to make the walk easy enough. Even so, Tommy still almost fell off a few times, wildly waving his arms over his head like a child pretending to be on a high wire.

When they reached Dr. Patel's tent, some of the workers were just beginning to switch on lanterns hanging from posts around the perimeter and in the camp's center. There was nothing remarkable about Patel's humble dwelling. It looked just like all the others from the outside.

"This is it," Priya said, standing on the narrow landing in front of the door. She pulled back one of the flaps and allowed the three to step inside.

The dark tent resonated with a foreboding vibe that each and every person felt creep through their senses, tingling their skin like a cool evening mist. Sean was the first to turn on his flashlight. He traced the bright white beam to a bed off to the side, then a desk at the other end with a lantern on it.

Priya had already moved over to the desk and picked up the lantern. She ignited the yellowish light, and the room instantly bathed in the warm glow.

They'd not been deceived about not being much to see in the tent. It looked like someone had come through and cleaned it, organized the loose items, and then left. If there was any sign of a struggle from the night Patel went missing, it had been covered up long before the visitors arrived.

Priya hung the lantern from a post in the center of the room to give equal light to every corner. "You may look through his things. Would you like me to stay?" She looked at Tommy.

He shook his head. "That's not necessary. We'll put everything back exactly as you see it."

"Then I will bid you good night. Breakfast is at seven o'clock in the morning. Things start pretty early around here because of the heat."

"Understood."

She gave a short bow and let herself out the tent's front.

When she'd been gone for a minute, Tommy put up his hands. "Shall we?"

Sean chuckled. "Notebook?"

"Notebook."

Adriana shook her head. She raised an eyebrow as if appraising the two. "You sure you don't want to be with him?" She directed her question at Sean, who laughed again.

"Shut it," he said with a wink.

The three stepped over to the little workstation and hovered over it. Tommy pulled the chair out and moved it aside so they could all stand close. Then he picked up the leather-bound journal and flipped it over to inspect the back.

There was nothing special about it. The book looked like any other journal that could have been purchased in the last fifty years, though due to the weathering of it the group guessed it was probably at least thirty to forty years old, maybe a few more.

Tommy set it back down on the desk and flipped open to the first page. The paper had faded to a brownish tint. Sketches in black ink filled the pages. Line after line of unusual symbols were bunched together between the drawings as if explaining what each picture was in a bizarre, long-forgotten language.

One of the images was of the god Vishnu in all his glory. As seen in so many of the renderings of the deity available online, he was holding a different item in each hand. Only one of them, however, was circled: the Gada. On the next page, there were three renderings of the mace, each one with lines shooting from it to symbolize some kind of power or perhaps the holiness of the relic. The latter seemed strange for a student of history and archaeology such as Dr. Patel to include. Yet there it was.

Sean's attention, however, wasn't on the drawings. He instantly recognized the symbols. His eyebrows pinched together, and his eyes narrowed. "Wait a second," he said.

"I see it, too," Adriana added. "The symbols from the drawing Dr. Patel sent Priya."

Sean nodded.

"If he's the one that sent it to her," Tommy interjected. He made no attempt to hide his doubt in the matter. He'd flown across the world in an act of good faith that she was telling the truth, that she wasn't an insane colleague who'd sent herself a strange message. That would be a pretty far jump over the edge to do something like that, so he leaned toward believing her. Just because he believed her, however, didn't mean he was without a shadow of doubt.

Sean rolled his eyes. He was more skeptical.

Tommy flipped the page to the next. It only contained a single drawing. It appeared to be an overhead view of a city grid, although it was crude, lacking any details as far as street names or buildings. There was, however, an X in the bottom-right corner of the image, located in a box that had dotted lines drawn into one area.

"Looks like a blueprint, doesn't it?" Tommy asked.

"Yeah," Sean agreed. "But of what?"

"A city?" Adriana offered. "Which one, I'm not sure, but it does look like a layout of an old town or city."

"Whatever it is, Dr. Patel felt like there was something important right here." Tommy tapped on the X. "I wonder what's there."

"Won't matter if we don't know what this place is."

"She's right," Sean said. "We have to figure out what all these symbols mean. It has to be some kind of secret language Patel discovered."

"Or invented."

Sean nodded at her. "Indeed. That's certainly in the realm of possibility."

"You're saying he invented an entire language to cover his tracks?" Tommy sounded incredulous.

"Not a language," Adriana corrected. "Just swapped out the lettering. I doubt he went all Tolkien with it."

The two men snorted at the reference to one of their favorite authors.

"So, if it's a cipher, we need the key." Sean came back to the conclusion he'd reached before.

"And that could be problematic," Tommy said with a sigh. "There's no telling where it could be." He looked around on the floor, pulled out a drawer to the desk, but didn't see anything in the first six seconds that made him believe there was a cipher key anywhere in the area.

"We'll look again after we finish going through this journal. Turn to the next page."

Tommy nodded and did as told. The next page in the book contained another drawing, this one of an old castle or fortress. It was a rough sketch, like all the others, with lines jutting off lines at haphazard angles. There was no mistaking what the structure truly was. Behind the castle, a sharply angled mountain rose above it, the pointed peak looming over the fortress and casting a shadow across the foot of the slopes below. As with the other drawings, there were more symbols.

Again, Tommy turned the page. A tall mountain peak with jagged lines meant to symbolize snow appeared on the right-hand side of the book. Other shorter mountains accompanied the tallest one. The details of this drawing were slightly better than the rest, save for a single line that shot out from the side of the largest mountain, probably an error by the amateur artist.

The groups of symbols ran along both pages, ending abruptly halfway down the page next to the image of the mountains. Tommy flipped the page and found that they'd reached the end of the professor's notes. The only thing that remained on the left-hand side of the book was the four symbols, the ones usually held in Vishnu's hands. On this page, however, they were alone, with no sign of the deity, as if floating in midair on the page.

Tommy turned the remainder of the pages in the journal and found they were all blank.

His eyebrows arched high on his forehead as he closed the book and then reopened it to the first page where the deity stood staring straight ahead with arms extended.

"So," he said with a dramatic exhale, "any ideas?"

Sean smirked. "Let's take a look around this tent and see if there's anything else the investigators might have missed."

"Okay. You think Patel might have hidden the cipher key in here somewhere?"

Sean's grin widened, and he glanced at Adriana.

She knew exactly what he was thinking. "We already have the key," she said.

Tommy pulled his head back and frowned in confusion. "We do?"

She nodded. "Yes. Patel sent it to Dr. Chaudhry."

12

THIRUVANANTHAPURAM

"This is insane!" Brock raged. He slammed a fist into the wall and punctured the drywall with ease. His hand disappeared up to the wrist. Then he pulled it out and dusted off the white powder now coating his skin.

"That was a little dramatic," Heather said. She kept her tone dry.

"How long can it possibly rain here?" he asked.

Brock and his team had been primed and ready to go into the temple the previous night. Everything was ready and in place. Then, out of nowhere, a thunderstorm had rumbled over the area and seemed to park itself in the sky above.

He knew that wasn't what happened. It wasn't even the rainy season, not that he knew of. But some kind of weather event was happening, and the consistent rainfall that had flooded the area for the last twenty-four hours was starting to whittle away at his patience.

"The forecast says the rain should move out sometime tomorrow morning."

"That's what it said yesterday."

"No," she insisted. "The forecast was for showers throughout the day and into the night.

"Yeah, and then it changed. It always changes. I don't think meteorologists have a clue what they're talking about."

She chuckled.

"It's not funny," he insisted.

"It's a little funny to see you have a tantrum like this."

She flashed a cute smile his way that diffused his anger, at least a little.

"Look," she added quickly, "this isn't going to ruin our plans. It's just delaying things a little. No big deal. We'll go in tomorrow night, and everything will be fine."

He shook his head and looked around the dusty room. They'd been cooped up in there for the last few days. He'd not grown up with money or luxury, but Brock had certainly become accustomed to those things during his years in Hollywood.

"No. We're going in tonight."

She arched one eyebrow. "You sure that's a good idea with the weather like this?"

"Doesn't matter," he said, waving it off with one hand. "I don't want to stay here longer than we have to. The longer we're here, the better chance we have of being spotted."

"And of you being recognized?"

He guffawed. "I would hope not. But yeah, that's always a possibility."

She knew his face and fame had stretched across the planet. He had fans in almost every nation with a theater. If he were to show up in a big city like Mumbai, there was no doubt in his mind he'd be mobbed by throngs of people wanting autographs and selfies. While he doubted that would happen in this town, he'd rather not take the chance. After all, he didn't exactly fit in with the locals.

"Okay, so let's say we do go in tonight. We'll have to account for the rain and any lightning that might be in the area, stuff like that. It's going to have an effect on our night-vision gear."

"It will cause the same problems for any security we run into."

"That's true. Still, I'd wager we are better equipped than they are.

Would be a shame to waste the advantage just because of the weather."

Brock paced to the wall with windows facing out toward the temple. He stopped, spun around, and then strode back. "It's not just about the weather!" Brock roared. "We are fighting against the clock here!"

The two other guards in the room flinched at the sound of his voice. It wasn't that they were afraid of him. Those two weren't afraid of anything. But he wasn't happy. That was never good for the guy writing the checks. If he wasn't happy, that could mean trouble for them. They enjoyed their work. More than that, they appreciated the pay. Brock was happy to spare no expense, especially on his security forces. He'd allowed Heather to handpick her team, telling her that money was no object. She'd gotten the best she could find in a cesspool known as the mercenary underground. These two were particularly good, at least for her needs. She wanted people with bad reputations in regard to their methods. Both of these guys fit that mold perfectly, each having faced criminal charges during their time in the military. Of course, their charges had been dropped. Shoved aside was more like it. Funny what a little money could do to sway the legal system.

They'd been facing a maximum of twenty years when Heather swooped in and offered them salvation. They'd been working private security for a firm operating in Baghdad when things went south on a convoy escort mission. The men were accused of opening fire on civilians. The truth, Heather had learned, was that the men did, in fact, do that, but with good reason. A group of terrorists had opened fire on their convoy, shooting from rooftops and windows of the buildings surrounding the vehicles.

The two men returned fire, taking out multiple targets in the process. Unfortunately, three civilians died during the firefight. The two were arrested and brought back to the United States, where they would face the military justice system.

Thanks to Brock Carson and his angelic assistant, that never happened. Now the men not only owed their lives to Brock but every fiber of allegiance they could muster.

That meant when he was unhappy, they would do whatever it took to make things right.

In the case of the weather, there wasn't much the two men, or anyone could do. According to their employer, though, the weather wasn't the primary cause for concern. Their ears perked up at this new revelation.

"Where is he?" Brock boomed. He threw his hands up into the air and let them fall to his hips with a clap. His voice echoed through the second-floor room. "How many days has it been since he disappeared?"

"Nine, sir," Heather answered. She almost never used a formal manner of speaking with him. They were beyond that, at least when they were alone. In the presence of other members of their team, however, she typically tried to act as professional as possible, only letting herself slip now and then, like when she had mentioned his tantrum. This was more than just a tantrum, and she knew it.

"And still no sign of him?"

"We have people on it." Heather took a stern tone, though she tried not to sound forceful. "We'll find him."

"If he was going to be found, it should have been done by now. The last thing we need is that loose cannon out there, especially if he finds what I think he's trying to find."

"He won't. You said it yourself. The Gada doesn't exist. If it did, you would have discovered it by now, right?"

She made a good point. Her comments slid a balm into his ears that melted his anger, at least a little.

"I suppose so."

"That's what you said before."

"I know what I said." He put his hands on his hips and twisted his head to look out into the darkness. Beyond the shanties and treetops, the golden temple sat in the night, waiting for them, beckoning them to come. "That mace is the only thing that can stop the trident. If he were to discover it, all our plans would be ruined."

"If he finds it, we kill him and take it. Then no one will be able to stop us." She moved closer to him, stopping inches away. She looked up into his eyes, suppressing the longing inside her.

"That would require finding him, wouldn't it?" He ignored her gaze. "How is it that someone like him can simply disappear?"

"Dr. Patel, it would seem, is cleverer than we first suspected. We had the camp under surveillance."

"And yet he managed to slip through."

He was getting on her nerves now, and she didn't appreciate his tone or the fact that he was sneering through clenched teeth at her.

"We will find him soon," she promised.

He shook his head. "You have no way of knowing that. The man has gone off the grid. He could be anywhere in this wretched country, hiding in the mountains, the desert, or even the slums of some big city. Do you know how many people live in India? A lot. Far more than the United States, and in a smaller area. He can blend in, disappear, and move around without anyone ever noticing." His head dropped, and he stared at the floor for a second. Then he shook his head. "No, Dr. Patel is gone. I doubt we will find him. The only consolation is that if he was on the trail of the Gada, he likely won't find it now. And if he does try to go back to his little dig site, we'll know it."

"You done?" She crossed her arms.

He looked up, about to lash out at her for speaking to him that way in front of the men.

She didn't let him get a word in. "We have word that a few experts have been brought in to help track down the professor."

The strained look in Brock's eyes eased a little. "Experts?"

"Not just any experts," she said. "They're bringing in Tommy Schultz and Sean Wyatt from the IAA."

His head inched toward her. "The guys from the International Archaeological whatever?"

"Agency. And yes, those guys."

His head twitched from one side to the other. "Why would they be brought in? They're security guys for the most part. Not investigators."

"That's true, but it seems they were convinced to take a closer look at the case of the missing Dr. Patel. Priya is the one who reached out to them. She must have given them a compelling reason to travel all the way over here."

"When do they arrive?"

Heather looked at the black watch on her wrist. "About eight hours ago. They should be at the dig site now."

Brock sighed. "I fail to see how this is good news."

She shuffled a few inches closer to him. She could feel the breath coming out his nostrils now, tickling the skin on her neck. "Because... if they find him, we can kill him. And if he happens to have stumbled on the location of the Gada, well, we can kill all of them and take it, thus eliminating the only threat to your plan."

He licked his lips and nodded. "I see." He turned and walked over to the wall and planted his hands on the windowsill. He stared out into the night for a moment. "This could definitely be a good thing for us. And has made my decision to go ahead with the mission tonight that much firmer." He spun around and faced the other three. "Get your gear together and be ready to move in twenty minutes. We're going into the temple. It's time to see what's inside this mysterious Vault B."

13

BHANGARH

S ean, Adriana, and Tommy stood on the landing just outside
Priya's tent. They'd asked for her, apologizing for the intrusion
to her privacy, but the woman hadn't answered or made an
appearance in the doorway.

Sean twitched his left shoulder forward, urging Adriana to take a
peek inside. She shook her head at the idea. "I'm not going to look
inside someone's place. That's an invasion of privacy."

"How private can it be?" he asked. "It's a tent."

"Very private. You want someone poking their head into my tent
later tonight?"

"Our tent."

"Not if you keep it up."

He pretended to be crestfallen, letting his lips curl into a pout.

"I'll do it," Tommy said, taking a step toward the doorway.

Adriana's hand shot out of nowhere to block his way. She took a
quick sidestep to position herself between him and the flaps to the
tent. "Um, no you won't."

Tommy chuckled. "I'm just kidding, Addy. Relax. She must be out
doing something."

"You three looking for me?" Priya's voice came from the shadows between two of the lanterns on the perimeter.

They spun around and spotted her walking up the plank walkway, a satchel in one hand and a flashlight in the other.

"Yes, we are," Sean said, clearing his throat.

"That didn't take long."

"What didn't?" He tried to cut himself off before he said it but couldn't stop his lips from moving. "Sorry, right. The investigation in Patel's tent. Got it."

Priya passed him a knowing smile. "So, I trust you didn't find anything?"

The three collectively shook their heads. They'd gone through the rest of the belongings in Patel's tent, checked the desk, the mattress, the small chest the man kept most of his clothes in, and even under some of the planks just to make sure he hadn't secreted something away under the movable flooring.

"We didn't need to," Adriana explained. "We already have everything we need."

"We do?" Priya cocked her head to the side and arched an eyebrow, befuddled.

"Well, you did," Tommy clarified. "I guess we did need this journal." He held up the leather book.

"How does that help us with anything?"

"We didn't know, not at first, at least."

"Remember the weird symbols on that letter Patel sent you?" Sean asked.

She nodded. "Yes. They look similar to the ones in that notebook. They don't make any sense, though. It's not a language I've ever seen before. Neither has anyone else, for that matter. And we're on an archaeological dig site, so there are a few of us around who know ancient languages."

The trio laughed.

"Fair point," Tommy said. "You mind if we step into your tent to show you what we found?"

"What we think we found," Adriana corrected.

Priya rolled her shoulders. "My tent is a little bit of a mess right now, and I don't have a good place for us to sit. Perhaps the mess hall would be better, one of the tables?"

"Sure," Sean agreed first. "Sounds good."

They made their way back down to the now-empty mess hall. The stoves on the big middle table were closed and shut off for the night. All the pots and pans had disappeared, along with the dishes. Raj was also out of sight. Sean wondered if he was in his tent, plotting what the meals for the next day would consist of, with visions of fried pastries, basmati rice, chicken, vegetables, and chutney dancing through his head.

Sean and Adriana sat down at the table on one side, Tommy and Priya taking the other. Tommy set the book down on the surface and peeled open the cover.

"These images," he started, "tell us that your friend, Dr. Patel, was looking for something."

"Something specific," Sean added.

"Right."

"Yes, that's what I wondered, but what is he looking for and what are all those strange symbols?"

"You don't happen to have the letter Dr. Patel sent, do you?" Adriana asked.

"Actually, I do." Priya pulled the satchel up from her side and placed it on the table. She unzipped the main compartment and stuck her hand inside. After a moment of searching through the contents, she found what she was looking for and retrieved the Ziploc bag with the letter inside it.

Sean and Tommy couldn't believe she was still carrying the letter around that way, but they held back their natural instincts to chastise her and tell her that the letter in her hands was quite literally the key to possibly finding her friend, along with whatever artifact he was trying to locate.

She pulled the letter out and pressed it on the table.

Sean gave a quick look up to the tarp above, making sure it wasn't leaking from the rain earlier in the afternoon.

"Okay," she said. "Tell me what this is all about."

Tommy spread out the pages of the journal and then pointed to the symbols on the letter. He counted them in his head and then looked up at Priya, then his friends. "Just as we suspected," he said. "There are twenty-six of them."

Priya shook her head, still not understanding what he was getting at. "So what? There are twenty-six. How does that help us?"

"There are twenty-six letters in the English alphabet," Sean said. "Each one of these represents a letter in that journal." He pointed at the leather book.

Priya's eyes widened. "You mean it's a code?"

The three guests nodded.

"A cipher of sorts," Adriana explained. "They aren't used very often in ordinary life, but in times of war and in the old days, ciphers were a common means of hiding secrets. It would seem your friend Dr. Patel had something he didn't want anyone but you to know. Sounds like he trusts you."

She bowed her head and nodded. "He does. Now I feel like I've let him down for missing this."

"Don't beat yourself up," Tommy said. He patted her on the shoulder. "Happens to the best of us. Besides, you're not really trained to figure out stuff like that. We deal with this sort of thing more often than most."

"That's why I knew you were the right people for the job." She glanced down at the book and then the letter. "With this..."

"Key. It's called a key," Tommy said.

"Key," she repeated, "how long do you think it will take to translate Dr. Patel's code?"

Sean and Tommy exchanged a questioning glance. Then they looked at Adriana.

"Few hours, maybe," Adriana said.

"Give or take," Sean added. "We'll create a master to work from, and that should make the translating process easier."

"And if we can make a copy of these pages, we can divide it up and go much faster. Although I guess you don't have access to anything like that, huh?"

"Certainly," Priya said. "We have a communications tent over there where the workers can chat with their families, print things, and make copies if needed."

"Sounds like a military setup," Sean quipped.

"That's where we got the idea." Priya beamed with pride.

"Good. We can make the copies and get to work in our tents. Should be able to get this taken care of before we go to sleep tonight, though we might have to finish up in the morning."

"Sounds good. I'll make the copies, and then you can get started." Priya's voice exuded excitement. "Thank you all so much. This is the most we've gotten out of anyone so far."

She took the book and hurried away from the table toward a tent in the front-left corner of the walled perimeter. When she disappeared from view, Tommy glanced across the table at his friends with a puzzled look in his eye.

"Strange, huh?"

Sean returned the bewildered gaze. "What do you mean?"

"The fact that she didn't consider that journal was one long code, a cipher from her close friend."

"Ordinary people don't typically think of things the same way we do. I doubt that possibility ever even crossed her mind." Adriana could sympathize—despite her talent at cracking codes just as well as the other two.

She knew the world of people around them usually just took things at face value, floating along through life as best they could, trying to make enough money to support themselves, make a difference to others, and eventually retire with enough to live on until they passed. Most folks weren't staring up at the symbols in a thousand-year-old cathedral, trying to figure out which symbols represented what and what numbers in an old book could be interpreted as something else. Most would have seen the symbols in Dr. Patel's notebook as nothing more than the mad ravings of a lunatic, or at best the imaginative doodling of a bored researcher.

"Well, either way, I'm glad we're here," Tommy confessed. "This is turning out to be a fascinating little trip. We've got coded messages, a picture of an ancient weapon that is purported to have superpowers, treasure maps, and great food. What more could you ask for?"

Sean cracked a smile. "You make a good point." He glanced out under the tarp and into the sky. The clouds were drifting away, now revealing patches of the starry night and allowing many of the celestial bodies to twinkle down on the earth below. "The weather even seems to be cooperating now after that harsh protest before."

"Don't jinx it, buddy," Tommy warned.

Sean let out a chuckle and eased back into his seat.

"There anything else unusual about all this to you guys?" Sean asked.

"Other than pretty much everything?" Tommy joked.

Sean laughed. "No, I mean about some of the people here."

Adriana grew serious. "You think one of these people had something to do with Patel's disappearance?"

"Could be. I'm just saying, whenever there's a ship, there's bound to be a rat on board somewhere."

Tommy didn't question his friend's instincts often, if ever. They'd known each other their entire lives, and Sean's senses on such things were almost always correct, despite seeming a little paranoid at first.

Leaning closer, Tommy lowered his voice as he spoke. "You think it might be Lidia?"

"Not sure," Sean admitted. "Could be her. Could be anyone."

"She did seem a bit...unfriendly," Adriana added. She twisted her head around. "And we haven't seen her since we got here. She dropped us off and disappeared."

"She's probably just very busy," Sean defended. "Picking up the three of us and bringing us here probably wasn't on her to-do list for the day."

"Then who?"

Sean didn't know, but it was the only theory he had to go on at the moment. From the time Priya said Patel went missing, he had the idea that someone working for them might have been involved. Yet everything they'd heard so far suggested that there was no struggle, which meant Patel could have left of his own accord. Sean hoped that was the case, that the professor was hiding out somewhere in the hills, or hundreds of miles away, searching through a cave for more clues as to the whereabouts of the Gada.

Sean snorted at the thought. An ancient weapon with the power to destroy or restore worlds. Or in the case of the mace of Vishnu, keep things in check, preserve the balance. He imagined an Indian archaeologist feeling his way through the darkness of a cave or some abandoned temple. The thought made him smile even though he'd never met the man before.

"I don't know for sure," Sean admitted, coming back around to the question. "For all we know, it could be Raj."

"The cook?" Tommy sounded incredulous and looked even more so.

"It's always the one you least suspect," Sean quipped. "But no, I honestly don't think it is him. If there is someone here in the camp that has anything to do with Patel's disappearance, I haven't got a clue who that might be. Not yet at least."

Adriana's eyes flitted up from the two men at the table, noticing movement at the communications tent. "She's on her way back."

The men understood the cue and changed the topic of their conversation back to the notebook as Priya approached. She carried a stack of papers in one hand and the journal in the other. She stopped at the head of the table and started dividing out the sheets until each of the three had an equal share of the workload.

"Thankfully, we had enough ink for all this," she said. "Sometimes, people make tons of copies and the cartridges run dry."

"Yeah, that is lucky," Tommy said and picked up a couple of sheets lying on the table in front of him. She'd also given them each a copy of the letter so they could have the key as they worked on their given assignment.

"So," Sean said, "I guess we should get to it. Let's see what our friend Dr. Patel was really working on."

14

THIRUVANANTHAPURAM

Heather peeked around the corner. The rain had subsided for the moment, giving way to a fine mist that seemed to spray from the sky. The hazy precipitation moistened their clothes, almost in a more annoying way than a straight-up downpour would have.

She spotted the first two guards, one on either side of the gate leading into the temple. The thick iron bars glared out at her, daring her to break in. She knew there was a heavy chain attached to a lock that kept the gate sealed during the evening hours. The two guards were armed with handguns, both holstered at their hips. They were far less imposing than the commandos that had previously occupied that post. For years, the commandos of the Indian military had protected the temple, armed with submachine guns, sidearms, and enough backup to take down a small town.

Back then, the temple was nigh impregnable.

Now, however, there were fewer men guarding the site. Not only that, those that were stationed there were nowhere nearly as well trained as the commandos. They were cops, so in that regard, they had their own strengths, but they were also men who hadn't been through the rigors, the tests, that forged an elite warrior's mettle.

While Heather was certain the cops were more than capable of taking down 99 percent of the world's criminals, she knew they were nowhere nearly competent enough to survive this night.

She stepped around the corner and strode forward. The silver sari she wore flowed around her, clinging to her shoulders, breasts, and hips as she moved. She walked straight toward the gate and the two men, knowing full well they would fix their eyes on her as she approached, although they wouldn't see the weapons she had strapped to her back and inner thighs. Perhaps that was better for them, dying without ever realizing what had happened. In some ways, it was how she wanted to go, in her sleep or via some kind of weird accident. Then again, Heather had always been a fighter, a warrior.

Since childhood, she'd never taken crap from anyone. She'd learned how to defend herself at an early age, fighting off bullies who thought they were too big for her to take down.

Initially, they'd been correct. She'd walked home from school with more than a few bruises on multiple occasions. But with every failure, every lost battle, Heather had learned from her mistakes.

Before long, she was the queen of the elementary school, then the middle school, and by the time she reached high school, no one bothered her. Ever.

She figured it was the time she took Paul Jones's arm and bent it over her shoulder, snapping the bone just below his elbow. That happened in seventh grade as a result of him trying to get her to show off her bra. When she refused, he pushed the issue, tugging on her shirt. Before he knew it, she'd grabbed his wrist, twisted her body, jerked him forward, and yanked down hard.

Heather could still remember the sound and feel of the bone breaking in the boy's forearm. She grinned at the thought as she approached the two guards. To them, she was flashing them a flirty smile.

She saw the stern looks on their faces melt as she drew near. Men were so easy. She raised one hand and waved her fingers in a coy way. Their shoulders sagged a little as they relaxed.

They never saw the two men appear from the shadows on either side, drawing long knives as they moved like ghosts—silent, floating through the misty air. The knife tips pierced the guards' skulls right in front of their ears. The two killers pushed the blades hard, thrusting them deep into the cops' brains, killing them instantly. Even as the two attackers withdrew their bloodstained weapons, the guards were dead, falling to the ground with a thud.

Heather never stopped moving, the sari flowing around her in the breeze. She lifted the skirt, revealing skintight black pants underneath, and grabbed a device from her belt. Letting the skirt fall back to her ankles a moment before she reached the gate, Heather lifted the object. There was a cylinder on the bottom, about half the size of a can of spray paint. The top of it had a trigger along with a gray button on the back, a nozzle on the front, and a couple of tiny tubes that ran to a short metal barrel.

She pushed down on the gray button and pulled the trigger, positioning the barrel no more than two millimeters from the chain on the gate. As she maneuvered the barrel closer to one of the chain links, she reached back and removed a pair of welding goggles that she'd hung from her sash prior to making her appearance on the street. She pressed them to her eyes and then made contact with the hot flame streaming out of the barrel.

The chain's link turned a deep red within seconds, then orange, yellow, and then the entire thing sagged suddenly as the flame severed the thick metal, cutting through it in less than a minute. Brock appeared directly behind her, and when the chain fell he dragged it quietly through the bars until it was free, then dropped it on the dead guard to his right.

He pulled the gate open with a gloved hand and stepped inside with Heather next to him. Once they were in, the two mercenaries accompanying them grabbed the guards and dragged them away into a dark alley, stashing the bodies next to a dumpster and then covering them with trash bags.

Someone would find them, likely the next day, but by then Brock and his team would be long gone.

The two men returned; one stood outside doing his best impression of a guard, while the other joined Brock and Heather.

She pulled the skirt up over her head and dropped the sari on the wet walkway leading into the temple, revealing the tight black tactical outfit that covered every inch of her slightly tanned skin. The only thing visible was her face and neck. Those disappeared when she pulled a ski mask over her head and gave a nod to Brock.

He returned the signal, and she moved forward, taking point.

Brock was in charge of the operation, but he wasn't so egotistical to believe that he should be running point in what was essentially a military-style raid. While he didn't like the idea of putting a woman out in front, in harm's way, she was the best of them and would handle any potential threats better than the other two guys, and definitely better than he would.

They moved down the corridor, keeping low in a crouched position to use the short stone wall to their left and right for cover. Passing a courtyard on the left, Brock stole a quick look over the wall's lip and saw four more guards standing around talking. He knew the commandos would never have been so lax on the job. Once more, he felt a wave of appreciation at the mistake the government made with the replacement of the elite fighting force with a more localized one.

The three moved with stealthy precision to the end of the corridor and hung a left. Each carried a handgun with a suppressor attached. Heather carried two weapons: a pistol in one hand and a knife in the other. As they rounded the corner, Brock immediately understood why she was holding the blade. They walked straight into a guard who was strolling down the next passage, about to turn the corner and head toward the gate.

The widening of his eyes was the only reflex he could muster before Heather's left hand shot up and pushed the blade through the bottom of his jaw, just behind the chin. The tip stopped somewhere inside his head, where she twisted it a half inch to the right and then jerked it out. The cop fell to his knees and crumpled in a heap before he could even gurgle.

Heather wiped the blade on his shirt with a deft flip of the wrist and kept moving. The wall wouldn't keep them out of sight for long if any of the guards in the courtyard busted up their little sewing circle and decided to do their jobs. She knew timing was everything, and the group of three would have to move fast if they wanted this to work. The other part of it was eliminating the threat. Even if they left one of the guards alive, he could call for backup. She knew that the commandos were still on call if needed. If those guys showed up, there would be trouble. She was good. So were her accomplices, but they weren't that good.

She scanned the corridor, moving faster now on the balls of her feet: four more guards to take out in the courtyard and likely dozens more on the grounds somewhere. But where were they?

That issue rang in her head like an alarm. There were supposed to be fifty guards watching over this site. So far, they'd only seen the two at the front, the one she'd just killed, and these four.

She reached the entrance to the interior portion of the temple and stopped at the corner before turning right to head down the next passage. She pressed her back against the wall and waited, keeping her eyes locked on the four cops in the courtyard. Brock and the mercenary who went by the name of Tre mimicked her movement and took up positions next to her along the wall, staying in the shadows to remain as invisible as possible.

Heather listened closely. She heard a familiar clicking noise coming their way. From the sound of it, there was more than one guard approaching. Footsteps on stone signaled at least two, and maybe more, marching down the hallway just around the corner.

One of the men was speaking in Hindi, chatting with someone else. They were not attempting to be silent; that much was clear. Then again, why would they have? They weren't the ones trying to break into the world's richest temple and steal a priceless artifact.

Heather raised a hand with one finger up, the other still clutching the deadly blade in her hand. She motioned to the guards in the courtyard. Brock and Tre both understood what she meant. The second the guards in the adjacent corridor appeared, there would be a fight. That would draw the attention of the men standing around just beyond the wall. An arched gate, much like the one over her shoulder, was opposite of them and hung open.

Heather glanced at her two partners and gave a nod. They returned the gesture and waited.

She watched the threshold separating the two passageways. The sound of the approaching guards grew louder with every passing second.

Then she saw it, the thing she'd been waiting for. The tip of a black boot appeared on the tiled floor. That was her cue.

She spun around the corner with the knife flashing in the dim candlelight that lit the next corridor. The sharp edge found the first man's throat and ripped into it, slicing through the carotid artery and jugular vein with deadly precision. Even as the man gurgled and grasped at his throat, she spun past him with a deft twist and jammed the blade into the next guard's neck.

He shuddered and twitched, at first reaching for his weapon and then the knife in his throat. Neither helped him. The damage was done as she removed the blade with a jerk. As the guard to his left fell to his knees, blood streaming through his fingers, the second guard toppled sideways, his shoulder striking the wall as he slumped slowly to the floor.

Heather figured there were more than two of them based on the conversation she'd overheard and the number of footsteps. She was relieved to see there were only two more behind the first. They reacted quickly, their training kicking in in an instant. The men raised their submachine guns to open fire, but she'd already begun the secondary assault. Knowing the men with her were already moving to handle the situation in the courtyard, Heather raised her 9mm and fired a round into the forehead of the man on the right. The tunnel echoed with the sound of the clap from the discharge. The guard fell backward onto the floor, dead in the blink of an eye.

The last guard saw his comrade taken down, and his instincts overtook his training. It was a classic mistake, one that she doubted the commandos would have made. Had it been one of those guys, he would have simply squeezed the trigger and poured a magazine of hot metal into her body, thus ending the mission right then and there. Not to mention her life. She liked to believe that wouldn't have happened, that she was faster than anyone she could face, but the reality was that a highly trained operative wouldn't have panicked, wouldn't have let the flight instinct overtake his fight.

The cop dove to his right and raised his weapon.

He's seen too many action movies.

Heather twisted sideways and extended her hand, both narrowing his target and taking aim. She squeezed the trigger once. The weapon discharged and sent a bullet through the guy's left eye. When he hit the floor, he rolled onto his face and lay still.

She spun back around, facing down the length of the corridor, weapon at full extension in case more guards appeared.

Behind her, Brock and Tre moved simultaneously as Heather attacked the four guards in the tunnel. They charged through the gate, catching the four men in the courtyard off guard.

Their heads twisted as they noticed the movement. Then their eyes widened with fear as they realized the men approaching them were pointing guns their way. Maybe they also saw the slaughter taking place behind the attackers where another masked figure was single-handedly terminating four of their brethren.

The guards never had a chance to react, other than a few twitches toward the submachine guns slung over their shoulders. Two of them had the weapons hanging at their lower backs.

Brock and Tre fired at the other two first, taking them out in a hail of bullets. By the time the remaining two men had grasped their weapons, it was too late. Rounds tore through the gaps in their armor, piercing their necks, heads, arms, and guts.

The four guards lay in a pile on the mosaic-tile floor.

Tre stepped over to one that was still writhing in agony and discharged his gun, planting a bullet in the man's skull. The guy stopped moving instantly.

Brock turned to face Heather and saw her keeping watch over the corridor. He ejected the magazine in his weapon and replaced it with a full one. Tre did the same. Then the two men trotted back across the courtyard and into the shadows of the passage.

"Well done," Heather said, sounding impressed.

"Where are the others?" Brock asked, knowing there were still plenty more threats to eliminate.

"I have a feeling we'll find them soon enough. This is the way to the vault, yes?"

He nodded.

"Okay then. Let's go find that relic."

15

BHANGARH

S ean rubbed his temples with both thumbs, fingers pressed
into his skull to give a little leverage to the digits and make the
pressure a little stronger. He'd been working on the encrypted
message for the last hour and was nearly finished, but what he was
seeing still gave cause for concern.

Dr. Patel's code was easy enough to decipher once the key was
applied. That wasn't the hard part or the reason for his current level
of anxiety.

"You see this, too, right?" he asked.

Adriana had been sitting across from him at the little desk, toiling
under the dim light of the tent's lone lantern. The group had split up,
retiring to their tents for the night to work on the translations and get
some rest. They would share their findings in the morning.

Sean hadn't necessarily thought it was a good idea to work on
something so mentally stimulating at a late hour, figuring it would
cause them to lose sleep. As it turned out, he'd nearly nodded off
several times.

"Adriana?" He said her name to snap her out of the fog she was in.

She was staring down at the sheet of paper with a pen in her right
hand. Hearing her name, she started and looked up. "Yes?"

"A little focused, huh?"

"You could say that. This is a fascinating journal. This Dr. Patel really did a lot of research."

"Uh huh..."

"But yes, I see it." She returned to his original question, at the same time confirming that she'd heard it, at least on some level. "It appears Dr. Patel was searching for some kind of clue."

"Three clues," he corrected. "All that leads to the same thing."

"The Gada."

The two twisted around in their chairs and looked toward the front of the tent. Tommy stood in the entrance, holding a stack of papers. "Sorry, I couldn't wait 'til morning."

He let the tent flap fall and stepped inside.

"Sure, come on in. We're decent," Sean joked.

Tommy's head twisted back and forth. "I saw you still had your light on and figured it was fine. You done working out your ends of the code yet?" There was a hint of excitement in his voice.

"Just finished," Adriana answered. "I assume you came to similar conclusions?"

"What conclusions?"

She tilted her head to the side and cast him a knowing glare, one that begged him to stop fooling around.

"What?" He put out one hand, still oblivious.

"That the good Dr. Patel was on the trail of something, the kind of trail we've seen before."

"See, that's why I wanted to work with the two of you instead of alone in my tent. I knew you'd have something I didn't."

The other two frowned at the comment. "You didn't figure out that the professor had pinpointed three clues that would lead to the Gada?"

Tommy's eyebrows lowered. "I mean, I figured maybe it was something like that, but you two had the introduction to his journal. I had the middle section."

"We have the end, as well," Adriana said.

"And?"

"It seems Patel believes that when you find the three objects Vishnu holds in his hands, it will lead to the great balancer, the weapon that can neutralize any threat and keep the world safe from harm."

"The mace."

Adriana nodded.

"All these lines are sort of a hodgepodge of thoughts the professor wrote down during his research, but most of what's here is stuff he believed was important in the search." Sean nudged his translations to the center of the table. "And the fact that he felt the need to encode everything he was writing and thinking...that means he was concerned."

"About someone following him?" Tommy asked. He found a stool near one of the beds and helped himself to a seat.

"And maybe worse."

"Yeah," Tommy said with a nod. "I was thinking the same. Only one thing makes a person come up with a cipher like this to keep something secret: fear."

"Now the question is; who is he afraid of? He must have known he was being watched, but by who?"

"I doubt we'll find that answer in any of these sheets," Adriana offered. "If we follow the bread crumbs, though, we might get it."

"Along with finding Patel," Sean added.

Tommy laid the papers down on the table and spread them out, rearranging them according to the order they were found in the journal.

"So," he said, putting his hands on his hips as he stared down at the paperwork. "It looks like a trail."

"Yep," Sean agreed. "Like we said, we've seen this sort of thing before. From the looks of it, we start here, with this place."

He pointed to the blueprint of the village Dr. Patel had sketched. "Any ideas where this is?"

"I have a few," Tommy admitted. "Despite the fact our friend Dr. Patel was poetic and deliberately vague, he wrote all these passages like one long riddle, each solution leading to the next until we eventually—hopefully—find the Gada."

He motioned to the first paragraph next to the schematics:

Here among the living dead, where curses thrive and echoes of ancient past drift like blown dust, the first holy relic sleeps.

There were some additional notations, things Patel was trying to work through as if writing down his thoughts. One particular section was of immediate interest. The first paragraph didn't contain a riddle, though it was just as puzzling as the previous one:

I've been on the trail of the Gada for many years now. I would spend time in the evenings or on weekends when I wasn't at the university or working for the museum. During those hours, often late into the night, I scoured the earth for clues as to the whereabouts of the magical mace of Vishnu.

Sometimes, I found myself asking why: Why should I spend so many of my days on this earth in search of an object that likely doesn't exist, that is most probably a device of myth?

The answer always comes when I see the things happening to people all over the world. Pestilence, disease, famine, war, death. If this weapon truly exists, perhaps it can once again restore peace to this world, bring balance, and save the innocent from evil.

My only fear is that if the Gada does exist, its brethren might, too. Last year at a conference, I met an interesting man from America who asked many questions about the Hindu religion, with particular interest in the holy relics of the trinity. Initially, I passed it off as curiosity, but now I'm not so certain. Were someone to find one of the other great weapons, such as the Trishula, the world could be in great peril.

That drives me forward and keeps me motivated on these nights where I feel my endeavor is fruitless.

An entry below that was dated a month later:

It would seem that my fears have come to fruition. Someone has learned of my quest to discover the location of the Gada. Even worse, I am now convinced that this person or someone else is also in search of the Trishula, a weapon of terrible power that could destroy the entire planet, at least according to the legends.

I've laid traps to see if I've been followed or watched. Sadly, my plans proved my paranoia justified. I was followed home yesterday evening from the university, and I've noticed a few things out of place in my office. I placed a pen and a piece of paper in an exact location marked by a simple line on the surface of the desk. When I returned from teaching a class, I discovered these items were moved. Someone tried to return them to their exact positions, but I know they were moved. From now on, everything I write will be encrypted. I've transferred all my notes and sketches into this journal to keep what I've learned safe, along with anything else I may discover along the way.

"So, he was being followed?" Tommy asked.

"Sounds like it."

"But by who?" Adriana asked.

"That's a good question. It also makes me wonder if they eventually caught him or if he simply slipped away in the middle of the night."

Sean pondered the situation. He rested his chin on three knuckles, letting the index finger run up the side of his jaw. "Personally," he said after silent contemplation, "I think the man got away."

Tommy raised both eyebrows, surprised at the sudden assertion. "Really? Why?"

Sean rolled his shoulders. "Everything we've heard so far tells us that there wasn't a struggle here in his tent. No one saw anything strange. This place, while not the most secure in the world, does have a minimal...very minimal security set up. And with all the people working this site, someone would have heard or seen something unusual. I mean, even if Patel had grunted or struggled, the tent next door would have likely heard it."

Tommy and Adriana nodded.

"So, you think he left?" Adriana asked.

"I do. When you read this, it says that he knew someone was on his tail. He even took action to confirm his suspicion. Does that sound like the kind of person that will let themselves become a victim?"

Tommy shook his head.

"Right. Doesn't sound like it to me, either. Patel was clever—based on this little journal. My guess is he took off that night and sent the letter to Priya, maybe the next morning."

"You think he's gone after the first part of the riddle?"

That was the portion of the mystery Sean wasn't so sure about. "If he did, he'd be putting himself in harm's way again. It's possible if he thought he could get there before anyone else, that he chose to track down these items that lead to the mace."

"But if he did that, and people were following him, then he would lead them straight to it." Adriana's objection made sense.

Sean had already thought of it. "Not if he threw them off the trail."

"Or maybe his escape wasn't an escape. Maybe it was his way of getting whoever was following him off the right track—just so he could put us on it with the help of Priya."

Sean and Adriana took a deep breath and blew it out through tiny holes in their lips, both making a low whistling sound.

"That's pretty deep, Schultzie," Sean said.

"Thank you." Tommy put his hands out wide as if to say, "It was nothing."

"There is one way we can figure out the professor's location...or at least where he was last week." Adriana glanced from Tommy to Sean and back again.

The two men didn't have a clue what she was talking about.

"Oh yeah?" Tommy asked. "How?"

"The letter. It has a stamp on it from the post office, a rubber stamp in ink. You saw it." She nodded at Sean.

"That's right. And it would have the post office and town where Patel would have mailed it." His voice rose with excitement as the realization set in. "Patel must have put her name and address on both parts, sender, and receiver, to throw anyone off the trail. They'd likely think she was just sending herself a note or something. Or they would ignore it entirely."

"So, we need Priya to show us that envelope. Once we do, we'll know where Patel went."

"And," Sean added, "if we're lucky, that location might be the first breadcrumb."

"To finding this town or whatever it is?" Adriana asked, motioning toward the schematics.

"Precisely."

"The others," Sean said. "He references the others. You think he was talking about the other items held by Vishnu in some of those images?"

Tommy nodded. "Makes sense. Especially when you work your way over to my section." He tipped his head to the sheet of paper in the center. "Reading through these paragraphs, it seems like you need to have all those other items together before the mace will do its thing."

Adriana snorted. "That your scientific explanation? The do-its-thing part, I mean?"

Tommy cracked a smile. "Yes, very scientific."

"He's right, though," Sean said. "Based on Patel's notes, we have to locate these other three things before we find the Gada." He pointed to the last page where the image of a shadowy mountain dominated the paper. "This passage suggests the same thing."

He pressed his finger to the paragraph.

When brought together at the holy mountain, the door will reveal itself to Vishnu's abode, and the holy weapon will share its light with the world once more.

"Pretty interesting."

The other two nodded in agreement.

Tommy set his jaw and crossed his arms. "I guess the first thing we need to do is get that envelope from Priya one more time and figure out where the professor went. It would be clever if he were to send it from a town near where this thing is." He motioned to the blueprint of the village. "If there is a town near there."

"Could we be so lucky?" Sean asked.

"We've been lucky before," Adriana said in a sultry tone. "No reason why it can't happen again."

"Any chance Priya is still awake?"

Tommy shook his head. "I don't think so. I noticed her going to her tent earlier. Just now when I came over, I saw her lights were out. She's likely asleep. Not that I blame her." The comment seemed to force a yawn out of him, and he stretched his arms high and wide.

"Let's all get some sleep," Sean suggested. "We can ask her about the envelope in the morning. Sounds like tomorrow is going to be a big day, so we'll need all the rest we can get."

16

THIRUVANANTHAPURAM

They'd made their way through the first chamber. It led down a set of stairs to a landing where Brock knew the first of the six vaults was located. He and his team had moved through quickly, bypassing that first staircase until they arrived in the next room, another chamber with high ceilings and a set of stairs descending down into the ground in the center.

The room was as unimpressive as the golden exterior was spectacular. There were a few symbols and decorations carved into the stone in the doorframe and along the walls, but by and large, there was nothing in the chamber that suggested there was something of value hidden below.

Brock knew that wasn't the case.

He stopped at the top of the stairs and glanced back over his shoulder. Tre was standing guard at the door with a big shoulder pressed into the frame. The man leaned his head out and took a quick look down the hall. There was no sign of anyone. No reinforcements coming to find those responsible for the dead in the corridors and courtyard. Not yet, at least.

Heather stood close to Brock a few feet away and staggered from his right shoulder. In one hand, she held a handgun. In the other, she clutched a cop, a straggler who'd strayed away from his post and stumbled into her arms. She'd been about to kill him when Brock—inexplicably—ordered her to stand down and let the man live.

She hadn't questioned his reasoning, not yet. He'd never mentioned anything about taking prisoners. This wasn't a situation where hostages would be an advantage, at least not that she could tell. Dragging dead weight around on a heist would slow them down exponentially, especially if the guy turned out to be trouble. He hadn't so far, but that could change when things started to heat up again. Up to that point in their mission, she'd killed several men in close quarters. In that kind of scenario, a hostage could cause all sorts of problems.

"Tre?" Brock said, still staring down into the dark stairwell.

"Yes, sir?"

"Cover the door."

"Done."

Brock turned on a flashlight and took a step down.

"You're mad," the prisoner said. The tremor in his voice underscored a fear deeper than the immediate threat of execution by means of a bullet. There was something else to it.

Brock sensed this strange sense of fear and twisted his head around, glaring at the prisoner. The man's lips quivered. Brock's lips curled in a devilish grin. "Afraid of the dark?" He reached out with a pocket-sized butane torch, pressed a button, and lit a candle on the wall. The little flame flickered for a moment, struggling to keep burning, and then steadied itself, casting a consistent yellow glow into the stairwell.

"It's not the dark I fear," the cop said. "There are far worse things down there than the dark."

Brock's grin widened, showing off his bright white teeth in the combined light of his flashlight and the candle. "I know. That's why we have you."

He turned slowly back to the stairs at his feet and began descending once more, stopping intermittently to light additional candles along the way. Behind him, Heather shoved the cop forward, forcing him to follow. Tre stayed at the entrance to the chamber in case reinforcements discovered their location.

It wouldn't take long for a patrol to discover the bodies in the courtyard or the ones in the tunnel. It was only a matter of time. By their best guess, based on watching the movements of the guards for the last few days, they had roughly ten minutes, give or take a few.

At the bottom of the stairs, Brock stepped through the antechamber leading into the main room where the door to the infamous vault awaited. He stopped on the threshold, just inside the doorway, and waited.

He could make out the images of serpents—more like dragons—wrapping their long, slender bodies up around the vault door. He noted the huge one sticking its head out at any trespassers, a snarling, gaping mouth issuing a final warning to any who dared consider an attempt to enter.

There was no mistaking what the architects of this place had in mind. Their goal was to ward off any who thought to rob the temple of its most priceless and powerful treasure. According to the tales that had been passed down through the decades, their ruse had worked—until now. Brock had no intention of letting some children's ghost stories keep him out.

He stepped purposefully through the archway, aiming his flashlight directly at the vault door straight ahead. His ears pricked as he heard the sound of Heather's prisoner scraping his shoes against the floor as he shuffled forward.

Brock's eyes lingered on an object lying on the floor where the tiles met the vault wall. The skeleton still clung to its tattered clothing. Shards of the fabric dangled, silent and motionless, from the bones. The skull was twisted to one side, the jaw open wide in a fearful, permanent gape as if still calling for help.

"There's another over there, sir," Heather said, her voice cracking the deathly silence of the room.

Brock looked to the right, shining the bright white circle on another heap of bones.

"You see?" the cop said. His voice wavered, bathed in fear. "This is a place of death. You must turn back."

"No," Brock said, "I'm not going to do that."

He loosened the tactical backpack from his shoulders and removed a strange gun. Its boxy frame and body looked like nothing the cop had ever seen. There was a canister attached to the top, about the size of a propane tank used for lanterns or camping stoves. Brock flipped a red switch on the side of the black weapon and nodded to Heather.

She shoved her gun's barrel deeper into the prisoner's back. The man grunted in protest, but his legs moved forward involuntarily, a natural response to the jabbing pain in his lower back.

The man's toe dug into the tile as he moved ahead and he nearly tripped. Heather grabbed one of his shoulders, though, and kept him upright.

"What are you doing?" The tremor in the cop's voice was growing. "This place is cursed! We are all going to die if we don't leave now."

Brock's eyes narrowed. Wrinkles streaked from the corners, almost all the way to his temples. "Well, you're not entirely wrong."

The prisoner eyed him warily, cocking his head to the side to ascertain the meaning of his captor's words.

Something made a sound from the darkness. Brock's lips creased. "There they are. Right on time."

The cop looked at Brock, then to the vault door, and back to Brock. "What are you doing? We need to go. Please!"

Brock shook his head. "End of the line for you, old boy." He used a mocking English accent to mimic the captive.

The sound grew louder, though not by much. It was a slithering noise with an intermittent flop thrown in now and then. Brock pointed his light at a small port in the wall to the left of the door, while keeping his eyes fixed on another one at the opposite side.

Hissing filled the room, the sound swelling to a whispery crescendo, like an army of ghosts approaching to perform their ghastly tasks.

Then Brock saw it, an eerie sight that sent a chill through his bones, though he dared not let on to the other two. He had nothing to fear. The sacrifice would be enough.

He steeled his gaze as the two glowing orbs neared, pushing through the black vent to reveal a smooth, scaly head. A long, forked tongue flicked out of tightly pressed lips. The snake slithered its way out of the opening until gravity did the rest and brought the body to the floor with a gentle smack.

The serpent's eyes locked on the prisoner, the nearest victim to his domicile. The snake's constantly flicking tongue fed it the heat signatures of the people in the room. Its focus, however, was on the closest target, the cop whose body trembled in absolute terror. The man's fear caused his heart to race within his chest. Beads of sweat dribbled down his forehead and the sides of his face, splattering on the tile around his feet.

"NO!" He begged to be relieved of his fate, but Heather kept the gun pressed hard against his back. His wide eyes gazed into the serpent's. He'd seen king cobras before. This variety, however, was different. It had a golden layer of scales covering its body, with black splotches along the back and sides. If the prisoner thought this was the worst of it, he was dead wrong.

More slithering bodies appeared through the vents, all driven by a communal urge, ancient instincts that pushed them to defend their home. Or was it something else, something more sinister?

This kind of behavior was uncharacteristic of snakes. It wasn't like them to swarm this way. They lived in perpetual competition with one another. Unlike creatures in other species, most serpents were extremely selfish by nature.

As more of the reptiles fell from the ventilation ports and slithered toward the prisoner, Brock stayed calm, watching them with a close eye. He was standing far enough away that the snakes barely noticed him, or so it seemed. Apparently, they were more interested in the closest, easiest target.

"Let me go! Please, I beg you!" The cop continued his begging, desperate pleas that fell on deaf ears. "I don't want to die!"

The last word out of his mouth came as a shriek as Heather

shoved him forward toward the approaching, leathery death. The man stumbled over the tip of his boot and lost his balance, falling headfirst into the writhing mass.

One snake snapped out at him in an instant, latching on to the man's neck before he had even hit the floor. Within seconds, a half-dozen more serpents lashed out, fangs brandished in the blink of an eye. They latched on to his arms, legs, hands, and face, each pumping their deadly venom into the man's tissues.

His screams of agony faded as the toxins did their vicious task with almost merciful speed. His body twitched and squirmed, still unwilling to give up the last gasps of breath in lungs that were rapidly suffocating.

The mass of snakes piled on to the victim, each issuing a bite to defend their turf. When Brock saw there were no more of the deadly reptiles exiting the vents, he shifted to the left, flanking the deadly mass.

Heather continued to move back and then around to the side where Brock had positioned himself. She kept her weapon trained on the beasts, watching with curious and horrified fascination.

The serpents were doing something, unlike anything she'd ever seen their species do before. While Heather was no expert on snake behavior, she was fairly certain they didn't hunt in packs like that. The more gruesome and disturbing part of the cop's fate wasn't the pack mentality. They were gnawing at the man's flesh, tearing skin and muscle from his body while he was still alive. Most snakes, as far as she recalled, consumed their victims whole as they had no teeth to chew their meal. Yet these beasts seemed to be doing just that— grinding sharp, small teeth in the back of their mouths behind the fangs, ripping into flesh and pulling it into their throats.

The cop had stopped moving on his own, but the arms and legs shifted and twitched as the snakes feasted on his body.

"Is he dead?" Heather asked.

"Yeah, I think so." Brock took a step forward and leveled his weapon, pointing the barrel at the writhing heap.

He flipped a button on the side, lighting a tiny torch on the tip of the muzzle. He pulled the trigger. A split second after, a stream of fire shot out of the gun. The compact flamethrower cast a swath of blazing death onto the serpents, bathing them in fire.

The flammable compound stuck to them like napalm. The snakes flopped around, biting at their own scaly skin in an attempt to put out the flames. Some rolled around on top of the others, but there was no stopping the inevitable.

When every single snake was burning, Brock pulled a bandana over his face and stepped back. Heather followed suit and watched the living pyre pour black smoke to the ceiling where it lingered briefly before finding a path out into the next room and up to the chamber above.

One by one, the snakes died off. Their bodies ceased their jerky movements, slowing to a few rolls and flops until the entire pile was nothing but a still bonfire of charred reptilian logs.

"Ugh," Brock said as he switched off the flamethrower. "The stench is awful."

"What did you think was going to happen?" Heather asked. She pinched the mask over her nose to keep from breathing in the foul odor.

"You're up," he said. "The second that smoke hits fresh air outside, we're going to have company." Brock shoved the weapon back into his gear bag and pulled out a roll of thick, gray material that looked almost like tape. He handed the first roll to Heather, and she immediately set to work.

She didn't need to be told twice. Heather was more than aware of the potential trouble that awaited if they didn't move quickly.

She took a second roll from the bag and hurried over to the door, carefully navigating the smoldering heap of dead snakes to her right. Fortunately, their ruse had worked. The serpents had pursued the cop far enough that they were clear of the vault gate.

Heather took the second roll and set it on the ground, while Brock took a third and began unraveling it. He pressed the sticky substance against the outside of the vault door's frame, running it around the vent on the left, creating a line that stretched up about six feet. She did the same, creating a parallel line and then, with the second spool, ran a horizontal strip that connected the two vertical ones.

Then she reached into her bag and took out small packet about the size of Brock's fist. She shoved the little satchel into the vent and flipped a switch on the top of it before pushing it deeper into the recess.

"You good?" she asked.

Brock nodded and pressed the thick tape a little harder at the top corner one last time.

"Yep."

"Okay then."

He grabbed his bag and slung it over his shoulder. She did the same, and the two hurried back to the antechamber on the other side of the doorway. Once they were through, the two ducked into the corners—one on either side.

"Cover your ears," Heather warned.

Brock did as told, cupping his ears with both hands while Heather pulled out a small black box from her bag. She flipped the safety switch on the top and then pried open the plastic cover that protected a red button. She glanced up at Brock one last time and gave a nod. He returned the gesture and she pressed the button, instantly covering her ears.

A deep boom erupted from the next room as the wireless detonators did their work, blowing the explosives with immediate effectiveness. A cloud of dust rolled through the doorway and spilled into the antechamber, mingling near the ceiling with the remaining smoke from the bonfire.

Brock lowered his hands, using one to disperse the dust by waving it around. His actions did little to get rid of the irritant, but he kept at it until the dust had settled, at least somewhat. Then he stepped around the corner and peered through the doorway.

Just beyond a dying cloud of dust, he could see the damage they'd done to the wall of Vault B. To the right of what was considered by most an impenetrable gate, a door had been created in the stone. The portal was about six feet tall and three feet wide, replacing the vent with a much larger version.

Brock stepped forward and raised his flashlight, casting the white beam through the heavy dust particles and debris. At first, he couldn't see much through the haze, but he pressed forward until he reached the lip of the new doorway. He stared through the short tunnel.

Beyond was something his eyes could scarcely believe.

He'd done it. Brock had broken into the forbidden vault.

17

THIRUVANANTHAPURAM

B rock took a wary step forward. He renewed his grip on the pistol at his side and held it at his waist as he moved through the opening Heather had blown through the wall.

"You sure you don't want me to go first?" she asked.

He shook his head. "No. I've waited for this day, the day I could get my hands on this incredible treasure."

He held his flashlight aloft, just over his shoulder, sending the bright beam through the settling dust and into the next room. At first, there wasn't much to see through the dirty fog. Then he caught a glint of something shiny with a hint of yellow. He didn't need to ask. Brock already knew what it had to be. Gold.

Cautiously, he pointed the flashlight down onto the floor as he reached the other side of the wall and paused for a moment. His hand twisted as he aimed the light in all directions, checking to make certain there were no traps set long ago that would ensnare him and his partner.

What he glimpsed was something that he could have never imagined in a hundred years.

The tiles on the floor were layered in pure gold, as if hewn from a mountain of the precious metal and carved in place, here, in this holy

cache. The walls were the same stone as the previous chamber but
with reliefs of golden trees, animals, and people carved into it. An
ancient story unfolded around them, laid out in golden majesty.
There was a sky, too, higher on the walls. Clouds of gold hung in the
heavens, surrounding the gods of the Vedas and Hindu lore.

Bronze censers stood atop marble pedestals along the wall, six in
all, evenly spaced to fully immerse the room in their bittersweet
scents. Between each pedestal, lined up one end against another,
were huge wooden chests made from thick oak. The handles were
coated in gold filigree. Each overflowed with piles of golden coins,
cups, candles, jewels, crowns, and gem-studded necklaces.

Brock caught himself holding his breath as he took in the sight.
Heather, too, had stopped breathing as she gazed upon the incredible
vision before them.

"They said this vault contained trillions of dollars' worth of
wealth," Brock whispered. There was a sort of reverence in his voice.

"Enough money to buy several countries," she remarked.

He nodded. "All a distraction from the true treasure in this room."

His eyes fixed on something in the back, standing alone against
the far wall. His feet moved without a command or a thought, but
with a desire. They carried him across the spectacular golden floor,
passing the chests of nearly unlimited wealth.

The vault was around one hundred feet long and about half as
wide. If he hadn't been so focused on the item in the back, he would
have easily been distracted by the enormity of the treasure
around him.

But Brock knew better. In the days of his youth, he'd wanted to be
rich and famous. They were the two motivating factors that had
driven him to work as hard as he had to become the person he was.
Yet there was something deep down inside that burned, a flickering
truth that kept his eyes locked on the one thing in the back he was
there to retrieve.

That truth was simple. No amount of money would do him or
anyone any good if the world was destroyed by mankind. With the
seas dying, the forests vanishing, and species of animals becoming

extinct every passing day, all the money and treasure in the world would be useless when there was no food to eat, no water to drink, and no safe place to hide.

He floated by all of it, walking on air as he crossed the room. He slowed, involuntarily, when he neared the strange object. He came to a complete stop a few feet before it and let out a breath he didn't realize he'd taken.

Heather came up beside him and halted. She'd been just as reverent in her crossing of the room, not out of religious respect but out of sheer astonishment. She'd never imagined a place like this could exist anywhere on the entire planet.

"Is that it?" Her voice remained quiet, just above a whisper, as if worried she would wake some ancient spirit or deity from a long slumber.

Brock dipped his head. "Yes." He took another step closer, shining his flashlight on the object. It gleamed in the light, flashing a yellowish glow that splashed off the treasures surrounding it. "The Trishula. The trident of Shiva."

He was overcome with the feeling that he should kneel before such a holy weapon, but he wasn't a religious man and the notion quickly faded from his mind. Still, he couldn't help but feel some kind of terrified respect.

The golden trident stood almost five feet tall, fixed into a hole in the floor that was the exact diameter of the shaft. As he'd seen in renderings, from thousands of years old to more recent, the entire weapon was made of pure gold. The Trishula alone would likely fetch millions of dollars, but that wasn't his purpose for being here. He did not intend to hawk the weapon to the highest bidder on the black market, or any other market for that matter.

He put the pistol back in its holster and took one last step toward the golden weapon, eyes unblinking, focused completely on the mysterious object. He hesitated for a second when his fingers were mere inches away from the shaft.

"What's wrong?" Heather asked.

He blinked after what seemed like an hour, his eyelids grinding like sandpaper across his eyes. His breaths came in short, shallow bursts, barely giving his lungs enough air with each rise and fall of his chest.

"This is the most powerful weapon known to mankind," he whispered. Despite keeping his voice low, the hissing of his voice still echoed off the walls and resounded for several seconds until dying away in the darkness around them. "This room, this treasure, this... trident, have not been seen in millennia."

She knew the history he'd shared with her. The stories of how the temple was built and the treasure it contained. Most of the structure around them wasn't thousands of years old. This room, however— Vault B—was different. Something about it told the two visitors that it was far older than the building around it. She had the distinct feeling it went back more than a few thousand years.

"With this trident," Brock said, "I will restore balance to the world. I will end those who seek to destroy it with their intentions or neglect. Billions will die so that those of us who understand this planet, and love it, can survive."

His fingers wrapped around the golden shaft, and he pulled up on it. Surprisingly, the weapon came out of its housing with ease. Brock held it aloft for a moment and gazed at the two curved outer forks of the trident. The sharp beveled edges narrowed to lethal points on the tips.

Suddenly, a grinding sound came from the wall. His eyes filled with fear as he glanced down at the hole in the floor. His breathing quickened as he glanced back at the door, forgetting for a moment that they hadn't come through the main portal. The entry they'd blown through the wall was still intact. Why wouldn't it be? He cursed himself for wasting precious seconds instead of trying to get out of what appeared to be some kind of elaborate deathtrap.

"What is that?" Heather asked, her head twisting around in all directions trying to locate the source of the rumbling. "Should we maybe get out of here?"

He nodded and took a step toward the exit. Then the sound

changed. They could hear stone grinding on stone. It was coming from the wall behind where the Trishula had been standing.

Brock lingered, staring at two massive square blocks receded into the wall. His scowl softened to a look of avid curiosity. He pointed his flashlight to the closest cavity and watched with wonder in his eyes as the block lowered from view, revealing something shiny on the inside.

He bent over at the waist and gazed into the hole, shining the light inside to get a clear view.

"What is it?" Heather asked, forgetting there was a new recess to the right she could have easily looked into.

Brock swallowed and stuck his hand inside.

"Are you sure that's a—"

"It's fine," he said, not letting her finish her question.

"Okay." She wasn't convinced.

He twisted his arm, jerked the shoulder, and began to pull something out.

When his hand emerged, a helmet of pure gold was clutched in his fingers. It was fitted with a piece of onyx in the forehead panel. The crystal was shaped like a teardrop.

Brock straightened up and extended the hand that held the trident. "Here," he said. "Hold this for a second."

She did as instructed, taking the weapon by the shaft with great care. She watched as Brock slipped the helmet onto his head and shifted it around until it was in place. It fit perfectly, almost as if it was made just for him.

Then he put out his hand once more, silently requesting the Trishula. She returned it and stared at him.

He raised the trident and inspected every inch of it, appraising the weapon with both admiration and fear. His eyes stopped on something along the shaft that was positioned midway down it. He frowned for a few seconds before he realized what he was seeing.

"What's that?" Heather asked.

A wicked grin parted his lips. "The trigger."

"Trigger? What does it do?"

Her question was abruptly interrupted by shouting in their earpieces.

"Sir, we need to move!"

It was the bodyguard they'd left at the front gate.

"Multiple targets coming in hot." His voice was cut off by the sound of gunfire. "Repeat. Multiple—"

The distant popping sound continued for another moment and then faded as quickly as it had started.

"Sir?" Tre's voice came through the radio. "They're coming in through the front gate."

Brock didn't need to be told who was coming. He knew. Heather did as well. The commandos had been called in. By who didn't matter. Brock figured this would happen if they didn't move fast enough. Now they were trapped. At least that's what the enemy would think.

What the commandos didn't realize was that they were running headlong into their own doom.

"What's in the other hole?" he asked in a hurried tone.

She ducked down and looked inside, then shoved one hand into the cavity. She removed a similar helmet, though slightly smaller. It, too, was fitted with a teardrop of onyx in the forehead.

"Put it on," he said.

She frowned, doubting what good that would do. "It's lighter than I thought it would be," she said, donning the protective gear. Once the helmet was in place, she looked to him. Despite the piece being incredibly lightweight for gold, it was still awkward to wear.

The matching helmets were designed with a cone shape at the top. They fit over the ears and the back of the head, halfway down the neck. Brock thought it odd that there were no ear holes, but he didn't have time to concern himself with the design of the helmets.

"Now what?"

"Come on," he said. "Let's see how this thing works."

He started toward the hole they'd blown in the door, but she stopped him. "No, wait. You heard the guys. Reinforcements are on their way, and you know what that means. The commandos have been called in. I can't take them all, even with your help."

He smirked at her and shook his head. "I don't expect you to. Like I said, it's time to see how this thing works."

He trotted toward the door, leaving his gear bag on the floor at her feet. She shook her head and picked up both bags, slinging them over her shoulders in a crisscross manner that created an X on her chest with the straps.

The two made their way past the charred bodies of the snakes and the dead cop, to the base of the stairs leading up to the second chamber. They saw Tre standing at the top with his back to them, gun pointed toward the exit.

He heard the commotion below and turned his head in time to see Brock and Heather, wearing golden helmets, rapidly climbing the steps.

Tre gave a nod, glad to see his employers were still alive and okay. He noted the trident in Brock's hand with a skeptical frown.

"Is that what you came for?"

Brock nodded. "It is. Come on, we have to move."

He headed for the door, but a firm hand clapped him on the shoulder. "They're coming, sir. There's no way out."

"We'll see about that."

Brock shrugged off his henchman's grip and charged forward toward the door. He passed through the first portal and entered the primary chamber where the staircase to the first vault was located.

Heather and Tre rushed after him. They skidded to a stop at the entrance to the chamber. Brock slowed to a stroll and looked around the corner. He didn't see anything, nor did he hear anything.

He shuffled out into the corridor and began walking toward the courtyard.

"What are you doing?" Tre protested, but it was too late. Brock was striding toward the opening at a quick pace.

Tre shook his head and rushed out to keep up. Heather was right behind him, taking a sidelong glance over her shoulder at the passageway in the other direction. No sign of trouble yet, but she knew that was about to change. No doubt, the commandos were sweeping the complex, spreading out to cover the entire area and then close into the center, tightening the noose until there was nowhere for the intruders to go.

Up ahead, Brock reached the T-junction in the passageway. To the left was the way out. To the right led deeper into the temple, probably to some prayer rooms and dorms. Those were just guesses, and it didn't really matter unless there was another way out in that direction.

Brock looked both ways and then moved left into the courtyard. High walls surrounded the grassy area, which was now littered with dead bodies.

Heather paid no mind to the corpses on the stone floor of the corridor as she crossed the tunnel and entered the courtyard. Tre was at her side and breathing heavily. He looked around as he and Heather put their backs to Brock and held their weapons out, arms fully extended.

Brock stood still, gripping the trident in both hands, a grim, resolute look on his face.

The courtyard was surrounded by high walls. Tree branches hung over the top in a few places, dangling dark green leaves into the courtyard. At the moment, all was still, seemingly in the entire facility. No breeze rustled the tree branches. No sounds of trouble echoed throughout the corridors.

It was an eerie peace, a calm before the storm. Brock knew as much, though he doubted his companions felt as much comfort as he. Brock held their escape in his hands. He didn't expect them to understand. They hadn't done the studying he'd done, spent time learning about the all-powerful trident of Shiva. In his fingers' grasp, he clutched a weapon of the gods. No number of guns could save his enemies from that.

The peace was broken in seconds.

He and his comrades heard the shouting first. It was followed closely by footsteps, boots clapping on the tiles of the passageways as soldiers charged through the building, drawing ever closer to the intruders' position.

"We can't take all of them, sir," Tre said. "We're going to have to surrender."

"No," Brock said. "When they get here, they will encircle us, yes?"

"I would."

"Good. Let them surround us, and then lay down your weapons when they tell you to."

Tre looked over his shoulder at the man to his back. Brock was still staring straight ahead. The moon peeked out from behind black clouds that beset the night sky, casting a shimmering golden glow from his bizarre helmet.

"I thought you just said we're not going to surrender."

"We're not. I'm simply telling you to let them think we are."

Tre turned back to face the oncoming enemies. "I hope you have a plan, boss," he muttered under his breath.

18

THIRUVANANTHAPURAM

Brock shifted his feet so he could face the courtyard entrance to the temple. He watched as the silhouettes of the commandos hurried down the corridors. One of them was shouting and pointing in Brock's direction. With the golden helmets he and Heather had donned, there was no way their triumvirate would go unnoticed.

Within seconds, armed commandos and the remainder of the police guard poured into the courtyard. Like ants flooding out of a mound, the soldiers surrounded the three intruders in mere seconds, each one holding a submachine gun or sidearm with sights firmly aimed at the thieves.

One of the men, apparently the guy in charge of the guard, stepped forward. He wore a crimson beret and held his weapon tight against his shoulder as he stopped a few feet in front of a line of his men. There were easily fifty guns trained on Brock and his partners, yet the blond man seemed unfazed.

"Put your weapons down and get on the ground!" the commando leader shouted, never letting his gun waver. It didn't even bob an inch as he stepped forward. His clean-shaven face was tight, clenched in a stern glare.

"Do as he says," Brock ordered in an even tone.

Heather did as instructed, lowering her weapon to the ground as she knelt, albeit reluctantly. She never took her eyes off the nearest gunman, glaring at him as if she could see through him to the back of his skull. She didn't have to look long to tell the man wasn't unnerved. The cops, sure, they might have been a tad thrown off by her intense gaze. These commandos, though, were a different breed. They were some of the elite in the Indian military, men who'd been through extensive training to endure things most others could not. Thinking she could get under their skin or perhaps make one of them shake a little was foolhardy. Not only that, it wouldn't do any good unless there was a longer play in Brock's mind that she didn't know about.

Unlikely.

In fact, Heather had no idea what he was playing at and what he thought was going to happen. She'd seen him in tough spots before, putting faith in things that she didn't understand. Most of the time, it didn't work out as he had hoped. Then again, those occurrences didn't involve fifty guns pointed at them. It wasn't her first time staring down the barrel of a gun. The early occasions were terrifying in more ways than one. Now, however, it was old hat to her. She'd become so accustomed to it that if a witness didn't know any better they'd say she was the one with a gun and the others were the targets.

Tre hesitated a little longer than the commando leader would have liked when it came to putting his weapon on the ground.

"I said drop it!" the officer shouted once more. His accent didn't have the British feel to it that they'd encountered so often, instead giving off the rounded sound of vowels and stunted Ts more characteristic of certain areas in India.

Tre's jaw clenched. The muscles popped out behind his cheeks as he pressed his teeth together.

"Do as the man says," Brock reminded him.

"I'm not going down without a fight."

"You're not going down. Just do it," Brock commanded him with a hiss.

"Fine."

Tre bent slowly at the waist and placed the weapon on the ground, then slowly lowered himself to the ground with his hands gradually moving toward the sky.

"I hope you know what you're doing," he added.

Brock stared through the officer as if he wasn't even there. His eyes blazed with the fury of a thousand suns. If Heather's gaze did nothing to the other soldiers in the group, Brock's at least made their leader confused.

"Put down the—"

"Trishula?" Brock interrupted. He kept his voice level, almost dark, but with a thick layer of arrogance aimed at the man's knowledge, or lack thereof. "You mean this?" Brock gave the slightest of nods toward the ancient weapon.

"Yes. Put that down and get on the ground, place your hands on your head!"

"You don't have any idea what this is, do you?" Brock asked.

The officer looked unsure of how to respond to the question. "I don't care what it is. Put it on the ground, or I will have no other choice but to shoot."

Heather twisted her head slightly so she could see Brock. Her own hands rested on top of the golden helmet she wore.

"I understand," Brock said. "Apparently, you don't know your history. Not to mention you must not be a very religious person. You see, this is the trident of Shiva, the great destructor."

"I know who Shiva is, you idiot. Put the...trident down and get on your knees!"

"Very well," Brock said.

He moved deliberately, lowering himself toward the ground with knees bent. He put some of his weight on the golden shaft to keep from falling over. Brock had put his faith in things before, even stuff of a religious nature. It hadn't worked out most of the time. Now, however, something was different. He couldn't put his finger on it. Actually, he could. His thumb rested on the button in the middle of the shaft. It wasn't just the button that gave him cause to believe in the power of this mystical weapon. It was as if some ancient voice was speaking to him from within, telling him that he would be fine, that he was in no danger.

His knees touched the ground, and he bowed his head.

"Now put that thing on the ground. Do it!"

Brock lifted his eyes and met the gaze of the officer. "It didn't have to be this way," he said in a matter-of-fact voice. "I would have let you and your men live. You could have walked away and gone home to your friends and families without ever facing death."

The confusion in the commando's eyes was palpable. One of the men took a wary step back, albeit outside the view of his leader.

Brock was lying, of course. He had no intention of letting any of these men live. His plan entailed the destruction of most of this filth-ridden country, along with many others in Asia. They would all pay for what they'd done to the planet. Then, perhaps when the dust settled, the world could renew itself once more and become the beautiful place it once was.

"I'm going to count to three, and if you don't put that thing down, I am going to shoot you."

Brock heard the threat. The man's voice sounded distant, almost as if it wasn't really there—a figment of his imagination.

"I warned you." Brock began to tip the trident forward. His thumb depressed the button on the shaft.

For a second, nothing happened. A surge of fear coursed through him, starting at his gut and resonating throughout his body. Then something else pulsed through him. It felt like his entire body had been flicked by a huge finger. An electric shock of some kind? No, he'd felt that before when, as a child, he'd accidentally touched a running spark plug. This had a warmth to it, like a concussion of heat that zipped through the air in a flat wave.

The commandos jolted back as if they were struck by the same bizarre force. Then the officer's head began to tremble as if being shaken by some invisible hand. Then it twitched from left to right, eyes wide with fear.

"Who said that?" He swiveled around, keeping the gun level, now sweeping it across the faces of his men. "Who said that!?"

To a man, every one of the commandos was acting the same way. They were spinning around in circles, searching for something. Some of them spoke. Others kept their lips sealed, but the unspoken words showed in their eyes, revealing their terror.

"Stop!" one of the men shouted. He squeezed the trigger on his weapon. The report cracked through the air. The bullet tore through the officer's neck and exploded out the back.

The man hit the ground with his knees. As blood spurted from his neck, he squeezed his trigger and poured hot metal rounds into the mass of his followers.

Chaos followed as the armed men turned on each other, each firing their weapons, turning the once-quiet courtyard into a firestorm of death. The cacophony was deafening, though the helmets worn by Heather and Brock seemed to dampen the sounds.

Tre, however, was forced to cover his ears. He winced in agony, twisting his head around from left to right. He, too, seemed to be experiencing the same symptoms as the gunmen.

Then, as suddenly as it had begun, the gunfight stopped. A haze of bitter gunpowder smoke lingered in the air, a pall over the grisly scene. A few of the commandos writhed on the ground as they pulled in their dying gasps. Most of them were motionless, the life already drawn from their bodies, never to return.

Tre screamed. "Who's there? What do you want?" He stood up straight again, his eyes fixed on the nearest dead guard, gun still in hand. Tre made a move toward it, but Heather saw and immediately understood.

He wasn't wearing a helmet. The Trishula hadn't had an effect on her or Brock, likely due to their helmets.

She got to her feet and stepped in Tre's way, smacking him on the side of the head with her elbow and dropping him with one blow.

The man fell in an unconscious heap to the ground at her feet.

Brock stood and surveyed the scene of death all around him. He glanced down at Tre, regarding him with a kind of sympathy.

"I suppose we should have found him a helmet," Brock said.

Heather breathed heavily for a second and then calmed down. She looked at the bodies of the guards and the commandos who'd come to aide them. Then she turned to Brock. "What did you do?"

Brock's eyes flitted to the trident still held in his hand. A wicked smile spread across his face. "I don't know, but we need to move. I have a feeling things are going to get very dangerous around here in a very short time."

19

BHANGARH

"Are those assault rifles?" Priya's question startled the three occupants inside the tent.

The three had heard her approaching. Dr. Chaudhry clearly hadn't tried to be quiet. Her boots had clomped on the boards outside like a small horse clip-clopping its way down a street. She also had a set of keys that dangled from her belt—a handy way to keep from losing them at a dig site but not a great method for stealth.

Sean turned and saw the woman standing in the doorway. She was wearing a tan button-up shirt, matching khaki shorts, and scuffed leather hiking boots. Her black hair was pulled back into a ponytail. She looked like she was ready to go on a safari. The only thing she needed was the hat and the Serengeti.

Adriana was busily checking her handgun at the little table along the far wall of the tent. Tommy was rummaging through one of the gear bags, checking his supplies.

"No," Sean answered her question.

"Because that's what they look like. Why on earth would you need those?"

Sean bit his lower lip. "Okay, first of all, they're not assault rifles.

Rifles, yes. Although with shorter barrels and uppers, they'd qualify as pistols." He noted the confusion in her eyes. "It's...complicated."

"They don't look like pistols; they look like assault rifles."

"Here we go," Tommy sighed.

Sean shook his head. "These are built on AR-15 platforms. The AR in that title stands for Armalite, not what you're suggesting. That was the company that developed the prototype. Now anything built on that platform is given the AR name. It's like an homage." He rolled one hand with a flourish to emphasize his point. It didn't impress her.

Priya tilted her head to the side and crossed her arms as if his answer didn't somehow make it better.

"Part B of that is those are not automatic weapons. They're tactical tools for a specific job."

"And what job is that? Starting a small war?"

Sean chuckled. "No." He paused for a second. "But you never know. Someone might start a small war with us."

She still appeared unimpressed. "You do realize we can't just go walking around India with you three carrying those things strapped to your shoulders, right?"

"Of course," Sean said. "Wouldn't dream of it. We'll keep these in this crate while we're here. Hopefully, this is the last time you see them."

She assessed his response and the innocent expression on his face. He shrugged as if she was the one who was crazy.

"So, why do you have them? And what's with those...things?" She pointed at the canisters at the end of the weapons case.

"Call it a safety net, first of all. And those are sound suppressors. Some people call them silencers. I don't really care what they're called. All I know is; they help save your hearing."

Priya let out an exasperated sigh. "Fine. Just don't go shooting up the country. I've seen your exploits." She pointed at Tommy as well. "I know that you two can get a little cowboy with things now and then."

"Hey," Tommy protested.

Sean snorted. "We only do that when the need arises. Let's hope it doesn't."

"Agreed."

Adriana had remained silent in the back of the tent as she finished checking her sidearm and then slid it into a holster.

"I've never seen archaeologists equipped like you three."

Tommy's shoulders lifted and then dropped back to where they'd been. "We're multitaskers."

Priya rolled her eyes. "Did you find anything useful last night while searching through the code?"

"We did," Adriana answered before Sean and Tommy could. "But we aren't sure what to do with it just yet."

"What's that supposed to mean?" Priya put out both hands, begging for answers.

"It means we need your help." Adriana stood and motioned to a series of papers spread out on the little table.

The response perked Priya's interest and she seemed to forget the previous discussion. "Oh."

She strutted across the floor to the table and looked down at it, placing both palms on the surface. She scanned the first sheet, then the second, and so on until she'd read all the translations the three had come up with the night before. When she was done, she stood up, a look of concern spreading across her face.

"Has anyone else seen this?" Priya asked.

"No," Adriana said.

The two men shook their heads. They loitered a few feet away, close enough to see the writing on the papers but not close enough that they were in the women's personal space.

A breeze flowed over the campsite and shook the tent fabric.

"Okay, good."

Adriana pinched her eyebrows together. Her lips pursed for a second. "Why?"

Priya walked back over to the tent door and looked out, sticking her head through the opening for a second to check both directions before pulling it back in and letting the flaps fall shut.

She returned to the group and lowered her voice. "I'm not sure, but I think someone in our group is still looking for whatever Dr. Patel was working on."

"The Gada," Sean said.

"So it would seem." She shook her head and placed a thumb and three fingers against her forehead, rubbing it in dismay for a moment. She looked stressed. "Before, I would have said that's a fool's errand, chasing after a mythical object like that."

"You don't believe in the legends?" Tommy asked. It was his turn to cross his arms and ask a question.

She shrugged. "I could take or leave the religious stuff. Some of it makes sense. Some of it doesn't. Scientifically speaking, though, I don't believe there is some almighty weapon that can save or destroy the entire planet. Is there a golden mace somewhere out there, buried in a cave or in the sea? Maybe. I seriously doubt it has any magical properties."

"A mountain," Sean corrected.

"What?" She sounded dismayed.

He motioned to the papers on the table. "According to Patel's notes, it will be found inside a mountain somewhere."

She nodded absently. "Fine. A mountain. Which one?"

"We'll get to that later. From the looks of his notes, we have to proceed through the order of things, the first of which is investigating the site he drew on that page." Sean pointed at the paper with the schematics on it. He returned his gaze to Priya. "Any idea where that is?"

She came back to the table and leaned over it once more, reading the passage from Patel's notes and then analyzing the drawing.

"Not offhand. But I know someone who might."

"I thought you didn't want to let anyone else know about this," Tommy said. Condescension rippled from the back of his words like the wake behind a boat.

"I don't. This person, however, I know I can trust. He'll know what that place is, I'm sure of it. I just hope he's not busy yet."

"Busy? It's not even eight o'clock in the morning," Adriana pointed out the time of day.

"We start early around here," Priya answered. "This man is very knowledgeable about local and regional lore. If the place on that map is real and the stories Patel mentioned of ghosts and curses is also something shared by real people, he'll know about it."

"Fine," Sean said. He only needed a few seconds of thought before agreeing. "Take us to this guy, whoever he is."

They trudged through the camp, using the boarded path that wound through the tents, fire pits, and outcroppings of rocks. They passed through the gate in the backside of the camp and into a narrow passage surrounded on both sides by stone walls that came up to their armpits.

Sean peered to one side and then the other as he walked along behind Priya. Normally, he wouldn't have been so uneasy at a dig site, but this was no normal occasion. Someone was after Dr. Patel and his information. Dr. Chaudhry's earlier paranoia that someone was possibly listening outside the tent only heightened his suspicions. If she was worried, then there was likely something to it.

The path opened up again, this time to a series of white tarps spread out over a broad swath. Wooden steps had been erected to allow workers to descend into the pits, where dozens of them were already busily working. Some were delicately scraping the sides of squared-off areas that resembled miniature quarries. Others were digging away with shovels and picks to loosen untouched earth. Several more were shaking sifters that sent a generous cloud of dust into the air while they kept the larger pieces of debris inside the screens.

"Over there," Priya said, pointing at a man with a long, thick beard that was streaked with white and gray; the quantity of which far outnumbered the black hairs the beard had once boasted.

She led the way over to where he was hunched over a table that looked like it had been thrown together with scraps from a landfill. It had a surface of plywood and two huge spools underneath it that had once carried cables or wires. The table didn't stand high, so the man looming over it looked to be in an uncomfortable position as he assessed a piece of pottery with a magnifying glass.

"Speck," she said as they approached.

Tommy and Sean exchanged a glance.

"Speck?" Tommy mouthed.

Sean responded with a shrug.

"Ah, hello, my dear," the man said as he straightened. He placed two hands on his lower back as if the strain of leaning over the table had caused a kink in the muscles. After a moment of rubbing them, he flashed a wide smile.

"Speck, these are my colleagues from the United States. They're here investigating the disappearance of Dr. Patel."

The grin on the man's face disappeared for a moment. "Any luck so far?"

Sean shook his head. "No, sir."

Speck cocked his head to the side in dismay then shook it. "That's a shame. I hope you find him soon. Good man, Ishaan. I enjoy working with him."

"Priya said that maybe you could help us with something, a clue that might lead us to Patel."

"Clue?"

Tommy nodded and spread the papers out onto the surface of the table where there were no shards of clay or other items cluttering it. He pointed at the first sheet and scooped the others back underneath it. "This," he said, "we need to know where this is. Do you recognize this site?"

Speck cast a wary glance at Priya, who gave a reassuring nod. He puckered his bottom lip and stepped to the side to get a better view of the drawing.

He craned his neck and then twisted the paper around. It took less than ten seconds for him to come up with an answer. "Sure. I know this place."

"You do?" Adriana asked. "Where is it?"

Speck raised his left hand and scratched his thick hair under the straw hat. "Well, that there is Kuldhara." His sharp Indian accent came through with an almost Southern twang, making his voice sound like a contradiction in terms. He rubbed his darkly tanned cheeks, still contemplating what this could mean, or at least that's what it looked like to the visitors.

"Kuldhara?" Sean asked. "What is it?"

Speck exhaled through his nose and bobbed his head to the side to prepare his explanation. "Well, it's an abandoned village. Nothing left there but ruins, mostly. There are a few towns within a short drive of there. Other than that, it's pretty much desert."

The three visitors thought about it for a moment.

Priya, too, considered his response. "Why would Dr. Patel place a drawing of Kuldhara in his notes?" she wondered out loud.

Speck didn't immediately answer. His eyes went from one person to the next as if waiting for them to come up with it. When he saw they weren't going to say anything, he took a deep breath. "The reason Kuldhara is famous is because of the hauntings."

"Hauntings?" Adriana asked, a frown crinkling her forehead.

"Sure. Lots of rumors about hauntings in this country. They say this fort is haunted, too, though I've never seen any signs of ghosts or spirits with ill intent."

That was a funny way of saying it, Sean thought.

"So, what makes people say Kuldhara is haunted?" Tommy asked. "I can see how this place would be spooky to some. What's so special about that location?" He looked around at their surroundings. The old fort stood above them, just over the next rise overlooking the dig site.

The older man had a twinkle in his eye, as though he was about to tell his favorite story.

"Kuldhara is a strange place," he said. "There have been several reported disappearances through the years, going back centuries. One place, in particular, claims the most fame in regard to the haunted tales."

"Yeah?" Sean asked. He tried to hide his skepticism, but he didn't know if it worked. He didn't believe in ghosts. He was a spiritual person, believed in a supreme being that built the universe. He could buy into any number of afterlife theories. Believing in ghosts, however, wasn't one of them. "What's this place?"

Speck stroked his beard and looked up to the ceiling of the tent as if drawn away by some distant thought from a time long since ago. "The well of Vishnu."

The others looked around at each other with confused eyes. Only Priya stood fast, staring at the man, waiting for him to go on.

"The well is claimed to be haunted by a spirit from many years ago, a dead Paliwal priestess who sacrificed herself to prevent the destruction of the village. It is believed that after an earthquake in the early 1800s, the people abandoned the area. The wells had run dry. Oppressive heat and a lack of rain made it impossible to grow food. So, the people left. When they did, however, the legend states that a Paliwal priest put a curse on the place, claiming that anyone who tried to settle there again would see the ghost of the priestess and she would haunt them for all time."

Speck let the story sink in and watched the reaction of his audience.

No one said a thing for a minute. Priya kept her expression stoic, but there was something in her eyes that told Sean she didn't buy a single word of what the man had just said, except maybe about the location of the map.

"Of course," Speck said abruptly, "those legends are propagated by the locals who seek to capitalize on tourists who are interested in such things. They even hosted a group of paranormal believers at one point. Those ghost hunters spent the night there in the village, claiming they saw several variations of dead spirits ranging from silhouettes in the night to glowing apparitions." His voice cut through the relative silence and the timid sounds of scraping, digging, and sifting from other parts of the dig.

"So, it's all just a gag to get people to visit," Tommy said flatly.

Speck shrugged and nodded. "It certainly sounds that way. I spent a summer there several years back, doing research on the culture, the people, their rituals, and the religion that dominated the region."

"What religion was that?" Adriana asked.

Speck grinned. "They worshipped Vishnu, of course."

The visitors each exchanged a knowing glance. If Kuldhara was the place Patel had drawn in his journal and the people who lived there were loyal followers of Vishnu, it certainly seemed the pieces were coming together. Throwing on a little mysterious lore about hauntings only made the possibility that much more tantalizing.

"So, guys," Tommy said, glancing from one face to the other, "feel like taking a little road trip?"

Speck let out a bellowing laugh. "It's more than a little road trip, my friend. Kuldhara is on the other side of the country."

20

LOS ANGELES

Brock stepped to the sliding glass door and entered the four-digit PIN on the keypad next to it. A moment later, the door slid open and a light gust of air blew over his face and hair. The artificial breeze smelled of tire rubber and metal with a hint of gasoline and other chemicals.

He walked through the door and into his basement garage. It lacked the dozens of high-end luxury cars that most wealthy people stockpiled. He'd seen them for himself, walking through the well-lit private showrooms where celebrities parked vehicles they likely never drove.

He never understood that, for the most part. They usually took limousines.

Brock glanced to his left and admired the two cars in his garage. One was a Tesla Model S. He loved driving that car, though it could only go so far. For his longer trips, he preferred the guiltier pleasure parked next to it. The silver Rezvani Beast was a work of mechanical and automotive art. The swooping, curved lines of the body wrapped around wide tires and a two-seat cockpit. The thing looked like it was ready to take off and soar into the far reaches of space.

He took his eyes away from the cars and focused on the reason he'd come down to his laboratory. That's what it was, in truth. Only a small portion of the basement was dedicated to the two vehicles. The rest of it was a high-tech marvel of science. Originally, he'd had it designed with the purpose of coming up with new fuels to work in existing combustion engines for cars. He'd hired two researchers who worked on site, five days a week, on the project.

They'd done thousands of hours of work, pilfering some of the research done by large corporations and grant-funded organizations. In the end, the answer had been right in front of them all along, and it wasn't anything they could patent or sell to the public. Ethanol was already being pushed by some, blackballed by others. Some touted hydrogen as the solution. Those were the two best answers Brock's team could come up with.

He'd been about to let them go, send them back to their lives to work for other companies. Then he discovered the legend of the Trishula. Brock had no idea how the thing worked or if it even existed.

Now, he had it in his possession, right here in his own home.

The only problem was, no one seemed to be able to understand how to recharge it.

He'd activated the weapon two nights before. The result had been incredible. Not only did every commando and cop surrounding him and his team end up killing each other off in a bizarre kind of paranoia-filled rage, people all around the city had reacted the same way. Media outlets across the globe had covered the shocking event, claiming that citizens within a two-mile radius of the temple had gone crazy and started to kill one another.

Brock and Heather witnessed the chaos as they lumbered back to their vehicle, dragging Tre as they escaped the temple grounds. The unconscious man had been dead weight and difficult to move. Getting him to and in the car was a total team effort that would have proved impossible for Heather or Brock had either tried it on their own.

Heather had to sprint back to their safe house to retrieve the truck while Brock stayed next to their bodyguard just inside the temple gate. The entire process seemed almost too much effort. More than once, Brock questioned whether it was worth saving the man or simply leaving him there to be ravaged by the citizens. Of course, he could have been merciful and put a bullet through the man's head, but that would have been a waste as well. Tre had proved a loyal employee so far, and useful. Brock could always hire more people; in fact, he needed to since one had just been killed. He already had a few in reserve back in Los Angeles watching his home.

Standing in his basement, Brock realized how close they'd come to being captured by the hallucinating mobs back in India. His security guy was recovering with nothing more than a bruise and a bump on his head. He sat atop a stool in the corner of the lab, watching the two scientists as they disconnected wires from Tre's skull and placed them on a silver table with caster wheels.

"Oh, Mr. Carson, just in time." One of the researchers, a guy named Adam Simpson, greeted him with a smile. The man was probably in his late twenties, early thirties at most. He had wavy red hair that flopped to one side of his head and shook as he spoke. Thick, black-framed glasses rested on his nose. He wore a lab coat but underneath donned jeans and a Green Lantern T-shirt.

The other scientist, a young woman by the name of Elma Donner, stood just behind his left shoulder, analyzing numbers on a computer screen. Her long, straight black hair hung down past her shoulder blades. She glanced back at her employer, offered a welcoming smile, and then returned to her work.

"How you feeling, Tre?" Brock asked.

"Better, sir," Tre answered. "Although I'd be a lot better if these two weren't making me their own personal guinea pig." He tilted his head to the left then right to get a good crack out of his neck. Then he swung his legs over the examination table and sat up straight.

"So," Brock turned his attention to Adam, "you sounded excited over the phone. What do you have for me?"

"It is exciting, sir." Adam sidled up to a metal stool next to a high-top table and sat down, folding his hands on top of one leg. "When you first told us about the symptoms the temple guards experienced, along with the symptoms the people in the city around the temple went through, we wondered if this thing had some kind of psychoactive effect on humans."

"Psychoactive?"

"It made them hallucinate," Elma said without looking away from her monitor.

"Right," Adam confirmed with a point of one finger.

Brock tried to understand. "So, when I pressed that button, the trident caused everyone around us to hallucinate?"

Adam nodded. "It's a little more complex than that, but yes. What actually happened is quite fascinating. I've never seen or heard of any technology like this in the world, and I've had access to some pretty awesome stuff before." His voice quickened as he grew more excited.

He stood up and walked over to where the Trishula was wedged into a stand designed to hold up Christmas trees. Several wires were connected to the golden surface, running to various machines.

"This thing is a kind of superconductor," he said, patting it on the side of the shaft.

"Superconductor?"

"Yeah, although there are some subtle differences between it and typical superconductors. The biggest is that this one doesn't send out a magnetic radiation field."

"That's a good thing. Right?"

"Yeah, for sure." Adam grinned at the question. "What it apparently does is fire off a surge of energy that disrupts the hippocampus within the human brain."

Brock arched one eyebrow. The lingo was starting to get a little thick. "I guess that's a bad thing?"

Adam chuckled. "It certainly could be. Based on the news reports of what's going on in India, I'd say yes. Although this is a fascinating discovery. Do you realize what you've uncovered?"

Brock knew he'd found a weapon of incredible power. That much was easy enough to answer. The rest of it, the technical speak and science talk, were a little fuzzy.

"So, you're telling me that this thing can cause people to hallucinate, right?"

"Sure seems that way. Not only that, when they do, it appears that they turn extremely violent. They must have perceived a threat of some kind and started to panic."

"I can attest to that." Tre was standing next to the exam table with his arms crossed. "I experienced it firsthand."

Brock was fascinated. "What did you see or hear?"

Tre's head twitched to the side once. "I didn't see anything; that much I know for sure. The voices, though; those were the really creepy part of the whole deal."

"Voices?"

"Yeah, like ghosts in my head, coming from all directions. They were saying threatening things like they were going to hurt me or kill me, and there was only one way to stop them."

"So, that's why you turned a little crazy for a minute."

"I guess so. I don't really recall what I did. I just remember hearing those voices."

"You don't hear them now?"

Tre shook his head. "No."

"His hippocampus seems to be functioning properly now," Adam interjected. "It appears that the effects of the weapon are temporary, albeit extremely dangerous. I definitely want to study this thing more."

The report caused a wave of thoughts and questions to crank up inside Brock's head. The possibilities of a weapon like this were incredible. Shiva's trident was the perfect tool to dismantle society and bring the world to its knees. It wouldn't destroy anything or anyone. Instead, the Trishula would flip a switch in the minds of humans, and they would do the dirty deed of killing each other and ripping apart society. Effectively, this thing could turn anyone in the world into a raving, murderous lunatic. There would be no witnesses, no way to stop the destruction. The world would tear itself apart, and Brock could sit back and watch it all happen.

He thought of the letter that he'd received from a mysterious benefactor, a person who'd claimed they knew the location of a weapon that could change the shape of the world

That letter led him to the golden temple.

At first, he'd doubted the authenticity of the communication, but when he received a phone call on his personal device, that tossed all his concerns out the window. The voice had been disguised by some kind of modulator, but it had been clear about what he was to do.

The stranger knew everything about him, about his desires to help the planet, and about his disdain for those who'd bragged about doing so much but in reality had done so little.

A fleeting thought of his former hero, slumped over in a chair, popped into his head. He'd killed the man without hesitation. That crime, too, had been perfect. The media believed Richard Farrow had taken his own life, a product of too much pressure in the spotlight.

Now that Brock had the trident, he wondered when his next communications from the mysterious benefactor would be. He had a feeling they were keeping close tabs on his progress despite a total lack of updates on his part. He had no way to do such a thing since there was no address on the letter he'd received and no phone number on his screen when the person called.

No, Brock would have to wait for them to reach out first if they did at all. Part of him wondered if all they wanted was to set things in motion and sit back to watch it all burn.

He shrugged off the thoughts, realizing Adam was still staring at him.

"So," Brock said, cutting the silence, "I guess that brings me to the most important question."

Adam nodded, though he wasn't entirely sure which question his boss was talking about.

"Can you make it work again?"

21

KULDHARA

S ean wiped the sweat from his forehead with a white towel from his tactical bag and then shoved it into his back right pocket.

Tommy used the sleeve on his shirt to do the same, removing perspiration from his face and head for the second time in five minutes.

The sun blazed in the cloudless sky above. Heat waves rippled in the distance, a mirage that hung constantly over the desert sand.

"At least it's a dry heat," he joked.

"I miss the humidity," Sean said, deadpan.

"You're the only person on the planet who has ever uttered those words."

The men trudged through the rubble scattered between the tattered remains of the abandoned village. The two of them, along with Adriana, carried their weapons in holsters on their right hips. The larger guns had been left in the SUV; they'd opted to keep them out of sight as opposed to drawing unwanted attention from any tourists hanging around. Subtlety was always preferable.

Priya had wondered why they were even carrying the AR-15s in the first place.

Sean explained again that their primary purpose in this particular mission involved investigation and security. He cited many private security firms who used these weapons on a daily basis, though he left out the dangerous locations where that was the case. Maybe he was being a little irrational. Truth was; he didn't want to have to use the weapons. Old demons were always around the corner in his mind, lurking in the shadows, begging to be loosed.

Kuldhara was a desolate place, barren and unwelcoming. Upon first glance, Sean understood why people no longer lived there. The searing heat seemed to suck the moisture from his body like a droplet of rain to the cracked, dry earth. He'd been in hot places before, some worse than this, but he never complained. It was part of the job, in fact, all the jobs he'd had in the last several years. You never got used to bad weather or inhospitable climates, but whining about it didn't make it any better, so he kept his mouth shut and tried to focus on the task at hand.

The two women were a few steps ahead of them, leading the way through the maze-like village.

Most of the mud-brick walls were about five feet high; some were lower, only coming up to the three-foot mark. Tommy held a copy of the ruins' blueprint in one hand, glancing down at it now and then to make sure they were going the right way. The truth was he was just as lost as the rest of them, save for Adriana, who always had a keen sense of direction.

Sean recalled getting lost in Lucerne, Switzerland once when he was there on vacation. He and several friends were visiting from the United States one summer, and he was separated from the group. He would have thought that with all the mountains, the fortress high up on the slopes, the river, and the unique architecture, that finding his way around that city wouldn't have been a problem. Yet there Sean was, late one night, wandering around for an hour until he found his hotel, where everyone was laughing as he approached.

That experience was one of the reasons he was more than happy to let the women lead the way, though he was a little surprised Priya wasn't familiar with the layout. Then again, it was a large country, and she'd been responsible for research in many regions. The odds were she'd missed a few.

Adriana led the way straight down an old passage that was littered with broken bricks and stray clumps of mortar. It all looked the same save for a few distinct differences with the layout of the dwellings. Most of them were nothing more than square structures pressed against each other to form what had to be tight living quarters.

Sean imagined what the village must have looked like when it was occupied at the height of civilization when children ran through the narrow streets and alleys, and the smells of turmeric, garlic, and chicken wafted above. It always struck him as odd that in most places like this, where time and Mother Nature had beaten the land, the roofs were usually nowhere to be seen. He'd thought about it before and was considering it again as they rounded a corner and proceeded down another channel of the maze. Finding a roof in the ruins of anything older than a few hundred years was usually rare, probably because timber rotted far faster than brick and mortar or stone. The materials were the kind that needed to be replaced semi-frequently.

He'd tried to be a good son through the years, helping his parents out financially when they needed it. They were both hard-working people, despite the fact they were retired and had been for nearly a decade. His mother, especially, struggled with relaxing and taking it easy. Those phrases weren't in her vocabulary.

If she wasn't working, she was busy with one of her many hobbies —which were actually miniature jobs in their own right. His father wasn't as intense but still found himself taking on various jobs in his workshop, building furniture and cabinetry. Sean was fairly certain he'd spotted a new arc welder in his dad's workshop the last time he'd visited. If his dad wanted to learn how to weld, that was up to him. As long as they were happy, Sean didn't care.

He snapped his mind back to the moment and surveyed the land over the tops of the ruins surrounding them. He chuckled to himself. All those distracting thoughts, springing forth from an observation about roofs.

Tommy touched Sean on the shoulder and gave him a tug with one finger. It was his way of silently telling his friend to slow down for a second. Sean turned to him with a questioning expression on his face, eyebrows stitched together and a stern grip to his lips.

"Hold back," Tommy said, watching as the women walked farther ahead, spreading the gap between them.

"What's up, Schultzie?" Sean whispered.

"You really think we're going to find something here? This place has been combed over more than Watergate."

The question seemed to come out of left field. "Not sure, man. But we've been lots of places that were heavily searched where we still ended up finding something.

"And what's up with Lidia?" Tommy changed the subject. "She's kind of...I don't know, rude?"

Sean hadn't considered the woman much after their initial meeting when she'd picked up the group at the airport and subsequently dropped them off. He hadn't seen her since. One of the guards that had been accompanying her was now, apparently, assigned to this trip.

Sean flashed a mischievous grin. "I think you have a girlfriend." He winked as he said it.

Tommy rolled his eyes. "No, dork. Not like that. I mean, what's up with her? She sure didn't seem friendly. Almost like she doesn't want us here."

"I'm sure we were just an inconvenience to her. You've run sites like that before. It's a lot to coordinate. The logistics must be a bear to manage."

"They can be, but again you're missing my point," Tommy hissed.

"How is June anyway?" Sean dug one more nail into his friend's patience.

"She's fine. Would you stay on topic?"

Sean snorted.

The two women were busy talking as they made the next left in the maze, apparently unaware that the men had fallen behind.

"Sure. What is your point?"

"Do I have to spell it out for you?" Tommy glared at his friend.

Sean's answer was a blank stare signaling he didn't know where this was going.

Tommy sighed, exasperated. "Doesn't she seem suspicious to you?"

Sean's unknowing gaze turned skeptical. "Why, because she wasn't as cordial as you'd have liked? She's not a concierge or a valet, Schultzie. She's got a job to do, and the three of us interrupted it. I wouldn't be all cupcakes and rainbows, either."

"Maybe," Tommy relented. "Still, there's something up with her. I can feel it."

Sean's eyebrows lifted, enhancing his unspoken skepticism. "You keep holding on to that feeling, pal."

They turned the corner and almost walked into the women.

Adriana issued a chastising glare. "Why are you two walking so slow?"

"Sorry," Tommy said, clearing his throat. "Just...taking in the sights."

She wasn't buying the explanation, but Adriana decided not to press the issue.

"It should be just ahead," Priya said. "Whatever it is."

There was doubt in her voice, and she didn't try to cover it up. Priya hadn't said much on the journey here. She'd spent most of her time on a laptop or her phone. The three visitors figured she was working, and so they didn't bother her. They could only imagine how much was on her plate, on top of driving them out to the middle of nowhere to investigate something that may or may not have been there.

Sean had gently suggested that she stay at the dig site and let them handle it. He'd wanted to say, "leave it to the professionals," but that would have given off the wrong signals.

When she'd insisted on coming after his toned-down recommendation, he didn't fight it.

Still, he couldn't help but get the feeling she was trying to push some kind of guilt on them. That sort of thing bounced off Sean.

Straight ahead, the remnants of the corridor rose to a crumbling archway.

"That's it," Priya said, pointing at the entrance.

The four passed through it and found themselves in a considerable area. It was far larger than the rest of the homes in the village, at least by a factor of ten. The room stretched twenty yards from left to right and was about half as wide. One end pointed to the east, while the other ran to the west. There was a fire pit made from red and brown rocks in the center. It appeared to be the only thing untouched by the last few hundred years.

"What is this place?" Adriana asked. She turned her head 360 degrees, assessing the space.

"A temple," Priya answered in a flat tone. "This was the town's temple to Vishnu."

A pall of reverence settled over them for a moment, but it didn't last long. The oppressive heat brought them back to the task at hand.

"I hope you know what you're looking for," Priya said, crossing her arms. "Would be a shame to have come all the way out here for nothing."

Sean stepped over a broken column that had tipped over long ago. It lay across the floor from south to north, shattered in two places. He moved toward the western side of the structure, his eyes scanning the wall for a clue.

"That's part of it," Tommy said as he moved to the opposite wall and mimicked Sean's search. "Sometimes, we travel great distances and end up with nothing."

Adriana stayed close to Sean, moving silently alongside him like a shadow. She remained quiet on the subject, choosing instead to focus on what she could see and hear around her. Her senses had saved her more than once, and out here, exposed in the desert among these ancient ruins, she had a sickening feeling that they were being watched. She knew Sean felt it, too, though he was trying to play it off with his banter and by focusing on finding whatever it was Patel had alluded to in his journal.

Her eyes flitted to the wall and the half windows that still remained. These walls were taller than most of those in the village. Around the entire area, the structures had collapsed over time, leaving the homes little more than a third of their original height. The temple walls, however, had remained largely intact and were still above their heads. That made seeing an approaching threat a serious problem.

"I'm going to head back here," Adriana whispered, jerking a thumb toward the door.

Sean's eyes flicked to her, and he immediately understood from the expression on her face. He gave a nod.

Adriana left him and wandered back to the doorway, slipping through as Priya's eyes were focused on Tommy as he made his way to the northwestern corner of the structure.

"I doubt you're going to find anything here." Priya pushed her sunglasses up to the top of her nose.

Sean ignored her statement, hiding his own concerns behind the reflective finish of his Oakley Turbines.

"It would have been pilfered a hundred times over," she went on. "Archaeologists have been here. Thieves probably went through it before they got here. Anything of value is long gone."

"Yeah, you're probably right," Tommy said. "But we have to leave no stone unturned."

Adriana listened from the doorway to the temple, her eyes narrow against the glare of the sun. Her sunglasses weren't as dark as Sean's, though her eyes weren't as sensitive to bright light as his. She panned the horizon over the ruined walls, making sure no one was approaching with malicious intentions.

Within the temple, Sean turned back and made his way through the rubble toward the other side of the room. It didn't take him long before he noticed the anomaly on the northeastern wall, situated in the center of the crumbling brickwork.

"What's that?" he asked, motioning to a stone tablet.

The object stood only a few, perhaps three feet high. It was fixed into a slot in the floor with dirt and rocks gathered around its base.

The tablet was almost flush to the wall, only separated by a narrow gap of less than an inch.

He worked his way through more clumps of debris on the floor and then stopped at the tablet, bending down to get a closer look.

Tommy joined him near the object and gazed at it, crouching next to his friend. They scanned the words they didn't understand and then noted the engraving at the bottom. A circle about four inches in diameter was chiseled there. It appeared to be nearly perfect in circumference, a task not easily accomplished, especially with tools from the Old World.

Priya wandered over and stood behind them. "They're scriptures from the Vedas," she said in a matter-of-fact voice. "They speak of Lord Vishnu and his purpose."

"To maintain balance," Sean said.

"To maintain it, yes, but also to enforce it."

"Enforce?" Sean looked up at her over his shoulder.

"Yes. It was his duty to make certain that balance was interrupted by no one."

Tommy's eyes lingered on the circle at the bottom. "What about this?" he asked, motioning to the carving.

She shrugged. "Probably a symbol of the circle of life. Of course, it could be the sun. From what I see in the writing, it doesn't say anything about it."

Her answer didn't impress either of the Americans.

Sean set his bag down and craned his neck to the side, getting a good look at the flat edge of the tablet. The stone was around two to three inches thick. Then he scanned the ground until he found what he was searching for.

He bent down and picked up a rock about the size of his fist made from hard sandstone. He scuffled back over to the tablet and reared back.

"Wait!" Priya nearly shouted. "What are you doing?"

Tommy did nothing to try to stop his friend. He could see where Sean was going with his line of thought and realized that if there was anything to find here, it was exactly where Sean thought it would be.

Sean whipped his hand around as though to smash the tablet with it—then stopped an inch from the surface. He grinned at Priya with mischief in his eyes. He tapped on the tablet with the rock. A hollow sound escaped from within.

Her eyebrows lowered. "It's...hollow?"

Sean nodded and then as quickly as he'd done before, brought the rock back and then drove it forward again, bashing the tablet with the sharpest edge. The surface of the tablet, where the disc was carved, caved in. Sean grinned as he locked his focus on the newly created hole. Then, with greater care, he chipped away at the loose fragments still clinging to the rest of the tablet's surface.

It only took him half a minute to have a cavity in the shape of the circle that had been there before.

"Well," he said, "I guess the thieves didn't take everything."

He and the others stared into the recess at the glimmering object within. A golden disc with notches engraved at random intervals rested inside.

22

LOS ANGELES

"That's the problem," Adam confessed. His voice wavered, trembling like a child's after being caught doing something wrong in a classroom.

"What's the problem?" Brock pressed. "Replicating the process?"

"Actually, that's not the only problem," Elma interrupted. She'd been hovering over her computer in the corner since Brock arrived. She stood up and turned to face them. Her lips were red as blood. A thin veil of makeup on her face accented her sharp features. Her skin was pale, like that of someone who'd spent most of her time in a lab like this one, far away from the harmful rays of the sun.

She walked toward the two men with a bit of swagger to her stride. Her black skirt hung down just above the knees; the matching blouse under her lab coat was cut in a V just below the neck but revealed nothing that would distract any of the men from their work or the discussion. It wasn't to say she wasn't attractive. Brock thought she was beautiful and was fairly certain Adam would never complain about his partner's appearance.

"What is the problem, then?" Brock asked, keeping rhythm with the conversation.

"Replication requires the weapon have some kind of power source."

"So?" Brock rolled his shoulders. "It worked in India."

She moved closer to the trident and removed some of the wires that were taped to it. "That's because it had been charging there for hundreds, likely thousands, of years. If Shiva or whoever it belonged to put it there long ago, this thing has been building up a powerful charge all that time."

Brock didn't follow. "I don't understand. There wasn't anything there to charge it."

"And that brings me back to the superconductor idea," Adam cut in. "In the ancient world, they had an understanding of static electricity that we are only now beginning to understand."

"I don't think we've even scratched the surface," Elma added.

"True," Adam gave her a sideways nod. "Be that as it may, the people or whatever they were that built this understood that there are pools of electricity that exist all over the world."

"Pools?"

"Yes. You can't see them, but they are definitely there, especially in dry, arid places. One of the more well-known regions is Egypt's Nile River Valley and the Sinai Peninsula."

Brock stared at him, still waiting for the point.

Adam sensed his urgency. "Anyway, we figure that one of those pools must have existed in that temple and powered this trident. So, when you pushed the button, you released that wave of energy and sent the surrounding area into a raving-mad chaos."

"Let me get this straight so I make sure I'm understanding what you're telling me. The static pools aside, you have no way to make this thing power up?"

Adam's head slowly turned side to side. "Unfortunately, no, not yet. We're working on it, though. We just need a little time. That's all."

Brock chewed on his lower lip. It didn't do much to suppress his frustration. He calmed his anger by reminding himself that it wasn't their fault. This was an ancient piece of technology that hadn't been seen in centuries, probably longer. No one on the planet would understand how it worked; at least that's what he told himself.

He sensed his face flushing red and noticed the two scientists' expressions. Adam was unnerved, while Elma appeared to be concerned—but not for her own safety.

"How long?" Brock asked, doing his best to keep the tone smooth and non-threatening.

"Not sure yet. Could be a day, maybe two."

"If we're lucky," Elma said. "The truth is this isn't like some simple car battery you hook up to a charger and jump-start. There's nowhere to attach jumper cables. It needs a geostatic pool to charge. That's the only way."

"We're working on creating a synthetic version of that, but we need a few days to have it up and running."

"Get it done in twenty-four hours," Brock said. He didn't need to make a threat. It was implied. In truth, he wasn't going to kill his lab team. He needed them as much as they needed the money he provided.

Finding scientists was easy enough, but finding people who could do what these two could, who held the same radical beliefs as Brock? That was another matter. He'd vetted them, filtered through stacks of candidates before choosing them. No way was he going to throw that out the window now. There was no time to replace them anyway.

"That's going to be pushing it, Mr. Carson. I don't know if we can—"

"Get it done," Brock said. He leveled his gaze at Adam.

"Yes, sir."

Brock switched subjects. "Good. Now, tell me why Heather and I weren't affected by that pulse sent out by the trident. I assume it has something to do with the helmets. She and I were each wearing one, while Tre wasn't."

Adam's fervor returned, and he visibly eased. "Yes, so glad you asked. And you're correct. The reason you and Heather were unaffected by the pulse was due to the protective helmets."

He turned to a table where the two helmets sat propped on

makeshift metal pedestals. "They're lined with a thin layer of lead on the inside, which is what protected you from the energy that disrupted everyone else's brain-wave frequencies."

"Okay." Brock believed he was following what the man was saying. "Sort of like those aprons you put on when you go get an X-ray."

"Exactly. Except these aren't X-rays, but yes, the principle is the same."

"What's with the black crystal in the forehead?"

"We believe," Elma said, "whoever made these items understood that onyx is actually a good insulator for electricity. "So, if the lead inside the helmet didn't help protect the wearer, the onyx on the forehead would have."

"Interesting. Are they safe to touch?"

"Yes, although we wondered why the people who made them would build them out of gold."

"Why's that?" Brock turned to her after staring at the helmets.

"Because gold conducts electricity," Tre said from the other side of the room.

Brock glanced at him and noted his casual grin, arms crossed in a matter-of-fact pose.

"He's correct," Adam confirmed. "Gold and most metals in that range of elements is an excellent conductor of electricity."

"So, while we were wearing those things, power was rushing over our skulls?"

"We're still investigating that," Elma stated.

That was a good way of saying none of them had a clue. Saying "I don't know" wasn't an option with Brock Carson. He had more money than anyone they knew and was an influential person on a cultural level across many nations. You didn't say "I don't know" to a person like that unless you wanted to end up floating facedown in a river.

"As long as they're safe to wear and touch, I don't care." He turned his attention back to the trident. "The more important thing is figuring out how this recharges. I have plans for this that have waited far too long. The world is dying, people." He assumed the tone of a great orator sending a message to millions of followers, despite the fact there were only three people in his immediate audience. "It's up to us to save it."

He noted the resilience on their faces, the grim determination that he'd hoped to see. Elma had no living relatives and few friends. Adam was the same, an orphan who'd put himself through school, living in a car during several weeks of high school until a social worker found out and put him in a home. Tre? Brock didn't care what his social status was. The man was a killer and completely committed to the cause. His disregard for life human life was good enough.

"Come with me."

The lab workers and Tre exchanged questioning glances and then followed their boss out of the basement. They ascended the stairs into a lavish living room that overlooked the valley through massive wall-size windows. Each piece of glass curved outward and had to be custom made to fit perfectly. The windows gave a sort of wavy effect to the exterior.

Heather was sitting in a deep sofa when the group appeared at the top of the stairs and filed into the living room. She stood and clicked a button on a remote. The flat screen on the wall over the modern fireplace flicked to life, and a moment later a map of the world appeared on the display.

Brock walked to the kitchen counter just behind the sofa and tapped the trackpad on his laptop. He wiggled the arrow around to make sure it was connected to the television. Seeing it move on both screens, he nodded to the others. "Have a seat."

They weren't sure where this was going but didn't mind a break from their toiling.

"I'm going to show you the master plan," Brock said. He clicked on the city of Hong Kong and then zoomed in until they could see an overhead view of the sprawling metropolis. "Hong Kong, Singapore, Mumbai, New Delhi, Bangkok, and many other huge cities in Asia are the primary culprits of the pollution that's destroying our oceans. Of course, there are major cities in every country that are guilty of other kinds of pollution. Some are dumping toxic chemicals into the air. Others are ripping apart forests, like in South America. The planet is on the brink of shutting down. With the weapon you two are studying downstairs, imagine what we could do in a densely populated area."

He let the words hang in the air for a moment.

"Setting off that device, like you did in India...millions could die within a short period of time." Adam said the words with a hint of wonder in his voice where there should have been concern. What did he care? The world and its people had done nothing for him save the lone social worker who had once given him a place to stay.

"Precisely," Brock said. "Our plan is to hit every major metro area on the planet, one at a time. Billions will die at the hands of billions. They'll all kill each other, and no one will be able to pin the crime on us. It's perfect."

"The only problem being that we still need to figure out a way to charge it," Adam added.

"And that this will be a slow attack." Elma turned and faced him with her arm up on the back of the sofa. "You're seriously going to fly to all these places to use that thing?"

"If I have to," Brock said. "I'm going to hit the most egregious offenders first. The Asian nations are responsible for the Great Pacific Garbage Patch that is looming just off our coast." He pointed out one of the curved windows toward the ocean in the distance. "Cleanup efforts are underway, but that won't stop them. They'll just keep dumping their waste into the water and letting it float east until it reaches our shores. It's dangerously close to the outlying Hawaiian Islands as we speak."

His voice deepened as he looked around the room at each person. His stare was glazed with anger. "It's time we teach them all a lesson. We will not let them destroy our world and our nation. Soon, there is going to be a lot more real estate and far fewer people to contend with. With the trident of Shiva, we are going to rid the world of those who are slowly destroying our world and restore balance."

23

KULDHARA

"We have trouble."

Adriana twisted and looked sideways at the other three as they huddled around the tablet in a corner of the temple ruins.

Sean looked her way first, standing from his crouch. His knees cracked simultaneously.

"How many?" he asked.

Sean didn't need to ask what she meant by trouble. He knew. They were on the same wavelength, as was Tommy. Priya, on the other hand, was green when it came to combat-type situations. At least that's what Sean figured.

He hurried back to where Adriana stood with a pistol now in her hand.

"I don't know," she said quietly, "but I noticed at least two. Over there. They ducked down when I looked in their direction."

"Yep," Sean said. "I had a bad feeling about this. Things were starting to get too easy. I should have known better."

"How would you like to handle it?"

He let an annoyed sigh escape his nostrils. "Would help to know how many there are."

"Sean?" Tommy asked. "What's the plan?" His voice was little more than a snakelike hiss as he held the golden disc in his hand.

Priya looked concerned. "What is it?" She asked the question the others didn't need to.

"It looks like we're about to have company. Not friends of yours, I'm guessing."

"What are we going to do?" Priya's panic came through in her voice and confirmed Sean's suspicion. She was an academic, a person accustomed to books, labs, study, and maybe a little fieldwork in a controlled setting. A firefight was no place for her.

"We need to get you back to the truck," Sean said. His gaze pierced her eyes, and Priya registered the seriousness of the situation in an instant.

Sean turned to his friend. "Tommy, get her back to the truck. Flank around the outside of this labyrinth." He looked back at Priya. "Call your driver. Tell him to have the engine running."

Sudden concern filled her chest and caught a knot in her throat. The driver. What if something had happened to him?

"Okay," she agreed.

"Go through that window over there," Sean pointed. "Stay low. Adriana and I will handle these guys."

"You don't know how many there are, though, do you?" Tommy asked.

"Don't worry about it. Just go."

His friend exhaled and then grabbed Priya by the shoulder. "Come on. It's about to get a little crazy here."

They took off toward the western window. Sean and Adriana took a position on either side of the temple entrance and waited. He took the easternmost side, while Adriana was on the west. Both pressed their backs to the old brick wall, minimizing themselves as targets for any enemies rolling their way.

Sean evened out his breathing, keeping it shallow and silent. Not that anyone would have noticed something that quiet. There was a hot, gentle breeze flowing over the landscape that did little to cool off the visitors, but it at least caused a gentle whistle in the masonry work where gaps had cracked their way through.

He watched Tommy and Priya slip over the windowsill and disappear around the corner behind the wall. There was a part of him that doubted the plan he'd given to his friend. If the people following them were smart, they would have circled around the exterior of the village and hemmed them in. Then again, maybe that wasn't entirely possible. Without tailing, observing which way the visitors went in the confusing maze of streets and alleys, it would have been extremely easy to lose a target.

Sean had bet on the latter being the case and that anyone who was there to follow or harm them would be somewhere close behind in the maze of walls and columns.

"How far?" Sean mouthed as his eyes met Adriana's.

"Twenty yards," she said without uttering a sound. "One o'clock."

He leaned around the corner for a second to get another look and then returned to hiding. The sun pelted his face, sending droplets of stinging sweat into an eye. He didn't dare brush it away, didn't dare move that much, instead blinking rapidly to get rid of the pain and temporary blur.

After waiting nearly two minutes, he started to wonder what was taking these guys so long. Had they got lost in the maze, or had something worse happened? He doubted they'd be lucky enough that trained hit men would somehow stumble into the wrong corridor and lose track of their targets. What if they'd doubled back to the SUV and trapped Tommy and Priya?

Sean didn't like that answer. He swallowed hard, his parched throat barely able to push anything down.

Patience had always been a virtue for him. It had saved his neck dozens of times through the years when others would have rushed into a nasty situation and found themselves cut down by gunfire. He'd been patient, too, when being held captive. Waiting to find an opening, a momentary opportunity had proved to be a valuable skill; one that has so far kept him alive.

Here, though, not doing anything could crash their mission or cause his friends to be killed back at the SUV. He couldn't simply sit there and do nothing this time.

Sean moved his lips, barely cracking them. "Follow me."

She gave a single subtle nod, and then Sean stepped out from behind cover.

He knew the corridor to his left was empty. There was only another three feet of path anyway, and no one had passed that direction. If anyone was waiting for him in the passage, it would be to his right or straight ahead. Based on what Adriana said a moment before, the enemy was to the right. He swept his Springfield .40-caliber around to the right and then left, making sure the area was clear. No sign of any trouble yet. The corridor they'd come through was also vacant.

Sean took a step forward, walking on the edges of his boots to minimize contact with the ground and to keep as silent as possible.

He slowed his movement as he neared the next corner on the narrow path. There was another entrance, this leading into a smaller dwelling across from the temple's southwestern corner. It might have been one of the priest's homes back when the village was a flourishing center of activity and culture. Now, it was little more than a four-foot-high pile of brick wrapping around an empty space.

Sean narrowed his eyes and listened, focusing his ears on any sound that was out of place. The constant warm wind made that task all the more difficult, causing a whistling to resonate in his right ear. The left ear, however, was shielded by his skull. Which likely saved his life.

He heard the scuffle of a shoe in some loose debris. Sean ducked as the gunman spun around the corner, wielding a Glock 19 in his hand. The weapon almost struck Sean on the top of the head as he spun, his boots kicking up dust and brushing rocks aside. His gun hand jabbed toward the man's chest, and he was about to squeeze the trigger when the man's free hand slapped up and drove the barrel of Sean's gun into the air. The muzzle let out a loud crack, but the round sailed harmlessly into the desert.

The hit to Sean's forearm was strong. A deep pain throbbed from within the bone. He never grimaced, never flinched. The second his pistol recoiled with a hand in the air, he pivoted and drove his opposing shoulder forward with the elbow leading the way. The elbow struck the attacker in the sternum and knocked him back, stealing the wind from his chest.

The guy staggered back through the opening and into the next room. Sean only now got a good look at the guy. His dark, reddish-brown skin gave away the region of the world he hailed from. It could have been right up the street. A red dot on his forehead told the world he practiced Hinduism. Sean stiffened and raised his weapon to fire, aiming at the shoulder of the man's gun hand. He was about to pull the trigger when he caught a glimpse of something dark to his left emerging from behind the wall.

He started to turn to address the threat, but Adriana was on it. A second gunman was vaulting over the four-foot wall, his foot flying at Adriana's head. She turned her shoulders and let the man fly by, immediately swinging her gun hand around. She struck the back of his neck with the bridge of her hand. The gunman grunted and stumbled forward, but he corrected with a dive roll and bounced to his feet as she squeezed the trigger.

The gun blasted its round, tamed by the silencer attached to the end. The bullet smashed into the brick wall just over the target's head as he dipped to the side and produced his own weapon. Dust and wall fragments rained down on him as he moved to get clear of a second volley.

The place was a shooting gallery.

Adriana ducked to the right, her finger twitching on the trigger once more. The target was out of sight now, but it was more of a warning shot than anything else—a less than subtle reminder she was still there.

Seeing she had the other guy under control—relatively speaking —Sean quickly brought his focus back to the guy in the room ahead. His hesitation had been minuscule, maybe a second or two. It cost him, though, as his opponent recovered and raised his weapon. Sean dove out of the way behind the wall as the gunman unleashed a flurry of gunshots.

One of the bullets sailed by Sean's head, missing by a foot. The round made a cracking sound as it passed, something he'd heard far too many times in his life. It was a noise most ordinary people would never hear or understand—the sound of hot metal breaching the sound barrier or traveling just below it, ripping through air particles on its short journey.

Pieces of the wall across from Sean exploded with every bullet that impacted it. Shards of mud brick showered him. Dust clouds billowed into the corridor, cutting visibility more with every shot.

Sean clutched his weapon near his face, ready to return fire. He glanced to his right at Adriana, who was creeping toward the corner where her opponent had retreated to and was now, likely, hiding in wait.

He needed to capture the high ground. It would expose him, but it would also give him the advantage of an unexpected angle. He poked his weapon around the corner and fired. The bullet missed the target wildly to the right, but it caused the man in desert tactical gear to duck for cover behind a fire pit in the middle of the room.

Sean glanced to his left, surveying the rest of the short alley. There wasn't much to go on, but he did have one idea.

He moved fast, careful not to make much noise as he skirted the wall, crouching low to stay out of sight. He reached the corner where the exterior wall of the compound joined the inner walls of the temple and the home across from it. He waited for a moment and listened. Not a sound.

Adriana was still locked in on the corner where the second gunman had disappeared. Something felt wrong.

Sean's instincts were usually on point with scenarios like this, and a sudden wave of fear washed over him, not for his own safety but for hers.

He threw caution to the steaming-hot wind, twisted his feet and bent his knees, then jumped, pressing his left hand on the top of the wall to his back. He vaulted over it, kicking his legs out high and wide to clear the upper edge. As he flew through the air, he whipped his sidearm around. His first target was going to be the man he'd been engaged with a moment before, but his eyes flashed to another threat, the gunman Adriana was hunting. He'd managed to slip through a window on the side, most likely, and was now inside the room with the other guy. He had now crept over to the wall shielding Adriana and was about to climb over it to fire down on her head. She was exposed at point-blank range and would have no way to defend herself. It would be over before she knew what had happened.

Sean changed the angle of his weapon in midair, from the first man to the imminent threat to Adriana. He squeezed the trigger as gravity pulled him down. His finger twitched one, two, three, four times, sending a barrage of hot metal at the unsuspecting gunman.

The guy heard the shots pop from his left. The first two missed, diving into the ground at his feet. The guy turned in time to catch one in the shoulder and the other in the leg, dropping him to the dirt, doubled over in agony as the burning pain pulsed through his body.

The original gunman Sean had been targeting immediately turned his attention to the threat and fired as the American hit the ground and rolled to his right. Bullets smacked into rocks close to Sean. Dirt erupted into tan puffs as he kept rolling until he was behind a rectangular brick edifice in what was previously a kitchen if he had to guess. At the moment, he didn't care what the thing used to be—as long as it gave him cover.

Sean pushed his shoulder into the barrier and waited a moment, silently counting the rounds he'd spent.

He listened intensely for a couple of seconds but didn't hear the man move. The only thing he heard was the whistle of the wind blowing over the walls and through the cracks in the brickwork. It mingled with the injured gunman's voice, groaning in pain from his wounds.

Sean pictured the remaining shooter holding his position with his weapon trained on Sean, waiting for the American to make a fool-hardy move.

Sean took a deep breath and then scooted to the right corner of the brick mesa. He was about to lean around the corner and take a shot when he heard three muted pops from the entrance to the domicile. There was another—a fourth shot—staggered by four or five seconds. Then he heard a thud.

Trepidation turned to relief. He knew the sound of that report. It was Adriana's gun. He risked a peek around the corner and then stood up when he saw the target was down on his back, crumpled against the wall.

"You okay?" Adriana asked.

Sean nodded, gazing at the Spaniard as she stood in the doorway with her weapon extended at the fallen target.

"I'm good."

"I'd say you owe me one, but you took out this guy for me." She cocked her head to the side for a second and then turned her weapon to the man who was writhing on the ground.

He raised his weapon and was about to shoot, but Adriana saw him first, dipped to her left, and blasted a crater into the gunman's upper arm.

The weapon in his hand fell to the ground, the fingers limp. He yelled again and dropped his head back to the hard earth.

Sean gained his feet quickly and rushed over to where the man lay. He kicked the gun out of reach, keeping his own weapon trained on the man's head.

"Don't move. I'd rather not put this bullet in your skull."

Adriana frowned at the comment but said nothing. She, too, held her sights on the man's head.

"Who sent you?" Sean asked. "You're in plenty of pain, but trust me, it can get a whole lot worse."

The man's crooked yellow teeth flashed in a gnarly grin. He started laughing, his chest rising and falling quickly. He shook his head. "You're too late. The end has already begun."

Then the man's head began gyrating violently, shaking in all directions as if he was being electrocuted. Then a calm came over him, and his head dropped back suddenly, hitting the crusted ground with a faint smack.

It was then that Sean noticed the trickle of white foam oozing from the corner of his mouth. He nudged the man's ribcage with the tip of his boot. The body barely moved.

"A cyanide pill," Sean said. "That's old school." He sighed, frustrated.

"Now we're back to where we were before."

Sean shook his head. "Not quite. We still have the golden disc. Let's just hope Tommy and Priya made it back to the truck safely."

An engine revved from just over the wall to Sean's right. Through the window, he saw the SUV skid to a stop on the dirt road. Tommy rolled down the window, obviously relieved his friends were okay.

"You get 'em?" Tommy asked, unnecessarily.

Sean nodded. "Yeah."

"Need a lift?"

Another nod. Sean glanced back at the two bodies as he followed Adriana through the crumbling window. One question kept flashing before his mind's eye: Who is behind all this?

24

KULDHARA

The driver steered the SUV out onto the main road, sliding it sideways on the dirt and gravel until the tires bit into the asphalt with a squeak. A veil of white smoke spat out from between the road and the rubber as the security guy hammered the gas pedal and sped away from the scene.

Sean and Adriana were in the back with Priya, both still catching their breath and looking back out the rear window to make sure they weren't being followed.

"Any idea who those guys were?" Sean asked. He grabbed a bottle of water he'd left in the cup holder when they got out and chugged half of it. Adriana did the same with her own bottle. The water splashed down their throats, soothing the dry, aching feeling.

Priya shook her head. She was panting, too, though probably for a different reason. Sean could see the look on her face from the back seat. She'd been unnerved by the sudden attack.

"No," she said. There was a tremor in her voice that caused the words to quiver from her lips.

"Okay," Sean said, glancing back again to make sure they weren't being followed. He took a glance at the guy behind the wheel. "What about you, Inik?" Sean asked the driver. "You recognize those two?"

The man shook his head. His beard was neatly trimmed and as black as his hair, which was the color of crude oil. "Never seen them before." His response came in thickly accented Indian.

"Okay, so that means it's not likely an inside job," Tommy asserted.

"Maybe." Sean wasn't convinced. "Someone on the inside could have hired those goons."

Priya sat next to the window, gazing out. Her lips were pinched shut, unwilling to say anything at the moment as she still tried to wrap her head around what just happened. There was a question, however, that she felt needed answering, for whatever reason.

"Those men back there...are they..."

Sean fixed his gaze out the tinted window, watching the desert brush race by on the plains that stretched for miles, interrupted only by the occasional rock outcropping or even rarer hill. "Yes," Sean said, answering the unspoken question.

"You...killed them?"

"One of them killed himself," Adriana said. "He bit a cyanide pill."

"That's old school," Tommy said.

Sean chuckled. "Yeah."

"What's so funny?" Tommy looked back over his shoulder at his friend.

"I used those exact words to describe it."

Tommy nodded, understanding, and then returned to facing out the windshield. "That's how brothers work."

Sean grinned. They had become close like brothers over the years. They may as well have been related, sometimes coming dangerously close to finishing each other's sentences.

Still, that didn't make Sean feel better about what had just happened. He'd planted two bullets in the man who'd killed himself, specifically with the purpose of not killing him. He'd worked through his issues and felt like he was in a good place now, one where he valued life no matter how bad a person was.

Maybe he was wrong. Maybe there were still people out there who should no longer be sharing the planet with the rest of the innocent population. Was he the judge of that?

Sean had a deep spiritual background, and he only believed in taking another life when it was absolutely necessary, usually in self-defense. His revelation in the last year had changed his thinking. He'd justified the actions of his past with a placard called necessity, but the truth was that Sean realized he enjoyed the killing, the power that came with it, the rush of it all. It was a sickness he knew he had to crush, or at least wrestle into submission.

He'd also come to doubt his skills as a trained killer. On top of that, he'd realized what had been pushing him all those years to find a way out of violent situations. There must have been something deep down inside him, tucked away in his subconscious, that drove him to find peace and solace, a place where his trigger finger and calm hand would no longer be required.

He'd tried to get away, leaving IAA temporarily to rent and sell kayaks and paddleboards in Destin, Florida.

The emerald water and pristine white beaches had given him a new sense of calm, though his business suffered and it never really made enough money to even float the rent. Not that he needed it. Sean had made a small fortune of his own over the years. He'd never have to pay for health or life insurance, and everything he possessed he owned outright.

Money hadn't been the issue for his place in Destin. Demons from his past were the cause of him abandoning that venture. He still kept a home in Rosemary Beach, a quiet little beachfront town that only stretched a few thousand yards before running into the next township of Alys Beach to the west.

He only made it down there a few times a year now, but each time he went he wished he could linger a little longer. Maybe it was time, time to leave all this behind. He'd tried that before, though, with no success. Sean couldn't abandon his friends. Tommy, the kids, Adriana, they were all family to him now. If there was one thing he'd learned that always stayed close to his heart, it was that you don't abandon family.

"Who else knows about Patel?" Tommy asked abruptly.

"What do you mean?" Priya replied with a puzzled expression. She was resting her chin on her palm, staring out the window when Tommy's question sliced through the silence.

Sean's ears perked up. So did Adriana's. They'd both been wondering the same thing. If Tommy hadn't asked the question, Sean would have five minutes later.

"Who else knows what your friend Dr. Patel was working on?" Tommy clarified. "He must have told someone other than you."

She shook her head. "No, I don't think so. Ishaan is...he's a very private person. He doesn't share many secrets with anyone."

"But he shared them with you," Sean insisted.

"Because he trusts me." Priya got defensive. "It's possible he spoke to someone else about this, but I don't know who."

"Lidia?" Tommy asked the obvious question. He clearly had something against the woman.

Sean wouldn't admit it, but her glaring absence after going through the trouble to pick them up at the airport and take them to the dig site was a little suspicious. Then there was the matter of her attitude. She seemed irritated that they were there to help in the investigation. Sean didn't want to pin blame on her simply because of those things, but two gunmen showing up at a place they were checking out and that only a handful of people knew about was reason enough for him to at least wonder.

There was, of course, another pawn in play. The one Priya called Speck. Outside of the people in this SUV, he was the only one who knew where they were headed.

Sean preferred to hope that it was one other possibility that was the reason for their trouble in Kuldhara. Someone had been watching Patel all along, tailing him, keeping an eye on his every move.

When he vanished, such a person would have gone through his tent and found nothing, but likely lingered in the shadows, waiting until someone else came along and picked up the trail. They would have known about Priya's trip to the United States.

That still meant whoever was behind this could be working for Priya at the dig site, but who it was Sean couldn't figure. Not yet.

"Dr. Farrington may be a lot of things," Priya said, answering Tommy's inquiry, "but I don't think she's a killer. Not to mention, I doubt she has the connections to send a hit squad after us. Besides, she's a friend. I don't think she has it in her."

"Anyone out there who had it in for Dr. Patel, someone he might have angered in the past that would be out for revenge?" Sean asked the question, but his eyes remained focused on the passing landscape outside.

Priya thought about it. "I don't know," she said after careful consideration. "Dr. Patel is well liked in the community. He's a good person. I would be surprised if anyone didn't like him. Off the top of my head, no, I can't think of anyone like that."

"Then someone is trying to throw us off the trail," he said, his tone matter-of-fact as if he'd just explained the sky is blue.

"What do you mean?"

"He means," Adriana cut in, "that there must be someone out there who doesn't want us to find the Gada."

"Okay, but why?"

"It's a weapon of immense power. Something like that could change the world in unimaginable ways—that is, if the legends about it are true."

Priya shook her head. "They're just stories. Myths. Nothing more."

"You don't believe in them?"

She considered her words carefully. "There are many things I believe in, in this world. Science. Reason. Logic. While I'm not against the notion that there could be powerful beings from space that created us, many of the things in the Vedas are a bit...out there for me. I was raised with it. By the time I reached university, I stopped going to the temple."

"Why is it so out there?" Tommy asked.

"What do you mean?"

"I mean, why are any theological beliefs too crazy to buy into? They're no less logical than trying to concoct a theory that the universe was spontaneously created by an unmotivated, unintelligent vacuum."

She considered his point. "I suppose."

"Maybe religion isn't perfect in any of its many forms. Organized religion has caused a lot of problems through the years, hurt a lot of people. Still, it's also helped a lot of people. It's fed the hungry, given clothes to the naked, put shelter over the homeless. Nothing is perfect in this world, but there are good people who are trying. Maybe they're working under a divine guidance of some kind."

"And maybe they're just good people," she countered.

"Sure," he agreed. "We may never know in this life."

Priya grinned. "Perhaps in the next—if there is one."

Sean listened quietly to the conversation. He had no intention of jumping in until they were done. When the cabin had fallen silent for more than a minute, he decided to speak.

"So, you still have the disc, right, Schultzie?"

Tommy nodded. "Yeah." Then he started checking his pockets. His hands moved faster and faster as he realized something was wrong. He looked inside his shirt as if it might be somehow hiding within the folds. Then he frantically checked in the seat pouch behind the driver's side.

"Schultzie? Please tell me you didn't drop the disc." Sean's calm tone faintly masked the swelling concern.

Tommy froze and then cracked a smile. "Of course I have it." He reached into his tactical bag and pulled out the shimmering golden disc.

"You're an idiot," Sean said with a shake of the head and a chuckle.

Tommy smirked. "I had you going for a second, though, didn't I?"

"Have you ever heard of the boy who cried wolf?"

Priya's eyes flicked to the mirror, looking at the two and their exchange. From her befuddled expression, the pinched eyebrows, the narrow eyelids, she had no idea what the boy who cried wolf was about.

"Oh come on," Tommy protested. "I was just joking around."

Sean let it go, still snorting a laugh. "You did have me going for a second there." His eyes fell to the disc in his friend's hand. He reached out and Tommy placed it on his palm.

The gravity pulled down on his arm as the weight of the gold settled against his skin. "Gold is always heavier than I expect."

"Same here," Tommy agreed.

Priya kept watching from the front with elevated interest.

Sean's eyes fixed on the patterns. There were symbols etched into the surface, as if done with a laser. There were no scoring marks, no jagged missteps in the cuts. They were absolutely perfect.

Sean cocked his head to the side, curious about another feature of the object. He ran his finger along the outside of the disc. Notches were cut into the edge, seemingly at random. Some of the cut sections were larger than others and separated by greater distances. Many were narrow and close together.

"What's with the notches?" Tommy asked. "That what you were going to ask?"

"Yeah," Sean said with a nod and a chuckle. "And these symbols... I'm suddenly wishing I had studied a little harder in college."

Tommy flashed a glance at the disc's surface and drew a deep breath. "Yep. Sanskrit. The original language of the Vedas."

Priya turned around all the way and stared at the disc. "It's written in Sanskrit?" Heightened excitement filled her voice.

The two men looked up at her. Adriana blinked, wondering where this would go next.

"Looks like it," Sean said. He handed the disc to her.

Priya took it gently in both hands, cradling it like it was the only child she'd ever have in this life. She scanned the surface, reading the ancient text as easily as she would a magazine.

Sean pursed his lips and glanced over at Adriana, clearly impressed by her ability to so easily read a language that had been dead for thousands of years.

"Incredible," Priya whispered. Her voice was barely audible over the constant whir of the air conditioning.

"What is?" Adriana asked. She leaned forward to get a better view.

Priya caught herself holding her breath, unintentionally. She continued to stare at the disc, eyes glazed over as if in a trance.

"What is it?" Adriana pressed.

Priya snapped out of the daze, shaking her head to one side. "It's another riddle. At least, I think it is. I'm not sure. It reads almost like a poem."

"And what does it say?" Tommy asked.

She swallowed hard, the lump rolling down the front of her throat until it disappeared at the base of her neck. "It talks of a love greater than any in the universe, a new beginning, and a place where love will reign for all time, where only the purest of hearts may walk."

"Okay...same as on that marker stone we found in the ruins."

"It also says that to find this dwelling and the bloom of life, one must first find victory by the sweat of Shiva's brow, an ancient home where the sun brings life once more."

Tommy stared ahead with a blank expression on his face. "I'm sorry, I'm not up on my ancient Indian history and culture. Any idea what all that means?"

She raised her head and looked out the windshield, then turned and stared him in the eyes. "I haven't got a clue."

Sean had been listening, but something caught his eye on the road behind them. He'd been intermittently taking a look back through the rear window, never fully settled on the notion that they weren't being followed. Then again, he was never really settled in situations like this, especially minutes after a gunfight.

Each mile they put between themselves and the ancient settlement gave him a little hope that they were in the clear, that there wouldn't be any issues. On the road behind them, however, countervailing evidence was rolling their way, closing the gap fast.

They'd only seen a few cars here and there on the desert highway. Most of them were vehicles going the other direction, possibly on their way to the ancient site to take a tour of the ruins or perhaps set up camp for a night of ghost hunting.

It was a desolate place, which made the white SUV in the lane behind them stand out like a gold coin in a pile of pennies.

He'd noted the vehicle a minute before, hoping that it was just another traveler out on the road to the middle of nowhere. It didn't take long for Sean to realize that wasn't the case. They were being followed, and whoever was on their tail didn't appear to be in the mood to simply lag behind and watch. The white SUV was coming for them, and from the looks of it, they were in a hurry.

"Um, guys?" Sean said, interrupting the momentary silence of the cabin.

The others looked at him, even the driver, who tilted his head sideways to get a quick glimpse before returning his eyes to the road.

"I don't mean to be clichéd when I say this, but it looks like we have company."

The others turned around and stared out the tinted back window.

The white SUV was closing fast, less than a quarter of a mile away.

"Can we outrun them?" Priya asked.

Sean took another look back, assessing the oncoming vehicle, and then shook his head. "No. I don't think so. That SUV is faster than this one. That doesn't mean you shouldn't try. I'd step on it if I were you."

The driver's foot mashed the gas pedal, and the cabin's occupants lurched back from the momentum.

"What good will it do to try to outrun them if we can't outrun them?" Priya demanded.

Sean was already in action. He had twisted his torso around and pulled himself over the top of the seat, into the back where half of the third row was open, the other half folded down to accommodate the case of weapons the Americans had brought with them.

"It'll buy us a little time," Sean said. He flipped open the clasps on the case and then pried open the lid. The AR-15s with black canisters on the barrels lay across the length of the box atop gray foam cushions.

"Time for what?" Priya wondered.

Sean removed one of the weapons and pulled back on the charging handle, sliding a round into the chamber.

"For this."

25

LOS ANGELES

Brock sipped his matcha green tea as he stared out over the city of Los Angeles. The hot liquid ran over his tongue then splashed into his throat, soothing the flesh as he swallowed.

He had his tea at least once a day, preferring to drink it instead of coffee from time to time. He found it helped keep him centered, focused, and energized. It was a routine that made the chaotic world around him seem to fall into balance.

Heather sat on the sofa behind him, reading a magazine and paying little attention to what her employer was doing. It had been two hours since they'd visited the downstairs lab, and she, along with Brock, figured it was going to take their little science team many hours, perhaps days, of work to figure out a way to charge the mystical weapon.

Thoughts of revenge simmered in his mind as he took another sip and slowly lowered the cup to his waist. A few birds flew by outside his window, one chasing another as they dipped and dove through the treetops and hills, disappearing over the ridge to the east. He considered the creatures for a moment and then returned to his previous line of thinking.

Brock never wanted to let go of the anger, the rage that burned inside him. What happened to his family was beyond unfair, though he hated to think of it in those terms. Unfair. What did that even mean? Life wasn't fair. People were thrown into myriad trials and tribulations over the course of their lifetimes. Sometimes, the troubles came in the form of natural disasters. Other events were man-made, either deliberately or accidental. What had happened to his family had been human negligence, an intentional decision to go ahead with an unsafe operating procedure that resulted in the destruction of coastline, the deaths of millions of sea creatures, and a loss of livelihood for thousands.

His parents were one such group, a part of the many whose lives were torn apart in a moment of greedy recklessness.

Brock looked down at his tea with silent contemplation. How long had it been since that terrible night? Four years? Six? Eight?

It seemed like yesterday when he received the news. He'd come home from class in his beat-up old Honda Accord hatchback, not the fanciest of vehicles, but it got him where he needed to go. When he arrived at the family home in the suburbs of Mobile, he saw the police cars parked on the street, the yellow tape wrapped around the big oak tree in the western corner of the front yard, and cops milling around. There was an ambulance, too, parked along the curb directly in front of the main entrance.

At first, Brock wasn't sure what was going on, if it had been a crime where someone broke into the house, or if something worse had happened.

He looked up toward the front porch and saw two EMTs wheeling out a stretcher with a body on it covered in white sheets.

Brock had frowned at the sight, still uncertain what was going on. A sickening feeling gathered in his gut, wrenching it with a burning, twisting grip.

Standing there in his lavish Los Angeles home, he could still smell the flowers in the garden and around the mailbox, still get a whiff of the freshly cut grass, the asphalt on the street, and the aroma of his car's old upholstery.

He had watched in horror, hoping against all things evil, that the person the emergency responders were wheeling out was a home invader, a burglar who'd been caught by his father and shot to death.

The two paramedics rolled the stretcher down the shallow sloping yard to the sidewalk. When they were within reach, Brock stuck his arm out to grab hold of the white sheets and pull them back so he could see.

"Brock?" his mother had called from the porch, wearing jeans and a button-up plaid shirt. "Come here, Son."

Her eyes were red from tears that must have been pouring for more than an hour. Her face, too, was flushed. She'd been through more emotional drama than anyone deserved. Now, this had happened, whatever this was.

He'd gone inside at her calling, ignoring the body on the stretcher for a moment, though his curiosity was piqued.

It was after he entered the house that his mother closed the door and gave him the tightest hug he'd ever received in his life. She began sobbing again, letting the tears drench his shoulders. It took her nearly three minutes before she could collect herself enough to tell Brock what had happened.

"Your father," she'd said amid a flood of tears. Her voice trembled, caught in waves of choking coughs.

That's when Brock learned what happened.

Out of work and unable to find employment elsewhere, Brock's father had drifted further and further into the seas of depression. He'd grown distant over the months following the oil rig disaster, his demeanor growing more despondent by the day.

After months of heavy drinking, draining all of his accounts until they were empty, Brock's father had taken the final, ultimate step.

When his mother uttered the words into his ear, he already knew what happened. He'd figured it out. All there was left to know was the details about how he'd done it.

At the funeral, Brock had remained stoic, intensely focused as the minister's eulogy droned in his ears like distant, unintelligible noise. He'd stared at the casket in the front of the church the entire time, his gaze never wavering. A tear escaped his eyes now and then, dribbling down the side of his face.

The graveside service had been especially hard on his mother. She'd choked and wailed for most of it. Occasionally, a relative or friend would put their hand on her shoulder as if that would somehow magically comfort her and bring an end to her pain.

Her eyes carried dark circles under them from the crying and lack of sleep over the last few days.

Brock had already cried his last tears as he watched his father lowered into the ground. The day had been surprisingly clear and sunny. Infernal heat pounded those who stood around the outside of the funeral tent's shade. The humidity of lower Alabama wrapped everyone in a moist heat. Brock had barely noticed. His mind had turned to one thing, the only place in his mind where he could find solace, consolation against the pain of what had happened to him and his family.

Revenge.

His interest in acting had grown from a time when he was young. He'd taken every drama class he could, every private acting session he could afford on his meager income from working at fast food restaurants and mowing lawns in the summer.

When his father ended his own life, his mother swirled the drain, herself sinking into an irreversible depression.

Brock knew that he could stay there and watch his mom go down the same path as his father, or he could do something that could both make their lives better and repay those who'd destroyed everything they had.

The acting jobs had been slow in coming until he got his break. Once that happened, he began funneling money back to his mom in Alabama, though he was fairly certain where those funds went.

She'd picked up an addiction to pills during the period of mourning after his father's death. A couple of oxycodones a day kept the doctors away, as did the sadness that seemed permanently rooted in her heart. Brock was glad to be away from it. While he loved his mother, he'd always been closer to his dad. Maybe that stemmed from the fact that he knew his mom had cheated on his father at one point, the affair fraying the delicate balance of their nuclear family.

He didn't outwardly hold it against his mother, but Brock always felt like his dad would still be around if that hadn't happened.

Maybe he was wrong.

He took another sip of the tea and noted a cloud in the sky over Downtown LA. Funny, he thought. He'd come from another LA, one that gave him nothing but grief and emptiness, to one that gave him a new hope. Lower Alabama wasn't a place where people made it big in the world, but it crafted a person's mind and resolve, steeled them against the elements of both nature and civilization.

Brock heard footsteps on the stairs, though he didn't turn around to see who was coming. He knew.

"Sir?" Adam's voice echoed through the living room, off the cathedral ceilings and glass, and into Brock's ears. "I think we have a solution."

Brock took another sip of his tea and then turned around slowly. "I'm all ears."

26

KULDHARA

Sean stared out the back window at the approaching SUV. The desert around them flew by in a blur to his right and left.

"Maybe they're just tourists in a hurry to get back to civilization," Priya offered from the front seat.

Sean shook his head, keeping his eyes on the vehicle. "I'd say that's a distinct possibility." Something in his tone made her think he wasn't entirely agreeing. "Except for the fact that I can see them getting ready to shoot at us."

"What?" Priya turned her head and looked into the side mirror.

Sean handed the rifle in his hands to Adriana. Then he grabbed one for Tommy and passed it forward, taking the last one for himself.

"Seriously, are you three really going to use those things?"

Her answer didn't come from the three in the back. Rather, it came in the form of a loud plunk against the tailgate door.

She started to ask what that was, but another look in the mirror told her what she needed to know. On cue, the mirror exploded into a thousand shimmering pieces of glass that splashed on the road as a bullet smashed into it.

The driver swerved to the right and then left, already taking evasive maneuvers as he'd likely been trained.

"Lower this window!" Sean shouted.

The driver eased his aggressive dodging moves for a moment and reached for the window button in the middle. Priya got to it first, apparently now convinced they were in trouble.

The rear window went down, and Sean raised his weapon. Tommy and Adriana rolled their windows down and poked their heads out, both leaning through the opening at a safe enough distance that they wouldn't fall onto the road below.

A gunman was leaning out of the front passenger side of the trailing vehicle, and a second was hanging out of the back driver's side. Both men had short black hair, sunglasses, and matching pale, almost tanned skin. Their weapons, like their hair, were black— albeit with a matte finish to the gunmetal. The submachine guns popped in the distance, sounding like nothing more than popcorn popping in an iron skillet when muted by the road and engine noise.

At that distance, their weapons were inaccurate, though still extremely dangerous. Even a gun with a short barrel could get lucky now and then from a distance. Then again, the enemy vehicle was rapidly closing the gap, and that "safe" distance wasn't going to last much longer.

Sean pressed the stock into his shoulder and raised the weapon. He'd outfitted each rifle with a red-dot holosight system for quicker reflex aiming and better accuracy. He'd always preferred the red dots for tactical situations, and scopes when he knew there would be more wide-open spaces during a potential firefight. The red-dot system was the one he considered the best solution for general use.

The dot inside the lens lined up with the driver of the SUV. Sean's thumb flipped the safety to the fire position without so much as the lightest tremble, keeping the dot squarely on the driver's chest, just below the neck.

His finger tensed on the trigger, and he squeezed.

The moment he fired the weapon, the SUV jolted up then down. The muzzle popped and sent the round sailing over the target by a good fifty feet.

"Sorry," the driver said. "Pothole."

Sean reset himself, ready to take another shot when the gunmen behind the driver opened fire in earnest. Their guns blazed, pushing hard against the men's shoulders as the braces dug in to keep the barrels from riding up over the target. Most of the rounds missed wildly. Some struck the asphalt. Many flew by Priya's SUV and into the sandy desert soil.

A few, however, pounded the back of the vehicle. Sean heard the familiar cracking noise of a bullet zipping over his head, the velocity of the round creating a breach in the sound barrier.

He stole a glance back and saw the round had harmlessly exited through the windshield right under the rearview mirror.

Relieved, but not at ease about the situation, Sean aimed again. This time, he didn't care if he hit the driver or not. He just had to send a message.

"Aim for the tires if you can!" Sean shouted at his companions in the middle seat.

Tommy and Adriana squeezed their triggers, their fingers twitching in quick succession as they fired the powerful 5.56-mm NATO rounds at the enemy vehicle.

Sean aimed at the hood of the car. One well-placed shot would puncture the radiator. He squeezed the trigger, and his suppressor can puffed with a muted pop. The round missed, a few inches high as far as he could tell, glancing off the slope of the hood.

The driver jerked his wheel to the right, and the enemy SUV lurched to the other lane. In the moment before the man brought it back into the proper lane, Sean saw there wasn't just one vehicle after them. There were two. From what he could tell, there were no more behind the second SUV, but that certainly changed the game.

The gunmen hanging out the windows clutched the edge of the rooftop to brace themselves as their driver swerved repeatedly to avoid the onslaught from Tommy's and Adriana's weapons.

The hood of the target SUV dipped down as the driver slammed on the brakes. The gap suddenly increased between the enemy convoy and the vehicle carrying Sean and the others.

"They're slowing down," Tommy stated the obvious.

"Only for a second," Sean said. "They'll catch up again." He knew what was coming next. With so few cars on the road, the two SUVs would come at them harder the second time, likely taking up both lanes to double the wave of bullets they could throw at their target. With that many guns, it was only a matter of time before one of them was hit or a tire struck, rendering their escape an impossibility.

"We need to lose them!" Sean shouted back at the driver. His voice sounded angry, but only because he needed to make sure he was heard over the road noise and weapons fire coming from within the vehicle.

Tommy ducked back in and grabbed a fresh magazine from his tactical bag. He ejected the first into the seat and then jammed the new one into the empty slot. A quick pull of the charging handle, and he was back to the window.

Adriana fired her last round and copied Tommy's actions, ejecting a magazine to replace it with a full one.

Even with the wind blowing in from the three open windows, the smell of gun smoke filled the cabin with its bittersweet, acrid fog.

"Any ideas?" Priya asked.

Sean fired the last of his magazine's rounds at the enemy, blowing out one of the headlights in the process. He turned around as he pressed the eject button on the side of his weapon. Out the window over his left shoulder, he saw a rocky hill in the distance, maybe a mile away. A dirt road wound its way up and over the ridge, disappearing over the other side.

"Get off the road," Sean ordered. "Take the next right."

"What?" The driver sounded doubtful. "There's nothing over there."

"There's a dirt road coming up. Take it."

"How do you know..." The man stopped his question short as he saw the turn coming up ahead. "You sure?"

"We can't outrun them, but we can use the terrain to our advantage!" Sean shouted back. He slid another magazine into his weapon with a click and jerked the charging handle, chambering the first of the new rounds.

Sean braced himself and glanced at his friends over his shoulder. "You guys better grab hold."

Tommy and Adriana ducked back into the cabin and grabbed the handles over the windows a second before the driver spun the wheel to the right. Their momentum shifted every occupant's weight to one side. For a second, Sean wondered if the SUV might tip over and flip into a deadly roll.

The tires left the asphalt as the SUV's body leaned heavily. As the rubber hit the dirt and gravel, it slid sideways. The driver stepped on the gas again, corrected the wheel, and accelerated forward in a power slide any professional rally driver would have been proud of.

The back end whipped one way and then the other a last couple of times before the driver straightened it out and charged forward along the dirt road.

Sean looked back, his feet wedged against the inside of the tailgate to keep steady. The two white SUVs would follow. He wasn't naïve enough to think they'd magically lost them by turning onto a side road. That wasn't the plan.

Sure enough, the two enemy vehicles swung onto the trail behind them and sped up, though now they were partially blinded by the billowing clouds of dust Priya's SUV was kicking up.

"What now?" Priya asked. Panic still filled her voice as she looked back into the rear of the cabin.

Tommy and Adriana were still perched in their seats, clutching weapons and looking back at the approaching enemies.

"Bump!" the driver yelled.

The SUV abruptly launched into the air, all four tires leaving the safety of the earth for a moment before the hood tipped downward and they hit the road with a heavy bang.

Tommy and Adriana were jostled from their seats, but with a hold on the handles above managed to stay relatively stable.

"Keep going!" Sean shouted. "They can't get two wide on this road, and it will be hard for them to see in the dust. The faster you can go the better!"

The driver kept his foot on the gas despite the heavy rocking back and forth of the vehicle as it hit more humps in the road.

Sean could see the first SUV hit the initial bump. The white truck flew into the air. It seemed to hang there for a moment before beginning its descent. The driver must have had a moment of panic because the front wheels twisted ever so slightly. Maybe the guy had lost his balance in the driver's seat and compensated with his hands. Whatever the reason, when the vehicle struck the ground the front tires bit into the earth and instantly yanked it to the left. The SUV swerved one way and then the other, tilting to the point of flipping over but not enough to finish the job.

The driver somehow managed to correct the problem and keep control, guiding the vehicle back onto the path ahead of the second. More clouds of dust rolled into the atmosphere from the near accident.

Sean stole another quick look through the windshield and saw they were getting close to the hill.

"Keep going up that ridge," he said in a stern voice. "We'll lose them up there."

"That's a narrow road," the driver answered. "We run into another car up there, it's going to be trouble."

"You see any other cars around here?" Sean couldn't help but feel like letting out a laugh at the notion. They hadn't seen but a few other vehicles and the odds of running into one up on this old desert dirt road were one in a thousand. At least that's what he told himself.

But anything was possible.

The driver of the first white SUV tried something radical, swerving off the road so his gunners could get a clear shot away from the column of dust rising up from their target's tires.

The plan worked—for maybe three seconds. The gunman on the driver's side poked his head out of the window and raised his weapon. For a fleeting moment, he had a clear angle and squeezed the trigger. The round struck the right rear taillight on Priya's SUV. Then the next moment, the white vehicle hit a huge dip in the desert floor. The gunman was jostled up, down, and then he fell out, his body tumbling in the dirt and among the rocks and brush until it struck a big boulder with terrible suddenness.

The remaining gunman ducked back into the cabin, thinking better of shooting on the bumpy terrain.

The engine whined as Inik revved it again, the vehicle once more leaving the ground, albeit only by inches this time. The occupants' heads all bobbed at the same time as the tires struck earth.

"Coming up on the hill. You still want me to—"

"Yes!" Sean said, cutting him off in midsentence.

"Okay."

The SUV reached a curve in the road where it bent to the right and ran parallel along the small mountain. Inik spun the wheel and stepped on the gas, driving it forward through the apex of the turn with expert skill. The back end fishtailed again, but all under the driver's control. He corrected the rear's action and straightened the vehicle, speeding down the new section of path.

He noted, along with everyone else in the SUV, that this section of road seemed smoother. The deep ruts and gouged potholes were no longer as prominent in the reddish dirt.

Sean propped himself up again, steadying his weapon to be ready for the two tails to appear behind them.

He didn't have to wait long. The first SUV spun around the turn, its rear whipping wildly from one side to the other as the driver struggled to keep it righted. Sean looked through his sight and aimed at the front right tire as the vehicle twisted and exposed the sidewall. Sean's finger tensed, then twitched backward. The rifle discharged, the muted report sounding more like someone striking a hammer on a wooden table.

In an instant, the tire exploded in a burst of white air blowing out of its bladder. Even through the dust, Sean could see the panic on the driver's face as he was now not only fighting the momentum and speed of the truck but the lack of a tire on one side.

He shifted his hands rapidly across the wheel, and for a moment appeared that he might save it, but the SUV lurched back to the left, the weight and velocity too much to put on one wheel. Everything slowed down as Sean watched the rim catch in the dirt. The back wheel on the same side was the next to dig in. The white body of the SUV lifted into the air and began tumbling side over side in a vicious roll that sent huge eruptions dust, sand, and debris into the air.

Through the mayhem, Sean saw one of the occupants thrown out of the truck, only to be crushed under it.

The wreck served two purposes. It took out one of the threats, and it slowed down the second. Maybe running away was still an option.

Inik reached another bend in the road and hit the brakes. He steered the SUV around to the left and began their climb up the mountain.

The road narrowed significantly. It was just wide enough for one car to have maybe two feet of clearance on either side. One wrong move and they would sail over the edge. If Inik was going to make that mistake, Sean hoped it would be now as opposed to at the very top.

A shiver of fear shot through him at the thought.

He looked back and saw the second SUV swerving around its partner and speeding up, heading toward the turn in the road.

Tommy stuck his weapon out the window and took aim. He fired several shots at the target, planting at least two rounds in the roof of the enemy vehicle before Inik reached another turn in the winding road. He slowed down again, this time catching Tommy off guard. The handguard on the barrel of his weapon banged clumsily against the window frame, and he fell back inside. Then a second later he was thrown against the door as Inik made the hairpin turn back to the right.

Adriana grabbed him by the shoulder to steady him. "You okay over there?" she asked with a hint of mischief in her eyes.

"Yeah, I'm good."

Inik accelerated again, kicking more dust out from the back tires.

The road grew steeper, nearing a 7 percent grade. Already, the height was starting to unnerve Sean. He risked a glance out the left back window and realized they were already at least a hundred feet up.

The hill was only five or six hundred feet high, hardly a treach-
erous mountain peak but still tall enough to scare the you-know-
what out of Sean. He felt himself pushing a little harder into the back
of the seat with his shoulders. Fear coursed through him, pulsing
with every heartbeat. His fear of heights had always held sway over
him, had perpetually been his kryptonite. Then again, at that very
moment, he had no one to blame but himself. It had been his idea to
go up the mountain pass. So far, it had proved to be the right call.
One SUV was down. One to go.

Of course, one slip by Inik at the wheel and they would all
be dead.

27

LOS ANGELES

B rock looked at a map of the world laid out flat against the wall with red and blue pushpins dotting the surface.

"Other than a map," he said, "what am I looking at?"

Elma crossed her arms and allowed her partner to explain.

"This is a map of the locations where there are geostatic pools of energy," Adam said. "You see the blue pins?"

Brock nodded. Would have been hard not to.

"That's where you can find them. Based on our analysis, if you take the trident to one of those places, we believe it will charge itself."

"You believe?" Brock sounded irritated. His tone crescendoed like a rising storm in the distance. "You believe? You come up here and offer me a solution to the problem of charging the weapon, and then you tell me all you have is what you believe?"

"Sir, if you'll only listen—"

"I don't want your theories, Adam. I want results. I need this weapon to be fully operational in the next forty-eight hours, or I am going to put a bullet in your head. Do you understand?"

Adam's face drained pale. "Yes, but sir—"

"I have paid you well, haven't I? Treated you well up to this point? Yes?"

"Yes."

"Then give me results."

Elma stepped in to interrupt. "There is a place not far from here, Brock, where we can test the theory."

Brock raised both eyebrows. "Really?" Now that was interesting. "Where?"

She moved over to the map and pointed at a blue dot. The pin was placed in San Bernardino, smack dab in the middle of the Mojave Desert. The location was a wasteland.

Brock had driven through it once on the way to Barstow. He recalled seeing no homes or towns, no place to stop for gas save for a couple of rundown old places that had closed long ago. At the time, he'd thought of how much it would suck to be stuck out there with a flat tire or engine trouble.

Now, however, the desert seemed to offer him a lifeline, a touch of hope that his plan could come to fruition. He stepped closer to the map and eyed the location.

"That's about ninety minutes from here, yeah?"

Elma nodded. "Something like that. We could load up the truck and take the trident out there to test it."

Brock was starting to like this idea. It could waste a day, but that didn't matter. He didn't have anything on his plate. He would have wasted it doing any number of unimportant things. This, however, was the driving motivation of his life at the moment. It had been for years. The long buildup potentially had an end in sight. If his two scientists were correct, they might have finally found what he needed.

"I assume you recognize the red pushpins." Elma's statement cut into his thoughts and brought him back to the present.

He stared at them for a moment and then grinned. "Yes. The targets."

There were a dozen on the map, and several were clustered in Asia, targeting Hong Kong, Bangkok, and a few other larger cities. Some of the targets were in India. Others were spread out around the world. Most of them were major metropolises. Los Angeles was not marked, but Brock knew the city's days were numbered. He was going to hit it, as well, though not at first. Giving the City of Angels a little extra time was the least he could do for the place that had made him who he was and had given him the resources to pull off this plan of revenge.

As luck would have it, most of the targets were located fairly close to blue pins where the weapon could be charged. Only a select few were separated by a large distance, but that was something he could work with. London, for example, didn't have one close by, but there was one in France. He could hit Paris and then migrate toward the UK, stopping to charge the Trishula on his way.

Revenge. He thought of the word. He was so close now he could taste it. Truly, he'd believed the hardest part would be getting the weapon out of India. While the extraction from the temple had been difficult, bringing the trident into the United States had proved simpler than expected.

Adam lingered close by, his fingers fidgeting in front of his waist as he waited to hear what his employer would decide.

"Get it ready," Brock said abruptly. "We'll take it into the Mojave."

Heather arched one eyebrow. "Won't we need a test subject or two to see if the thing works? I mean, it's not like a bomb where you know if it went off."

He'd already considered her point. "Yes. We will need guinea pigs. And I have the perfect people in mind."

28

KULDHARA

Adriana watched out the window as the second white SUV sped along the narrow dirt road below. They were only one turn back now, though Inik was nearing the next just ahead.

Down on the plains below, the dust whipped into a frenzy by the car chase was now blowing freely across the desert in massive clouds of red and tan. She stuck her gun's barrel through the open window and took aim, squeezing off three, four, five more shots at the target, again mostly missing but a few diving through the roof of the enemy's ride. Whether she hit any of the occupants was impossible to tell.

Inik repeated the same process he'd already completed multiple times, slowing down at the next curve and then accelerating through the apex. The SUV surged forward again, a bit faster than the driver expected this time, and the back end whipped around.

The back-left tire slid across the dirt surface, kicking up rocks and dust as it spun and ground its way toward the edge. For a second, Sean thought they were going over. His heart pounded in his chest as it seemed the anxiety of decades was finally coming to fruition. All his fears of falling or going over the edge of a cliff were being realized.

He felt the SUV sag for a second as the left tire dropped over the edge.

Tommy and Adriana both squeezed the handles over the doors. Priya did the same.

Sean simply pressed his feet harder into the back corners and pushed one hand against the side of the back seat's wall.

Inik didn't panic. He felt the mistake the moment he made it and continued pressing down on the gas even as the back swung out over the sharply sloping ledge. The vehicle continued to drift and it appeared the entire back was going to be lost, which would undoubtedly send the SUV over the edge and tumbling down the mountain.

The driver gripped the steering wheel with white knuckles as if he'd rip it from the column. Somehow, the back-right tire dug in as Inik continued correcting the oversteer. The rubber bit into the dirt and propelled the SUV forward toward the relative safety of the right-hand side of the road and the slope leading up to the top of the hill. A quick shift back to the left and the vehicle was straight again, zooming up the road toward the next turn.

Sean exhaled, not realizing he'd been holding his breath for the last ten or fifteen seconds. He blinked rapidly, overcome by relief that they weren't dead. At least not yet. Death wasn't something that he spent much time fearing; although any threat usually came in the form of a gun pointing in his direction.

Heights, however, held sway over his mind and body like nothing else. There was something utterly terrifying about falling or tumbling down from a high place. He couldn't explain it and had never truly gotten to the source of the phobia, though he certainly had a few guesses.

Just as Sean was starting to breathe normally again, Inik slammed on the brakes and the SUV skidded to a stop, blocking the road in a diagonal line.

"What are you doing?" Sean asked and sat up. He looked over his shoulder and realized the problem before Inik could respond.

He'd worried there might be another vehicle coming down the

mountain from the other direction. It had been the biggest cause for reservation to his idea. This, however, was something he hadn't considered. There was no way he could have. Perhaps, if he'd thought more about where they were in the region, it might have come to mind.

He snorted derisively as he stared through the windshield at a herd of sheep, dozens of them, walking aimlessly down the road toward them. Two shepherds stood behind the flock of woolen-clad beasts, staring at the SUV with concerned curiosity. One looked angry, though it might have just been the blinding light of the sun causing his eyes to stay narrow, his face tightening into a scowl.

Sean saw the dust cloud below being thrown up by their pursuers. They were about to reach the turn. Within seconds, the enemy will have caught up. Then, it was anyone's guess as to how things would turn out. He unclipped his magazine and counted the rounds left. Still plenty, with another full mag in his rucksack. He pushed the magazine back into the weapon and took aim, placing part of the handguard on the edge of the back window to stabilize it. He closed one eye and pressed the stock to his shoulder, lining up the red laser dot on the rock wall at the apex of the turn.

The SUV's front left quarter panel appeared first as the driver guided the vehicle through the curve. The rest of the hood came into view, the windshield and the body of the vehicle next. Sean waited. He calmed his breathing instantly, forcing out the panic from a moment before and plunging himself into an exercise he'd done so many times before.

His breaths came in shallow, silent streams: in...out. Repeat.

He put the red dot on the driver of the oncoming SUV. It was less than a hundred yards away now, not an easy target, but the driver had nowhere to maneuver. Any sudden movement would result in either a long, deadly plunge over the edge or an abrupt crash into the steep slope on the other side.

The red dot remained on the driver's chest. Sean's finger tensed on the trigger. Then he squeezed.

Nothing happened.

He frowned and pulled the trigger again with the same result.

"Oh no," he said. He pulled back on the charging handle and looked into the chamber. The round had jammed. "Seriously?"

Before he could reach into the chamber and remove the problematic round, Adriana was already in action.

She pulled the handle to the door and kicked it open. She slid easily from the seat and onto the dirt, her boots sending miniature clouds of dust up from the surface. She stepped forward, weapon in hand, and raised the stock to her shoulder.

The enemy driver hammered down on the gas, accelerating even faster. The SUV surged, and the motor roared. Fifty yards. Forty.

Adriana didn't wait for the perfect shot. She trusted the instincts, skills, and wisdom she'd learned long ago as part of her training. Her teacher had taught her to never wait for the perfect shot because if you did, it would never come. Instead, he had said, the best shot is the one you take when it feels right.

She lined up the dot with the driver, squinting with one eye and staring through the scope with the other. With zero hesitation, she squeezed the trigger.

The canister on the end of the rifle popped. She pulled again and again, firing multiple rounds into the cabin of the onrushing vehicle.

The driver took the first two bullets to the chest. The third went through his neck, his body shuddering from the force of impact, then from the vital organs being torn to shreds. The man slumped forward onto the wheel as a gunman appeared through the sunroof. He was about to fire as the driver's weight tugged the steering wheel to the left. The sudden movement threw off the shooter's balance, and he wobbled to one side.

Adriana emptied her magazine, pouring every round she had into the SUV despite the fact that the occupants' fate was sealed.

The truck careened over the edge, seeming to hang in midair for a moment before the weight of the motor pulled it into a nosedive.

Inside Priya's ride, everyone watched in astonishment as the other

SUV smashed into the road below, nose first, then flipped end over end, toppling across the edge of the next slope and disappearing from sight in a cloud of smoke and dust.

Adriana walked around the back of the vehicle and looked down the steep hill, listening to the sounds of metal crunching and twisting, glass shattering, and the truck's motor whining then grinding to a stop.

Satisfied with her work, she returned to the open door of Priya's SUV and climbed in. "We should head back," she said, subconsciously noting the sheep still blocking the road. "We need to find out who those men were."

Priya said nothing, still seeming to be in a state of shock from all this.

Inik, however, composed himself and threw the SUV into reverse. Back at the turn, there was a little more shoulder room on the side of the road, and with a few three-point turns, he was able to get the vehicle going the other direction.

He guided the SUV back down the road, through the section of dirt that had been dug out by the grill of the enemy's truck when it made the first impact.

Down at the bottom of the mountain, Inik turned the SUV through the last curve and steered toward the enemy vehicle—or what was left of it.

The white SUV was resting on its top. The steel frame had been exposed as much of the exterior had been ripped and twisted away in the crash. A stream of black smoke poured out of the vehicle's bottom, probably from where some piece of the engine had cracked and was now burning oil.

Inik slowed down as they drew closer to the wreckage. Most of the dust from the pursuit and the subsequent destruction was now floating off into the atmosphere, spreading out and disappearing in the distance. When he was a hundred feet from the wrecked car, he stopped and put the SUV into park.

"What do you want to do?" he asked, never taking his eyes off the mangled vehicle. Through one of the busted windows, he could see the legs of the gunman who'd popped out of the sunroof. His upper body wasn't visible, crushed under the weight of the totaled truck and pinned to the earth by the roof.

The other occupants were difficult to see. One body was crumpled on the ceiling and was nothing more than a mass of twisted arms and legs.

"We'll check it out," Sean said. He grabbed his .40 and set down the jammed rifle.

Adriana and Tommy stepped out, the latter walking around to the back and opening the tailgate so Sean didn't have to climb through the open window.

The three kept their weapons at the ready, around waist high and aimed forward toward the wreckage. At the slightest sign of trouble, each one of them would raise and fire, easily cutting down a threat if necessary.

Sean was in the middle as they approached. "Fan out," he said to the other two in a low voice.

The others did as instructed and split off from him to flank both ends of the SUV. They moved around cautiously, investigating the crash to make sure none of the occupants posed a threat. Sean reached the driver's side and crouched down, his weapon pointing into the cabin. On the other side, Tommy and Adriana met in the middle, Tommy taking the front and Adriana the back seat. The three knelt down and stared inside.

They already knew the man in the sunroof was dead. The driver, too, was a goner, the blooms of crimson staining his white shirt; a matching thin trickle leaked from the corner of his lips. Lifeless eyes stared down at the floor.

A passenger in the front was harnessed in with his seatbelt, still clutching a semiautomatic submachine gun. His neck was bent in an awkward direction, eyes glazed over in death's grip.

Two more were in the back, unmoving. One was in the third row, though his feet were still dangling over the second seat, splayed out in two severe directions. His legs were clearly broken.

"He must have been thrown into the back," Tommy observed.

Sean didn't say anything. It was the correct assessment. The other body was a female. A bullet hole in her head had ended her life. One of Adriana's shots must have snuck through the front seat and hit the woman.

Each one of the dead people in the crashed SUV wore similar clothes: white shirts with black windbreakers over top of them and matching pants and combat boots.

Satisfied they were all dead, Sean stuffed his pistol back in its holster and leaned in closer to get a better look. He tilted his head to the side and reached into the woman's jacket pocket, careful not to disturb the body. He pulled back the fabric and found a thin booklet inside. He retrieved it and stood up, opening the pages. He didn't need to see what was inside to have a fairly disconcerting answer as to who they were.

The woman's identity might have been a fake. It was a high probability based on the assumption he was quickly formulating. He closed the booklet and gazed at the cover. The burgundy leather was embossed in gold. There were five stars with a wreath over the top of them. Below that were several characters that he couldn't read, but he didn't need to since the translation was directly below each row. Even then, Sean didn't need the translation. He recognized the stars and wreath. It wasn't his first time seeing this kind of passport.

His mind flashed back to the past, distant memories he'd wished weren't there. Nevertheless, they were, and at the moment they served him well.

"They're Chinese," Sean said loud enough for the other two to hear.

Adriana was checking a gear bag that had fallen to the ceiling, which was now the floor to the vehicle's occupants. She pulled the rucksack out of the wreckage and set it at her feet, then went back in to see if there was anything else of interest.

"How do you know they're Chinese?" Tommy asked, making his way back around to the side where Sean was standing. He rounded the front of the SUV and saw what his friend was holding. "That a passport?"

Sean nodded and held up the booklet for his friend to see. Then he handed it to Tommy so he could inspect it.

"Definitely Chinese," Tommy quipped.

Sean rolled his eyes. "Like I said."

"What are they doing here?"

That was the million-dollar question, and Sean only had a fifty-cent answer. "I'm not sure."

"You think they had something to do with Patel's disappearance?"

Sean had been pondering that very thing since the second he spotted the passport. "Possibly, but why?"

"If they got word that Patel was searching for the Gada, it's possible the Chinese would make a play for a weapon like that, mythical or not."

"True," Sean agreed. "Look at you, sounding like an operative."

Tommy's face blushed. "Whatever. Anyway, who are they?"

Sean knew that answer, though he didn't want to voice it. If the Chinese had sent one team, they would send more, especially when this group didn't report back. Getting out of the area became an immediate necessity.

"MSS," Sean said without emotion.

Tommy's brow furrowed. "What? What does that mean?"

"Ministry of State Security," Adriana answered as she came around the back end of the vehicle. She was hefting a black rucksack in one hand. She set it down at the men's feet and crossed her arms. "Chinese intelligence and counterintelligence agency."

The last part turned on the lightbulb in Tommy's head. His eyes widened at the epiphany. "You mean like CIA and KGB?"

The other two nodded.

Tommy ran a hand through his thick brown hair. He'd started sweating the minute they'd left the air-conditioned SUV. He glanced back and saw Inik and Priya sitting in the front. Priya was leaning forward to try to get a better look at what was going on.

"What is Chinese intelligence doing here? And why are they trying to kill us?"

More million-dollar questions, Sean thought.

He knelt down next to the rucksack Adriana had found and opened one of the zippers to the main compartment. He pulled back the flap and rummaged through the inside. There was a flashlight, a pair of Chinese 9mm pistols, something he figured to be a detonator, and a black folder. He pulled out the last item and opened it, resting the spine on the top of the gear bag.

Sean stared curiously at the sheets of paper inside the folder. They were dossiers. There were pictures, too, black-and-whites of each person in his group. The ones for him and Tommy were complete, including the known city of residence minus the address, and a bit about their past.

Adriana's only featured a photo. In her file, it said Name Unknown, along with a similar entry for most of her details. She'd gone out of her way to maintain international anonymity, keeping several passports and other identification papers to ensure no one ever really knew who she was—present company excluded.

"Like I said," Sean reiterated, "if they think there's even a remote chance that this Gada exists, they'll want it. China is already one of the few remaining superpowers in the world. A weapon like that could put them on top, assuming the thing could do what the legends say."

"I thought the Gada was a weapon that brought balance," Adriana said. "It was Shiva's trident, the Trishula, that destroyed the world."

She brought up a good point. And wiping out the planet's population wouldn't benefit the Chinese, either. They had too much riding on many of the world's nations for trade, commerce, and support. It was the great check and balance that kept them, along with most countries, in line.

"Maybe they don't want it to attack anyone," Tommy said, his voice low, almost reverent. "If they are concerned someone is going after the trident, perhaps they know this is the best way to defend against it."

"That would rule them out of being involved with the disappearance of Patel," Adriana said.

"Maybe." Sean wasn't convinced. He glanced down at the dossiers again. "Whatever the reason, they certainly did their homework on us." He twisted his head and looked back at the SUV once more. His eyes met Priya's staring back with questions oozing from them. "For now, it doesn't matter. We need to move. The farther away from here, we get, the better."

29

MOJAVE DESERT

Brock stood with his hands folded behind his back, the knuckles of his left hand resting against his belt as he did his best impression of standing at ease.

He also did his best to ignore the sweltering heat of the late-morning sun as it blazed high in the sky overhead, not a cloud to be seen to offer the briefest respite of shade. Being in the middle of a forbidding desert, there were also no trees around. The best they could hope for was a rock outcropping that stood tall enough to offer a splinter of shadow.

Brock sought no such refuge. He wasn't there for comfort.

His four-door Jeep Wrangler hardtop was parked nearby, the heavy-duty off-road tires covered in a thick layer of fresh dust. The black rims, too, sported a coating of light brown.

Heather stood next to the vehicle. She held a Sig Sauer Rattler in her hands with a strap slung over one shoulder. The weapon swung gently at her waistline as she watched the approaching convoy of two black Chevy Tahoes rumbling down the dirt road toward their position.

Brock's eyes scanned the horizon, as did Heather's, searching for any sign of trouble beyond the approaching SUVs.

They saw none.

The two vehicles bounced on the rough road but maintained a steady pace as they neared.

Elma and Adam sat in the back of the Jeep, waiting and watching. Behind them in the Jeep's rear was the Trishula, wrapped in a heavy white blanket to keep it protected from the sunlight. It was a precaution the two scientists weren't sure they should take or not. In the end, they'd gone with erring on the side of caution rather than risking damage to the weapon. Not to mention that if someone were to spot the thing in the back of the Jeep, they might try to steal it without knowing what it truly was. Some areas of Los Angeles were crime-ridden, and driving around with a giant golden relic in the back was sure to draw attention.

The convoy arrived amid a swirl of dust that had followed the two trucks across the plains. The drivers remained inside until the dust cleared before getting out.

They stepped out onto the parched earth. Six other guards in long-sleeve black shirts and Kevlar vests got out, as well. They surrounded the back doors of the first vehicle in a semicircle. One of the men reached out and pulled open the door.

Inside, an older man with sagging, wrinkled skin looked out into the bright sunlight. He winced and held a hand up over his face to shield his eyes from the painful rays that seemed to pierce his pupils more harshly by the second.

"Out you go," one of the guards said. He grabbed the man's wrist and yanked him out, letting him fall face first to the ground. The old guy landed on his elbows, which sent a new surge of pain through his arms and shoulders. He grimaced but pushed himself up. Clearly, there was still a hefty portion of pride inside this one.

Brock remained stoic, unmoving, as he watched two more people removed from the back of the SUV. They were all men, all probably in their early to late sixties, not old by most standards but certainly older than Brock and Heather.

The man who'd been dragged out first took a step forward as the others were marched around the back of the SUV and shoved into line behind him, each standing off to one shoulder.

They were all in business suits, expensive ones at that. Brock imagined the clothing alone was worth several thousand dollars. Never mind the cufflinks the men wore. The guy in front had diamonds embedded in his, glittering stones that shimmered and flickered in the light of the sun. The others were plain by comparison, made from 24-karat gold and crafted into the shape of coins the size of silver dollars.

Brock didn't judge the excess, not harshly anyway. He did, however, have another judgment to issue the three.

"Hello, Mr. Hazleton," Brock said. He stood fast, unmoving as the older gentlemen appraised their captor.

The old man looked curious. After a moment of analysis, he determined who the man was who was speaking to him.

"Brock Carson?" Hazleton asked.

"In the flesh." Brock put out both hands as if to say "surprise."

"The actor?" The wrinkles across the man's forehead revealed the fact that he still wasn't sure if it really was Brock. On top of that, he likely wondered what in the world he was doing out here in the middle of nowhere.

"Please forgive me if I don't offer you an autograph."

Hazleton's confusion deepened, evidenced by the stern expression on his face, the quivering lip, the narrowed eyelids, the reddish burn in his cheeks.

"What is this all about?" Hazleton asked. "Are you behind this? We were taken out of a very important meeting. When these...whatever you call them...dragged us out of the conference room, we found two of our security guards dead on the floor." He motioned to the henchmen Brock had paid to apprehend the three.

"Yes," Brock said. "To answer your question as simply as possible, I am the one behind your abduction."

Hazleton shook his head, the loose skin under his neck jiggling as he did so. "Then you're going to be in a great deal of trouble, Sonny. Do you have any idea who I am?"

Brock's head rocked back and then dipped forward in a single dramatic nod. "Of course, I know who you are. You're Stanford Hazleton. You run one of the largest oil companies in the world. From what I've read, you make a lot of your money down in the gulf. Is that right?"

Hazleton didn't see where this was going, but he decided to answer anyway.

"Yeah. So?" He had a sharp Texan accent. "I've never been one to get excited about ordinary people who pretend to be someone else on camera."

Stanford Hazleton was one of the most powerful oil tycoons in the world, including among those in Saudi Arabia and some of the other mega-producers in the Middle East. He'd been shrewd with his investments over the years, piling up mountains of cash with his diverse portfolio so he could buy some of the larger deposits of crude. Venezuela was his next target. He'd already purchased enough of the drilling rights to be the biggest player, not only in Central America but also in the entire Western Hemisphere, if not the world.

To Hazleton, it was a game of power. Once you had so much money, there was nothing left to play for except more of it to see who could get to the top. Then, of course, there were the political implications. Several had suggested he run for president, but he'd scoffed at the notion, preferring to pull the strings from behind the curtain. Money was easy enough to make, and it was just as easy to lose if you weren't careful and didn't make the proper investments over time.

He'd fostered extremely profitable relationships and guided politicians in the way that best suited his interests, and as a result, his empire had grown tenfold over the last fifteen years.

It was amazing what money could buy.

There were rumors—always rumors—that he'd been involved in some murder conspiracies, eliminating people on his meteoric rise and many more after. Competition wasn't something Hazleton appreciated. He used hard tactics to take over other businesses that couldn't match him dollar for dollar in the court of law. Those who could fight him and, at the very least, postpone their company's death, typically met unfortunate ends.

Brock was well aware of these rumors. He knew they were much more than that. A man like this was the perfect criminal, loaded with more power than a king and enough money to buy his own country. Yet here he was, in metaphorical chains along with his cronies.

The other two, one with thinning brown hair and a dark tan— likely from spending three hundred days a year on a beach or golf course—looked the more nervous of the three. He was in his mid-fifties and was clearly not accustomed to being pushed around. He struck Brock as the type who did the pushing, a bully in the corporate world. That was his role, after all. He was Hazleton's lead attorney, always on retainer so he could be called at the drop of a hat.

The other was closer to Hazleton's age. He was a master at propaganda, twisting and weaving stories for the media and the public at large to buy into whatever lies they wanted to feed the world. He had a crown of wispy gray hair on top of his speckled scalp. Deep lines cut into his skin, running from the corner of his eyes. Heavy bags under them told of a life spent staring at computer screens and fleeing the light of the sun in exchange for artificially lit boardrooms.

It was these three who, in Brock's mind, were responsible for what happened to his family. They were the cabal that had destroyed tens of thousands of lives, including his father's.

Not only that, they continued to destroy, wrecking the planet with their new drilling sites that seemed to be popping up daily despite a global push toward renewable resources. It was only a matter of time until these three repeated their ghastly mistake from the gulf. Or something far worse.

"I know you couldn't care less about actors and celebrities of my ilk. Most of us offer nothing of real value to the world."

He paused as the older man narrowed one eye, assessing what Brock was getting at.

"I just have to say," Brock went on, "what an absolute thrill it is to have you here, Mr. Hazleton. You have built an extremely impressive

kingdom for yourself, one that spans the globe penetrates governments, and has infested the entire known world."

The last part sent Hazleton the signal he was looking for. "I know
you and your other tree-hugger friends don't like me, boy. So, let's cut
the bull. I don't have time for this." He looked around at their
surroundings. They were twenty miles from anything or anyone.
"Whatever this is." Anger bubbled inside him and infused his words.

"I'm sure you have a very busy day ahead of you. Although I have
to admit, my security team here found yours to be a bit...lacking. I
honestly thought it was going to be a lot tougher to kidnap you. I
digress..." Brock threw up his hands, finally changing his stance.

He paced a few steps to the right and then twisted back to face the
three prisoners.

"What's all this about, Brock?" Hazleton grumbled. "I'm a very
busy man."

"Oh, I know, sir. Believe me, I know. You have more wells to dig,
more money to make, more of the planet to ruin for ours and future
generations."

Hazleton snickered, his head rocking back an inch or two as he
did so. "Please. The planet ruins itself, Son. I don't see you
complaining with your SUVs and the jet planes you take all over the
planet." He waved a hand at the vehicles behind him. "You wouldn't
have any of that if it wasn't for men like me." He jerked a thumb at his
chest. "And morons like you do just as much damage as the rest of us.
No one put a gun to your head. You don't like driving or flying? Try
walking, and see how far that gets you."

The guy was hard as stone; Brock knew that going in. Hazleton
hadn't become the ruthless tyrant he was by being soft.

"Fair point," Brock said. "Of course, there's always a plot twist,
even in real life."

He watched the man's reaction, gauging it carefully before
continuing.

"You see, Mr. Hazleton. Stanford. Do you mind if I call you
Stanford?"

The man swore, unleashing a slur of expletives. Then the threat came. "When I'm done with you, you won't be able to get a part in a pawn shop commercial."

Brock nodded. "Stanford. Stanford. Stanford. Is that any way to speak to the man who is going to decide your fate?"

Hazleton's stoic grimace cracked. A hint of doubt clouded his eyes.

"You see, there's more to it than just all the planet-raping and pillaging you and your cronies do. For me, killing you is also personal."

The older man's eyes narrowed. "You don't have the guts, kid."

Brock pouted his lips and nodded. "You know, a long time ago I'd have said you're right. And honestly, it took me a while before I could build up the—guts, as you said—to do it, but it doesn't really bother me to take another human life." He pulled a pistol from a side holster and pointed it at the man, lining up the sights with his forehead.

"Make no mistake," Brock sneered, "I would enjoy nothing more than killing you myself after what you did."

Hazleton snorted derisively. "Then do it, boy. Draw down and shoot me. I don't think you have it in you."

Brock grinned. "You have no idea what I am capable of, or about my past."

The last part caught Hazleton off guard.

"My dad was an oil rig worker in the Gulf. He lost everything because of the decisions you three made. You knew it wasn't safe to drill there, and you did it anyway. My family lost everything. My father..." Brock choked, but he fought through it as any good actor would. "My father saw friends die, people, he'd worked with for decades. He ate a bullet. Because of you."

Hazleton's confidence melted before the eyes of every witness. Realization set in, stark and harsh like the landscape around them. He wasn't walking out of this desert alive.

"So, that's what this is really about, huh?" Hazleton asked. "Your old man offed himself, and that's our fault?" He shook his head, still as brazen as ever. "Maybe your old man shouldn't have picked a line of work where the elements could so easily wreck his career. Or perhaps in a place where no one drills for oil." He waved a hand. "It doesn't matter. What do you want, kid? Money? Is that it? You want to extort me? Your kind got your settlement checks a long time ago. It's not our fault your family blew the money on booze and flatscreen televisions. We paid for our mistake. Get over it."

He started to turn, but one of the guards behind him pressed a barrel into his lower back, causing him to freeze.

Brock lowered his weapon and shoved it back into the holster. "You see, I could kill you," he said. "But I have bigger plans at play here. See, I can't let people like you go on destroying this planet. So, this is where the big plot reveal comes in." He waved one hand around in a circle with a flourish. "I'm going to take out all of you. Not only that, I'm going to eliminate billions of offenders worldwide. The planet will reset when I'm done. Global warming will end. Nature will take over again. And balance will finally be restored."

Hazleton shook his head. "You're insane."

"Maybe," Brock said, tilting his head to one side for a second as if considering the possibility. "But there won't be many people around to tell me that when all this is done."

Hazleton's eyebrows pinched together. "What are you talking about?" There was a hint of concern in his voice mixed in with the curiosity.

Brock raised one finger, and a mischievous grin slid across his lips. "I am so very glad you asked, Stanford. This is your lucky day." He turned and motioned to Elma and Adam, who'd been lurking next to the Jeep for the last few minutes.

Hazleton looked over at the man and woman. They were dressed in casual attire, like a couple ready to hike into the desert. The woman wore khaki shorts and a white button-up, short sleeve shirt. The man had longer khaki shorts, hiking boots, and a flannel shirt with the sleeves rolled up. He was holding something long and slender in his hands, something wrapped in white sheets. The woman gripped two strange-looking cones. He couldn't tell at first, but he thought they were some kind of helmet.

Elma and Adam walked over to Brock. Adam handed the covered

item to his boss and then slunk back to the Jeep, where he leaned into the back seat and pulled out a modified football helmet. It had metal flashing on the sides, wires running through blocked ear holes and a dark visor over the eyes. The thing looked like a ridiculous science experiment produced by a crazy old inventor.

Adam slipped the helmet over his head and reached into the vehicle, pulling out another.

It was then Hazleton noticed the guards were also wearing helmets. He'd not given it much thought before. Mercenaries sometimes wore protective headgear when going into combat. Now he saw them pulling flaps down over their ears from the inside of the helmets and buckling them under their chins. They, too, pulled down visors over their eyes.

"What is this?" Hazleton asked the dash of concern in his throat growing.

"You're about to find out."

30

JAISALMER, INDIA

S ean pulled back one of the thin, faded red curtains and peeked out through the narrow opening. Their vehicles were the only two near the building. Besides those, only three others occupied the sparse parking area. One was a beat-up old Volkswagen Beetle. Another was a Datsun pickup truck that had to be at least forty-five years old. The last was a Lexus IS 300. Sean admired the latter, realizing, too, that those three vehicles pretty much summed up society in India. There were the haves, and then a whole bunch of have-nots.

He recalled watching documentaries about Mother Teresa feeding the hungry and helping those in need. It was always astounding to him how many people in India were absolutely dirt poor, living in squalor—almost unlivable conditions. His eyes fluttered for a moment, rethinking the term dirt poor. Every nation had poverty. People were hungry all over the planet. Here, however, it was a little more in-your-face than he was used to.

That wasn't to say it was everywhere. Recent studies showed that India was no longer leading the world with people living in extreme poverty, a distinction that had been theirs alone for far too long—not that anyone would ever want to win that title. Nigeria had recently far exceeded India in the number of people living in desperately poor conditions.

And the gap was widening significantly as Nigeria's poverty rate continued to escalate, while India's was shrinking, bringing more and more people into better living conditions by the day.

Sean hadn't researched it enough to try to understand why the drastic change was occurring, but he was glad it was. He hated seeing people living in the dirt, on the streets, in lean-tos and shanties. Especially children.

Over the course of his career in special ops for the government, he'd developed a thick skin for most things in life. His empathy had all but been sucked dry as a result of what he'd done for a living. For the most part, Sean didn't regret that—losing sympathetic feelings for others. It kept him alive, had saved his hide on numerous occasions.

That wasn't to say he was completely callous. When it came to those he loved, he cared fiercely about their well-being and happiness. His family, friends like Tommy, Adriana, and others, and a sparse few in the periphery of his circle mattered to him more than anything.

It was strangers he had trouble connecting to, which had resulted in his ability to forget the faces of those he'd eliminated in the past.

As he'd passed some of the shanties, the people sitting in the oppressive heat on paper-thin mats or simply on the dirt flies biting at them, Sean was struck by the severity of it all. The absolute hopelessness those people lived in was staggering.

He'd never mentioned it to Tommy—his insensitivity to almost everything in life. And to his friend's credit, Tommy never pried. Schultzie was the best kind of friend that way. He was always there when needed but also understood the boundaries best not crossed, although Tommy certainly must have had his suspicions. He may have even been correct.

Only Sean knew the truth.

Losing his girlfriend in that motorcycle accident so long ago had changed everything about him.

It was his fault she'd died. Through the decades, he'd pushed the guilt as far down into the depths of his soul as he could. He'd dated in college but never got more than four or five months into a relationship before he torpedoed it and wound up looking like a jerk.

Jennifer's death was on his conscience for the rest of his life—no matter how hard he tried to run away from it.

A career working for the government, chasing down bad people and making them pay, served two purposes in his mind. The first, he felt, was the more prominent of the two. It was a dangerous job. He didn't care if he lived or died. Hadn't since the accident. It should have been him—after all—not Jennifer who died. Being in a situation where death was all but inevitable suited him perfectly.

Something deep inside, though, kept him surviving. No matter how many times he'd found himself in impossible situations, he'd managed to narrowly escape. After six years in Axis, he'd had enough of dodging bullets and staring down barrels. He'd convinced himself that he'd finally paid his penance, that he could retire to a life of taking it easy with his friend, flying around the world in search of ancient artifacts instead of killing people.

In the end, running away from the problem hadn't helped things one bit. In fact, he'd recently come to understand a sinister truth about himself. He actually liked the killing.

Did Jennifer's death have something to do with that, too?

He couldn't answer that honestly to himself, though he thought it probably did in some twisted way.

One thing he knew, though, was that for years he'd been a callous, non-empathetic soul who only tried to do good simply because it was right. Now and then, however, he found himself caring about total strangers, concerned for their well-being. Then he had met Adriana.

She'd taken a wrecking ball to his heart and mind, tearing down ancient walls built so thick long ago that no one could break through. Adriana had, though, and she'd worked her way into every fiber of Sean's being to the point where he was having more than one existential crisis.

He peered out the window at a family sitting on the street corner just outside the parking lot. They were praying, legs crossed and hands pressed together. There was a boy, a girl, what looked like their grandmother, and an older man.

Sean wondered what their story was, why those two children were with people obviously too old to have birthed them naturally. He feared something may have happened to the parents, a tragic end perhaps, though he certainly didn't wish that. Not on anyone.

Maybe the mom and dad were at work and they hung out with the grandparents during the day, praying for passersby on the street in exchange for a few coins. The kids looked dirty, from Sean's position, as if they hadn't bathed in several days. Maybe longer. He let the curtain fall and turned back into the room, suddenly unable to take the visual. A lump formed in the base of his throat and caught above his chest, tightening everything to the point that his breathing turned shallow.

He slowed his breaths to a more deliberate pace and counted to ten, visualizing big white numbers on a black backdrop in his mind. It was an exercise that he often used to calm himself down. He feared the day it would no longer work.

"You okay?" Tommy asked. His friend was sitting on the edge of one of the two queen beds. The women were in the next room, separated by an open intermediary door. The guards were in the next room over, behind the headboard in Tommy and Sean's room.

"Yeah," Sean lied. He wasn't okay. He was pretty far from it.

Tommy didn't press that one. "Shame we couldn't stay at the Fort Rajwada," he said. "Much, much nicer than this place."

Sean knew the spot his friend was talking about. Fort Rajwada was one of the nicest hotels in the city of Jaisalmer. It had been used for a long time by Indian royalty, only converting into a public hotel in recent years. The marketing team behind the hotel's success flaunted the notion that tourists could get a "royal" experience and a taste of the way things used to be for the ultra-wealthy leaders of India's past.

Fort Rajwada was a gem in a barren desert, like a shining

diamond in a mud field. It stood out above the homes of the common people, perched on a short rise that gave it the only decent views in the city. Not that there was much to look at. Aside from a small shopping district where an open-air market appeared to be thriving, there was much poverty to behold in Jaisalmer. Hundreds of homes looked to be on their last legs, ready to collapse at any moment. Then there were the street urchins, the pickpockets, and the homeless. Fort Rajwada seemed to float above it all like some heavenly creature looking down on the world with disdain and a haughty air about it.

Sean was glad they'd picked this place. He enjoyed the finer things in life, but here in this town, where so many seemed to be without, he felt better about staying in this dump.

The hotel was only four stories tall and looked like it could be condemned sometime in the next decade. Inside the room, long cracks ran up the wall from the floor, arriving at a ceiling that was peeling away amid a yellowish tint of cigarette smoke from the previous decades when such a thing was prolific.

Sean had another reason for choosing this location, though, aside from the personal stuff.

"I know it's not the best," Sean said, "but we talked about it. This place gives us a good vantage point if someone comes after us again. That hotel was so big, too many places for an assassin to hide and escape once their work was done. Here, it's smaller, more compact. We can see into the parking area, and if someone's coming down that hall, we're going to hear it on that creaky, uneven floor."

Tommy chuckled and nodded. He'd noted the noisy flooring on the way in, boards that were warped so badly from years of neglect that they creaked like rusty hinges. "Granted."

Adriana walked through the open door between the rooms. She was checking something on her phone and looked up to meet Sean's gaze. He stared at her, admiring the way the jeans hugged her legs and hips, the smooth skin of her neck as it emerged from the collared white shirt hanging from her shoulders. Her eyes, though—those eyes so deep and dark, mysterious and forbidding, yet tender and full of passion—they were what drew him in every single time. There was something new in them, though, a hint of pain he'd never seen before. They'd barely had any alone time together, at least to talk about whatever had been going on in the last several months. They had discussed menial things, but she was holding something back and he wasn't sure when would be the right time to press that issue. Now certainly wasn't it. Soon, perhaps, he'd ask her what she'd been up to, where she'd been. How she had found him was one he didn't need to ask. Her skills were equal to his, maybe even a little better. He'd heard about her training from a young age, how she'd been brought up to defend herself with any and all means possible. Adriana, no doubt, could give Sean a run for his money were they to engage in hand-to-hand combat. He grinned at the notion, knowing that day would never come. Probably a good thing since she would likely kick his butt.

Priya was right behind her as Adriana entered the room.

"So," Adriana led off, "Priya and I think we have a few interesting things for you to check out. Not sure if any of it will lead to what we're looking for, but it's worth a shot."

Priya nodded and handed a sheet of paper to Tommy. He scanned the scribbled notations and then set it on the desk for all to see as Sean moved over to stand next to Adriana.

The scent of her perfume wafted into his nostrils, dizzying his senses for a moment with the intoxicating aroma of some kind of exotic flower whose name he didn't know. It was all he could do to lock his eyes on the desk in front of her and focus on the paper.

"So, this is a list of locations?" Tommy asked.

"Correct," Priya said. "I've been trying to work out the part concerning the ancient home, one where the sun brings life once more—as the riddle states. There are many ancient sites in this land, as you all know. Old ruins litter the country from the vast deserts to mountainous regions and even a few locations along the coast. I wrote down as many as I could think of that were heavily influenced by the sun, even sun worship, but as far as anything definitive...I'm not sure."

Sean's eyes ran down the list of towns and cities. He recognized one or two, but not many. There were fourteen names written on the paper. Maybe that was a good start, but it hardly got them far.

"The question is," Priya cut the silence, "how do we narrow them down?"

"We've been working on this for the last hour," Adriana added. "I know you two have seen as many if not more riddles of this kind than I. So, any thoughts?"

The group had been at the hotel for nearly two hours. The sun was setting and every one of them could feel fatigue pulling on their bodies, begging them to get some rest. The combination of the exhilaration, the adrenaline from the chase, the heat in the desert, and the long drives had taken it out of them. Now mental strain was taking its toll as well.

Sean ran both hands through his hair. "Schultzie, you want to lead off or should I?"

Tommy rolled his shoulders and snickered at the baseball reference. "I've been running through it in my head since we got here. I do have a few questions for Priya since she likely has a better understanding of the ancient cultures than the rest of us."

Her eyes softened at the compliment.

"So," he continued before she could thank him or say anything that would make him feel more awkward than he already did, "we need to understand the symbolism of this culture and the way it was hundreds, even thousands of years ago. It seems like there are a few symbolic items in this sentence."

Priya's head moved up and down, a subtle acknowledgment that he was a correct.

"The dwelling is likely a literal place," Sean said, piggybacking off Tommy's thought. "The ancient home, same thing."

"So, they're not one and the same?" Priya asked confusion written in the lines on her forehead and from the corners of her eyes.

"I don't think so," Sean said, giving one shake of the head to the left. "You notice how there is a distinction between the two?" He pointed at the lines written above the list of cities. "To find this dwelling," his finger ran down to the last part of the sentence, "skip the middle and go to the end where it says one must find an ancient home. That's two distinct locations, probably separated by a significant distance, if I had to guess."

"Wow," Priya said, astonished she'd not considered that before. "I never thought of it like that. I was under the assumption both places mentioned were the same."

"Probably not," Tommy added. He went on. "Now, we have the bloom of life. Easy enough to figure out what symbol that part is talking about."

"The lotus," Adriana said with confidence. "The next piece of the puzzle."

"Right," Tommy said. "So, the clue to where we need to look comes from the next section. By the sweat of Shiva's brow and the part about finding victory." He looked up from the paper. "Any idea what that could mean? I know that in some cultural religions, legends, and myths, a deity's sweat or tears are often thought to have created lakes or rivers. Is there a place where the Vedas speak of something like this or maybe a region where this kind of belief is prominent?"

Priya thought hard for a minute. She rubbed the edge of her jaw with one finger as she pondered the riddle and Tommy's question. "There are many such rivers here in India. The Ganges is worshipped as a goddess. To try to figure out which one this riddle could be referring to would be...extremely difficult, to say the least." She fumbled through her words as the complexity of the puzzle overwhelmed her mind.

"And this is where we come to the place where the last piece reveals its importance," Tommy said.

"Last piece?"

"The victory," Sean chimed in. "If I had to guess—and I'm sure Tommy feels the same—I'd say we're looking for a place where there's a river dedicated to Shiva or with some kind of legend about his sweat creating the waterway, and that has historical significance in relation to a military victory, a moral victory, or some other kind of victory—if there is such a thing."

"I doubt it has to do with sports," Tommy quipped.

"Right."

Priya's brow furrowed as she considered this new information. Then her head slowly started nodding, picking up speed as the answer confirmed itself in her mind. "Yes. Yes, that's it. The victory. City of Victory." Her voice grew more excited with each syllable.

Sean and Tommy glanced at each other with uncertainty.

Adriana lifted an eyebrow at the woman.

"City of Victory?" Sean asked. "What's that?"

Priya couldn't get the words out fast enough. She swallowed, moving her head in all directions with excitement.

Finally, she found what she wanted to say amid the jumble of thoughts pushing their way toward her lips. "The City of Victory. I know where it is. And it's directly on a river that was once believed to be produced by the sweat of Shiva. I can't believe I didn't think of this before."

Sean and Tommy gazed at her with a sort of pride in their eyes, the kind a parent would when their child first learned how to ride a bike.

"Great!" Tommy exclaimed. "Where is it?"

She started to get her phone out of her back pocket when Tommy's phone started ringing.

He fished the vibrating device out of his pocket and checked the screen. It was the lab back in Atlanta.

He held up one finger, signaling he needed a minute, and turned away, walking over to the window. "Hello?" he said, pressing the phone to his ear.

"Tommy? It's Tara. Did you see what happened?"

Tommy shook his head. Then he turned back over his shoulder, looking at the others with a concerned expression on his face. "What do you mean?"

Sean recognized the look in his friend's eyes. He mouthed, "What's wrong?"

Tommy lifted his shoulders then lowered them.

"I'll send you the link to the news feed. You need to see this."

31

MOJAVE DESERT

B rock stood there, six feet away from Hazleton, staring into his eyes with an icy, vengeful gaze.

"This," Brock said, shaking the covered staff, "is what will change the world." He peeled back the layers of fabric until the trident was revealed; its shimmering golden tips flashed in the sunlight. The sheets fell away to the ground in a heap.

Hazleton admired the Trishula, not aware of what he was seeing but certainly mesmerized by the weapon crafted from precious metal.

"What's that?" he asked, doing his best not to sound impressed.

"Again," Brock answered, "I am so glad you asked. This," he leaned the staff forward, "is called the Trishula."

"What are you going to do with that? Stab me with it?"

Brock chuckled. "No, Stanford. You really don't have much of an imagination, do you? No, I'm not going to stab you with it. See, I need you three to conduct a little test for me."

Wrinkles creased Hazleton's forehead. "What are you talking about? What test?"

"This weapon is so much more than what it appears to be on the outside. First, though, take a look around. Doesn't look like much, does it?"

Hazleton said nothing, but his eyes flitted left to right, taking in the desert around him.

"Pretty much a wasteland." Brock twisted his head around, pretending to see it all for the first time. "I can understand why the government chose places like this to test their nuclear weapons back in the day."

"Are you going to get to the point anytime soon, or is your plan to bore us to death?"

Brock's grin widened. "So impatient. I want you to understand that you are going to be at the forefront, the beginning of a new age." He glanced over his shoulder at the two scientists by the Jeep. They were both wearing similar helmets now. Heather had put hers on a few minutes ago. "My research team over there believes that this place and many others like it all over the world have special qualities about them. Apparently, unbeknownst to me, something called geostatic electricity builds up naturally in pools, especially where there are dry, arid climates. At least, that's what they tell me." He spotted the bewilderment in the other man's eyes and kept going. "Why is that important? What does that mean for you? I'm sure those were the things going through your head, still are most likely. Well, I'll tell you."

His hand slid down to the button and circled around it, teasing it for a moment before letting his palm ride up a few inches. "See, this isn't just some brute-force weapon, as you so insinuated a moment ago. Sure, it could probably be used for that. But it's so much more. Did you happen to see the news in the last day or so?"

Hazleton didn't see where this was going, and he was rapidly growing tired of his captor's ability to beat around the bush. "I don't watch the news much. Only business."

Brock's head bobbed in several directions, mocking his prisoner. "Well, this has quite a bit to do with business. At least, it will going forward. Surely, though, you saw what happened in India at the golden temple."

Hazleton's eyes widened for a moment, then returned to suspicious slits. "I saw something about it but didn't get all the details.

Bunch of people went crazy or something. Started killing each other. Local police and military were even involved. They quarantined the area." As he said the words, relaying the story, the man realized how much he actually did know about the bizarre occurrence.

"Very good, Stanford." Brock filled his tone with sarcasm like a king's goblet filling with wine. "You did see it! How do you suppose that happened?"

The man shrugged. His associates had been quiet the entire time, neither knowing what to say.

"What about you two?" Brock asked, turning his line of questioning to them. "Any clue what happened?"

They shook their heads but said nothing. Brock expected nothing less. They were mere corporate yes-men, put in place to advise. Their advising of Stanford Hazleton proved to be nothing more than agreeing with his assessments and plans whenever asked. In return, they were well paid, lived lavish lifestyles filled with every luxury they could have ever wanted. Small price to pay to have it all.

"I thought not," Brock said. He turned and took a step back toward the Jeep. Elma handed him his helmet and he slid it on with one hand, jiggling it over his ears so it fit snug.

"Are you expecting a visit from an alien species or something?" Hazleton joked. "You look ridiculous in those things."

Brock's answer was a nod to the guards surrounding the three men. They all backed away, creating a much wider circle around the prisoners. One stepped forward, a submachine gun held in one arm, a cardboard box tucked under the other. He held the box out in front of the three men and tipped it over.

Three RMJ tactical tomahawks fell out onto the ground. The blades clanked against each other as they hit the dry earth in a puff of dust. The sharpened edges glinted in the sunlight, honed razor-thin.

Hazleton bowed his head and looked down at the weapons. The curved metal blades, or beards as they were known, came to a sharp point at the bottom. A deadly spike, often used for rescue operations to break windows or rip away metal, protruded from the back of the blade.

"What are these for?" Hazleton asked. He noted there were three weapons, one for each of them.

"Before you say anything else," Brock interrupted, "no, I don't expect you three to fight me or any of us with those. We'd simply shoot you, and that would be the end of it. That would hardly be fair. And earlier, when I said I'd like nothing more than to shoot you for what you've done, that wasn't entirely true. A close second, but not the number-one way I'd like to see you die."

Hazleton's expression turned grim. He chewed on his bottom lip, waiting to hear his fate. The two men next to him were less stoic. Their lips trembled. Hands shook. They didn't like the way this was going.

"We're here in the desert," Brock said, "because I need to test this weapon, to make sure these scientists of mine are correct about how best to charge it. They claim that there is a big pool of static electricity right here, in this very spot." He waved one arm around as if showing off his own property. "Of course, we can't see it. One of the many invisible forces in the universe. We can, however, see its effects. If they're right," he pointed at Elma and Adam, "this weapon will now be fully charged, and we will all be in for a show. Well, you three won't, but the rest of us will."

"And if it doesn't charge?" Hazleton growled.

"Then I let you kill my two scientists and send you on your way."

Hazleton started to speak again, but Brock held up one hand to stop him. "I think we've talked enough, Stanford. Don't you? It's time to see if they're right. And if they are..." He started laughing a deep belly laugh. "Well, that thing you saw in India is just the beginning."

Hazleton finally connected the dots. "You...you did that? With that...thing in your hands?"

"Yes, Stanford. That's correct. When I hit this button, it will send out a signal that will disrupt the frequency of your brain waves. All of us will be immune, of course." He tapped on the side of the helmet with the nail of his index finger. "But you three...well, let's just say my money is on the tanned guy there."

He pointed at the youngest of the group. In turn, the man's eyes darted back and forth between Brock, his boss, and his coworker, as if assessing what his first move should be.

Brock's hand slid back down to the button, and he let his thumb brush it gently. "I have to say, Stanford, it's going to be a real pleasure to watch you die after all the lives you ruined. My parents were good people. You destroyed them. Now I'm going to destroy you."

"You're insane!" Hazleton boomed. He took a threatening step forward. "Do you know that? You talk about lives ruined, and yet you're saying your plan is to kill billions? You're crazy. You're all crazy for following this nut job!" He waved an accusing finger around at the entire group.

"Perhaps," Brock said. "But I'm the monster you created."

His thumb depressed the button, and a gentle pulse resonated out of the Trishula. It was almost unnoticeable, like a waft of air washing over the mesa and then disappearing as quickly as it had arisen.

Brock and the others retreated a little farther. The guards remained in position with their weapons drawn and aimed at the men in the center. The gunmen opened back into a semicircle, moving so that an outcropping of boulders was to the captives' backs.

Hazleton shook his head and placed a palm to his temple as if massaging a headache. Then he glanced down at his feet, at the tomahawks in the dirt. The once-determined, death-defying look in his eyes was gone, replaced with a mistrusting panic. His right hand shot down, and he wrapped his fingers around the nearest toma-hawk's handle. He started to grab one of the others, but Tan Man lunged forward and kicked Hazleton's hand away, striking him in the wrist with the tip of his fine Italian leather shoes.

Hazleton snapped back, retreating for a moment and rubbing his wrist with the opposite thumb while his fingers still clenched the weapon's handle against his palm. He sneered at Tan Man, the guy who'd served him so loyally for the last decade or so. The two said nothing, instead letting the intent in their vapid eyes do the talking. Their minds had been scrambled save for one pervasive thought. The trident wrecked human reason, destroyed any sense of right or wrong, danger or safety, replacing everything with the desire to kill.

Tan Man lunged forward first, erring on the side of aggression. He raised the tomahawk over his shoulder and swung hard at Hazleton's neck, ready to end the fight with one quick blow. The older man, to his credit, was nimbler than his associate would have imagined. He ducked to the side and whipped his own weapon around in a backhand attack, aiming the pike on the end for Tan Man's back. The younger of the two was off balance from his attempt, a fact that likely saved him. The pike's tip grazed his expensive suit jacket and tore through a section of skin. The hit sent a stinging pain through his body but did little more than cosmetic damage, and only served to heighten his anger.

He spun around in time to raise his weapon and block a downward blow that would have sunk the sharp edge through the top of his skull, splitting his head in two. The bigger man gave an inch. Then, a split second later, shoved hard.

Hazleton flew backward, staggering and flailing his arms to maintain balance. He hadn't seen where he was going, and a moment before he fell onto his tail he felt a heavy thud accompanied by a sharp pain in his shoulder blade.

Hazleton grimaced and let out a grunt. His legs weakened, and he felt the world spinning around him. Then his vision blurred, a haze streaking through his pupils as he saw his former associate charging toward him. Then Hazleton looked back. Fresh pain screamed from the wound in his back as the third man yanked the tomahawk from his flesh and bone. He dropped to the ground, the pain in his back temporarily replaced by an abrupt shock to his knees. Then he fell forward. He felt the warmth of the earth reverberating through his cheek. A fleck of dust floated into his eye, but that was the least of his worries. He could barely feel his extremities. Was he paralyzed? A twitch in one of his toes told him he wasn't, but close to it.

Tan Man averted his attention to the last enemy. He'd never liked the other. A snooty, well-to-do Ivy League graduate who had held it over him like a whip whenever there was legal trouble. The older of the two, somewhere between Hazleton's and Tan Man's age, was fitter than his employer. He spent three days a week jogging and three more doing bodyweight exercises. He was lithe, wiry, athletic.

Tan Man's bulk made him an imposing figure. Muscles flexed inside his expensive suit jacket. He slowed his approach and addressed the cumbersome clothing, removing the blazer with a whip of the left arm and then the other. He tossed the tomahawk from one hand to the other as he circled his lone remaining enemy.

He snarled, spittle spraying like venom through clenched teeth.

The older man said nothing but held out one hand and motioned for him to make his move with a flick of his fingers.

Tan Man charged. Two huge steps and he was on the other, swinging his ax sideways in a dramatic curve. His anger and overconfidence were both misguided. The older man easily sidestepped the advance and slashed down with his own blade. The handles clanked loudly. The force of the blow drove the tomahawk down in Tan Man's hand. Were his grip not so tight, he would have surely dropped it. The damage, however, was done.

His momentum, combined with the counterattack, left him exposed. His face was waist high to the enemy. Though it was only for a second, being hunched over in a fight to the death was nearly the worst position to be in. The enemy raised his knee hard. When the kneecap struck the target, it crumpled Tan Man's perfect nose instantly, driving it back into his face and between his eyes.

Blood gushed from the wound, and Tan Man's vision instantly fogged. Instinct took over, and he put his free hand over the shattered appendage to stem the flow. He immediately realized his mistake and twisted his head to look up and see the enemy standing over him with his tomahawk raised. The next instant, the opponent swung. Tan Man moved to block the attack, but his foot slipped and he rolled forward.

The enemy did not expect such a clumsy move. He jumped into the air to avoid the rolling attack, but as he leaped, Tan Man's ax flopped through the air and caught him in the groin.

He yelled at the top of his lungs and fell in a heap, the parched earth now soaking up thick, dark crimson fluid in multiple places.

The fight forgotten, the man clutched his groin in agony, writhing back and forth in the dust and rocks. His face contorted as he looked up to find Tan Man hovering over him, tomahawk dangling in his fingers. His face was smeared in red from the nose down and from ear to ear. More still drained from his nostrils, but he'd recovered from the blinding pain and was now ready to finish this.

The older man's fingers searched around him in a panic, and he was now abruptly, jarringly aware that he no longer held his weapon. His right hand found it first, behind his hamstring, as his digits wrapped around the handle once more. He started to bring the blade around to fight the imminent attack.

His defense was too slow and far too late.

Tan Man whipped the ax blade down hard, plunging the curved point deep into his enemy's skull.

The man's eyes went blank. The body, neck, and head shook for a moment. Then the legs and spine gave out, and he fell to his side, killed instantly.

Tan Man gasped for air through his mouth, his nostrils blocked by caked blood. His head swayed back and forth with his torso, gravity pulling hard on his mass. He noted someone watching over his right shoulder. A man with a gun stood there, looking at him. Tan Man heard a voice urging him to kill again. He couldn't fight it. A primal instinct called to him, begging him to take more life, to spill more blood on the desert floor. More voices filled his ears. All of them said the same thing.

His lips moved, barely more than flutters in a hot breeze. "Must. Kill. More."

No sooner had he uttered the words than something heavy hit him in the side of the neck. The blow knocked him sideways; he fell to his knees, then onto his side. He wanted to raise his arm, to find the source of pain searing through his neck. But he couldn't move it. He reached around with the other hand, the surrounding desert once more melting into a blur. His fingers crawled over the base of his neck like a spider until they found what was causing this new pain.

His index finger touched the metal first. Then the others joined in, running along the flat side until it reached the handle. He tried to swallow, tried to gasp for air, but it did nothing to help. He felt something warm running down his neck, to his chest, soaking his shirt. Tan Man felt faint. He fought the encroaching haze, but it was no use.

With a last sickening grunt, he fell over onto his face.

Hazleton stood over the body. He wavered for a moment, pain echoing from his shoulder blade. He'd watched the two battle each other as he allowed his confusion and pain to subside a little. While they were fully locked in combat, Hazleton had grabbed his weapon and snuck up on them. Whoever won would be his victim.

He stared at his former associates, seeing them in a way he never had before. They were evil—devils, even—demons of this world that begged to be killed. They'd begged him, hadn't they? It was their voices asking to have their lives taken.

Then he heard more voices. They were coming from all directions. Hazleton turned and found several people standing around him in a half circle. He'd seen them before, at a distance. They were holding guns, pointing them in his direction. He recognized the men, mercenary scum. Every single one of them stared blankly at him. Their lips didn't move, but he could hear their voices. How? How was he hearing them? Hazleton didn't know, but an instinct buried deep inside him begged to be unleashed, demanded blood.

He twisted his head from one side to the other, trying to figure out which one to kill first. Then something flew through the air and struck him in the chest. The tomahawk had sailed end over end until the spike hit him in the center of his ribcage. He looked down at the weapon protruding from his chest and then up to the person who'd thrown it.

Brock snorted and wiped a tear from his cheek. He breathed heavily as he stared at Hazleton, eye to eye.

The dull pain in the older man's chest swelled and pulsed through his body. He coughed and suddenly felt weak. Blood mingled with his spittle as it struck the dirt and was absorbed by the earth. He dropped to his knees, clutching the handle with both hands. He yanked at the weapon, but it was stuck, and his strength evaporated by the second.

As Stanford Hazleton fell backward, his legs bending at a painful angle, he could still hear the voices repeating the same phrase—over and over. He stared into the cloudless azure sky. Then it turned silver, then gray, then darkness approached. He closed his eyes to usher in the coming night, still hearing the voices in his head.

"Kill. More."

32

JAISALMER

Sean, Adriana, and Priya hovered around the desk just behind where Tommy was seated.

Tara had sent him the link to a news report out of India. He quickly set about opening his laptop and logging in to his email. A few clicks and they were taken to YouTube, where a regional news outlet had covered the story. The headline read, "Mass Murder in Thiruvananthapuram." Tommy didn't want to try to pronounce the name of the town. He had a feeling his two friends thought the same and imagined their feeble attempts to sound it out in their heads.

The video began to play and he tapped the volume button to hear what the middle-aged woman on the screen was saying. She was speaking in heavily accented English.

"Tonight's top story comes to us from Thiruvananthapuram, the site of the Sree Padmanabhaswamy Temple, famous for its vast stores of wealth valued at over fifteen billion pounds sterling."

The camera switched to a gruesome sight. Bright lights had been set up on tripods in the middle of what looked like a plaza. A golden temple shimmered in the background, appearing iridescent in the glow of flashing cameras and vehicle headlights.

There were dozens of bodies strewn across the ground, each with dark cloths draped over them so the faces were covered. Even with the attempt to hide some of the bloodshed, Sean instantly recognized puddles of congealed blood pooling around the dead. Guns lay on the ground next to some of the bodies. An occasional arm, hand, or leg escaped the death shrouds that covered the victims.

"What in the world?" Tommy uttered in a whisper.

His answer came almost instantly.

The anchor continued: "This horrific tragedy is being classified as a potential act of terror, though no one is claiming responsibility. The usual terrorist organizations have been eerily silent in regard to this incident.

"Authorities are still investigating the cause of the massacre that cost the lives of over fifty guards here at the temple. More bodies were found inside the temple complex, one who died from snakebites. It appears the reason investigators aren't a hundred percent sure this was a terrorist attack is that it also involved what could only be described as the most significant theft in the history of the world."

The screen changed to a shot of an inner portion of the temple where stairs led down into a dark chamber. Investigators were at the bottom. Some were in hazmat suits. Others were simply in windbreakers and blue rubber gloves and shoe covers.

"The incredibly famous Vault B, long believed to be impenetrable, was broken into by the suspects in this heinous crime. It is yet unknown what they took since cameras malfunctioned once the walls were breached. Scientists are working around the clock to understand what happened to the electronics during this most critical moment of the crime."

Tommy looked up at Sean. Sean returned the glance and then looked back at the screen.

"Police said only one witness survived the attack. That person has been taken into protective custody and is being interviewed to gather more details about what could have happened.

"It also appears that whoever broke into the vault did not take much, though it is impossible to know the full inventory of what might have been in there. Early estimations are that the treasures within this chamber are valued in the tens of billions and perhaps hundreds of billions. Still, the tragedy of this night looms over what is known to be a peaceful city. A prayer vigil has been arranged outside the temple grounds for later tomorrow evening, once the crime scene has been fully evacuated."

Sean crossed his arms and continued staring at the monitor as the video came to an end.

He took a step back and then turned, walking over to the window for a moment. He pulled back the curtain and gazed out into the early Jaisalmer night. An additional car had joined the sparse collection in the lot, an old Honda Accord with fading red paint.

"Why did Tara want us to see that?" Sean asked. He let the curtain fall back and looked over his shoulder at the other three. "What's so important about that particular story?"

"We're here in India," Tommy answered. "She probably wants us to be aware that something dangerous is going on. You heard the report. Terrorists are likely the culprit."

Adriana shook her head. "They don't operate like that. Terrorist organizations almost never steal anything. They do it for religious zeal, for extremely self-righteous reasons. They're not thieves—not typically, anyway."

Sean raised an eyebrow. Since when was she an expert on terrorism? He let the question go, filing it away for later with the others he'd been putting off for the right moment.

"She's right," Sean agreed. "This isn't the MO for a terrorist hit. They would have slaughtered everyone and then left, posted a comment on Twitter or something, taken credit for it. Breaking into this...vault or whatever it is, is not a terrorist's style."

"Okay, but maybe this group is different. You know? They're evolving all the time to counter whatever the free world is doing to combat their tactics."

"Yes," Priya interjected. "And you heard the woman on the news report. She said most of the treasure was left intact. They weren't even sure if anything was taken."

Sean didn't like it. There was something about all of this that stank, drowning out the lingering sweet smell of Adriana's perfume.

"Why would someone break into a place like that and not take anything? They must have taken something." He rubbed the back of his neck where it met the base of his skull. Stress sometimes caused him to have headaches, and he could sense one coming from this perplexing turn of events. "What do you know about that temple?"

Priya thought for a second and then shrugged. "I know they have placed a potential value on its treasure stores around a trillion American dollars."

The words sucked the air out of the room. Tommy blew a whistle through pursed lips.

"There are six vaults," she went on, "five of which were opened after the government finally decided to grant permission. The treasures discovered within were incredible. No one is quite sure why such a large amount of gold and jewels were stored there, though there are some interesting theories."

"You said five were opened," Adriana noted.

"Yes," Priya gave a nod. "The sixth, known as Vault B, has never been touched. It is sealed from the inside, and no one knows how to open it. Not to mention, permission has never been granted. It's one of the reasons there were so many guards stationed there...to protect the temple and its vast resources, but also to keep anyone from trying to get into Vault B."

"I don't understand," Tommy said. "If there is so much money in there, why not figure out a way to open the vault and pull all that dough out? Imagine the good it could do for your country."

Sean immediately thought of the extreme poverty he'd witnessed in his short time there. He had the exact same sentiment as Tommy. What could a few hundred billion do for the good for those struggling in this nation?

Priya's head tossed back and forth dramatically. "That's not all. There's a legend—a warning, actually." She corrected herself.

"A warning?" Adriana shifted her stance.

"It is said that whoever breaks the seal to this vault and opens the door will unleash incredible destruction on the world. Some have said it will release a plague. Other, more extreme ideas even go as far as to say that Shiva himself will return to destroy the planet so that Brahma may return to create it anew."

"Okay," Tommy said, his voice littered with doubt. "Some of that sounds a little crazy."

"It's not so crazy," Sean said. "There are lots of great examples in history and science where things once thought to be silly in the Bible, or in other spiritual texts, have been proved to be possible. Just look at what we found in Armenia." He motioned to the laptop monitor. "We just saw the evidence of that sort of inexplicable stuff in the video."

Tommy glanced at the screen then turned back to face his friend. "You think the two are related?"

Sean didn't know for sure. And he certainly didn't have a definitive answer. Still, there was something strange about the massacre at the golden temple. "Those men," Sean said, pointing at the screen, "the ones guarding the temple; who were they?"

Priya needed a moment to think before she remembered the answer. "I believe they were commandos. No, wait. Some might have been commandos; however, the commandos were relieved of the primary duty of guarding the temple and had been replaced by city police. That happened several months ago. The commandos were on standby in case something...like this happened."

"Lot of good it did," Tommy said.

"They would have been called in," Sean realized, ignoring Tommy's comment. "Those guys are highly trained. They're like the Special Forces we have in the United States. It would take an extremely skilled unit of equal talent and training to take them out. Even with all the terror schools popping up across the globe, most of the terrorists don't have the know-how, tech, or systems to make this possible."

"Maybe they had them outnumbered," Tommy offered.

"Could be," Sean admitted. "But that's not a terrorist thing, either. They usually operate in small cells to remain anonymous, not ripple the pond. Their tactics are guerrilla. A group large enough to over-whelm these guys would be easily noticed."

The room fell into a deathly silence. After a minute of reflection, Tommy broke it. "So, you think that whoever got into that vault may have unleashed something...sinister, like a plague?"

Sean abruptly spun on his heel and walked back over to the computer desk where the other three were stationed. "Move," he said to Tommy. "I need to check something."

Tommy stood up as bewilderment washed over his face. "Sure, go ahead."

Sean eased into the seat and let his finger tickle the keys for a moment. Then he clicked on the trackpad and started typing. He ran a search for more information on the incident at the golden temple. Several results filled the page, and he clicked on one that was unre-lated to the video they'd just seen.

"What are you doing?" Priya asked.

"Detective work," Sean answered, monotone. "I'm looking for images of the crime scene."

"Why? What good will that do?"

Sean took a deep breath, scanned the page, and then clicked the back button. He selected another article and then scrolled down, panning over the images of the crime scene. Most of the pictures featured cops standing around blocking off the area. There was police tape everywhere. Emergency crews could be seen working to clean up the scene. Sean zoomed in on one image and leaned closer to get a better look. Then he shook it off and kept scrolling.

"He's in the zone right now," Tommy answered Priya's disregarded question in a whisper.

Her eyebrows lowered. "What does that mean?"

Sean clicked on another result. "It means I'm trying to figure out what killed these men." He didn't look away from the screen as he spoke.

"How are you going to do that?"

Sean pointed at the monitor, to an image of dozens of covered bodies on the ground. "These men were highly trained, well organized. The cops, too, had training for situations where they would be attacked. This is not organized. Not at all. See how the bodies are all over the place? Some are next to each other. Others are at a distance. It's chaotic."

"So? That's what terrorism does. It makes people panic, causes chaos."

"Not these guys," Sean said. "They know how to react, how to defend themselves. You know better than any of us about that. Tensions with Pakistan have always been high in this part of the world. They're known for routinely harboring terrorists. Because of that threat, your country's police and military forces are well equipped to deal with that sort of thing. This isn't the work of terrorists," Sean said. "There's something else going on here."

"What then?" Tommy asked. "You think it was whatever got unleashed from that vault?"

"I don't know," Sean said, "but I intend to find out."

"What are you going to do?" Adriana asked, sounding suddenly concerned about his intentions.

Sean sighed and spun away from the computer. "You three need to stay on the trail of the Gada. There's still a chance it could lead us to Patel."

"What do you mean, you three?" Tommy asked.

"I'm going down there." He jabbed his thumb at the computer screen. "And I'm going to find out what happened."

"I don't understand," Priya said. "What does that have to do with finding Dr. Patel and the Gada?"

"I don't know," Sean admitted. "It might be nothing. But you said there was something cursed in there, something that could wreak havoc on the planet, cause worldwide destruction."

"It's a myth," she said, "nothing more. I hardly believe in ghost stories, Sean."

"Yeah, well, we have a few dozen dead cops and Special Forces guys in a temple where some kind of forbidden vault was opened, a vault that is attached to a mystery you've apparently heard of." He leveled his gaze to meet hers. "I don't believe in those kinds of things either, but at this point, I'd say we don't rule out anything yet."

"Maybe you don't have to go all the way to the temple to find out what you need to know," Adriana said.

Sean turned to her. "Yeah?"

"You have a friend with connections," she said. "Maybe it's time you give her a call."

Sean shook off the suggestion. "I'm not sure Emily can get to the bottom of this from where she is."

Emily Starks, the Axis director, had access to people and places most government entities did not. She operated behind the veil, deep within the shadows. Her agency was small, easy to manage logistically, and ultra-secret. She answered only to the president of the United States. Funded through a number of covert channels and hidden funnels, Axis agents didn't have to go through red tape to get things done when the need arose.

Sean had worked with Emily for years before she became the director. She'd begged him to stay, nearly every time the two chatted or spent any amount of time together. Now and then, Sean called in a favor with his old partner when he needed information or when he was in a pinch. Sometimes, more often than he preferred, that assistance involved some kind of bailout.

"I wasn't talking about Emily," Adriana corrected.

Sean's eyebrows scrunched together. Then he realized what she was saying. "Oh. Her."

Adriana nodded. "Yeah. Her."

33

JAISALMER

Sean held the phone to his ear as he stood by the window in Adriana and Priya's room. He stared out the window, watching as he always did in situations like this, a hawk keeping a lookout for prey—or a threat. He already knew sleep would be at a premium that night.

He was accustomed to that. Years of working in the field, undercover, and immersed in dangerous situations, had taught him to work on minimal sleep and recover when the job was done. Usually, he could do that—get home and catch up over the course of a few days. Lately, though, he'd been having trouble sleeping at all times.

On cue, he yawned and cupped his hand to his mouth.

"Hello?" The woman's voice came through the earpiece in a professional, authoritative tone.

"Yes, Madame President. It's Sean Wyatt."

"Ah, Sean. Right on time. Director Starks said you'd be calling now."

"Yes, ma'am, I'm terribly sorry to bother you."

"Sean, my predecessor has filled me in on everything you've done for our nation during your years with Axis and beyond. You never need to apologize to me. If you're calling, it must be important and... forgive me for assuming this, a potential matter of national security?"

Sean licked his lips and turned away from the window. "It might be. I'm not sure yet. This is way below your pay grade. I know you have people for this kind of thing, but I need a favor."

"Name it."

President Gwen McCarthy was a straight shooter if Sean had ever seen one. She came from Chicago's South Side, grew up amid a hotbed of drugs and gang violence, and forged a business for herself that propelled her to heights no one from her background could have ever imagined.

She got involved with local politics first, then moved on to the state level before running for governor of Illinois. She'd been reluctant to run for president, but the party wouldn't stop knocking at her door until she said yes.

The election had been close, but in the end, Gwen became not only the first female president of the United States but the first black woman to rise to the office. Former President John Dawkins, a personal friend of Sean's, had endorsed her campaign, so it was no surprise he'd told her about Sean and their special relationship.

"There was a strange incident in India. Bunch of—"

"The massacre at the temple." She cut him off. "Yes, I saw. I... assume you had nothing to do with that?"

Sean almost chuckled, but he thought better of it. "No, ma'am. I did not. But I'm trying to figure out what happened."

"And you thought the first place to check was with the president of the United States?"

She didn't sound annoyed, but she didn't try to hide her bewilderment, either.

"No, ma'am. But I do need to speak to someone with connections here in India."

"You're there now?"

"Yes, ma'am."

"And you're sure you didn't have anything to do with that incident?"

This time he let the chuckle escape. "I'm sure."

"Well, if you think this could affect us in some way, I'll lean on your expertise in that matter. What is it you'd like to do?"

"I need the truth about what happened down there."

"The truth?"

"Yes, ma'am. The kind of truth only a person in your position is privy to."

Silence filled the line for a moment. Sean hoped she was considering his request, but he didn't get his hopes up. Not much, at least.

"What kind of information are you looking for, Sean?" President McCarthy asked, her tone returning direct.

"Something is fishy about the reports I'm seeing in the media. I know not to trust everything they put out there, but I find it odd that so many well-trained soldiers and cops were taken out so easily. I want to know what really happened."

The call plunged into silence once more, though for a shorter period this time. "I'll make a call to one of my people," she said. "I think I understand what you're getting at, though I'm still new at this, Sean. I was only sworn in a few months ago."

"Yes, ma'am. Any help would be appreciated. Thank you."

"No problem. I'm happy to help. Any friend of John's is a friend of mine. I look forward to meeting you in person soon."

"That would be lovely."

"Expect a call in the next hour. Don't wait too long to answer, or he'll hang up. Is there anything else I can do for you?"

"No, Madame President, that was it. Again, I hope this isn't a bother."

"Not at all, Sean. If it's a matter of what you deem as national security, that's good enough for me. Your résumé tells me you're a man who knows a thing or two about that stuff—more than I do, that's for sure."

"You'll get your sea legs soon enough."

She offered a short laugh. "I hope so. Have a good night, Sean."

"Yes, ma'am. You as well, Madame President."

She ended the call, and he stared at the screen for a moment.

"What a strange world I live in," he whispered, "where I talk to presidents at the drop of a hat." He snorted. "Then again, they're just people when it's all said and done. People doing a job."

He turned and walked back into the other room where Tommy and the two women were waiting for him.

"Well?" Tommy asked, his eyes full of hope.

"Nothing yet. She's got a guy who's going to call me in the next hour or so. Said he'll probably know what happened."

Tommy still wasn't sure the media was wrong. It may well have been a terror attack, but Sean had good instincts when it came to this sort of thing. There was still one major problem in his theory, though, that Tommy couldn't come to grips with.

"Do you really think that what happened at that temple somehow links to Patel's disappearance and to the Gada?"

Sean shook his head. "No. I'm connecting some dots that are not even remotely close to one another. Long shot, but I think Patel stumbled onto something he wasn't supposed to, something sinister."

"Yeah, we figured that. Thus the disappearing act."

"Right, but what if someone came around, asking about the..." he turned to Priya, "the weapon Shiva used. A trident. What was it called?"

"The Trishula."

"Right." He snapped his fingers. "The Trishula. What if someone was asking about it, real curious as to what could have happened to the thing? What if Patel got suspicious? Or maybe that someone wanted to know about the Gada? Why? Why would someone come around asking about mythical weapons that likely don't exist?"

"All good questions," Adriana admitted.

"With no viable answers," Tommy added.

Sean turned to Priya. "Do you have any details about the Trishula, how it worked, what it did? Or the Gada, for that matter?"

"No, not really. It was said that the trident of Shiva was an all-powerful weapon that brought destruction and chaos to the world."

"Chaos," Sean said the word quietly to himself.

His phone started ringing, and he looked at the screen. "That was fast." He hit the answer button and walked back into the other room. "This is Sean Wyatt."

"The president said you had questions." The man's voice was gruff. Sean could tell he'd been in the political trenches for at least a few decades. The accent was Midwestern, probably Iowan if he wasn't mistaken.

"Yes, sir. About the incident in India."

"Yes, she told me. You need to understand that what I'm about to tell you must not be shared. It's private. No one outside of me and two others on my team knows about it."

"Understood. I know how this works, sir. I'm impressed with how quickly you reached out."

"Yes, I know you know how this works. But you're a civilian now, so that changes things. Also, when the president asks me to do something, I don't beat around the bush. I like to get things done and move on to the next thing. I'm sure you get that."

"I understand."

"The witness, the lone survivor of the attack—he claimed it was carried out by only three people. Two of them were wearing strange-looking golden helmets."

That was odd. Okay, odd was putting it mildly. It was downright bizarre. How had only three people in weird helmets taken out dozens of well-trained cops and commandos? That didn't compute with him in the least. He hoped this guy on the other end of the line could shed some light on that very question.

"How is that possible?" Sean asked, voicing his thoughts in case the man wasn't going to answer them first.

"We're not sure how they did it, but we know what they did. The survivor was taken to a hospital where he, at first, claimed to be hearing voices. He had to be restrained upon arriving. The initial diagnosis was schizophrenia. Then the episode seemed to pass. As if whatever he was feeling simply wore off."

Sean had a background in psychology. He'd studied it extensively in college and after his time at the university was done, just because he enjoyed learning about human behavior. It certainly helped forge his skills as an agent and helped him understand people better, like the man talking to him on the phone. Sean's instant read on him was that this guy didn't waste time, probably had a clean, orderly home, and was not liked by many of his peers.

Regarding the situation at the temple, however, this agent's explanation didn't add up. Sean knew all about schizophrenia, the symptoms, and how to treat it. He was pretty certain the hospital had administered the appropriate drugs to the victim. That would have been their first way of dealing with it. But this guy on the phone said it simply wore off. That didn't happen, at least not often, with that sort of disorder. It was there for the long haul.

"Schizophrenia doesn't just wear off," Sean said, hoping he didn't offend the guy giving him information.

"That's what everyone said. I'll leave that to the shrinks. I'm just telling you what I learned."

"So that's why they're using the terrorist story," Sean said in a hushed tone. "They don't know what happened."

"Bingo. You know the routine, Sean. Misdirection. Give the public a faceless enemy to be outraged at so that there is a sense of justice later on down the road. You know, pin this one on the people responsible for another attack."

Sean knew all too well what he was talking about. He'd seen the cover-ups firsthand, atrocities swept under the rug. It was another reason he'd wanted out. Despite all the good Axis did for the world, it was still part of the machine, albeit a small one.

"Right. What did the guy say when he came back around?"

"Nonsense mostly. He kept saying all the others were telling him to kill. Over and over again, kill us. Kill more. That sort of thing. He claimed it took over his mind, that he couldn't resist it and, oddly enough, didn't want to. Like his brain had been taken over by some kind of strange virus."

Sean frowned. He ran a hand through his short blond hair. A virus? How could someone do that? And what was with the helmets the attackers were wearing?

He visualized the scene from the images he'd seen online: the bodies, the emergency crews, cops standing around.

Golden helmets?

It sounded like something out of a weird science fiction story. He half expected the guy on the phone to start talking about little green men.

Then Sean had a new question pop into his head, the answer to which might hold the key to solving this strange story.

"What did the witness say happened? He claims he heard voices telling him to kill. How did all the others die?"

"That's just it," the man said, his voice as gruff as ever. "He confessed to killing some of them, though he claims he didn't do all the murders. Claims that they all started trying to kill each other. It was a bloodbath, Sean. Some of them were shot, others were beaten, a few stabbed. Every single cop and Special Forces soldier in that group started attacking each other. Weirdest thing I've ever heard of, and I've been in this business a long time, pushing thirty years."

"Thus the story about terrorists. Can't have something like that getting out to the public."

"Nope. You know what would happen if it did."

"Panic. Chaos." The last word in Sean's head lingered on the tip of his tongue for a few seconds as the realization hit him. "Destruction."

"Yep. I have to let you go, Sean. Getting another call."

"Yes, sir. Thank you." Then he stopped the man. "Oh, one last thing?"

"Go ahead." He sounded irritated, like a guy who'd been in that gig for way too long.

"The attackers, did they have any kind of weapons, anything unusual they were carrying with them?"

"Yeah. Actually, they did."

Sean's ears perked up.

"Said one of the thieves that broke into the temple was carrying a trident. He said that the guy holding it pressed a button on it or something. Then there was, like, a pulse of energy. I don't know. Sounds crazy to me."

"A trident?"

"Yeah, I know. Sounds stupid. Listen, I gotta go. Good luck with whatever you're trying to do here."

"Thank you."

The offer of gratitude went unheard. He'd already hung up. Sean stared at the phone for a second, still not sure he could believe it.

Everything the man on the phone just described was something out of a psychologist's nightmare. If he'd heard correctly, and he was pretty sure he had, the thieves who broke into the golden temple had used a powerful weapon, a trident—the same weapon wielded by the Hindu god Shiva. There was no chance it was a coincidence.

This was what Patel had feared. Sean knew it. The professor must have been in a race against time, against these thieves, knowing full well what the Trishula could do if it was discovered by a nefarious character. But who? Who would do such a thing?

Terrorists? Sure. There were always extremists looking for some kind of doomsday weapon that could wreak havoc on the free world and kill millions of innocent people. But this, this didn't sound like them. He'd never seen or heard of any terrorist organization operating in this manner. Then there was the part about the helmets and the pulse that the witness had felt.

The helmets must have insulated the attackers somehow, though he wasn't sure how that would work. It was the only explanation as to what the man on the phone said. If they were wearing weird head-gear, it had to serve a purpose.

Then Sean considered the pulse once more. He thought hard about it, wondering what kind of power the ancient device would have to harness such a thing, and for what purpose. Gears turned in Sean's brain. The symptoms, the attack, the myth about the trident— all of it came together.

Sean struggled to remember what he'd learned in school. There was something about brain waves. He knew that was it. It had to be, but he couldn't quite recall the details. His mind was brilliant with its ability to remember all sorts of things. Sometimes, it was close to eidetic. With this particular detail, however, he struggled. When he had a chance, he'd have to look up information on brain waves and their effect on a human mind in regard to schizophrenia.

He slid the phone back into his pocket and turned to the door leading into the other room where his companions were sitting around the computer, talking and working through more solutions to the riddle.

A single thought returned to Sean's mind, overshadowing all others. It was dark and foreboding, a monstrous storm cloud that evacuated everything from his brain. Someone had discovered the Trishula, and he had a bad feeling about what they might have planned next.

34

LOS ANGELES

Brock placed the Trishula in the hole his assistants had cut into the floor and gazed at it with silent admiration.

Adam attached a few wires to the surface with some tape and then hurried over to his computer station to check graphs and lines occupying the screen in four sections.

It only took him a couple of seconds to get the readings. He stood up and turned to Brock with a wide grin on his face. "It's fully charged."

Brock nodded, mirroring the pleased look his scientist shared.

Elma, too, had a satisfied expression on her face. She stood by the wall with arms crossed, lips turned up in a sly grin, and one foot crossed over the other.

"Excellent," Brock said. "I'm impressed, you two. You were spot on." There was a jubilance in his voice, like a proud father doting on his children, except he sounded like a kid, too. "I can't believe that worked. How did you know?" He glanced at Elma, who he figured to be the brains of the operation.

"Good research," she said.

"You got that right!" He jabbed a finger her way, accompanied by a wide grin.

He watched as Adam removed the helmets from a black plastic case and set them on a table in the middle of the room.

"I'm especially impressed you two were able to make a couple of extra helmets to work just like the originals."

The other three pieces of headgear weren't anything spectacular aesthetically, but they functioned as planned and that was the important part. Brock couldn't have his own people killing each other, or him for that matter. Especially him.

He wandered over to one of the helmets and picked it up in both hands. He held it high and turned it over to see inside. It featured the usual cushions a football helmet would contain, with a few additional modifications. The ear holes were covered in gold filigree. The inside, too, was lined—although with a lead liner Adam had cut from an X-ray technician's garment normally used for protecting patients. The top surface had been coated with a thin layer of gold as well, nothing more than a foil sometimes used for baking decorative cakes. Adam had wondered if that would do the trick: it was pure gold so he figured it would be fine. Even so, the gamble was fully his to take. If it hadn't worked, he'd likely be dead right now.

Brock set the helmet back down and gave it an appreciative nod. "Fine piece of work, you two. You did well."

"Thank you, sir." Adam spoke up first. Elma simply acknowledged his compliment with a nod of her own.

"I guess that means our next objective is to select a new target."

Everyone listened closely, watching as Brock made his way over to the giant map on the wall.

They were all tired, worn out from the drive to the desert and back. Not to mention the toll the sun and heat had taken on their bodies. They all needed rest, and it was getting late. Darkness had fallen hours ago. The last thing any of them wanted was to have to start planning their next move.

Brock, however, seemed rejuvenated, energized by the fact that his new toy worked. "We need to choose our next targets carefully," he said. "One with a massive population but that will also allow us to get to our next one quickly."

"And still be able to recharge the weapon," Adam added.

"Right. So, let's see…" He tapped his chin with one finger as he scanned the map, going over city after city until he stopped at one in Asia. He took one step closer and pressed the finger to the city of Shanghai. "This one. We'll hit Shanghai."

Tre was leaning against a counter, palms pressed into the edge when he heard Brock say the name of the next target.

"Shanghai?" he asked with minimal effort to mask his concern.

Brock spun around, hands out wide. "Absolutely. It's perfect."

"It's…in China."

"So?"

Concern lines stretched across Tre's forehead. His dark eyes pried at Brock's to see if he really didn't understand the problem. "Brock, that city is huge. There are like…thirty million people there."

"Yes, I know. That's why I picked it. Most bang for our buck."

"In China."

"Yeah, you mentioned that. What's your problem with hitting China?"

Tre merely shrugged. "I have no issue with taking a swing at the Chinese. What I do have an issue with is how we get in. That country isn't exactly easy to sneak into. Will be a challenge."

Brock strode over to his head of security and slapped him on the shoulder. "Then I guess it's a good thing I have you on the team. No one knows that stuff better than you. Find us a way in. You and Heather definitely know the ins and outs. Make it happen."

He turned and glanced at Heather with a wink.

She offered a wry smirk in return.

"Seriously, guys, you got this. Do something simple, like we're going into the country to take them a gift or something. You know, for a museum. Tell them we found some antique vase and think it's Ming dynasty or whatever, but we need the experts to verify it for us."

Tre thought for a moment. "Actually, that might be exactly what we do."

"Really?" Brock looked surprised. "Because I was just spitballing there."

Tre shook his head. "No, I think that's exactly the thing to do. If we roll up in there with a big golden trident and some weird helmets, that could raise suspicion."

"But," Heather took over, "if we come bearing gifts, especially from a famous actor, there's no way they'll hold us up in customs. They'll push us right through."

"We'll still need weapons, sidearms at the very least." Tre's voice grew stern. "Even with this thing"—he motioned to the Trishula —"we need to be able to defend ourselves if necessary."

"I have connections in Shanghai," Heather said. "They can get us whatever we need weapons-wise."

"Connections?" Brock asked.

"Triads. I took out a rival for one of the leaders. In exchange, she said I could have whatever I needed whenever I was in town again."

Brock raised both eyebrows at this new revelation. "You took a contract for a gang leader?"

"I did a lot of things before I came to work for you. Money is money, and killing is killing. I'm good at the latter, which, in turn, makes me more money."

He nodded. "Yes, it does." Then he spun back around and faced the map once more, and walked closer to it. "We'll need a place in the center of the city to have the biggest impact."

Adam was bent over his computer, staring at the screen. His fingers flew across the keyboard, the clicking sound echoing throughout the basement lab. After several seconds, Brock turned to him with a chastising look on his face.

"What are you doing? Writing a novel?" He put his hands on his hips.

"Um, no?" He said it like a question. "I was just...well, we might not need to do the whole museum, fake vase thing after all."

"No? Why's that?"

Adam spun the computer's monitor around so the rest of the group could see it. Even Elma stood up straight and moved to get a better view.

The widescreen displayed the information page of a website. It was the main site for the Shanghai Comic Con, a huge, international cosplay convention that brought cosplayers and props enthusiasts from all over the planet to the city for three nights of costumed debauchery.

"So...it's like the Dragon Con or Comic Con of China?" Brock asked, his eyes rising to look at Adam over the top of the screen.

"Yes."

"How did you know about this?"

Adam still sounded nervous. "I...um, because I've always wanted to go to it. I love doing cosplay."

"Really?"

"Guilty pleasure." His shoulders raised then fell.

Brock returned his gaze to the monitor. He scrolled through the pictures from the previous year. Some of the costumes featured on the site were extravagant. He imagined the designers and builders must have taken months to make them. There were, of course, a few that were bare minimum, but he was impressed by the detail of many. There were giant mech outfits, others donning their favorite science fiction villain wear or hero gear. Many of the women were scantily clad in things that would make a bikini model blush, covered in bright body paint and tiny bits of cloth or vinyl. He immediately recognized why Adam thought this convention was their perfect cover.

"People will be flooding the city from all over. Security won't be as tight with all these crazy costumes coming in."

"Exactly. We can just slip all this gear right through customs. They'll never suspect a thing."

Brock's head bobbed up and down. "Make it happen." He panned the room. "Get some rest tonight. Tomorrow, we're going to China."

35

HAMPI

The SUV's engine roared as they sped down the road. It was anything but a short drive from Jaisalmer to Hampi, which was why Sean and the others had elected to charter a flight out of Jaisalmer to the regional airport in Karnataka. Driving would have taken over thirty hours, and Sean knew they didn't have that kind of time. The clock was ticking faster by the second. Somewhere in the world, the mysterious thieves who'd broken into the golden temple were doing one of two things: getting prepped for another attack, possibly on a large civilian population, or they were going to sell the weapon to someone who would carry out the attack. He had no way of knowing which, but both had the same horrific ending.

The plane had definitely seen better days, an old cargo jumper from the 1950s. The interior was cramped and uncomfortable, with hard, straight seats that jiggled every time the aircraft hit even the tiniest bit of turbulence.

Sean's fear of heights didn't usually cross over to flying, for whatever reason. He never understood why that was the case, but in this one his fears did trickle over that line just a smidge. Black smoke poured out of the engine on the right, either a sign that the thing was about to catch fire or that it was burning as much oil as fuel. Maybe both.

He wasn't the only one relieved when they landed safely on the cracked and patched tarmac near Hampi, a small town along the Tungabhadra River. The second they'd stepped out of the poorly ventilated aircraft, they were throttled by the hot sun blazing in a cloudless blue sky above. Fortunately, the SUV had already been arranged and dropped off just outside the hangar.

Sean looked out the window at the passing city. It was much smaller than the places they'd seen so far. The homes and businesses were old, most probably built in the 1950s or close to that era—just like their plane. There were a few, more modern structures—an office building here and there, an apartment building—but much of the city was old, especially the structures that mostly caught Sean's eye.

Ancient temple ruins were scattered along the riverbanks and on the plains, surrounded by lush, bright green trees and tall, red outcroppings that jutted up from the earth to form a series of rocky hills around the entire area. One particularly tall structure stood high above everything else. The stupa rose out of a massive temple complex atop a plateau overlooking the valley.

Sean stared at it with admiration, always bewildered at how the ancients were capable of building such things with primitive means. He'd always wondered about that: if humans thousands of years ago were using rocks and sticks for construction, or if they somehow had access to technology that modern humanity was just now learning about.

"Turn here," Priya said to the driver.

The other bodyguard in the front of the vehicle pointed in the direction she was suggesting to confirm.

Sean continued looking out through the back window to make sure they weren't being followed again, however, he had the uneasy feeling that that is exactly what was happening. He'd knocked off the rust over the years, been more alert than ever in recent times, but as good as he was he knew there were younger, more ambitious villains out there who were pushing the boundaries of agents' skills. And

Sean was no longer a government agent. Hadn't been for nearly a decade now. Nothing forged, and honed, an agent's abilities like being in the field. There was no substitute.

He took another glance out the window to the right as the driver turned onto the next street.

Pedestrians strolled casually down the sidewalks in both directions. Many looked like tourists, cameras hanging from their necks and fanny packs attached around their waists. Some carried backpacks. Others pushed strollers occupied by infants. None of them seemed to be in any particular hurry. A select few wore orange robes, probably marching their way to some holy site for a pilgrimage. There were others, of course, there for the same reason, but dressed in more typical day-to-day clothing.

Up ahead, through an opening in the trees that lined the road, Sean saw the river once more.

The Tungabhadra River stretched 330 miles across the state and into other regions of the country. Not far from where they were, two smaller rivers joined to form the larger Tungabhadra, though that explanation wasn't why they were here. It was the legend of the mighty river that had brought this group to Hampi.

As Priya had relayed the story, the river had been formed by the sweat of Shiva. An interesting point, considering they weren't on the trail of Shiva. Or were they? Sean had learned a good bit about Hinduism in the last few days, not only from observation but also from reading as much as he could during their journey. That reading also helped him to fall asleep at night.

In many places, there were shrines to Shiva, but there were also those to Vishnu, even some to Brahma. Shiva, however, seemed to have a devout following in certain areas of the country, a fact that fascinated Sean since the deity was one bent on destruction. He wondered how people could worship such a god, but he let it go, deciding his attention should be on more pertinent things.

They passed through a section of the town where ruins lined the streets, surrounded by government fences and low-lying walls. Thick trees with broad canopies blotted the ground with shade where visitors sat, getting momentary relief from the hot sun.

"Over there," Priya pointed to a parking spot along the side of the road. "Park there." The place she motioned to was near the base of one of the taller mountains in the valley. Its surface was dotted with enormous rock outcroppings, boulders, and small scraggly trees.

The driver did as instructed, slowing down and flipping on his blinker to let the two cars behind them know his intentions. He expertly backed the SUV into the spot and then pulled forward, executing the parallel parking job in one easy maneuver.

The occupants poured out of the vehicle and onto the sidewalk, instantly immersed in the dry heat the region had to offer, making the cool air conditioning of the SUV seem like a distant memory.

Priya stared down a long dirt walkway toward the river where an outcropping of huge boulders rose from the shore. There were a dozen or so people loitering around the site, some taking pictures, others simply gazing at the beautiful setting at the base of the mountain.

Around three sections of boulders, stone pillars rose from a base supporting a stone roof. The structures looked like miniature temples.

Sean and the others had seen images of the site before getting on the plane to fly to Hampi. They'd each done quick web searches and were immediately surprised at the rich cultural and religious history this little region had to offer.

To his back, where the tallest stupa rose into the azure sky, enormous temple complexes dotted both sides of the few main roads leading in and out of the city. Clearly, there had been something about this place—a calling, perhaps, that led religious and spiritual leaders to build shrines to their gods here. There were Buddhist, Hindu, and even a few other temples dedicated to smaller religions, but each had their place, and seemingly, all lived in harmony with one another.

"Shame we aren't going to get to see that complex," he said to Adriana.

"Mmm," she hummed in agreement.

What was it about this valley in the desert, this oasis of life and spirit that caused people living so long ago to dedicate it to something larger than themselves?

"There's the entrance to the cave temples," Priya said.

"Then we should get moving," Tommy said, reading Sean's thoughts. "The longer we stick around in one place, the easier targets we become."

Priya shuddered. She didn't like the idea of being a target and made no effort to hide that from the others. The two security guards tightened their belts and glanced around, as if that would help them spot someone hiding out, watching and waiting for a chance to snag their prey.

"Stay here with the car," she ordered the guards. "I don't want to draw too much attention."

The men were reluctant, confused by the order, but nodded and climbed back into the vehicle.

"Yes, but we're not going into those caves."

"We're not?" Tommy frowned.

"No," she shook her head. "We're going up there." She pointed to the top of the mountain looming over them and the caves below.

Sean's head craned back as he took in the intimidating sight. The higher up his eyes went, the worse his fears became, growing inside him like a balloon ready to burst.

The group moved up the path at a rapid pace. The entrance to the cave temples was only a few hundred yards away, but it felt farther. Exposed, out in the open and knowing the Chinese MSS had come after them before, didn't make it feel any safer.

Sean checked over his shoulder more than a few times as they made their way up the path and veered off to a narrower dirt trail that led to the foot of a tall, rocky hill at the base of which were the gigantic boulders and the stone pillars.

"This is it," Priya said. "It has to be."

Sean arched an eyebrow. "It doesn't have to be. We could be wrong about this." He noticed people walking along a narrow path that wound its way up the mountain. At the top, he could make out tiny specks, more visitors who were carelessly standing on the edge of the precipice, unaware that they were inviting a horrible fate.

She shook her head. "Sure, that's always possible, but I can feel it."

Sean didn't say anything else, but he felt it, too—a strange beating in his heart, tugging him somewhere. Why? He'd not felt something like that before, an invisible force pulling him to a destination. Or had he? Maybe it was just his phobia telling him not to climb the mountain. Every fiber of his being agreed with that assessment.

He and the others stepped closer to the entrance of the nearest of the three temples. An image of a deity was carved into a rock panel wedged between two of the columns. "That's Buddha," Priya commented.

Sean and Tommy noted the figure, the folds of fat draped over his thighs, the joyful look on the chubby face, the bald head, and the earrings dangling from his ears. There was no question who the sculpture was meant to represent.

"Over there is the temple for Shiva," Priya said, pointing at another entrance. It was shaped similarly, with a triangular façade to the roof propped up by ancient pillars. Part of the roof was leaning to one side, evidence of age, weather, and maybe even an earthquake or two.

"Always remarkable to me," Adriana said, "how these old structures are still standing after so much time." She hadn't said much since they'd arrived. On the flight, she and Sean barely spoke, each keeping something from the other, each knowing that to be the case.

He reached out his hand and touched her palm with his fingers, brushing across it gently. She looked over at him and smiled, squeezing his hand in hers as they trudged through the packed dirt and low-cut grass toward the third temple cave entrance.

This one featured a different deity on a front-facing panel. He had a rounded belly, though not as bulging and pronounced as the Buddha they'd seen a moment before. This one had a slightly more muscular upper body and legs and wasn't sitting peacefully with a happy look on his face. This figure was standing with feet shoulder width apart and one hand in the air over his head in triumph. The other hand was extended to the side, clutching a long creature in his hand with a firm grip.

"A cobra," Tommy said as they stopped close to the panel. "He's holding a cobra." He turned to Priya. "Why is he holding a cobra?"

"The cobra was one of the creatures associated with Shiva. In fact, in some of the lesser-known myths, cobras were his servants, his protectors—his guardians."

"That news report said that one of the people killed at the golden temple died from snakebites."

She nodded. "Yes. There was an expedition there in the early 1900s led by a renowned archaeologist named John Portman." She turned her head away from the entrance and faced the others. "He hoped to open Vault B, without the Indian government's permission, of course."

"What happened?" Adriana asked.

"He and his team went into the antechamber. They snuck down the stairs and into the room where the entrance to the vault was located. Portman claimed that snakes poured out of walls around the gate. According to the story, one of his men was overwhelmed and killed right away. Apparently, those particular cobras were extremely aggressive. They attacked and latched on to the victim, killing him in minutes as more and more of them pumped their deadly venom into his bloodstream. Portman was the lone survivor. The two men with him died from their wounds. After that, no one was permitted down there. Security was tightened, until recently." Her head turned back to the carving on the stone panel.

No one said anything for a minute. The story was a grisly one and sobering.

"You don't think there are any snakes in this cave, do you?"

"No," she said with a faint laugh. "This place is visited by thousands of people every year." Then she turned and gazed up at the top of the stony mountain. "But of course, anything is possible."

36

HAMPI

The town of Hampi was home to some of the most ornately designed temples in the world. The little city had become renowned for the variety and beauty of its holy places from the past. Hundreds of stupas lined the walkways in the courtyards of the Hampi Temple. Well-manicured lawns and paths provided a serene visiting experience for tourists. It was refreshing to see ancient ruins so well cared for, considering so many all across the world had fallen into disrepair over the years.

The cave temples, by contrast, were much smaller on the outside and nowhere near as spectacular as some of the larger, more opulent temples on the plains, especially up on the plateau overlooking the valley.

Those temples at the base of the mountain had been built out of convenience, using natural rooms and chambers carved by time and pressure. Perhaps it was laziness by the builders or maybe just careful planning. They'd built the entrances so that visitors coming to worship would feel like they were entering a holy place. It wasn't that the structures on the exterior weren't magnificent. They were, in their own way, smaller versions of some of the famous Greek and Roman temples from thousands of years ago. Their design could have been some kind of homage to those powerful cultures from history.

Inside those caves, candles burned along the smooth walls hewn by the hands of time and people. The builders had taken what they were given and smoothed away the rough spots, making the inside of the caves look more like real temples. The walls were straight and flat along their surfaces. Emblems of the gods from the Vedas occupied recesses between sconces that pooled flickering light into the chamber.

Sean longed for the safety of those simple caves below. A lump in his throat hung there like a golf ball, making it nearly impossible to swallow or breathe. He stared out at the terrifying and glorious scene before him. He had to crouch low, bending his knees to feel a little more secure so high above the valley floor.

They'd climbed to the top of the mountain via a narrow path that wound its way from the river basin all the way to the peak. Hundreds of tourists and pilgrims were there, some taking pictures and video, others offering prayers to their deities for guidance, comfort, peace, blessings, or healing.

The sun had reached its zenith an hour before and was now making its journey across the sky toward the horizon. Sean imagined the sunsets were pretty amazing up here, though it was certainly one of the last places he'd want to be after dark. The winding path to the top hadn't been so bad as long as he focused on the mountain to his side and the dirt under his feet. Without many drop-offs, he felt a little more comfortable with this climb than he had with others. In some ways, it reminded him of the hike to the top of Stone Mountain near Atlanta, though that one was more of a straight-up hike to the top of a giant rock. He shuddered at the memory of taking the tram during one, particularly horrifying trip. At least by walking he'd been able to take the heights gradually. The tram was a box hovering hundreds of feet above the ground, held up by nothing more than a metal arm and some cable. He didn't care what the tensile strength of the cable was. It was terrifying.

This mountain, too, caused his knees to go weak. He could feel them wobbling with every step, the muscles, and ligaments keeping him upright having turned to jello before he had reached the summit. It was nothing, though, compared to that stupid tram ride.

Priya stepped over to the edge and looked out, putting the bridge of her hand to her forehead to shield her eyes from the glare of the sun. She took in the view for a minute, admiring it for the first time. In all her work in India, she'd never visited the top of this mountain. She'd been to Hampi before and toured the temple grounds down below, but had never taken in the vistas from this location.

Tommy and the others followed, leaving Sean in the rear as he continued to gaze tentatively at the surrounding countryside and the basin below. He was distracted by tourists getting—what he believed to be—too close to the edge.

The moment passed, and Tommy turned to Priya. "So, what's up here? You said there was a temple cave, but it's not like the ones down below?"

She shook her head. "No, there is a cave just around this peak." She pointed at a rocky summit that rose above the top where they stood. A few brave souls were climbing around on the rocks, free-climbing short distances and then lowering themselves back down.

Sean knew there was no way he was doing that and hoped that wasn't what she meant.

"I'm still thinking about that serpent carving down below," Tommy said. "The one held by Vishnu." His comment broke through the surface of Sean's fears and put his mind onto something else for a moment.

"The snake," Sean said, "has been taken by Vishnu. It's a symbol of removing the power from his destructive brother, Shiva. This is where we find the next piece to the puzzle."

Priya's lips creased, and she raised one eyebrow, impressed with his assessment. "Very good, Sean."

He blushed, and for the most fleeting of moments forgot how terrified he was perched on the mountaintop. That memory returned a second later as he saw another tourist walking near the edge. One of the strange facets of his phobia was that he not only feared for his own safety but was also desperately concerned for the safety of others. He'd had nightmares about watching other people falling from great heights and never wanted to see that in real life. Out of all the horrific things Sean had witnessed, that was the one he dreaded most.

The precipice wasn't a sheer drop-off, at least not at the top. There were no vertical cliffs with thousand-foot falls, though there were certainly some long drops just below the natural landings that staggered the face of the hill. That fact was likely why he wasn't lying on his side in the fetal position. He recalled the staircase in Bhutan leading up to the Tiger Monastery. That journey had taken him nearly an hour to climb simply because he couldn't make his muscles work. Sean's fear of heights was very nearly paralyzing his one true weakness.

"Shall we?" Tommy broke the group's silence and motioned to the path wrapping around the tall rocks. A middle-aged Indian couple came around the turn, the woman had her long black hair pulled back into a ponytail and the man's wavy black hair was swept to one side. They were wearing jeans, T-shirts, and sneakers. Hardly equipped for a long day of hiking, but they appeared comfortable.

Sean straightened his legs and followed the others. He looked back over his shoulder at the trailhead, making certain no one was tailing them, but also because he didn't want to face the path ahead. From the looks of it, the trail leading to this temple cave went dangerously close to the edge, disappearing, in fact, onto the rocks, with visitors required to traverse the boulders to reach the destination.

Adriana lingered toward the rear to stay close to him. She reached out and wrapped her fingers around his hand and held him tight. "It'll be fine," she said. "Just stick with me."

A light breeze blew a loose strand of brown hair away from her head. The scent of her perfume washed over him once more. And for the shortest of moments, Sean was no longer afraid of heights. He could have fallen ten thousand feet in that instant and been fine.

The rest of the group fell into single file as they worked their way over a rounded boulder and around the curve in the rocks. They came to a flat area where several visitors were standing around looking out at the view. Some were taking pictures with their phones. Fewer had actual cameras, taking what they surely believed were professional-quality photographs.

As the procession rounded the turn, Sean got that queasy feeling in his gut again and leaned to the rocks on his right to keep his balance and stay focused. He couldn't help but think maybe he should have been the one to stay with the SUV down at the bottom.

Soon, though, the path veered away from the drop-off and toward the center of the mountain, where the gigantic pile of boulders rose up from the peak as if placed there by some enormous hand tens of thousands of years ago. The rocks were stacked haphazardly, some lying across others at sharp angles, others teetering horizontally, still more propped up vertically. How they'd gotten to this point in such a formation was simply fascinating.

Then Sean noticed the thing that was most out of place in this otherwise perfectly natural setting. A staircase, carved from indigenous stone, led up through a narrow passage in the rocks. The stairs were cut smooth, angled flawlessly, a clear piece of human engineering from the ancient past. How long ago they were built no one in the group was certain, but they were old. Everyone knew that much.

Priya trudged up the steep stairway, hugging the right side to allow other visitors by as they descended back from the mountaintop. Rays of light poked through huge cracks and holes between the boulders overhead. Tommy suddenly felt the very real sense that they were walking under hundreds of tons of loosely fit rocks.

The boulders had formed a natural tunnel of sorts. It was cooler along the path now that they were in the shade. The massive stones, too, worked as insulators, absorbing the heat of the sun on the top and dissipating it through their dense molecular structure so that underneath the temperature was easily five degrees cooler.

Bracing himself on the face of a boulder as his toe caught on one of the steps, Sean tripped, nearly falling forward into Tommy.

Adriana had shifted behind him to make him feel a little safer, though it did little since he also had to worry about her falling.

Once they were halfway up the steps and in the shadows, though, he could no longer see the long drop to the basin below, and his fear of being so high quickly evaporated.

"You okay?" Adriana asked.

He swallowed. "Yeah. Not seeing out there makes it better."

"And being under tons of heavy rock held up by nothing more than gravity doesn't frighten you?"

Sean chuckled. "Not as much as falling over a cliff."

The steps veered to the right and then back to the left until they reached a stopping point where another cluster of rocks was stacked. At the base, a stone doorway stood to greet visitors. The door frame was made from the same stone as the boulders surrounding it, with painted red lines along each side and across the header. The frame seemed to be holding up the entire structure if it could be called that.

"This is it," Priya said. She turned to face the other three and then continued inside.

Tommy appraised the rock formation and shook his head. "I have a very bad feeling about this."

"Relax," Sean said with a nudge in his friend's back. "If I can make it up to this point, you can go a little farther into some cave that could easily crush us at the hint of an earthquake."

Sean passed his friend and walked into the darker area beyond the threshold, followed by Adriana. She winked at him as she passed.

Tommy rolled his eyes. "And here I was trying to be nice to you about the whole fear-of-heights thing." The others disappeared inside, leaving him talking to himself.

He raised his hands and let them fall to his sides with a clap. "Fine."

The interior of the tunnel was half cave, half stone forest. Slivers between the rocks overhead provided streams of light that poured in and illuminated the meandering paths through the bizarre temple. There were larger holes, as well, that allowed thick rays of sunlight to splash onto the floor and the temple walls.

Everyone had to duck down, bending at the waist to make it through some of the low overhanging rocks inside the passage. There were sections, too, that were narrow, so much so that in a few places Sean and the others had to turn sideways to shuffle through.

"I have to say," Tommy said as he ducked under another rock overhang and made his way forward, "I've never been in a cave like this before."

Sean chuckled as he bent down to progress through the narrow gap in the rocks. "Yeah, a cave in the air. We've been in our fair share through the years, but nothing this high up. Not that I recall." He didn't say it, but Sean silently prayed they wouldn't have to explore another place like this again.

The passage opened suddenly to what appeared to be a large chamber. The rocks overhead had seemingly bent and molded themselves into a room where more ancient pillars adorned the walls. Paintings of various Hindu deities decorated the rocks. There were shrines cut into some of the hard surfaces where piles of melted wax told of when candles had burned in the past, possibly recently.

"Wow," Adriana said as she stood up straight and turned around to take in the sight. "It really is a temple in the clouds."

"Yes," Priya agreed. "This," she emphatically pointed at the floor, "this is the temple, the ancient home the riddle speaks of."

"You're sure?" Tommy asked. "I mean, I hope so because that was a long, difficult hike."

She nodded slowly. "This location is one of the oldest holy sites in the region. These paintings on the wall"—she pointed at something that appeared to be a rendering of one of the deities, but it was blobbed and almost shapeless—"these have been dated to the earlier Indus Valley civilizations. They predate the Tamils by thousands of years."

"So," Sean said, "this is one of the first places where Hindu religion was observed?"

"It wasn't the first, but definitely one of the earliest, yes. Hinduism originated in the north, near the Indus River."

"Good to know," Sean said. He had his hands on his hips and was looking up to the ceiling where a single hole in the rock formations allowed a beam of light to shine onto the floor. It reminded him of the oculus in the top of Rome's Pantheon.

"The question is," Tommy interrupted, "where is the lotus?"

Priya took in a deep breath and exhaled slowly. "That, Tommy, is where the work begins. I don't have a clue."

37

HAMPI

The four spread out in the vast space, each taking a quarter of the room to search for any sign of the lotus. There were flowers painted on the walls in different places. Some weren't paintings at all but carvings engraved into the stone underneath cutout recesses where stone idols sat waiting to be worshipped.

Sean turned on his phone light to get a little extra help and began scanning every inch of his territory.

The room's floor was mostly flat save for a few spots where huge slabs of rock had fallen at some time in the past. It was an unnerving thought to consider that could have happened at any time.

There were five other tourists in the chamber, all doing the same thing, more or less. They were happily inspecting the carvings, the wall paintings, and enjoying the experience of ancient architecture in the pillars and headers within the temple. Two of the visitors were taking selfies with their phone, the bright flash sending a streak of blinding light throughout the darkened chamber for a moment before it plunged back into relative darkness, broken only by the sun's rays shining through the gaps in the roof.

Sean kept sliding to his left, as did his companions. They closely inspected the surface of the boulders from floor to ceiling, but as he kept moving he realized there was probably nothing here that even closely resembled the lotus they were looking for. If it was a golden object, like the disc they'd found at the ruins in Kuldhara, they should have seen something by now, a hint to where the thing might be.

In Kuldhara, there'd been a tablet with strange writing and an odd indentation that told them something was within. Here, though, Sean and the others discovered nothing that would further their quest.

Sean reached the point where Adriana had begun a few minutes before. He stopped and turned around, looking back at the others. With hands in the air, he shrugged. "Anything?"

Tommy finished his section last and spun around. "Nothing. You?"

"No."

Adriana and Priya said the same.

Sean sighed. "Well, I found some stairs over in that corner, but it doesn't look like it goes anywhere."

A young woman, probably in her mid-twenties, looked over at Sean. She was wearing faded jeans, sneakers, and a white T-shirt. Her curly light brown hair dangled around her ears and grazed her shoulders. She had a happy look on her face, the kind of look people in their youth often wore because the world hadn't yet stolen away all their dreams. The jaded side of Sean called it naïveté, though maybe that was a tad on the hateful side.

"Oh, it goes somewhere. There's another chamber up at the top of the steps." The girl asked the question in a cheery voice that sounded both aloof and informative at the same time.

"What chamber?" Sean asked. He turned suddenly serious once more.

"Yeah," she said, her accent clearly English. "That back corner over there has more steps. You go up those and through another door. Takes you into a tiny little prayer room or something. Not sure what it was. I'm not big on Hinduism."

"Then why are you here?" Sean asked out of curiosity.

She shrugged. "I don't know. I like to travel, and some of my friends wanted to see this place. I'm always up for a little adventure."

"Ah. I see."

"Anyway, you guys seem like you're looking for something. Maybe it's in that room. What are you looking for?"

Sean narrowed his eyes. "A weapon of immense power." He decided the truth would throw the girl off enough that she'd shut up and leave him alone. Not that he didn't appreciate the information. He'd had no idea there was another room. "Thank you for your help," he added quickly.

He walked by the girl as she continued to stare into the space where he'd been standing a moment before. The look in her eyes showed she was trying to wrap her head around what he'd just said, and whether or not he was messing with her. By the time she decided he was joking, she spun around and saw him ascending the steps to the secret room.

"Be careful," she warned. "Those are slippery."

"Thank you," Sean said without looking back.

Adriana and the others glanced over to the corner as Sean disappeared through the dark entrance at the top of the short staircase.

He shined his light ahead, quickly realizing that this new area had no natural light source of its own. Sean had to bend down a little to get through the short arch in the doorway. His boots slid a little on the smooth surface of stone beneath his feet, proving true what the girl back in the main chamber had said about it being slippery. He wasn't sure why that would be since the area was mostly dry and hot, with relative humidity being low. Sean pressed his hand against the rock wall to his left, leaning into it with his elbow, and kept going.

The passage from the stairs was short, only fifteen feet or so before it opened into another circular room. Sean spun around in a circle, flashing his light on the walls as he gazed into the hollowed-out rock.

The space was a cone, shaped much like the stupas in the valley below, and like others, he'd seen before in other countries. This rose to a ceiling about twenty feet above. Sean panned the entire chamber, spinning in circles more than once until he'd inspected every inch of the area surrounding him.

He was surprised to find the walls bare, with nothing carved into them, and no paintings as he'd seen downstairs in the other room. If this was a temple, it was a simple one, built with minimalistic design in mind.

Then, as his eyes drifted downward, he realized what it truly was. Sean saw the indentation in the floor. There was no doubt as to what it could be. This upper level was no temple. It was a tomb.

He took a careful step forward, head turning side to side to make sure he didn't miss something that could fall and hit him or that he would trip on, and moved into the center of the room where a long rectangular indentation was cut into the floor. It was covered in dirt, packed hard by the centuries but dry and untouched by weather.

Who could have been buried up here in this place? They must have been someone of extreme importance to deserve such an honor. Just carrying the body up the mountain would have been an incredibly difficult and strenuous feat.

Then there was tradition. Sean knew his history, knew a good deal about other cultures but was he mistaken in recalling that most Hindu burials were cremations? Or was that only for certain castes of society?

That last thought caused him to wonder if he was truly looking at a gravesite or if there might be something else buried beneath his feet.

He glanced back over his shoulder, but there was no sign of the others. Maybe they were engaged back in the main room. The temple had grown quiet, too quiet for his liking. The darkness seemed to envelop him, save for the pale white beam blazing from his phone.

Sean bent down to one knee and dug a finger into the earth. He found it was pliable and scraped away a small trench. Again, he looked back over his shoulder, this time concerned some local official would be standing behind him, ready to arrest him for disturbing an ancient historical site.

He cupped his hand and used the bridge of it to scrape away more dirt. This second layer was harder, but he was still able to move some of it, creating a wider ditch.

Sean stood up again, satisfied he could work with this, and set down his gear bag. He unzipped the secondary pouch and fished out his hunting knife. The gray handle contrasted with the black coating over the steel blade within the sheath, but he did not intend to dull his knife in the dirt. The sheath would work just fine.

He knelt down in the center of the rectangular indentation and started scraping away at the surface, working faster now that he had at least a minimal tool for the job.

It was much easier than using his hands, and the dirt moved readily under the hard edge of the sheath. He was glad he'd not replaced the factory one with a new leather one, which would have likely been too soft for this particularly odd job.

Sean kept digging, occasionally wiping his forehead with the back of his hand as the temperature in the room seemed to increase the harder he worked. He knew that wasn't the case. It was his temperature that was climbing, but he was fine with that. Five minutes into the job, he hit something solid in the center of the little pit and froze. He glanced back over his shoulder, now more concerned that his friends hadn't come up to join him or at least to see what he was doing.

He sighed and looked back into the hole he'd made. The edge of something was poking out through the surface. Was it a bone, a piece of a skeleton buried here long ago? Or was it something else?

Sean swallowed and decided to dig a little more. He dug faster with renewed vigor, scraping away the layers of dirt until he saw more clearly what his scabbard had initially struck.

He held his light closer to the object; the yellow glint from it sparkled in the darkness. There was no mistaking it. There was gold buried here, but why?

He brushed aside more of it and took in the entire object. It was propped in the folded hands of a sarcophagus sculpture. Sean couldn't see the rest of the figure, but the hands were large with long, thick fingers cradling the golden object with palms turned up.

Sean leaned close and dared to touch the object, pinching one of the petals between thumb and forefinger. He pulled gently, worried that even the slightest disturbance would break the delicate-looking object.

He put the phone in his mouth and clamped down on it with his teeth to keep the light on the golden flower. Then he used his free hand to steady the base of it as he pulled it away from the sarcophagus.

Once the object was free, Sean took the phone out of his mouth, thankful the flower had come away so easily since his jaw was quickly starting to hurt. He held the device in one hand again and inspected the surface of the flower. The petals were delicately crafted, mimicking a real lotus with elegant curves, intricately carved details, and a gold that must have been as pure as anything produced in modern refineries. In the center of the flower, more Sanskrit was inscribed on the yellow surface.

Sean didn't know much of the ancient language. Tommy had studied it when they were in school together, but even his grasp of it was sketchy, hence allowing Priya to translate for them.

He frowned. Where was Priya? And the others?

Sean stood up and spun around. He'd sensed someone approaching despite hearing nothing unusual. He'd been trained to know when he was being followed when there was a threat coming his way. It had been ingrained in him, and now his senses were telling him something was wrong, very wrong. He'd been alone too long, far too long for his liking. Normally, Sean wouldn't be unnerved by that. He was accustomed to being by himself in all kinds of situations. At the moment, however, he wished one of the others in his group would appear in the tomb's doorway.

Surely, one of them would have been curious enough to see what he was up to. The fact that no one had come up only served to heighten the growing concern in his mind.

Sean cursed himself for leaving the others in the first chamber, embarking on his own to investigate something he thought curious.

He looked back at the floor where he'd discovered the grave and the golden lotus, glanced down at the object, and then decided to see what was going on back down below.

There were no sounds of scurrying around, a struggle, nothing that would have immediately concerned him. However, the lack of anyone talking at all also caused him to worry.

Sean hurried back over to the entrance and poked his head through. There were a few lights dancing on the floor and walls below, though all he could see was their deformed circles moving back and forth. That was a good sign. His friends were probably just being reverent in an ancient place of worship.

Then he considered what he was holding in his hands and decided it was probably best if other visitors didn't see it.

He set down his tactical bag, opened up a pouch that was roughly the size of the golden lotus—about five inches in diameter—and carefully slid it inside. He secured it with a bandanna to give the object a little cushion and then lifted the bag and slung it over his shoulder.

He was about to step out of the doorway when two bright lights flashed in his eyes. Instinctively, he raised one hand to shield his vision from the blinding glow.

"Whoa, you mind shining those somewhere else, like not in my face?"

"Don't move." The order came from a voice with a heavy accent. It was definitely Far Eastern, but which country wasn't immediately clear. The words were sharp. Even though the other person had spoken only two words, it was enough to put a region to the accent.

Sean stayed perfectly still for a moment, his hands remaining close to his face.

"Put your hands over your head." The man was almost yelling now. His voice echoed through the cave, bouncing off the walls in a harsh pitch.

"Take it easy," Sean said. His thoughts initially went to his friends in the chamber below. Were they okay? What had these people done to them?

Then the next thought was of the lotus in his backpack. They would go through his bag. That much was certain. They'd find the golden object and take it. More than likely, that was why these men were here.

Sean raised his hands slowly. He made out the faint outline of a submachine gun in the guy's hands; the make and model weren't immediately clear, though he thought he recognized it. It had to be a Type 05. The unique curve of the rear-fitted magazine, the forward grip, the muzzle break—he could glimpse all of that in the corona of the man's beam. It was a newer weapon, one that had largely replaced many of the old models used by police and military in that part of the world.

That fact gave away exactly where this guy was from and who he worked for, although Sean had already come to that conclusion before seeing the weapon. It was the only thing that made sense, at least in his mind. Based on the prior incident on the road from Kuldhara, he knew precisely what had happened. While Sean believed they'd eliminated the threat from China, that apparently wasn't the case. He considered the weapon holstered at his side, but there was no chance he'd even get the thing out of its sheath before being cut down by this highly trained killer. He'd be dead before he hit the ground. The MSS had found them, tracked them somehow, and now Sean and his friends were their prisoners.

38

SHANGHAI

Brock hovered by the railing with his palms pressed against the cold metal, fingers wrapped around the curved steel. He stared out the window at the sprawling city below with a look of satisfaction on his face.

Heather was next to him, arms crossed and a foot farther away from the glass that ran the length of the wall to give visitors a full view of the city from the observation deck. Four men in black stood a dozen feet behind them on the stairs leading to another platform. Tre was one of them, watching the entrances and exits with hawk-like eyes. The other three were handpicked by him, mercs he knew he could count on, brothers that had served with him in half a dozen tours all over the world. They'd been in the thick of it, done things that would give softer soldiers nightmares and send them spiraling into the throes of PTSD. Not Tre, and not these guys. They were hardened to the point of monsters, and that was exactly what Tre wanted by his side when things got real.

In 2015, the Shanghai Tower had surpassed the one in Dubai for the title of highest observation deck in the world. The building reached an astounding 2,076 feet into the air, often photographed stretching high above the clouds during the more humid parts of the year. The tower included 106 elevators and lifts capable of reaching speeds of up to 46 miles per hour. While the structure was the second-tallest building in the world, it was hardly second rate. The swooping, curved designs allowed high winds to slide over the surface and peel off the other side, an important consideration when building something 128 stories tall.

One of the more fascinating pieces of the structure was that it was a building within a building. The core was wrapped by a shell of steel and glass that spiraled into the sky. Designed in cooperation with an American architectural firm as well as a renowned Chinese architect, Shanghai Tower was a wonder to behold for anyone visiting the city —whether for the first time or the hundredth.

Brock watched the cars on the streets far below as they zipped back and forth about their day. People going to or from work, running errands, or simply out for some fun. They had no idea what was about to happen to him. He couldn't help but feel like he was standing on the cusp of something incredible, history about to be made, the likes of which the world had never seen except for stories from myth and legend.

Tens of millions of people were about to die, and they all had it coming.

Sure, there were probably some innocents down there among the ants running around on the streets and sidewalks. But that's how life worked. Innocent people died sometimes. And when it was for a good cause, did that really make their deaths senseless or in vain? He thought not.

Shanghai was one of the worst offenders when it came to polluting the sea, the air, and the Earth itself. Every single day, enormous volumes of garbage were piled up in vast landfills or dumped into the water. There was no telling how many species of land and water animals had been lost as a result of this single city's reckless disregard for the planet.

How many citizens had lost their livelihoods, just as his parents had when the oil spill in the gulf had ripped everything from them?

He knew it wasn't a small number.

Fishing villages along the coast had suffered through the years. Some of the fish managed to survive but were too toxic for consumption, which meant the fishermen had to go farther for an untainted catch. Doing so resulted in lower profits for them and a lesser quality of life for those who were already barely scraping by.

But their suffering would soon be over. Brock would see to that. Thirty million people were about to be thrown into a cauldron of chaos the likes of which they could have never imagined.

His only regret was that he couldn't hit the entire city in one strike. Adam and Elma had deduced that the effective pulse range of the Trishula was only around a thousand yards. After that, the frequency it discharged faded and didn't have the same effect. A few people might notice something in their heads, a strange misfire of a synapse or something, but would likely not fall prey to the schizophrenia that gripped those closer to the weapon.

It was no matter. All he needed to do was light the match. After that, tens of thousands of people in this densely populated area would go insane, all obeying the same repetitive command in their minds telling them to kill.

Maybe thirty million people wouldn't die. Perhaps it would only be a million or two, but that was a good start. And just when things started to settle down, he'd hit his next target. He'd already chosen it, though he hadn't yet told Heather or the other members of his team. He wanted it to be a surprise. Why? He didn't know. Call it the mischievous part of him. Or perhaps it was the drama he enjoyed. He was an actor, after all. He liked to keep secrets and build suspense, even if it was just for his own pleasure.

"Quite the view, isn't it?" Brock said abruptly. He gazed out at the city, the mega skyscrapers, the giant apartment buildings, the businesses, the waterways cutting through sections of the city filled with boats that teetered back and forth, the lush green mountains that hugged the city in their embrace, wrapping around them like a blanket of forest.

"Yeah," Heather agreed, "it sure is something. Shame it's going to be burning tomorrow."

Brock snorted derisively. "There's no shame about it. Cities like this are a testament to both the ingenuity of humans as well as their careless disregard for what they're doing to the world when they create it."

She nodded. "There's that."

Heather cared about his mission—or whatever he called it. Not as much as Brock, but she did believe in it. Her unspoken reason, the true purpose behind her helping him, however, was far darker.

She'd seen the things humans were capable of at every level. She'd been abused as a child, in almost every conceivable way. It had hardened her against men for a long time. And it caused her to detest the weakness of women who allowed it, women like her mother.

There were times when her mother had sat in the corner sobbing while her father would beat her. Heather knew her mother could hear it when Uncle Johnny came over and wanted to spend some alone time with the little girl. For a long time, Heather was a broken toy, a shattered young woman who flinched whenever a boy so much as brushed against her in the hall at school.

That all changed one fateful day when she'd finally had enough. She was walking home from school, her junior year in high school, when she heard a strange noise coming from under the bleachers of the football stadium.

It sounded like someone was in a fight. One of the voices was a girl's accompanied by the distinct sound of a guy telling her to shut up.

She veered off the path and found one of the boys from the high school team on top of one of the cheerleaders. She was telling him over and over again to stop.

Heather faced the demons of her childhood that day, seeing her weak mother, her violent father, her wretched uncle, all of them at once.

She'd noticed a piece of rebar propped up against one of the bleacher supports a few feet away. Her thoughts had gone back and forth from the imminent sexual assault to the hunk of metal.

Heather dropped her bag and picked up the rebar. She stalked over to the two on the ground. The girl's clothes were nearly all ripped off at that point. He was tugging at her underwear and had already pulled his own pants down.

He noticed Heather approaching out of the corner of his eye and warned her to get away, to leave them alone, that it was none of her business.

In a moment that changed her forever, she ignored him, stepped forward, and swung the rebar as hard as she could. The dense metal rod struck him in the temple. The boy fell over onto his side. His body started twitching. His eyes rolled back into his head, and then he went still.

The girl screamed as she saw the boy stop moving. Her eyes darted back and forth to Heather and then to him.

"Shut up," Heather had said. "Get your things and get out of here."

"You...you killed him." The girl trembled in disbelief.

Heather wasn't sure about that. Her intentions hadn't been to kill him. As he continued to lie there on the rocky surface, unmoving, she realized that was a growing possibility.

"You killed him!" The girl was screaming now. "Why did you kill him?"

Heather turned to her and stared into her eyes with disbelief. This idiot was upset about a rapist being murdered? "He was trying to rape you," she'd said.

"I loved him."

Heather couldn't believe the girl's response. It sickened her, made her think of her mother, so weak and cowardly. What was it about these women who allowed men to do whatever they wanted to them?

Anger bubbled up inside of her. It was a rage greater than she'd ever felt toward her father, maybe even toward her uncle. Women like this were just as much of the problem in Heather's mind. Her mother never tried to stop what happened, never had the courage. Heather had no intention of letting this weakling allow that to happen to another child someday. She looked into this cheerleader's future and saw it as plain as day. She'd be just like her mom.

The rebar swung itself repeatedly until the cheerleader, too, lay motionless. Heather didn't fully realize what had happened until she looked down at her hands, dirty with rust and black metal residue. She glanced at one body and then the other, then dropped the rebar and ran away.

She'd spent days, weeks, wondering if the cops would ever pin the murders on her, but they never did. They called it a crime of passion but never found the jealous suspect. The case went cold after a few years. There were no witnesses, no one to betray Heather's actions.

She realized soon after that other than the fear of being caught, she felt no remorse, no emotions whatsoever at the killings. In a strange way, she felt...good about it. The only thing that resembled the smallest pinch of guilt was about the girl. She'd been innocent, but Heather knew that would change as she grew older. She'd have allowed her children to experience the same things Heather had, and that was unacceptable. It was appalling. She wouldn't tolerate that.

Going into the military had sharpened her skills, forged her into a weapon. When she got out of the service and went into private contracts, she'd had no idea an opportunity like this would present itself. Yet here it was. Brock Carson, a world-famous actor, was giving her a chance to help punish humanity for their sins. While his justice was for other atrocities, she could enjoy it just as much for her own reasons.

She looked out over the city of Shanghai, knowing there were thousands, hundreds of thousands of people, maybe millions who were just like her father, her mother, that football player, that cheerleader. She would purge the earth of them and in doing so build a stronger civilization where those things didn't happen anymore. Women could be strong. Men would be honorable. Or maybe they wouldn't. Maybe none of that would happen. As long as she made them all pay, she was satisfied.

And if a few billion people happened to die along the way, so be it. They were no less innocent than her mother, bystanders letting it happen right in front of their eyes without a Good Samaritan in sight.

"When are we going to do it?" Heather asked. Her voice was calm, unemotional as if she was asking when they were going to call an exterminator to get rid of a rodent problem.

Brock turned to her, a cryptic smirk on his face. "When would you like to do it?"

Oddly, he was the only guy that ever treated her like a superior. He'd given her opportunities, true enough, but the thing that endeared Brock to Heather was a kind of respect that she'd never felt before. She loved him for it and would go to the ends of the earth for him because of how he'd treated her.

Once more, he was giving her the reins, letting her make the call as he'd done so many times in the past. Maybe he was afraid of her. Maybe he simply knew that she was intelligent with tactical decisions. Or perhaps he simply wanted to give her a taste of revenge that he knew she so badly wanted.

"First thing Monday morning. People will be on their way to work. The streets will be packed. That will give us the most bang for our buck."

His smile broadened. "Excellent, though...that's still two days away. No matter; you're right. That will give us the biggest bang. And it will give us time to make sure we have everything prepared. Let's get set up and ready for Monday morning, then." Brock stepped over to her and placed a hand on each shoulder, gazing into her eyes. A loose strand of brown hair dangled over one of her ears, and he brushed it back. "Soon, they'll all pay for what they've done."

She nodded. "Yes. I've waited a long time for this."

39

HAMPI

The skin on Sean's wrists stung from the plastic zip ties digging in, rubbing the flesh raw in seconds.

The MSS agent behind shoved him down the last two steps, and he stumbled forward into a cool, dry room. He tripped in the darkness, lost his footing, and crashed hard onto the floor, his shoulder hitting with a painful thud. He was lucky he didn't hit his head or face. Still, he grimaced from the impact. Concrete, definitely concrete.

His first instinct was a snappy comment that would have, in all likelihood, pissed off the Chinese agents and resulted in some kind of threat or punishment, but due to the overwhelming confusion at the situation and the pain in his shoulder, he kept his mouth shut, thinking better of it until he could get a handle on things.

He wriggled around and tried to sit up, but another agent in black stepped over to him and dangled a pistol over his head, letting the barrel waver back and forth, not that Sean could see it.

Suddenly, the hood over his head was ripped away. He blinked furiously for several seconds, trying to acclimate to the bright lights in this new place. His eyes darted around, taking in the setting. There were several lights dangling from various places in a cracked ceiling.

The air was dusty, with a smell of the past such as he'd detected in abandoned or condemned buildings, dilapidated structures and sheds that hadn't been used in a long time. As the blurriness in his vision began to subside, Sean took in his surroundings, becoming quickly aware of where they were and who was there.

They were in a basement. Based on the time spent in their captors' vehicles, he guessed they hadn't left the region. The drive had only taken twenty minutes. Sean guessed they were close to Hampi, perhaps in a larger town, but not far from the ancient temple sites.

Once he was caught, they'd bound his hands and yanked a hood down over his head. He heard the agents telling tourists that he and his friends were terrorists and that they were being arrested. How anyone believed that a bunch of Chinese MSS agents had jurisdiction in a remote Indian settlement was beyond Sean, but he supposed their weapons bought them just as much validity as any badge ever could.

Tommy, Adriana, and Priya were on their knees, lined up next to the wall to Sean's left. Two agents were standing guard over them with weapons ready to cut them down at a moment's notice if the prisoners tried anything foolish. Sean wondered about the wisdom of firing the weapons in this place. The guns were equipped with silencers, but even with those attached, it could get loud in a room surrounded by cinder block walls. Not only that, a stray shot could ricochet dangerously around the room and hit an unintended target. Unlikely, but still a thought.

Sean knew that MSS agents were highly trained, just as he was. They were, in many cases, the front line of defense—and often, offense—for the Chinese government and military. It was preferable to use their talents and skill sets as opposed to waging an all-out war, especially when the latter could result in financial catastrophe for the burgeoning nation.

A figure in the corner caught Sean's eye. It was a woman dressed in black, like the others, but in this case, a business suit. She was the Chinese version of Sean's friend Emily Starks, clearly the one in charge of this operation if not the director of the MSS itself. He doubted the latter could be true. Someone of that station wouldn't be out here in the field dealing with a few Americans looking for an ancient artifact. Or would they?

The more that strange things happened in this case, the more Sean's belief in the Gada grew. The mere fact that the Chinese intelligence agency was here was proof enough that even they believed.

Sean remained on his side, staring at the woman he figured to be the one calling the shots. In his mind, he chuckled at the pun. He hoped whoever she was, she wouldn't actually call for shots. Dying in a basement somewhere in India wasn't what he had planned for this mission.

She gave a nod, and a firm hand grasped him by the shirt and hauled him up, propping him on his knees.

The smart aleck in him couldn't be held back any longer. He turned his head and looked at the man who'd picked him up, also likely the guy who'd shoved him down the stairs.

"See? You have to clean up your messes. Let that be a lesson to you. Don't shove people downstairs unless you're going to help them up after."

The man appeared puzzled by the comment but said nothing, taking a step back and pointing his pistol at Sean's head.

"Good to see your sense of humor is still on point, Mr. Wyatt." The woman spoke in a cool tone, but it wasn't the sound of her voice that spooked Sean. It was the notion that she knew who he was.

That shouldn't have been shocking to him. He was on many hit lists around the world. There were likely, at any given time, two or three dozen people looking for him to exact revenge for one offense or another from his past. Why should the Chinese be excluded?

"I'm sorry," Sean said, "I don't believe we've met. I'm Sean Wyatt, as you apparently already know, but I didn't catch your name."

He twisted around and mocked extending his hand to shake hers.

She shook her head.

"I didn't give my name."

"No, but I figure you will. You're MSS, right? Sorry for the agents we killed in the desert. That what this is about?"

The woman stepped forward, hands folded behind her back. From his vantage point, it was difficult to tell how tall she was, but he guessed around five feet four inches. Her silky black hair was pulled back into a tight bun. She wore matching black glasses, though they could have been just for appearances, so thin were the lenses.

She stopped three feet away from him and looked down.

Tommy, Adriana, and Priya were watching from the other side of the room. Sean stole a glance at them. None of them appeared to have been tortured—not yet, at least. That would happen before long, though, which meant he needed to find a way out of this mess. These agents weren't the kind to make mistakes.

He'd had a run-in with an MSS operative once before. They were both after the same target, luckily, but Sean had noted the impeccable methods used by the other asset. The man had been ruthless, cunning, and when it came to finishing the job, he'd taken the shot when he had to without a second thought. It had always bothered Sean a little that he hadn't been the one to take out the target. That was the competitive side of him. Now, he didn't care. In fact, he was glad he hadn't done it. One more soul haunting the notches on his belt was something he didn't need, no matter how wretched a person they might have been.

"My name is not important, Mr. Wyatt. The fact that you killed some of my assets is neither here nor there. While I'm not happy about it, that is not why we have you here, in this room." She waved a hand around in a twirl before placing it back with the other behind her waist.

"No? You brought us here to ask us stupid questions and then shoot us?"

"There are no such things as stupid questions, Sean," Tommy said with a chuckle. "Stupid people who ask questions, sure, but no stupid questions."

Sean snorted a laugh. "Yeah, he's right. My bad."

She narrowed her eyes, and he could tell the woman was tempted to slap him. Sean and Tommy always dealt with life-or-death situations like this one in the only way they knew how: with laughter. That old saying about having to laugh so you wouldn't cry had been a valuable tool throughout the years.

"You were a government agent before, weren't you?" She stood up straight after asking the question. "Which agency...escapes me, but you worked for the United States in some kind of covert capacity." Her accent, while clearly Chinese, wasn't as flawed as many he'd come across. She spoke clearly, cohesively, and with more than enough menace in her tone to get the point across that she wasn't amused.

"We've all had lots of jobs over the course of this life," he said. "You never know who did what."

"I know," she said. "I know you took many lives in your service. I know that you were once a dangerous man. It took us a long time to figure out who you were, but there was no mistaking it when I saw you this time around. The Southern Ghost, they called you. I never really cared much for the moniker. I don't think giving the enemy nicknames does anything but heighten their legend, which can make an agent sloppy if a confrontation arises."

"You're right to think that." Sean kept it to himself that he thought the nickname was pretty corny, yet cool at the same time. "What do you want with us? Why were your men following us?"

"That, Mr. Wyatt, is a question best answered by someone else."

Sean scrunched his forehead, caught off guard by the answer. Did that mean she wasn't the one in charge of this little operation?

A door opened directly in front of Sean, and another figure was marched in. The man didn't have his hands tied, though he was clearly a prisoner like the rest of them. He had dark brown skin that looked almost gray in some places. His black hair also had streaks of gray in it. While he was probably in his sixties, he didn't look older than forty-five.

"Ishaan?" Priya said abruptly. Her voice was full of both relief and concern. "What are you doing here?"

Sean frowned. "Dr. Patel?"

The man nodded. "Yes." He turned to Priya. "Hello, my dear." There was a sadness in his voice.

"What is going on?" Priya demanded. "Why did you take him?"

The woman in the black suit snorted a derisive laugh. "We didn't take him," she said. "He came to us."

40

HAMPI

"What are you talking about?" Priya roared. "Let us go! Let him go!"

One of the guards moved closer to her, brandishing his weapon. She quickly quieted down.

Patel drew a deep breath and sighed. "They didn't take me, Priya," he said. "Not initially, at least," he added with a degree of venom. "I went to the Chinese government for help."

"Why on earth would you do that?" Tommy asked.

Next, to him, Adriana was staring down the nearest gunman, probing him for a weakness that was not easily revealed.

Patel turned to the Chinese woman. "Is this really necessary?" He motioned to the others. "They're not going anywhere. You took their weapons. They are here to help."

"They killed my men," the woman said. "By all rights, I should execute all four of them. Maybe even you. So far, you've presented no evidence of what you claim."

"Evidence?" Sean asked. "What evidence? What is this about?"

Patel swallowed. "I'm sure this is all very confusing."

"You're right, Ishaan. It is!" Priya shouted. "I thought you were dead or kidnapped. Instead, I find out you went to the Chinese for help!"

He put up both hands and lowered them repeatedly to get her to calm down. "I know how it looks. Please, just listen."

"You know how it looks? Because it looks like you sold us out, Ishaan."

"I didn't sell you out!" He raised his voice to overcome hers. "I found an artifact."

She calmed down for a moment. Her breathing, however, was still coming in quick bursts. "What artifact?"

He nodded and licked his lips. "I found the seashell of Vishnu."

The room fell silent as though a bomb had gone off and everyone was waiting for the fallout.

"The what?"

"I left...a few weeks ago, remember? When I said I was going out of town for a few days to investigate something?"

Priya flipped through her memories. It didn't take long to recall that one. "Yes. Are you telling me you left the dig site to go look for something else?"

"That's exactly what I'm telling you. I found a clue at the site. I thought it was nothing and figured I'd be back in a couple of days. No big deal. You and Lidia do a good job of managing everything when I have to go somewhere. So, I knew the dig was in capable hands."

He paused to catch his breath. "I found the seashell down on the coast, in a cave."

"This shell," Tommy interrupted, "is it made out of gold?"

Patel answered with an emphatic nod. "Yes. Pure gold. And there's a riddle engraved on it, in Sanskrit. It speaks of a mountain home, a place where only the gods can go and where the purest of heart may tread. It also says that the mountain cannot be climbed by mortal men and that death awaits any who try to reach the top."

"Almost sounds like whoever hid that seashell doesn't want anyone trying to find the final destination."

"Or that is the final destination," Sean quipped.

"Why?" Priya asked. "Why did you go to the Chinese after you found this shell?"

Patel exhaled through his nose. "Because, Priya, I fear that the mountain in question lies partially in Tibet, in the Himalayas."

"Tibet?" Sean asked. "So, you figured out where the Gada is?"

"I wasn't sure. That's why I left clues for Priya. And I see that she found some of the best historical sleuths around to help."

"I brought them in to help me find you, Ishaan. I can't believe you were fine."

"You sound unhappy about that."

She shook her head. "It's not that. I just...I was worried."

"I understand. But I'm fine. I went to the Chinese because I wanted to go through the proper legal channels, especially if your findings confirmed my suspicions. I also knew that according to the riddles we would need the five pieces to access this shrine on the mountain."

"Which mountain?" Sean asked.

"It's called Mount Kailash," Patel answered. "It isn't as high as Everest, but it's formidable and has been declared unclimbable by many experts."

"Nothing is unclimbable. There is a world of idiots out there who I'm sure would love to give it a crack." Sean spat the words. He'd never understood people who tried to get their jollies by tempting fate in high places. Not him. He's had enough thrills to last a lifetime, and if he didn't he could always go to an amusement park or get on the back of one of his motorcycles.

"No," Patel said, "this is a holy mountain. It is unclimbable because the gods made it so. No one has dared try it, and no one will. Thousands of people go there every year on a pilgrimage. They walk around the holy mountain, reciting prayers along the way. Most believe the walk should be done in one day."

"Sounds exhausting," Tommy said.

"It is. And it is rejuvenating. I've done it." He paused for a moment. "The mountain isn't only holy to Hindus. Buddhists, too, hold it as a sacred place. There is no question that this mountain is special. If two different religions believe that, then it is unlikely a coincidence."

"That's also hardly a scientific deduction." Tommy tried not to sound rude, but he couldn't help it. Just because there were a bunch of people who believed the same thing didn't make it true. There were, after all, millions of people who had believed the earth was flat at one point in time.

"That's fair," Patel said. "You're correct in saying that. I would say the same thing if I hadn't seen what happened."

Sean's head twitched to the side. "What are you talking about?"

"The attack in southern India, the one the media is calling a terrorist attack."

Sean kept his lips tight. He knew what had actually happened there, but he wasn't about to show his hand. Not yet, at least. He wanted to make sure this guy was on the up and up, not secretly working for the Chinese.

"Surely, you saw it on the news or heard about it?"

"We heard," Adriana spoke for the first time since arriving in the basement. "We also know the truth."

Patel's eyes narrowed. "You know the truth? The truth the media would have you believe?"

She shook her head. "We know about the Trishula. We know it was taken from the temple and used on the guards."

"So, you know what it's capable of."

Heads nodded.

"The Gada is the only weapon that can counter it," Patel said. "Once I found out someone was trying to find the Trishula, I knew there was something more to it and if that weapon was ever discovered there could be only one way to stop it."

"Hold on a second," Sean said. "You said someone was trying to find the Trishula. How did you know that?" He made no attempt to hide the suspicion in his voice.

"A man," Patel said and then swallowed, "a man from America approached me about it. I...I knew who he was, so I didn't think anything of it at first. I figured he was trying to work on a plot for a movie or something."

"Movie?" Tommy wondered.

"Yes, this man is a famous actor. He...he called, asked if he could come by the dig site to ask a few questions."

"So, someone from Hollywood flew all the way to India to meet with you?"

"I suppose so."

"You didn't think, oh, I don't know, that was a little odd?" Tommy's voice rose and echoed around the room.

"I did. But I was willing to meet with him anyway. Initially, he did say it was for a movie. It was only later that I realized his intentions were less than scrupulous. He started the conversation innocently enough, asking about what we were looking for at the site, what we'd found so far. I didn't tell him about the clue to the seashell. I never mentioned it to anyone until I found it. Eventually, he got around to the real reason he was there. By that time, I could tell all the other stuff was small talk. His body language, his eyes, all of it suggested he didn't care about anything else other than the trident of Shiva, the Trishula."

"And what did he say?"

"He said he'd found a clue that led him to believe he knew the location of the Trishula, that it was hidden in the golden temple in the forbidden vault."

"And he wanted you to get him access to it from the Indian government," Sean said, connecting the dots. "He figured a prominent archaeologist like you could rub the right shoulders and get him in to have a look around. Then, once he was inside, he could steal the thing and walk with it."

Patel seemed a little dazed. "Yes...yes, something like that. When I realized he was serious about finding the trident, I...I didn't know what to do. So, I did the only thing I could think of."

"You told him you had no pull with the government."

"That's right," Patel admitted. "I lied to him. The truth is, I do have a little influence, but I doubt I would have been able to get anyone into the forbidden vault. It's been protected by the government for more than a hundred years."

"So, he left? Just walked away and accepted your answer?"

"I knew that the guy was serious. He had no intention of simply letting this idea go. He had men with him. And a woman, too. She appeared to be the head of his security force."

"Private security. This guy must be a heavyweight in Los Angeles."

"He is."

Sean put the rest of the puzzle pieces together. "So, this guy leaves you and goes to the temple, breaks in, takes the Trishula, and uses it on the guards there. They go nuts, kill each other, and he and his cohorts manage to slip out of the country."

"Yes," Patel said. "That's exactly what happened."

"This actor," Tommy said, "he got a name, or you just going to keep us in the dark about that, too?"

Patel's head swiveled back and forth. "Of course, I was going to tell you his name. You'll know who he is. He's one of the most prominent actors in the world. The man who approached me is Brock Carson."

Sean's head spun. "Brock Carson?"

Patel nodded. "Yes. The very same."

"I don't believe it. Why in the world would he do something like this? I know actors can be a little cuckoo sometimes, but a heist like that? He has everything in the world he could ever want."

"It wasn't about the money," Adriana said. Everyone in the room turned to her. "Reports suggested nothing of financial value was taken. And he didn't steal the Trishula because he wanted something new for his collection of rare artifacts and relics. If that was the case, he wouldn't have discharged it."

"What is his purpose, then?" the Chinese commander demanded. "Why are we here? I lost good agents because of all this. I want answers, or I will have you all executed. Starting with you, Dr. Patel."

She pulled a pistol out of a holster and pointed it at his head.

The man was clearly not accustomed to having a gun pointed at him. He quivered. Sean could see his legs trembling as he put up his hands. "Please, I...I don't know everything."

"What does this man want with that relic?"

Sean had already been thinking about it. He knew the story behind Brock Carson's rise to fame. He was actually one of Sean's favorite actors. He loved the kinds of movies Brock did. They were full of action, humor, and they didn't take themselves too seriously. All of the memories of those films faded away.

Sean recalled the story about how Brock came from the Florida Panhandle, not far from Destin and Fort Walton Beach, just across the state line if he remembered correctly. Brock was the son of a fisherman, and his family had been devastated by the oil disaster that polluted the beaches, killed wildlife, and wrecked so many livelihoods. Somehow, Brock had emerged from all of that to become a mega-successful star. There was something tragic, though: seemed like his father committed suicide or something. Sean couldn't recall exactly, but he knew there was a tragedy in there. Could that be the motive? Why else would Brock Carson want an ancient relic with the power to wreak havoc on the world?

"We need to find him," Sean said.

The woman with the pistol looked down at him. "Why?"

"You heard what happened?" Sean spoke fast, knowing his life and the lives of his friends could hang in the balance. "This thing... this weapon, it can force people to kill each other. I have information, information from a high-ranking government official that this was no terrorist attack. Brock Carson used the trident. It sent out some kind of...frequency that manipulated the brain waves of the victims. It altered their thoughts. They started killing each other. Do a little digging. You'll find out I'm telling the truth." He leveled his gaze. "You have to trust me."

"Trust you? You killed my men. I should end this right now."

"You heard Dr. Patel," Sean urged. "He knows where the Gada is. It's the only weapon that can fight this thing. It alone can neutralize whatever Brock is planning, and unless I miss my guess, it's revenge."

She took convincing. "Pfft. Revenge? He's done nothing to China. He has no reason to."

Sean shook his head. "Think about it. Brock Carson is a huge advocate for the environment. His dad's life came to an end because of what happened with the drilling accident in the gulf. Maybe... maybe he wants to wage a war against humanity, rid the planet of people. There are nut jobs like that out there. And China hasn't exactly been the best environmental steward in the world. You've done your fair share of polluting, as have most nations."

"You're stalling. And I'm tired of this." She pulled back the hammer on the pistol. Her finger tensed on the trigger.

"Run a scan," Tommy blurted.

"What?" She turned her head away from Sean for a second.

"A weapon like that will have an enormous energy signature. It probably has to be charged or something."

"He's right," Sean added. "To put out a frequency in a big enough radius would require a significant amount of power. The witness who survived the incident at the temple said the thieves were wearing golden helmets and that they were unaffected. But the pulse went out over a pretty wide swath. Most people were asleep at the time, but there were a few other stray cases of people experiencing the same symptoms throughout that part of the city. If I had to guess, that weapon is probably putting out a significant magnetic signature of some kind. I know your government has the sensors and tech in place to find something like that. Just run the scan and see what you come up with."

"This is ridiculous. Your time is up."

"Fine. Imagine that thing going off in your most populated cities. Have any relatives in Beijing? Hong Kong? Shanghai?"

The last one struck a nerve. Sean saw her flinch. It was subtle, almost unnoticeable, but it was there.

"Run the scan, Agent. And let us find this Gada. It's the only thing that can neutralize the trident. We find that we can stop this thing from killing millions of people all over the world. Maybe more. Who knows what he has planned?"

"You're guessing," the woman said flatly. "You're putting out theories that have no foundation whatsoever. How does your saying go, grasping at straws?"

"Maybe," Sean admitted. He shrugged. "Maybe I am. I don't want to die, and I certainly don't want you to kill my friends over there. But if we're right, you could have a massive catastrophe on your hands with no way to stop it. No weapons, no intelligence, no medicine that can make this go away. Your people, my people, people all over the world will start killing each other. Your own men here will do it if they're within the pulse radius. You can take the chance that I'm wrong. Or you can team up with us and help us find a way to save everyone from what might be Armageddon."

She considered his words carefully. Silence hung in the room like a thick fog.

Sean was certain she was going to kill them all.

"Very well, Mr. Wyatt. Dr. Patel did come to us. That might be your saving grace. He approached us so we would know about what was happening and to make sure he did things the right way. I'm willing to overlook what happened with my agents in the field. It's their own fault they're dead. We'll chalk it up to thinning the herd, as you Americans say."

It was the second time she'd used that phrase, and it was already getting annoying. At this point, Sean didn't care if she called him Vicky. They had to get out of here.

She turned to one of her men and started issuing orders in Mandarin. Sean didn't catch much of it. His Chinese was out of practice. He picked up a few words here and there, something about checking with their headquarters about something. It was probably her asking about the scan that Sean requested.

Then she swiveled around and barked at the rest of the guards as the first one scurried through a door and up a set of stairs.

The remaining guards began untying the prisoners.

Sean felt the circulation course through his fingers and hands. The rest of his companions were equally as relieved to have their bonds removed, each wrenching their hands and clutching their fingers back and forth.

"I think we may be able to expedite that scan Sean was talking about," Tommy offered. "If I may."

The woman in charge arched one eyebrow. "Fine. The second I find out this is all a ruse to try to get free, I'm going to execute every one of you myself."

"There is one other thing," Patel said, ignoring her threat.

All eyes turned to him. "I don't know that what we're looking for will be found at Mount Kailash."

Every face in the room that understood him twisted in confusion.

"You just said that's where you think it is," Tommy objected.

"I know, but there's another possibility, one that is more likely."

"Hit us with it."

"There is a mountain to the south of here, a place that is sacred to multiple religions, but especially Hinduism. It was built to honor Kailash and was named for that very purpose, the Kailasa, or Kailash, Temple."

Priya's eyes widened. "Yes, that's right. Home of the Ellora Caves."

"Caves?" Sean rolled his eyes.

"Yes, there are hundreds of them. Although only a handful are open to the public."

"Why do I feel like we're going to end up in one of those that isn't open to the public?"

"It is possible," Patel said, "that the Gada was taken there thousands of years ago—if someone had been able to discover it on the holy mountain."

"You just said no one has climbed it."

"True," Patel admitted with a nod. "However, it's possible a righteous person—a priest, perhaps—made the journey to Shiva's abode and took the weapon."

Sean sighed. "So, which is it, guys? We need to make a decision. Are we going to Tibet, or are we going to this other place Patel mentioned?"

"I think the Kailasa Temple is our best bet," Priya chimed in. "It has the most historical significance, plenty of places to hide something like the Gada. I don't know of any caves at the mountain, though admittedly I've never been there."

"No, you're right," Patel confirmed. "I've never heard of any there, either."

"Which would make hiding something like that a little trickier." Sean considered the options and then stared over at the Asian woman. "Sounds like we're not going back to your country yet, lady."

41

JAIPUR

Once they were out of the basement and under the open sky, Sean pulled out his cell phone, with MSS permission, and called Emily.

The blue sky overhead was fading into pale whites, oranges, and pinks as the sun set. As the phone rang against his ear, he wondered how long they'd been in the basement. He'd never been unconscious, but he also didn't recall being in the car that long, or downstairs for more than twenty minutes.

"Hello, Sean," Emily said.

"Em. Hey, it's Sean."

"Yes...I know. I just said, 'Hello, Sean.'"

"Yeah, it's Sean."

"Are you messing with me?"

"A little." He glanced at the Chinese female MSS agent and winked. The woman didn't know how to take it and simply shook her head at him.

"Ugh, what do you want?" Emily asked. "You know I have a job, right? And it doesn't entail bailing you out of sticky situations every other week."

"Okay, first of all, ouch. That hurts, Em. You know you can always call on me for help."

"If that was the case, then you'd be here right now in Atlanta, waiting on your next assignment."

She'd been trying to get him back on board with Axis ever since he had walked out of the door. He'd come back once to help with a project that involved an old Nazi experimental weapon that turned up in Argentina. That was the last time he'd worked for Axis, and she knew it might be just that: the last time. He was content with his role at IAA, and prying him away from that would take something she wouldn't wish on anyone, like a personal tragedy of epic proportions.

"Second," Sean ignored her, "Last time I asked you for a favor was, like, six months ago."

"If you don't count the call before this one and me buying you coffee last week."

Sean sighed. "I said I was sorry. I left my money clip in the house."

She chuckled. "What do you need today, Sean?"

"This is a hard one, actually."

"Oh, really?" Emily sounded intrigued. He could picture her sitting up a little straighter in the chair at her desk.

He didn't wait for her to ask about it. "I need you to track a flight passenger for me, or better yet, a flight."

"Okay..."

"The passenger is a celebrity. Brock Carson."

He waited for a moment in the silence, watching the group walk from the derelict building to the Chinese SUVs parked along the street. They were in an old industrial part of town where textile mills and fabric-processing plants littered several city blocks.

"The movie star?"

"Yes."

"Um, and why do you want me to track him?"

"We have reason to believe he's up to something, something pretty bad. You know about the incident in India?"

"The terrorist attack?"

"Yeah, well it wasn't a terror attack."

"I thought not."

"We think Brock is the one responsible. He broke into the temple, stole an ancient relic with the ability to mess with people's brain waves, and then left the country. Not sure where he is now, but my concern is that he's going to go after a bigger target."

Silence spilled from the device once more. "You do realize how insane all of that sounds, right? Ancient relics that alter brain waves? Brock Carson a criminal mastermind? Come on, Sean. I think you and Tommy have been playing in the dirt a little too long."

"I figured you'd say that. And you're right, it is crazy. Except right now I'm in the custody of some MSS agents who also believe that's what happened, along with a highly esteemed colleague of Tommy's who is helping us find a solution to counter this weapon."

"Okay, give me a second here. I'm trying to wrap my head around all this."

Sean visualized her putting her fingers against her forehead and rubbing the skin deeply with her fingers.

"He likely has a private jet. Since he's based in LA, you can probably narrow it down to LAX and the Ontario airport. Just take a look at the logs from the last couple of days, maybe the last week. Let me know what you find. That's all I'm asking."

She sighed. "Fine. I'll put someone on it. But you realize this is like ten you owe me, right?"

"Nine tops."

She chuckled. "Fine. Whatever. Need anything else? A back rub? Maybe a pizza delivered?"

"Thanks, Emily," Sean said, ignoring her joke. "I have to go. Nurse Ratchet is giving me the death stare."

"Who?"

"I'll tell you later. Gotta take a ride with Chinese intelligence."

"Yeah, I still don't know what that's about."

"Bye. Call when you have something."

"You're welcome."

Sean ended the call as she was finishing her snide goodbye.

"Sorry," he said, staring at the woman by the SUV. "We should know something in the next hour."

In the car, Sean had learned the woman in charge was Ming Lao, although getting that much out of her had taken a bit of prying on his part, with no small amount of charm as well. She'd calmed her abrasive demeanor, at least a little. That wasn't to say that she was all cupcakes and rainbows. The woman still kept a permanent scowl on her face and remained, for the most part, nontalkative, except when she was on the phone. Sean assumed her calls were mostly with MSS headquarters or whoever was in charge in some remote location of China. Based on some of the words and phrases he caught in Mandarin, his assumption was correct.

They'd only been driving for twenty minutes when Sean felt his phone vibrating. Adriana was sitting next to him, and she glanced over to see who was calling. Ming also turned around in the front seat and eyed him suspiciously.

He glanced at the screen. "It's Emily," he said, holding up one finger. "That was fast," he said into the device.

"You know me. Efficient."

"True."

"Well, your cockamamie theory might have at least some validity to it."

"Yeah?"

"Brock Carson took his private jet to Mumbai last week. Returned to Los Angeles a few days ago."

"Really?" Getting the confirmation still didn't make the wild theory add up in his head.

"There's more," Emily said. "He left the country again yesterday. Flew to Shanghai."

Sean blinked rapidly as his brain kicked into gear, running through a series of stats and data about the enormous Chinese city. "That's a metropolis."

"Thirty million-plus." Emily's statement sent a shiver through his skin.

"Thirty million people," Sean repeated. "If he sets off that weapon in the middle of the city, it could have cataclysmic effects. Millions would die."

"Why would he do that? I don't understand the motive."

"Me, either," Sean admitted. "I'm still trying to wrap my head around that. I can't help but wonder if this has something to do with his past."

"What do you mean?"

The driver of the SUV steered the vehicle through a security gate where he stopped and handed his credentials to the guard. The man scanned the paperwork and then opened the gate, motioning the driver through.

At the far end of the tarmac, a white jet was sitting outside a well-lit hangar.

"His father's fishing business was ruined by the drilling disaster in the Gulf years back. I remember seeing something about it on television or online. Can't recall. I just know that his father ended up killing himself after the family went bankrupt. His mother was never the same, either. Not sure what happened to her. Somehow, Brock climbed out of that mess and made something of himself. I think they were from Mobile."

Emily went silent for a moment. The SUV rumbled toward the jet and the hangar. Sean could make out some of the crew fueling the plane and going through some final checks.

"Sean, you still there?"

"Yeah. I'm here."

"I don't see how this could be a coincidence."

He didn't know what she was talking about, but his curiosity spiked. "What? What's a coincidence?"

"Some campers found three dead men in the Mojave Desert yesterday. They'd been dead a couple of days from what the coroner said. Seems they all got in a scuffle and murdered each other, though one of them appears to have been killed by a third party."

"I...don't follow what this has to do with the Brock Carson deal."

"I'm getting to that. The dead men were the ones in charge of the oil company that caused so much damage to the environment. They were pretty much directly responsible for that, the aftermath, and the scant payouts the people along the Gulf Coast were given for their troubles."

The dots connected quickly now. "These men, you said it appeared they were involved in a scuffle, as in they attacked each other?"

"That's what the report suggested," Emily said. "I wouldn't have thought anything about it before except for what you said about Brock and his family. They were directly affected by all that."

"So, he used the trident on them as a test run," he muttered.

"The what? Did you say trident?"

"Nothing," Sean said, snapping his head back and forth to get his mind back on track. "If he has revenge on his mind and he's not satisfied with killing the people responsible for ruining his family's life, and his, then that must mean—"

"He's going to go after bigger targets, targets who have committed the same crime. Isn't he a big environmental activist?"

"Yes. Yes, he is."

He could hear keys clicking on Emily's computer. The SUV pulled up behind the fuel truck and came to a stop.

"Time to go," Ming said, twirling a finger in the air.

"One second," Sean insisted. She scowled at him but got out of the car and left him alone, instead directing the people in the other vehicle on what to do. The MSS agents scattered, some grabbing luggage and gear, others rushing onto the plane.

Emily's voice came through the phone again. "Sean, I'm reading an article that suggests marine pollution from the Chinese mainland could be seven times worse than originally estimated."

"Sounds like Brock has found his next target."

"This is incredible," Emily said, her tone absent. "I can't believe how much pollution they dump into the ocean."

"And it drifts east, toward Hawaii and California. You've heard of the Great Pacific Garbage Patch, right?"

"Yeah, but I had no idea it was this bad."

"That floating island of trash is the size of Texas, Em. And it's coming from Asia. Shanghai is just the first target. I'll bet he's going after Hong Kong, maybe Shenzhen, and that's just in China. India is a major polluter, too. I'd wager he'll hit Mumbai after Shanghai. After that, who knows?"

The group began boarding the aircraft, ascending the stairs into the cabin. Sean found a seat facing forward toward the cockpit; a direction he preferred to face when flying in private jets. Something about flying backward unnerved him, and he didn't know why. Adriana sat next to him with Tommy taking a seat across from the two. Priya and Patel sat across the aisle.

The plane's interior was luxurious—tanned leather seats and walls, ceilings with decorative buttons, and cherry wood armrests and appointments contrasting the beige leather.

Sean raised an eyebrow as he looked around the jet and leaned closer to his friend as if about to share a deep secret. "Looks like communism is working out just fine for certain groups of people in the People's Republic."

Tommy chuckled. "Technically, isn't it socialist?"

Sean rolled his shoulders. "Same difference. Either way, this is a nice ride. Every bit as classy as your Gulfstream."

"Hey," Tommy protested. "I love that plane."

The two laughed as the support crews finished their final checks, stowing the baggage and locking the cabin door. A few minutes later, the jet taxied down the runway and launched into the night, en route to the Kailasa Temple and the home of the gods.

42

AURANGABAD

The sun peeked over the mountains to the east. Scattered wispy clouds hung in the sky, sliding gradually across the atmosphere above. The bright blues and whites added to the scene below that played out before the visitors—gentle slopes and mountains of lush green grass, dark rock, and dense forests.

Sean and the others had arrived in Aurangabad late the night before. They'd driven from the airport into the city and found modest accommodations for the remainder of the night—or, as it turned out the morning.

They'd gotten little more than a nap on the plane, but it was enough to keep them alert for the drive to the massive lake where they could get more appropriate sleeping quarters.

A nearby lake had glistened in the early morning rays of the sun, its glassy surface rippling gently in the breeze as the group loaded up their vehicles for the drive through the valley toward the mountains.

Along the drive, Sean's demeanor declined rapidly as the convoy ascended into the thinner air of the high elevations. He hoped they wouldn't be traversing some terrifying goat path across a mountaintop. As they neared the Kailasa Temple area, though, he was relieved to see that there were no such threats waiting for him.

The cabin of the vehicle remained largely silent during the short drive north to the region that was home to the ancient temple. Most of the occupants were busily reviewing as much information as they could on the magnificent structure.

Sean was shocked to learn that the Kailasa Temple was the largest single megalith on the planet. The religious site had been constructed using a vertical method, meaning it had been carved from the top down. As he scanned through the images he'd found online, that fact grew more and more impressive by the second. The planning involved in building such a place would have been overwhelming. Then there was the time involved in progressing the project. The greatest of care would have been taken to make sure no mistakes were made. Every single statue, pillar, wall, step—everything had to be absolutely perfect on the first try since it would be impossible to rework a blunder. When building something from components that were imported, construction crews could simply remove a mistake and replace it with a new piece. With a megalith like this one, that wasn't an option.

The result was one of the most impressive structures on the planet, built thousands of years ago with techniques long forgotten to the annals of history.

Priya was in the very back row with Tommy, looking at the seashell Patel had produced.

"He left something out," she said abruptly.

"What?" Sean turned around, curious.

"The part about the secret door?" Tommy asked. He seemed to be following along.

"Yes." She looked up from the golden conch, surprised. "I didn't know you could read this." She pointed at the Sanskrit carved on the seashell.

He blushed. "I don't...I mean, not really. I know a little."

"If you can read the part about the secret door, then you know more than a little."

"You're better at it than me. We should probably stick with your translations, just to be safe."

She grinned at the compliment and then went back to reading the script. "This says that the secret door to the home of the gods may only be entered by the purest of hearts."

"There's that line again," Sean said.

"Yes," said Priya, and went on, "and that the three keys will unlock the gate."

"The four keys," Tommy interjected, "that must mean these three items we have on hand. The disc, the conch, and the lotus, plus...." His voice trailed off. "The weapon itself is the last key," he realized.

"Correct. At least, I hope that's correct. Otherwise, we're making a trip into Aurangabad for no reason."

"Not to mention a lot of people are going to die," Adriana added.

Up ahead, they could make out the outline of a colorful archway painted in white and faded red. There were already hundreds of cars in the parking area at the base of the mountain, and pilgrims were making their way through rows of stone stupas leading up to the archway. The mountain disappeared behind other smaller peaks and then reappeared once more between them.

The driver guided the SUV down to the parking lot and found a space near the end of a row of cars. The second vehicle in their convoy arrived and parked next to them, the men inside pouring out a moment later.

"Where is this secret door?" Sean asked as he opened his door. A blast of warm air greeted him, and he was immediately glad they weren't in the Himalayas along the border of Tibet and Nepal.

Priya tapped on the conch. "It doesn't say."

"What do you mean it doesn't say?" Sean's frustration showed on his face.

"It just says that a sacrifice must be made in order to find the door."

"Sacrifice?" Ming asked.

"Easy," Sean said, turning to face the woman. "It doesn't mean you have to kill one of us." He hoped. He was joking, but there was something in her tone that said she was hopeful.

She shrugged and walked to the back of the vehicle where one of her men was handing out packs of supplies. They had snacks and water for the hike, and everyone was armed, which likely made them the only ones on the mountain to be so, considering it was a holy place for peaceful worship.

Sean went to the back of the vehicle and took a black bag. The agent handing them out looked at him with suspicion. Sean ignored him and rummaged through the bag to check the contents.

"Hey," he said to Ming. "Where are our weapons?"

She snorted. "You think I'm just going to give you a gun so you can shoot me with it?"

Sean shook his head. "Listen, lady, if you want us to help save your country, which is what it looks like we're doing here, then you're going to want to give me a gun, and my friends, too. Killing you won't do a thing for me or them. We need your help just as much as you need ours right now."

He lied. They had absolutely zero need for the Chinese contingent at the moment, but they might later. They were in Chinese-administered Tibet, but that wasn't the big issue. If they had to go to Shanghai, that could be a problem and one that Ming could solve for them—if she was feeling generous. He wondered if that was ever the case for the prudish commander.

She considered what he said. The breeze picked up and ruffled a sparse few strands of her black hair that had escaped from the bun. She said something in Mandarin, and the man by the tailgate frowned, obviously unhappy with the decision. She barked at him again, and the man snapped into action. He reached into a box in the back and retrieved Sean's weapon, as well as the others.

Sean handed them out, passing guns to Tommy and Adriana, then one to Priya. She stared at it, clearly uncomfortable with the idea of carrying a firearm, but took it reluctantly and stuffed it in her inner coat pocket.

Sean and the other two checked the magazines, the chambers, and then put their weapons away. The last thing they needed was to startle a bunch of peaceful worshipers on pilgrimage.

"Shall we?" Adriana asked, looking at Ming.

The group made their way down the path that ran adjacent to the gravel parking area and next to a row of stones.

They reached the stupas and looked up the slight grade to the archway that marked the path to the temple. It had some kind of religious significance, Sean knew that much, but he didn't bother asking what it was.

Dr. Patel and Priya were just in front of him, walking nervously behind two of the MSS agents. There were two more at the rear, led by Ming. Sean couldn't help but still feel like they were prisoners of sorts, being marched to a destination where they would be executed or thrown into a hole.

The warm, humid air made the hike far more difficult, and by the time they reached the archway, every single person in the group was breathing hard, even the fittest of the MSS agents. The vibrant green mountainsides surrounding them reminded the visitors of an alien world, a beautiful yet desolate place save for the humans daring to tread there. While the air was almost tepid, it had a pleasant scent to it, laced with flowers and leaves, much like Sean recalled from his homes in Tennessee and Georgia.

Fortunately, the crest of the hill was just beyond the archway, and once they were over the top the rest of the walk was flat or slightly downhill.

From the top of the rise, the group could see down to the temple, and to a person, everyone stopped for a moment, not only to catch their breath but also to admire the view of what was one of the most incredible sights they'd ever seen.

The stone temple had been cut out of the mountain itself, gouged from the rock and shaped carefully by expert hands until the stone was no longer rough, jagged peaks and slopes, but an elegant work of art dedicated to the spiritual mysteries of the universe.

As the group progressed toward the site, more details appeared. The main and largest stupa was surrounded on the right and left by four smaller towers—strikingly similar to the obelisks of ancient Egypt—two on each side. The gray-brown stone temple complex was unlike anything they'd ever seen before. Rather than removing the rock from the mountainside and building something there in the vacant quarry, they'd simply skipped one step in the process and hewn everything as it was. This was a symbolic move as much as one of convenience or out of aesthetic purpose. By carving the mountain into a place of worship for the gods, the temple was just as holy to believers as the mountain itself. The stone within the towers, the stupas, the shrines, down to every pillar that lined the walls within the peripheral walkways, was a piece of purity, just as it would have been when placed there by the hands of the deities.

When the procession reached the entrance to the temple, Ming ordered the men in front to halt. They did so immediately and spun around, awaiting their next orders.

Sean and the others also turned to see what she was going to say.

"Where to now?" she asked, a sardonic hint in her voice.

"We need to find an altar," Tommy said. His answer was definitive, leaving no room for doubt except as to where that place might be. "We should split up to save time," he added.

"I don't think so, Mr. Schultz," Ming sneered. "I'm sure you and your colleagues would love that."

"It's not that you're not a delight to hang out with," Sean said. "I mean, that trip here was a peach, but he's right, we can cover more ground if we split up." He thought quickly. "You should go with Tommy." His friend started to protest, seeing exactly what Sean had just done by sticking him with the unfriendly MSS commander. "Take a couple of your men and Dr. Patel, and check out that side over there. I'll go to the right with Adriana and Priya and your remaining guys. Meet there in the middle under the main shrine, and if we find anything we can go from there."

"And if we don't find anything?" Ming asked. Her right eyebrow lifted slightly as if there was some sick part of her that hoped they would come up empty-handed so she could pay them back for killing her agents.

"Then we check the main temple," Sean said.

"Shouldn't we send someone in there first to take a look around?"

"If you want. It's your show, lady. I'm just offering suggestions. You want to split into three groups? Fine. I just thought you'd be more comfortable with two, you know, not dividing your forces too thin?"

She seemed to consider his statement and then gave a nod. "Very well. We split in two groups." Ming stepped closer to Sean. "I hope this isn't part of some silly plan you've concocted."

"Plan? To what, escape? I thought we were working together now, Ming. You know, two superpowers teaming up to save the world?" He slapped her on the shoulder. Her body shuddered from the friendly blow, and her head bobbed slightly. "We're not trying to get away from you. We're trying to help you. So, you're welcome."

He left it at that and started walking to the right toward the path that ran behind two towers and in front of a row of columns underneath a stone overhang.

Ming rolled her eyes and then motioned to two of her men to follow him. Adriana and Priya hurried to catch up. When she did, Adriana glanced back at the MSS commander.

"You don't seem to like her very much," she said.

"Who, Ming?" Sean asked, looking back over his shoulder. The two agents had caught up as well and were following them closely.

"Nah, she's a hoot," Sean said.

Adriana eyed him, suspiciously. "She wants to kill us."

"Yeah, I know. But she won't. Not now that we're helping to save her nation from a zombie apocalypse."

"How can you be so sure?"

"I'm not. Just call it a hunch."

"That's an awfully brazen hunch to go on, Sean. These people are killers." Priya didn't lower her voice. She didn't care if the guards with them heard what she was saying or not.

The other group split off and went the other direction, looping around behind the first tower on the left side and the set of stone steps that rose up to an entrance to the main temple.

Sean walked around the curve and stopped in the middle of the wide stone path that led around the carved buildings. Reliefs of Hindu deities were cut into the rock on both sides. The intricate detail was immaculate, right down to the eyes, noses, ears, fingers, toes, and even the jewelry the figures wore.

From what he could tell, the carvings represented stories from the Vedas, legends, and tales of powerful gods who warred in the heavens and then forged the earth with their own hands, creating the human race in the process. There were more stories cut into the stonework, some of the great rulers, others of magnificent warriors, all right there for all visitors to see.

To the right, Sean noted the columns cut from the same stone. They appeared to be supporting the mountain itself, wedged between the earth and a rock overhang. He wondered what the symbolic significance was of that piece of the temple grounds, but there wasn't time to waste on peripheral historical things like that. He had to find the altar that led to the secret door. The lives of thirty million people hung in the balance, maybe more if Brock Carson was successful with his first large-scale attack.

Brock Carson.

Sean wouldn't have thought it possible. Then again, why wouldn't it be? He'd watched, silently, over the years as Hollywood and Nashville produced more and more stars in the entertainment firmament, stars who believed their opinions mattered more than ordinary people. They voiced their beliefs and ideas on massive platforms, and those platforms gave the ideas traction—whether they made sense or not.

He'd recently read an article about a smallpox outbreak in the United States that was almost exclusively due to one particular collection of idiots who suggested that parents shouldn't vaccinate their children. The fear, largely unsupported by science, was that vaccines could cause autism. There'd been no real proof published about such a thing, and the notion sparked outrage from the medical community.

It made perfect sense.

People with a louder voice than others and with an extremely large following could gain momentum for their ideas, but there was something else that could be gained: greed, lust, and a thirst for revenge.

With a large enough ego and a strong enough motive, it wasn't inconceivable that a movie star with money and connections would eventually use those weapons for nefarious purposes.

Most of the time, famous people used their scope of influence for good. Sean thought of Sting, the guys from U2, and several actors and actresses who'd built foundations to help feed the hungry, save the rainforests and keep people from murdering innocent endangered species. He admired those folks, even contributed to their causes with regularity.

Sooner or later, though, a bad egg would pop up in the bunch. It seemed Brock Carson was that bad egg.

Sean strolled along the columns, inspecting the walls for any sign of an altar that might be the one they were looking for. Adriana and Priya took the other side, assessing the foundation wall of the temple as they circled around.

He figured they wouldn't find anything out here. Priya likely came to the same conclusion. She, better than any, would know where the altars would be in a place like this. Still, it was important to be thorough. The fate of the world hung in the balance. And time was running out.

43

AURANGABAD

The two groups met at the back of the giant stone temple after working their way around each side.

Tommy put both hands out wide. "Nothing. You?"

Sean shook his head once. "No."

"See?" Patel insisted. "I told you there won't be an altar out here. There are likely several inside the temple, though."

"We know," Sean said. "But it was worth checking."

"We're wasting time," Ming interrupted. "We should keep moving."

Sean pursed his lips and looked at his friend. "Look at Miss Ming here. Yes, ma'am. Right away."

He started off toward the front of the building again, this time in a mock march.

Tommy chuckled and shook his head. Sean was goading the woman, and Tommy knew it. He'd seen his friend do it on numerous occasions when they were in sticky spots. This wasn't necessarily one of those moments, but the troublemaker in Sean couldn't help himself. If anyone ever tried to impose their will on him, their rules, Sean's natural reaction was to act childish to the point that the antagonist would become frustrated and lose their composure. More often than not, this resulted in opening a weakness within a villain. In this case, Tommy wasn't sure if Ming was still the villain or on their side, but he suspected Sean was performing his usual ruse just in case.

Ming motioned for her men to catch up to Sean and they rushed forward, one lining up on either side to make sure he wasn't trying to get away.

The group reached the front of the temple and stared up at the enormous structure with its pyramidal shape and rounded dome cap. The arched doorway into the temple was dark despite the bright light of the morning sun showering its rays down on the mountain.

Sean glanced at his watch. They'd already spent nearly forty minutes investigating the area. It seemed like they'd only been there fifteen at most. Then again, that was how things usually went on missions, especially when time was not on their side.

"Shall we?" Sean said, motioning to the others.

Patel nodded, took one swallow, and then led the way into the temple.

Inside, the air immediately grew cooler, dropping several degrees and causing a shiver to shoot through Ming's body. Along with the daylight pouring in, candles burned along the walls to light the way.

Inside, a statue of Shiva stood in the center of a great room. The floor was cut smooth from the mountain rock, as were all the columns and archways inside. The ceiling rose in the shape of a huge dome, high above the floor, and was adorned with various holy figures from Vedic lore.

At the base of the idol, the ground was covered with flowers; an assortment of food such as pastries, bread, and vegetables; and more candles. There was a dish in the center of it all, at the feet of the deity, that contained bills and coins—an offering plate for the gods.

"This would be an altar, right?" Sean asked.

"Sort of," Priya corrected. "It is where offerings are placed. Many Hindu temples around the world have something similar for the different deities."

He recalled visiting a Hindu temple in Chattanooga during the Hindu festival of Diwali. One of his friends was a practicing Hindu and had invited him to join the festivities. There were group songs and prayers, an array of food like Sean had never seen, followed by an interesting procession as the men walked around the back of the symbolic representations of the Hindu deities reciting more prayers to usher in blessings and another bountiful year.

He'd thought it odd that the women were separated on one side of the room and were permitted to walk around the prayer circle only after the men were done, but then again, other religions had their own cultural quirks, too. He'd been impressed with the sincerity and reverence of the festivalgoers and promised to do it again sometime in the future when he wasn't out of town or working on a project for IAA.

"What we're probably looking for isn't this place, though," Priya continued. "We need to find something that isn't easily found."

Tommy bit his tongue at the oversimplification, choosing not to say anything disparaging.

"So," Ming said, "I suppose you want to split up again?"

"Now that's a good idea," Sean said. "Same teams or you want to pick again?"

Adriana chuckled under her breath.

Ming ignored him and motioned to the others.

"Actually," Priya said, "I don't think that will be necessary."

Ming had already started walking away with two of the agents, apparently to investigate one side of the temple's interior.

"No?" Tommy asked.

Priya's head swiveled side to side. "No. It isn't here."

All eyes shifted to the professor and then back to her.

"What do you mean it isn't here?" Tommy demanded.

A sudden splinter of fear pricked at Sean's gut. They were in the wrong place. They should have gone to Tibet and Nepal to search the mountain there. They'd wasted a full day, and now there was no chance they could find the Gada in time to stop Carson's evil scheme.

"I mean it's not in this temple," Priya said. She turned to Patel. "The home of the gods isn't in this temple. This place was built by men, long after the deities left this world."

"And I thought she didn't believe in that stuff," Tommy said as an aside to Sean.

Priya didn't hear him and went on. "The mountain is their home. And this place was built to honor Kailash."

"By that logic," Patel said, working his way through the problem, "that means we have to look in one of the caves."

"Not just any cave," she said. "This entire complex is dedicated to Shiva, lord of destruction."

"Right."

Sean had thought it odd that they would be searching for the mace of Vishnu in a place dedicated to Shiva, but he'd gone along with it, assuming that if he and the others were wrong, they'd have been corrected.

"What's your point?" Ming asked. She was growing impatient, and everyone could see it from the drawn expression on her face.

"Her point is that there is only one section of this complex that is dedicated to Vishnu," Patel said, taking over for his protégé. "There's a cave, and it's in the back of the temple."

"Weren't we just back there?" Adriana asked.

"Yes, but I didn't think much of it until Priya came to this realization. We're not here for something that belonged to Shiva. It's Vishnu. And the only place in this entire structure that is dedicated to him is a small cave in the back."

"Let me guess," Sean said, "we can't get in there."

Patel shook his head. "I'm afraid not. It's blocked off."

"Oh, the one with the iron door in front of it and a padlock?"

"Yes, that's the one," Patel said. "It appears we've reached a dead end."

Sean snorted a laugh. "Seriously? You think a door and a lock are going to keep us from going in there? Think about it, Professor. The fate of the world is at stake. If we get arrested for breaking into a barricaded cave entrance, I'm pretty sure we're still doing the right thing."

"Not to mention I didn't see any cops around on the way in," Adriana added.

"Exactly."

Patel sighed, contemplating his solution.

Ming motioned for the agents to move back toward the exit.

"Where are you going?" Patel asked.

"We're going to open the door," she said, curtly. "Are you coming with us or what?"

For the first time since he'd met the woman, Sean noticed a hint of mischief in Ming's demeanor. Was he seeing things, or had she even offered Patel a wink with her response?

Didn't matter. At the moment, he was with her.

The group made their way to the exit, leaving Patel alone for a moment. He let out a long exhale and slapped his hands to his hips. "Oh, screw it."

He trotted ahead to catch up with the others.

They made their way around to the back of the temple again, this time as a group. When they reached the rear wall, Patel stopped and gazed through the gaps in the columns. There was a darkened corridor beyond, under the lip of the overhang. It wasn't easy to see inside, but there were outlines of darker openings along the inner passage wall. One of them was blocked by a metal door, a steel lock hanging from a hook and looped through another one that was bolted into the rock. Over the metal door, a tiny figure was carved into the stone. It was only a few inches tall, half that in diameter. The carving was the image of Vishnu.

Sean took a step into the cool passageway and looked in both directions. There were no tourists, no worshippers to be seen. The hall ran about a hundred feet from one end to the other and was dotted with caves. Most of the openings were too small for a person to get through, but there were a few that could easily accommodate a curious tourist or a wannabe spelunker.

He took a few more steps and drew closer to the blockaded door. With his left hand, he lifted the padlock and examined it. He let it fall gently to the wall and looked back at the rest of the group, who'd joined him in the passage. It was crowded in the narrow thoroughfare with so many people standing in one place.

"You guys got something for this?" Tommy asked the MSS agents.

They looked around at each other, and then Ming spoke. "We have some explosives. Shouldn't take much to blow this lock."

Sean shook his head. "Seriously? With all these people around?" He motioned to the area outside the corridor. Tourists and pilgrims were milling around, gazing at the architecture and the marvelous construction. "No, we need something quieter." He looked at Adriana.

"I got this," she said with a wry grin.

The group hovered around as she reached into her boot and pulled out a thin tool. The piece of metal split in two, revealing a minuscule trench in the center where a tiny rod was lodged. She took the pin and clenched it between her teeth, then shoved the first pick into the lock, then the second. Holding the two picks with one hand, she removed the pin and shoved it into the padlock's keyhole. She twitched it to the right, then the left, and suddenly the lock fell free, hitting the stone floor with a clank.

She shoved the lock pick kit back in her boot and glanced at Ming. "Glad you didn't check my shoes," Adriana said dryly.

Sean chuckled and tugged on the door. "Come on, everyone in before someone sees us."

One by one, the members of the expedition shuffled into the cool darkness of the cave. Sean was the last one in and closed the door behind him. Then he paused, opened the door again, and picked up the lock from the ground. The last thing they needed was to be trapped inside. Better to put that somewhere no one would find it.

Flashlights bloomed to life and illuminated the passage. Unlike the smooth stone of the exterior where, thousands of years ago, workers toiled tirelessly for a perfect finish, these walls were cut rough, carved almost as if in haste. Sean understood why. They weren't walls anyone was supposed to see. This tunnel was man-made; that much was clear from the jagged remains of stone that jutted out in various directions, unlike the more rounded rock of a natural cave.

Tommy took the lead as the group snaked their way through the passage. He'd done this a million times, or at least it seemed like that.

He and Sean had joked about their underground experiences several times over the years. Of course, they not infrequently ended up in subterranean tunnels. If things were hidden out in the open, then they'd have already been found.

The corridor narrowed at a bend, and every member of the party had to turn sideways to get through. One of the larger MSS agents scraped his chest and back against the walls as he passed, but he was able to make through—barely.

The group continued trudging ahead for what seemed like an hour. Sean couldn't help but wonder how far back in the mountain this tunnel went. He imagined the workers slaving away in the darkness, cutting these passages for a purpose they likely didn't understand. It must have taken them decades, maybe more, to get all of it completed. The temple alone was an astounding masterpiece of ancient engineering and human determination, but these tunnels were no less impressive, simply by their sheer length and the volume of rock that had to be removed.

That was another one of the mysteries he'd read about regarding the Kailasa Temple. No one seemed to be able to figure out where the ancient builders had taken all the stone they had removed from the site. Perhaps it was dumped in a canyon somewhere and then erosion had covered it.

Sean snapped his head to get his focus back on the job at hand. He glanced back at the agents behind him, then returned his gaze to the front of the long procession. He was suddenly overcome with a bad feeling, one that he'd encountered many times before. He hoped the premonition was wrong, but Sean had one thought that kept making its way to the front of his mind.

They were all going to die in this darkness.

44

AURANGABAD

The group spilled into the underground chamber, each person grateful to be out of the ever-tightening passage and into a room where they could stretch and have some space around them. They'd been marching through the subterranean passage for nearly half an hour, and with every passing minute, the tunnel seemed to close in around them.

The distinct smell of rock as old as the planet mingled with the scent of moisture, a musty odor that permeated the large room even though there was no sign of water.

Every single person in the cave pointed their light toward a single object that occupied a central position along the back wall. They quickly examined the rest of the room, the engravings of the Hindu godhead, the minor deities, and the great leaders of the religious movement from so long ago. Those figures were cut into the rock just as they were outside, surrounding the temple and within it. Here, however, they all stared toward the far wall and the incredible visage that rose from the floor.

A statue of Vishnu had been hewn from the mountain's stone. The deity was in a sitting position, on a throne, each of his four hands extended out in multiple directions. The face was stoic, staring straight ahead with a grim sense of purpose in his eyes, lips sealed in a tight crease. It wasn't a smile or a frown, simply a neutral expression, as if waiting for the visitors to make their move.

Patel was the first to approach the idol. He cocked his head to the left and examined it closely, noting a platter at the deity's feet where offerings could be placed.

"This is incredible," he said.

The statue was around six feet tall, and that was in a sitting position. While the stone obviously wasn't going to get up and stand, Sean imagined it to be twelve feet tall if it did. The ancients who designed it likely thought that Vishnu truly was twelve feet tall, such was the regard given to gods by mortals.

Priya was the next to step closer, and the others followed, forming a semicircle around the sculpture.

"His hands," she said, "they're empty, save for the mace."

She pointed out the thing that Sean and the others felt was a glaringly obvious piece of information. Three of Vishnu's hands were empty. The fourth, the lower right hand, held a stone mace, as a king would hold a scepter—more symbolic than an actual weapon.

"Is that what we're here for?" Priya asked.

"No," Tommy said, stepping forward. "I don't think so."

"I thought you said this place would hold a weapon that could stop whatever it is the actor is planning." Ming spoke with intensity now, a bubbling anger rising up from deep down inside. She was not only frustrated but fearful.

Sean imagined this hardened woman must have family or friends in Shanghai, maybe somewhere else in China as well. He saw through the tough exterior. Inside her anger dwelt a seed of fear, not for herself but for her people, or as he believed, family.

"It is…I mean it should be," Tommy said. "We just have to figure out what to do next."

"The offering," Patel said, pointing at the tray at the feet of the deity. "It's the sacrifice the riddle spoke of."

The tray was around two feet long and about half as wide. Sculpted from the same mountain stone as the statue, it was also

about an inch deep, easily capable of holding the three golden artifacts Sean and the others had retrieved.

"You think we put them on that thing?" Tommy asked.

"Yes. It's the only answer." The words tumbled out of his mouth.
He spoke rapidly, a sense of urgency filling him that the others hadn't
seen before.

"It's not the only answer," Tommy argued. "We need to be careful
with this. I doubt whoever built this place and designed a tricky
riddle to find it would make it easy to get the mace."

"It's just a piece of stone," Ming said, her voice rising. She brandished her pistol and waved it at Patel, flicking it to the side to indi-
cate he should move away from the statue. "You brought us all down
here for nothing. And now my people are going to die because of it.
We came to the wrong place. There is nothing here that can help us."

There it was. The pain Sean had sensed in her tone. It was
coming through more clearly now. She cared about someone in
China. Who it was didn't matter. These weren't the emotions grown
from a sense of duty to country. This was personal.

"We should have gone to the mountain in Tibet," she added.

Patel shook his head. "No, you don't understand."

"Put the weapon down," Priya said.

Everyone turned, surprised to see she'd managed to sidle backward and position herself behind Ming. In her right hand, she held a
pistol with the muzzle only a half inch from the back of Ming's skull.

"What are you doing?" the MSS commander asked. "My
men will—"

"Your men will drop their guns, as well."

Sean, Tommy, and Adriana watched the drama playing out with
disbelief in their eyes.

Priya, formerly nothing more than an archaeologist thrown into
an element she had no business in, was now confident, cool, and
appeared ready to kill without reservation.

"Do it!" she shouted at them. "Drop your weapons, or I kill her
right now!"

The agents hesitated. Each held a gun pointed straight at Priya.

Had they wanted, they could have ended her right then and there within seconds, but not before her finger twitched and pasted Ming's forehead on the statue.

Ming said something in Chinese, her breathing shallower than before. She'd not seen this coming, and it had her afraid. This soulless iron woman was afraid of dying.

The agents hesitated another few seconds and then one by one lowered their guns to the ground.

"Kick them over here," Priya said.

The men did as told, sliding the weapons across the floor until they were all at Priya's and Ming's feet.

"On your knees," she said.

Sean watched what was happening with wonder. He couldn't believe it. He started to reach down and scoop up some of the pistols when he noticed Patel turn his body. There was something in the man's hand.

Sean turned his head and saw what it was. Patel was holding a gun.

"Leave those there, Sean," he said. "You won't be needing them."

Then everything hit Sean at the same time. The color drained from Tommy's face. Adriana simply stared at what she now knew was their real enemy.

Sean straightened slowly, hands at his sides. "What are you doing, Professor?" He didn't have to ask. He knew exactly what was going on. Nothing Patel was going to say would be a surprise. Sean had seen this story before. It was the old double cross. They'd been used.

The motive wasn't yet clear, but that would come. He knew it would. Sean just had to keep them talking, and the fact that he and the others weren't already dead meant that Patel and Priya weren't sure what was coming next and that the Americans might still be needed. The Chinese, however, were in immediate danger.

"Do you really have to ask, Sean?" Patel sneered. "You're a smart guy."

"I have some guesses."

Priya snorted. "I'm sure you do."

"Do you know how much money I make at the university, Sean?"

"In rupees or dollars? Because I gotta be honest, the conversion-rate thing is really confusing to me."

Patel snickered. It was a foul sound, laced with wickedness.

"Always joking around," Patel said. "I've heard that about you, that you can't keep your mouth shut."

"No, I'm being serious. I really suck at converting other currencies to dollars and vice versa."

Patel waved the gun as a signal to Sean to shut up.

"Fine," Sean muttered. "I guess we can assume it's not a lot."

"No, not a lot. That is putting it mildly. And do you know how much time I spend out in the hot sun at those dig sites?"

"Probably more, I'm guessing."

This was good. Sean had him talking. Now he had to figure out how they were going to get out of this.

"More than it's worth. And what do I get? My face on the cover of Archaeology Magazine?"

"That would be—"

"No!" Patel cut him off. "I don't even get so much as that. And it wouldn't pay, anyway."

"So," Tommy said, "all of this was just one big scam so you could collect a treasure you believe is here."

"Very good, Tommy," Priya said. "The mace of Vishnu doesn't hold any secret powers. It's a golden staff, nothing more, but we're willing to bet the Indian government would love to have it and be willing to pay almost anything for it. Symbolism, you see."

"Except there is no golden mace," Ming spat. "It's made of stone."

"You shut up," Priya said, pushing the muzzle into the back of Ming's head.

One of her men started to take a step forward, but Priya saw the move. "Don't," she ordered, and the man froze.

"It's here," Priya said. "Initially, we believed that it could be in Tibet, which would mean we'd need a little help from the inside with the Chinese. Letting them know about a potential national security threat was easy enough. Ishaan alerted the proper authorities, and you and your team showed up shortly after." She pushed Ming's head forward an inch. The Chinese woman winced at the slight pain.

"Of course, we needed to move quickly and were stumped by these ridiculous riddles. Then we got to thinking..." She put one finger to her chin, mimicking the thought process about calling Tommy and Sean. "Who in the archaeological community is really good with this sort of thing? Your exploits have gained you international renown, Tommy."

"And Sean," he quipped. "Don't forget Sean. He helps a lot."

"Shut up."

"Okay then."

"You two have been invaluable to this project," Patel said. "Honestly, I doubt that we could have done it without you."

"I guess that means you're going to let us walk out of here," Tommy said, his voice full of sarcasm.

"No," Patel said with a snort. "You're all going to die down here. And Priya and I are going to be rich."

"I knew I sensed something in your voice about him," Sean said, cutting off the professor. "There was an...affection. You two are a thing, aren't you?"

"Dr. Patel is a brilliant man," Priya said. "I love him and would do anything for him."

"You're like half his age," Tommy said.

"Well done," Sean added with a nod to Patel. "Living the dream."

"Both of you shut up. It's time to collect our prize. The keys, give them to me." Patel's voice boomed through the chamber.

"Fine," Tommy said. "They're in my bag. Look for yourself."

Every eye in the room locked on Tommy as he set the bag down the floor and gently nudged it toward Patel. "Here you go."

Sean's right hand slipped into his pants pocket. He'd put one of the flash-bang discs in there earlier before they ran into the MSS agents and before any of this had gone down. He kept one there most times when he was in the field, just in case of an emergency. It was getting to be an old trick but one that had served him well, getting him out of tight situations when there was no other way. Curiosity, however, kept him from withdrawing it just yet. He wanted to see how this was going to play out.

Patel stepped over to the bag, still holding his weapon tight in one hand, waist high, and grabbed the loop on the top of the pack. He pulled it closer to the statue and opened the main compartment, using the residual light from everyone's flashlights to see inside.

First, he pulled out the disc, then the lotus flower, and placed them both on the tray at the feet of the idol.

Then he slipped his own pack onto the floor and fished out the golden conch. He held it up in the pale glow of the flashlights and admired it, the yellow metal glittering.

"This," he said, turning to Priya, "this is what we've been waiting for. Our lives are about to change, my dear." He turned to Sean. "And we have you and your friends to thank for it. We will be wealthier than we could have ever imagined."

"You sure you don't just want to sell those things?" Sean asked. "Could probably fetch a pretty penny...er, rupee."

Patel shook his head evenly. "No. The Gada is why we are here. We will never have to set foot on another dig site again, not in another classroom, ever."

He turned halfway around, keeping the weapon in his left hand pointing randomly at the prisoners. The other slowly lowering the seashell down to the tray. He placed it on the stone surface next to the other artifacts and then stood up straight to watch.

Nothing happened.

After three seconds, a frown streaked across his face. Priya mirrored his reaction.

Ming started chuckling. It wasn't a pleasant sound, cracked and tired.

Patel was about to speak, probably to the effect of why it wasn't working, when something clicked deep within the statue's base. The tray began to move, inching its way down toward the floor, producing a grinding sound.

Priya's eyes widened, a mystified smile spreading across her lips.

Patel stood back, his feet positioned on a great tile in front of the statue.

When the tray finished its descent, there was a thud from somewhere deep in the mountain. It was then that Sean realized the subtle, almost unnoticeable differentiation on the floor's surface. The entire corridor and most of the chamber was cut from the mountain itself. This pad, however, where Patel stood, was separate. The seams were extremely thin, but there was no mistaking it. This tile wasn't part of the rest of the floor.

A rumble thundered from within the mountain. Then another loud thud.

"This is it!" Patel exclaimed, turning his head back to look at Priya.

One second, the professor was standing before the group, a look of greed-driven ecstasy on his face. The next second, the floor opened up and swallowed him. His hands flew into the air as he dropped through the tile that swung open, dangling on ancient hinges no one knew were there.

Priya's wonder-filled face flushed pale in an instant. "Ishaan!" she shouted as she lunged forward to try to save the man she loved. She slid to the edge on her hands and knees, looking down into the dark abyss below. She heard Patel screaming as he plummeted, but she couldn't see him. Then, as suddenly as he'd fallen into the hole, his screams ended with a faint smack.

"No!" Priya shouted.

She started to rise, but a foot caught her on the rear and jolted her forward. She felt her weight disappear as she tumbled into the opening and down through the darkness of the pit. Her screams were higher than Patel's, horrifying, haunting sounds that echoed up from the cavern below and resonated in the chamber until she, too, hit the floor hundreds of feet below.

Sean and his friends looked at Ming, her leg still held up in the follow-through of her kick.

The woman hadn't hesitated. Just like Sean, she'd waited for the right moment, a sliver of opportunity to take action. When it presented itself, she'd done what had to be done.

She lowered her foot to the ground, staring into the gaping hole with a look of disdain. Then she turned to Sean.

"I had a bad feeling about them," Sean said. "Could never put my finger on it, but something was weird."

Ming nodded. She bent down and picked up the nearest pistol, then pointed it at Sean. "I, too, mistrusted them but decided it was worth looking into. Now, here we are, in the wrong place and with no time to get to the true mountain."

"What are you going to do, kill us and leave us here?" Tommy asked. "We didn't lie to you."

Ming shook her head. "No. You didn't. You were betrayed just like us." She flipped the barrel around and grabbed it, then extended the weapon to Sean. "I have a feeling you're going to need this. We have to get back to China and find this Brock Carson before it's too late."

Sean took the weapon and stuffed it in his belt. "Okay then."

Adriana stepped forward, careful not to startle Ming or her agents. "Not before we get the Gada," she said.

Ming didn't understand. "You saw; this was a hoax. There is no mace of Vishnu."

"I wouldn't be so sure about that," Tommy said.

Adriana stepped onto one of the statue's legs, carefully looping it around the waist to keep her balance. The pit loomed just to her left as she reached down and picked up one of the golden keys. She took the disc first and stood up straight. A quick look at the palms of the idol revealed where each item was to be placed. The disc went in the right upper hand, where a circular indent held it securely.

Next, she took the seashell and placed it in the top left hand where the imprint was carved to match the base of the conch.

The third and final key, the lotus, had a matching base cut into the bottom left hand of the idol. Adriana took the flower and held it over the idol's palm. She took a deep breath.

Tommy wanted to stop her. Sean wasn't sure what to do. He'd seen her die before, or so he had thought at that moment. It was something he never wanted to witness again. He trusted her, though, and he knew she was aware of what she was doing.

Adriana placed the flower on the hand and stepped back, lowering herself off the statue.

Another deep rumble came from within the mountain, this time behind the statue. The grinding noise came to life again. Now it was the deity itself that was moving. Once it had lowered itself a foot into the floor, it stopped and froze in place, the top of the base now flush with rest of the floor. Behind it, an arched recess—dark and shallow —was revealed.

Everyone turned their beams toward the cavity, the bright white blooms flashing on something gleaming and sparkling in the darkness.

They all crowded around the hole, except Sean, who kept at a safe distance to stare at the yellowish metal object propped in a stone stand set into the wall.

There, in the depths of the mountain, they'd found the lost mace of Vishnu—the Gada.

45

AURANGABAD

The plane's engines roared, and the occupants' heads rocked toward the rear as the thrust kicked in. The wheels thundered down the runway, and within fifteen seconds the plane's wings started to push against the air beneath them, lifting the sleek jet into the air.

Once they were airborne, the pilot banked hard to the left, circling upward before straightening out and setting a course due east.

The Gada was safely on board, locked in a thick plastic case and being watched by two of Ming's men. She'd been on the phone with Beijing since leaving the Kailasa Temple complex, giving orders, sharing information, and asking questions.

She'd not taken a second to let the rest of the group know what she'd heard or what was going on. All they heard were the short bursts of her responses in Mandarin as she said yes or no to whoever she was talking to on the other end of the line.

The plane leveled out at its cruising altitude, and some of the agents got up to move around the cabin. Some of them chatted, whispering to exclude the Americans from their conversation, although Sean and Tommy picked out a few choice words here and there.

"They should be thanking us," Tommy said after a glance over his shoulder at three guys standing in the back next to the bar. "We saved their nation."

Sean tilted his head to the side and lifted one eyebrow for a second. "We haven't saved anything yet. If Ming can't locate Brock and that weapon, we might already be too late. If it works like the Trishula, we need to get the Gada as close to the epicenter as possible."

"You're right," Tommy said. He stared down at the floor, losing the conversation in his thoughts.

"You okay?" Sean asked. "You seem...a little distant."

Tommy shook his head. "Yeah, I'm good. I just...I didn't see that coming with Patel and Priya, you know? That one caught me way off guard."

Sean nodded. "It got me by surprise too, buddy. Don't beat yourself up."

"Oh, I'm not. It's just, I never get used to seeing that sort of thing. Two colleagues, there one minute, gone the next. It's strange."

"They were bad people," Adriana said, interrupting. "They needed to die. They would have killed all of us, and then millions of people all over the planet wouldn't have had a chance."

"You're right," Tommy said. "Still...." He stood up and turned toward the back of the plane where the three men were still hovering around the bar. "I need a drink. You guys want anything?"

Sean snorted a laugh and shook his head. "No, thanks. I'm good." Adriana also declined with a turn of the head.

Tommy made his way to the back of the aircraft and started chatting with the agents. Whether or not they understood each other wasn't clear, but for the moment they seemed to be getting along.

Sean leaned back in his chair and put his head against the headrest. He let out a long sigh. The whine of the engine was the only thing that remained constant amid the occasional yes or no in Chinese by Ming.

"What's wrong, Sean?" Adriana asked abruptly.

He raised his head and looked over at her. She was staring deep into his soul with her deep brown eyes.

"What?"

"Something's wrong with you," she said. She placed a hand on his. "You haven't been the same since I got back."

He drew a breath through his nose. "I'm fine." He wasn't lying entirely, but he also wasn't being completely honest.

"No, you're not. I know you. Something happened while I was gone." There was a splinter of sadness in her voice. "Do...you still love me?"

Sean let out a relieved laugh. "Honey, of course I still love you." He leaned over and kissed her on the cheek. "Why wouldn't I?"

She took two breaths and then turned her head. "I don't know. Because I disappeared for almost a year? We never saw each other? Barely spoke? That makes things difficult."

He couldn't deny that. He'd been wondering where she'd gone, why she was so short and coy during the rare moments they did speak. "I never stopped loving you." He meant it. That part was the entire truth. "But yeah, it was hard sometimes. And then..."

"Then, what?" She feared what he would say next, that he would tell her he met someone else, that he'd fallen out of love with her and decided there were greener pastures elsewhere.

"You're right," he conceded. "Something did happen."

Sean told her of the search for the Templar treasure, how it had led them to Oak Island and then eventually, a secret archive of the Freemasons located in a discreet area in the nation's capital. Then he told her about what happened to him personally, how he'd come to grips with the fact that he enjoyed killing, enjoyed it to an almost sociopathic level. He told her how he'd wept, how he didn't want to take lives again, and then how he'd eventually come to grips with his sins and the ghosts from the past.

There was a measure of guilt in his eyes as he finished his confession. "I...nothing has changed, though, Addy. Here I am again, taking lives."

She stared evenly at him, without judgment or chastisement. "And are you enjoying it?"

He shook his head.

"You don't crave it?"

Again, his head turned.

"Then let it go, Sean. Some of us in this world are blessed with unique skills, talents that have been forged in the fire by time and excruciating work. We are here for a reason. People like us, we are rare but necessary weapons against tyranny and evil. If there were none like us, the world would be chaos. Crime would run unchecked. Murder, terrorism, rape, all of it would be in play without someone to make certain those with wicked intentions were reminded that destroying civilization comes with a cost."

He knew she was right, but he still couldn't accept what was wrong with him on the inside. "I know all that. And I accept that role, every day I wake up. It's just...what's wrong with me? I don't want to like taking the lives of others."

"Nothing is wrong with you, Sean. You said you went to therapy."

"I did."

"Then keep going until it's all worked out. Do whatever you need to do. And I'll be here for you. I don't plan on leaving again."

Sean nodded and licked his lips. He wanted to ask where she'd been, but thought better of it.

Turns out, he didn't need to.

"It's time I tell you where I was and what I was doing."

He raised his head and met her gaze.

Adriana told him everything about the organization known as Shadow Cell that June worked for. He was both surprised and not at these revelations regarding their friend June Holiday. He'd noticed something about her, something that wasn't so innocent, so incapable of handling herself in any kind of fight. She'd hidden it well but not enough that he didn't take note. And that meant something.

Adriana relayed the story about the Red Ring, how she'd gone all over the world chasing down a new breed of terrorist organization.

He'd heard about the epidemic in Sweden, the attacks at the soccer game, the bombings in Liverpool, and the other details she mentioned. Sean never knew that behind all of it the woman he loved was trying to stop it, putting her life on the line to make the world a safer place.

It wasn't dissimilar to his days with Axis. He understood it and didn't need her to explain why, especially after she told him what she'd seen after the terrorist attacks in Paris. Sean understood perfectly.

The last fact, however, caught him off guard. He had no way to see it coming.

"You were trained by...a ninja?" He asked the question without masking the disbelief in his voice. "I thought they were...I don't know, extinct."

"Hiding for hundreds of years, exiled, but not dead. My father had me trained at a very young age with them. Originally, they were purely assassins," she explained. "Now, they are keepers of the peace, a deeply spiritual order." She told him about the diseases they worked tirelessly to cure along with their training in the deadly arts.

Sean couldn't keep his mouth from gaping open at the revelation.

"I...I don't know what to say. This is all..."

"Scary?"

"No," he shook his head. "It's kind of amazing."

She let a smile stretch across her face. "It doesn't frighten you?"

"Honey, the only thing that frightens me is high places and certain snakes."

"You freaked out about that spider in the house that one time. You shrieked like a little girl."

He chuckled. "Well, it surprised me. I didn't know it was there. Just like I didn't know this stuff about you. But it doesn't scare me. Nothing about you scares me." He leaned close and kissed her on the lips again. "I love you."

"I love you, too."

"And I love the both of you," Tommy said from over her shoulder. He was holding a whiskey glass half filled with an amber-brown liquid. "But I miss June." He took a swig of the whiskey and winced as the liquid burned his throat on its way down.

"June loves you, too," Adriana said. "She told me to tell you she'll be back in the States soon. She's just finishing up some things in the UK."

"Great Britain? What's she doing there?"

He hadn't heard any of Adriana's story.

"I'll let her tell you all about it," she said with a mischievous smirk and a wink.

"Fine," Tommy took another sip. "No one tells me anything."

"We have him," Ming said, interrupting the conversation.

Everyone turned to face her as she stood from her seat in the front of the plane and approached, still holding the phone in her hand. "We found Brock Carson."

"You did?"

"Well, we found an energy signature that is out of the ordinary. You were right; it's magnetic in nature. It's in Downtown Shanghai."

"Great!" Sean said. "Call in the cavalry, and we can go home."

"No," Ming said, "that won't work."

"What do you mean it won't work? You said you know where he is."

"We do. But there's a problem."

"Problem?" Sean arched one eyebrow.

She nodded. "Yes. He's barricaded himself in the Shanghai Tower. They've booby-trapped the entire floor where he's staying. There's no way to get to him without knocking down the upper third of the building or hitting it with a missile."

Sean knew those weren't options, for a variety of reasons. "So, he's going to set off the Trishula?"

She nodded. "Earlier today, a video was broadcast across most of the media outlets around the world. It was a threat. He warned the world that because of our reckless disregard for stewardship of the planet, he was going to make humanity pay and let Mother Nature start over. We didn't need the scans to locate him. He made the video in one of the villas in the Shanghai Tower."

"So, we need to get there with the Gada and neutralize it."

Her head turned slowly one way and then the other. "I don't know if we'll make it. He said he was going to activate the trident at sunrise tomorrow."

"Then I guess we need to hurry. Are they evacuating the citizens?"

"My government...they don't believe it's possible. While they've seen what happened in India, they aren't willing to risk mass hysteria over something that may or may not be a reality. They don't understand."

Sean swallowed hard.

"If Shanghai falls," Tommy said, "there will be no stopping him. He'll go from city to city until all of humanity is murdering each other."

Sean turned his gaze to Adriana and then back to Ming. "Then I guess we should hurry."

46

SHANGHAI

Brock stood on the balcony overlooking the city. Police helicopters had come and gone, flying around the top of the building like flies around a bull for the last few hours. The aircraft had disappeared, and a thick blanket of clouds had covered the city below. Only the highest buildings peeked through the fluffy white shroud. In the sky above, a half moon shone brightly, illuminating the tops of the clouds with its eerie glow. More stars than usual were visible on this night. Typically, the city's light pollution blotted out most of the heavenly bodies, save for the moon. The stars were brighter tonight, though, the atmosphere's residual glow from the artificial light below muted by the low-hanging clouds.

Heather snuck up behind him, padding her feet softly on the smooth, tile floor. She wrapped her arms around his waist and pulled him tight.

She'd never loved a man in this life. None had ever given her reason to. Brock, however, was different. He'd not pushed her away, not forced her into anything. He let her be who she was and fostered that, nurtured it to become more than she ever imagined.

Now, here they were, on top of the world, ready to give the planet a new start, a new beginning.

She recalled seeing a movie about that at one point. It wasn't well done, but she'd watched it until the end. It was a film about a tribe of natives living in Central America. They'd unwittingly welcomed the Spaniards to their shores, a move that had resulted in catastrophic and widespread illness, and eventually, the death of most of their once-powerful nation.

"What are you thinking about?" Brock asked, lacing his fingers through hers as she squeezed his abdomen tight.

"A bad movie," she answered.

He chuckled. "Must have been one of mine, then."

She laughed. "No. Another one. One where the natives welcomed certain death into their land without knowing it."

"Sort of like they've done here, huh?"

She nodded.

"A Trojan horse, of sorts," Brock said. "By this time tomorrow, millions of these people will be dead. They'll no longer pollute the waters, support the oil companies with their cars, and dump trash onto the land. They will be the first to fall."

"Where to after Shanghai?"

He grinned. "They'll prep the other cities here in China. We'll go west, to Mumbai. Hit them next. What the Indians have done to their land, their waters, and subsequently the rest of the world's water is unforgivable. They'll pay just like the rest. From there, I'm thinking New York City would be a good place to go."

She nodded. "It won't be easy. Homeland Security will be on full alert, especially after we hit two major cities."

"Nothing worth doing is ever easy. It wasn't easy to become an actor, but I did it. I worked, took side jobs, sacrificed. And here we are, in the penthouse of Shanghai Tower, all because of hard work."

"Indeed."

"Now this next phase...It will be harder than anything we've ever had to do before. But it's the only way, the only chance we have of resetting the planet and getting things back to the path nature intended."

She didn't bother arguing with him. She knew the real reason behind why he was doing this. He was bitter, a broken toy that didn't want any of the other toys to get any playtime. His life was torn apart, the foundations blasted away. He knew who was responsible. And while it should have been enough to get revenge on those men by watching them kill each other, it wasn't close. He was on a mission, one that would essentially end humanity and all its cruel intentions.

Was it cruel to perform attacks like this? Maybe. But soon, only a precious few people would be left. They would be lost in a world without technology or the knowledge to recreate it. During their intellectual growth, humans had also devolved to the point where basic survival instincts and intelligence were all but lost. Brock estimated that of the survivors, only a fraction of them would make it until the end of the year.

Heather and the rest of Brock's team would be safe. They were all protected from the effects of the trident's power. She would watch the world tear itself apart by his side. All the men who ever wronged her and women like her would die. Those who didn't would be left with a sparse reality, one that offered them no reason to keep on living. Many would likely take the easy way out.

As long as most of them paid, she was fine with that.

The sound of helicopter rotors thumped in the distance. They were coming back.

"I knew they wouldn't stay away for long," Brock said. He turned his head and gazed over his shoulder into her eyes.

"What can they do?"

"Aside from bombing the building? Not much. And I highly doubt they'll resort to that. They don't have the guts. The building is far too expensive, and there are too many innocent people down below. They'd have to evacuate dozens of city blocks." He looked out again at the white blanket below. "No, right now they're trying to figure out a way onto our floor and into our suite."

"You mean the decoy ones, right?"

"Exactly. They have no way of knowing that Mr. Jones's room is now being occupied by us."

He'd gone to the trouble of booking two suites in the hotel before arriving. Both were penthouse villas, but they were on opposite ends of the building. The one they were standing in was on the very top floor. The decoy was on the lower penthouse level one floor below.

If and when the cops found a way in, they would also discover that the entire floor was empty.

By then, it would probably be too late anyway. The surrounding area would be infected with the zombie-esque brain wave change that would result in the deaths of so many people.

If the cops got there at the right time, they, too, would turn murderous. That would be a sight to behold.

"We should go inside," Heather said. "No reason to give them an easy target or let them know where we are." She knew that there would be snipers on the helicopters, looking to take out Brock at a moment's notice.

The cops would be looking in the wrong place, that much was certain, but if they saw him, they'd easily recognize him.

He'd burned everything to make this happen. By putting out the video and stating his demands, he made it known to the world exactly what his intentions were and the price to be paid for disobeying him. He was going to unleash the power of the Trishula anyway, whether governments tried to clean up their act or not. The truth was, the planet was too far gone and making a few simple changes wouldn't be of any benefit. It had to be wholesale or nothing.

Brock nodded at her, and the two stepped inside, closed the sliding door, and drew the curtains. Tre and some of the other men were in the next room over, probably asleep for the night while two stood guard in the hall.

Heather looked up into his eyes. She placed her hands on either side of his face, just above the jawline. They locked lips for a moment, and then he pulled away. "When all this is over, you're going to be the queen you deserve to be."

She smiled at him. "I know."

47

SHANGHAI

Ming led the team off the plane, down the stairs, and onto the tarmac. The weather was miserable. Thick black clouds boiled overhead, churning as they slithered across the sky, dumping sheets of rain onto the earth below.

Sean pulled up the hood of his rain jacket and tugged it tight against his head.

The others did the same as they disembarked and stepped into the deluge.

Within thirty seconds, they'd all piled into a fleet of black Mercedes-Benz sedans and were speeding away from the hangar, heading toward downtown.

"Didn't realize it was the monsoon season," Sean said, looking out the window at the storm pelting the area.

"It's not," Ming said.

The clock on the dashboard said it was five o'clock in the morning. Sunrise would be soon. Everyone in the convoy knew what that would mean.

Unfortunately, Ming had said the Chinese government was being stubborn about the potential attack. While she'd given definitive proof about the abnormal magnetic spike in the area, no one seemed to believe it was a threat. All electrical devices were working. There was no sign of anything radioactive. If Carson was in possession of an explosive device of some kind, they wouldn't know it.

Ming got the distinct impression her government was calling the bluff, a dangerous game that she knew they shouldn't be playing. She'd seen the evidence. They'd seen it, too, but they didn't believe it was what she said it was—a Hollywood actor with a golden trident that could alter brain waves.

They might as well have laughed her off the phone.

Ming and the rest of her team were essentially on their own.

She had connections in the city's police department and had called in some of their helicopter units to have a look at the building. They'd flown around near the apex for almost half an hour, circling the penthouses and a few floors below. The report, of course, had been "nothing unusual." There was no cause for concern, at least that's what the cops believed. They had no idea what was up there.

The ride into downtown was a quick one. At that hour of the morning, there were only a few people out on the road, but that would change in forty to fifty minutes when rush hour began. And it was Monday, which she knew was particularly bad when it came to stop-and-go traffic.

The Shanghai Tower rose high into the air over the city, the top disappearing in low-hanging cloud cover that seemed to separate the elite of Shanghai from everyone else. Ming had heard those jokes before. She was on a government salary. Most of the populace were on set incomes. Only a select few seemed able to participate in the game of capitalism. They were the ones with the penthouses, the high-rise condos, and the mansions along the waterfront.

Socialism—for the masses, at least—had been a largely failed experiment. Ming often wondered how long it would be before their bubble burst. She knew the United States was in massive debt, as well, and it was only a matter of time until things went south for them, too, which would undoubtedly pull China down. Or the other way around.

At the moment, none of that mattered. She'd sworn to fight for what was there now, not what might be or might not be in the future. At this second, the lives of tens of millions of people were at stake, and she and this band of Americans were all that stood in the way of disaster.

They reached the Shanghai Tower and found a sparse collection of cops loitering around the base of the building. There were two outside the entrance, but Ming was shocked to find that their lights weren't on and the building hadn't been cordoned off. It was almost as if the city was only doing the bare minimum to fulfill their obligation to her and her agency.

They parked along the curb, and Ming got out. She strode purposefully toward the nearest cop by the door and held up a badge as if to tell him to get out of the way and go back to doing nothing.

Sean and the others didn't know her well, but it was easy to see she was upset. He, too, was surprised by the lack of law enforcement around the building. They clearly weren't taking this terrorist threat seriously.

To back that up, Tommy had scrolled through the IAA social media pages and checked the news feeds. Sure enough, most of the world thought Brock Carson was joking or trying to get publicity. Some believed he was setting up a role for a new movie, a type of guerrilla marketing that many entertainment companies were now employing with tremendous regularity and effect.

Memes aplenty had popped up all over the internet. Some were poking fun at Carson, while others, and not few in number, were begging for more of his threat videos.

What had been intended as a villainous move with an unachievable ultimatum had gone viral and was a huge hit.

Sean knew that would only serve to make things worse. He looked to the right and saw a car pull up. It had a sticker on the front that he couldn't read, but it looked like something he'd seen on a ride-share car before.

The back door opened and three young women got out. They were screaming and pointing to the top of the building, or where it might be beyond the clouds. They immediately started taking selfies with their phones. More cars pulled up to drop off riders. As Sean reached the entrance to the building, he realized what was going on.

These citizens were jumping on the bandwagon, thinking the entire thing was a big publicity stunt and were more than happy to give their attention to one of the world's most famous actors.

Sean caught up to Ming and tapped her on the shoulder. "You need to get these people out of here."

She looked at the crowd beginning to form in front of the main entrance. She sighed and shook her head. "There's nothing we can do about that. They're going to come. Everyone thinks Carson is about to make a big announcement about a new film or something. You couldn't keep the fans away if you tried."

He was impressed with her assessment and with her knowledge of international fandom, but he couldn't suppress the worry in his mind. The more people who gathered at the base of the tower, the worse this was going to be.

The group entered the side of the building and hurried across the lobby to the elevators. The second Ming pressed the button to call a lift, Sean abruptly realized what they were about to do. A sickening lump formed in his gut and his legs went weak. He felt the color drain from his face. It was all he could do to clench his fists and hope he didn't fall down.

This tower was one of the tallest buildings in the world and seeing Ming press that button reminded him that they were about to go to the very top.

Ming had called in a bomb disposal unit on the way from the airport. It was one of the few things she had direct control over, when necessary, through the agency. The men were already there, on the first penthouse level.

The doors opened, and everyone stepped inside. Sean moved more slowly than the rest, and Adriana gripping his hand to reassure him did little to ease his concern. There was nothing that could take away this incessant phobia. The elevator doors slid shut, and the lift took off, slowly at first. But as it ascended, the speed increased to an almost dizzying level. Sean was accustomed to going fast. He'd taken his motorcycles on more than one see what this baby can do trips to the grocery store and back. He'd ridden the famous Dragon's Tail in Deal's Gap, North Carolina, just a few miles from Robbinsville. Speed wasn't a problem—unless he was rocketing toward the top of a tall building.

Tommy put a sympathetic hand on his shoulder as they watched the floor-indicator lights zip by on the readout above the doors. When they reached the one-hundredth floor, the elevator began to slow until they arrived at their destination, 127. This was the floor where Brock Carson had checked into and where he'd set up his little headquarters for the attack.

Ming stepped out of the elevator and froze.

The bomb squad was there, blocking the hallway as a robot rolled down the carpet toward the room that, she figured, was Carson's.

"We've detected several devices on this floor," one of the men in armor told Ming. "You should go back down until we've cleared it out."

She knew they were good. The explosives would be dismantled and rendered harmless—unless one of them blew.

Ming glanced at her watch and then at Sean. "It's almost sunrise," she said. "We need to get to his room and stop him."

Sean glanced back at the men carrying the black case with the Gada inside it. His mind was racing. At present, there were no windows save for at the end of the corridor, and he couldn't see very well out of them from this vantage point. His fear of heights had dissipated slightly since getting off the elevator. He hoped it would remain that way.

"He's not on this floor," Sean said abruptly.

Ming, Tommy, and Adriana stared at him, all wondering the same thing.

"What do you mean he's not on this floor?" Tommy asked.

"It's a decoy," Sean said. "I've seen it before. Heck, I've done it before when I was worried someone was coming for me. You rent a room on one floor and another on a different floor."

Adriana shook her head. "Then where is he?"

"I'd wager he's still around here close by. This is the penthouse level, right?"

Ming turned to one of the bomb squad guys and asked in Mandarin. She turned back to Sean. "There's one more penthouse level above us."

"That's where he is."

"How do you know?"

"Because this guy has a chip on his shoulder. He came from nothing, and now he has an ego. No way he's going to be second floor from the top. Not his style. And what better place to watch anarchy ensue than from up there?"

It was possible Sean was wrong. Truly, it was an educated guess, but something was up. Why all the traps on this floor? To confirm, he had another question.

He pointed at the cop running the bomb disposal operation. "Ming, ask him what kinds of explosives these are."

She gave an exasperated sigh but did as requested. When the man answered, she turned back to Sean. "He said they resemble mines. You Americans call them claymores, he said."

Claymores were designed to send a horizontal blast out and away from the source. While there was any number of dangerous anti-personnel mines that could jump up and explode, from the Bouncing Betty to the kind that was just buried in the ground and exploded vertically, the claymore was a specific directional mine.

Those kinds of explosives wouldn't damage the floor above. They would wreak all kinds of havoc in this corridor and for these rooms, but the top floor would be relatively unaffected. Same with the ones below.

Sean looked back at the agents who'd carried the mace up the elevator in its plastic case. Then he flashed a glance down the long corridor where the windows were. The first rays of sunlight peeked through and splashed on the floor and walls.

"We need to get this up there now," Sean motioned to the case while speaking to Tommy.

His friend nodded and grabbed one handle. Sean grabbed the

other, but one of the agents shook his head and pushed his hand aside.

"Now isn't the time for a power play," Sean said. "He's going to set that thing off. Let us take care of this."

The men looked to Ming for their orders. She considered it for a moment, longer than Sean would have liked, and then nodded once.

Sean flipped up the latches and grabbed the handle to lift the lid and set it on the floor. Inside the case was a soft black foam cushion cradling the golden mace. The Gada had a shaft about two feet long that narrowed in the middle and widened at the base and near the top where it expanded into a vase-like shape. It was one complete piece with no openings on either end.

Sean reached into the case and picked it up. He was surprised at how light the object was. It might have weighed ten pounds, which was pretty heavy, but not what he would have thought for something made of gold.

He hefted the object in one hand, cradling the wide end of the mystical weapon with the other. He flipped it around, twisting it to examine it once more. They'd looked it over when they found it in the temple cave, but there was something about it Sean didn't understand. How did it work?

The only thing he could figure was that, somehow, the Gada simply absorbed the signal that was sent out from the Trishula. Was that possible? Or did they just fly halfway across the world to find a golden object that was of no help?

There was only one way to know, and time was running out.

48

SHANGHAI

B rock stood on the balcony, the Trishula in his right hand, its base resting on the platform by his feet. He looked east as the sun came up over the horizon. The bright yellow, nearly white rays glistened on the waterways and the connecting sea. Mists rose from the forests in the hills and mountains, joining the clouds already on the rise toward the higher altitudes of a crystal clear sky.

Up here, he was above it all. The sounds and smells of the city below were drowned out by a constant wind that whispered in his ears. Not that he hated any of that. The food in Shanghai was phenomenal. He'd enjoyed the last few days here and thought perhaps someday he would return when most of the population was dead. The people who'd founded the city so long ago had certainly picked a beautiful spot.

He turned to his right and caught a mote of light glancing off Heather's helmet. He winced and then grinned. The helmets were ridiculous-looking things, gaudy and awkward, not to mention uncomfortable. They were designed for function, nothing else. The modified helmets Adam and Elma had rigged at Brock's request were at least a little more comfortable, with padding built in to keep them snug against the wearer's skull.

Brock looked back into the suite where his security team waited. Two of them were stationed on either side of the door. Tre and one other were closer, standing in the living room just inside the sliding door to the balcony. Then there were the two outside the room. One was positioned by the elevators in case a threat came up to the top floor. Sure, there were other people renting rooms up there, but Brock wasn't taking any chances. Another man was placed at the opposite end of the hall, where a bench sat next to a wide window that gave visitors a panoramic view of the city. There was another, more sinister reason for the guards in the hall. Brock knew that when the pulse went out from the Trishula, the occupants in the other rooms would begin killing each other. The survivors would spill into the halls, continuing their hunt for more bloodshed. The guards' orders were to kill anyone who entered the hall, no matter who they were or what age. Brock doubted there were children up here, but if there were, he didn't care. There was no mercy left in him, no patience, and no empathy. He'd surrendered fully to his mission, and there was no going back.

The final section of sun cleared the horizon and was fully visible.

"It's time," Brock said. His finger hovered over the button on the trident, tickling the smooth golden surface. He watched as a cloud drifted over the face of the sun, casting a thin shadow across the city for a few seconds before it cleared to the other side, once more bathing Shanghai Tower in a warm glow.

Heather touched his arm, squeezing his bicep firmly in her grasp.

He looked back at Tre. The bodyguard adjusted his helmet and gave a nod. Brock didn't have to ask. He knew the men in the corridor outside were already equipped and ready to go.

Brock drew in a deep breath and exhaled one last time. The air wasn't exactly clean but certainly cleaner up here in the rarefied space than it was down below, where smog hung thick over the streets and permeated the buildings.

"To a new world," he said.

His finger depressed the button on the trident. He felt the gentle brush of the pulse as it shot through his body and coursed throughout the building and beyond.

Suddenly, the building shook violently from the top all the way down to its foundation.

Brock frowned. Then his eyes shot wide with fear. Something was wrong.

He turned to Heather for answers, but she had the same questions in her eyes. Then the building answered.

The tower bent hard, swaying to one side. Brock and Heather instinctively took a step back from the ledge as the building seemed to bow in that direction. They felt gravity pulling them toward the railing and tilted their torsos back to fight it. Then, as suddenly as it began, the movement stopped.

But only for a second.

The skyscraper paused and then began to sway in the other direction. The movement threw the suite's occupants off balance and sent Brock and Heather sprawling through the door and into the living room. Brock's foot caught a corner of an area rug, and he tripped. He tumbled onto the floor and rolled until his back hit the sofa and stopped him. Heather stumbled into the room and managed to brace herself against the bar. Tre had steadied himself against a corner wall, leaning into it with his shoulder. The guy across from him was on his tail, sprawled out and struggling to get up. The two at the door had wedged themselves into the corners of the foyer and were desperately trying to keep steady.

The building reached the zenith of its motion and then continued onward to the other side.

The occupants felt the pull of gravity once more, now dragging them toward the door leading into the hallway.

Brock managed to scramble to his feet and hold on to the sofa.

"What is going on?" he shouted.

Heather didn't have an answer. She was too busy trying to stay on her feet.

Klaxons started to blare, signaling an evacuation order.

The realization hit Brock even as he shuffled over to the kitchen and grabbed the edge of the granite counter to stabilize himself. He saw a clock with a pendulum on the wall and knew what had happened.

The world's tallest buildings were usually built with a damping system. This system was designed to counter the swaying motion that a tall structure would inevitably face from winds, planetary movement, and simply from being so tall with so much weight. Damping systems were usually constructed with a heavy pendulum that would counter the swaying motion. So, as a building moved one way, the pendulum would swing the other and reduce the movement to an almost imperceptible level. Without such dampers, people could easily lose their balance and experience seasickness on dry land.

Brock could feel the bile rising in his throat as the epiphany came to light. He fought off the nausea and tried to think.

He'd read about this place, the Shanghai Tower, and about its unique eddy-current damper. It was a fascinating piece of engineering, but also an elegantly simple solution to the problem of keeping such a tall building stabilized.

The pendulum was built with one thousand tons of steel plates that were surrounded by powerful magnets. When the building moved too much, the system activated itself and countered, but also used hydraulics to slow the pendulum's movement so it wouldn't overcompensate. The result was that anyone on the top floors of the tower would feel almost no movement at all, which was an incredible feat.

There was only one conclusion that Brock could come up with. The Trishula had caused the damping system to malfunction.

He assumed that the structure was built to withstand some swaying, that the engineers had planned for a contingency such as this, but that didn't keep fear from creeping into Brock's mind.

His original plan had been to stay put, there in the hotel, and let everyone in the surrounding city blocks start killing each other. Eventually, they would spread out and head farther into the city, hunting down more victims. When that happened, Brock and his team would board the helicopter waiting below on the helipad, and they'd make their getaway.

Now, he wasn't sure that was an option.

The elevators would be shut down. At least that's what he figured. That's how those things typically worked. When there was an emergency like a fire or earthquake, often the stairs were the only way out. He cringed at the thought of descending all those stories to reach the floor with the helipad.

This new turn of events had just upped his timeline. Perhaps there would be no triumphant viewing of the chaos down below. That would have to wait for another time.

Now, they needed to get out of here in case things got worse.

49

SHANGHAI

Sean reached the top of the stairs and nearly vomited. He and the others had felt the pulse. He knew that meant Brock had activated the device. Had the Gada worked to stop its deadly frequency from disrupting brain waves all across the city?

It must have. He still felt relatively normal, aside from the sudden wave of nausea that hit him. Was this one of the symptoms?

Adriana braced herself on the railing and climbed a few more steps to the top where Sean was wedged in the corner. Tommy clutched the railing against the opposite wall. Ming and three of her men were doing the same.

Alarms were piercing their ears from the ceiling above and down below. The annoying sounds signaled the need to get out of the building.

"What happened?" Sean asked, shouting as loud as he could, both to be heard and to help him forget his nausea.

He felt the building moving, and his legs weakened. He felt his bowels shudder. His face flushed white, and he held the door latch with white-knuckled fury. Here he was, 128 stories up in a building he knew he had no business being in, and now it was moving. A hundred horrific scenarios played out before his eyes within seconds.

From the top of the structure snapping off and falling to the streets below, to the whipping building tossing him and others out of the windows, none of it was pleasant and only served to further Sean's sudden wave of panic.

"We have to get out of here!" Ming yelled. "The damping system has failed!"

Sean knew what she was talking about. He was vaguely familiar with those systems. They were pendulum-operated in most cases. He'd read about them as a result of a sick fascination with his phobia, wondering why buildings swayed and then how humans were able to counter that phenomenon.

Ming's revelation was a terrible one, and his only thought was that they were all going to die up here in this tower. Reason flew out the window, and Sean caught himself hoping that was the only thing that did.

This entire scenario was playing out like something from his nightmares.

There was a steel resolve in his mind, though, that overrode all the fears, the panic, the crippling paranoia. The Gada had worked. He and the others weren't attacking each other, driven to madness by some ancient code unleashed in their minds. If they left now, they would be safe, probably. The inherent problem with that, however, was obvious to Sean. If they escaped, that meant Carson could, too. If he got out of the building, he had the resources to vanish once more only to pop up and attack another city. Without knowing the next target, Sean was keenly aware that the Gada wouldn't be able to stop another attack. The weapons, it seemed, needed to be in the same area.

"Go on!" Sean ordered. "Get everyone you can out of the building! Emergency teams will need all the help they can get with the evacuation."

Ming hesitated. "What are you going to do?"

The fears screaming at him from the depths of his subconscious vanished into a thin veil of resolve. "I'm going to get Brock Carson."

Sean turned without waiting for her to respond and reached for the door handle. Behind him, Tommy and Adriana stayed close, each gripping a weapon in one hand and the railing in the other. He'd learned a long time ago not to try to tell his friends to stay behind, to go where it's safe. Adriana, Tommy, and Sean were three sides to a triangle, the strongest structure in nature. Together or nothing. That was how they operated. He glanced at Adriana, his jaw set firm. He didn't want to lose her. Every time they went into a dangerous situation, that fear overwhelmed all others. She could handle herself. He knew that. He also knew that sometimes, even the best were unlucky.

"Ready?" he asked.

They nodded and Sean pulled on the latch.

He flung the door open and was struck on the shoulder by a heavy object. The building had swayed a little the moment he'd opened the door, so when the guy flying through hit him, Sean's torso twisted naturally to compensate for the lack of balance. The guy had been in the corridor just beyond the exit. As he fell down the stairs, a gun flew out of his hand and clattered down the steps until it reached the landing next to the unconscious body of its owner. Ming had just rounded the first corner when the guard appeared, striking his head against the railing and then numerous steps as he tumbled.

She looked up at Sean.

He shrugged. "See? We're good."

She shook her head and ordered two of her men to check the body.

When she glanced up again, all three of the friends were gone, the door closing slowly behind them.

Sean made the mistake of turning to the right first. There was a long window looking out into the city. It took a fraction of a second for Sean to be reminded of just how high up they truly were.

He felt the bile return to his throat and he choked it back, snapping his head around. The fear melted as he saw Brock Carson and several others running down the passage in the other direction. One man stayed behind. He was in a tight black Under Armour shirt, black cargo pants, and boots, and had a submachine gun in his hands. As Brock and his entourage were vacating their suite, the guard noticed the movement at the other end of the hall amid the chaotic sounds of the klaxons and the swaying motion of the Tower.

The man raised his weapon to fire, but Sean was a quicker draw and unleashed a quick shot that cracked by the man's head and sank into the wall. The guard leaned sideways, realizing he was exposed and that he needed to find cover. The door pulled closed as he tried to shove his way in, and his shoulder barged against it with a thud. The blow jarred him, but that wasn't the worst of his troubles.

The barrage of hot metal zipping toward him was.

Sean, Tommy, and Adriana each fired their weapons.

Five bullets from their combined barrels tore into the guard as the three stalked toward him, spread out wide across the breadth of the corridor. His body shuddered as the hot rounds struck, two piercing his chest, one in the pelvis, and one in the gut. He slid down against the door and slumped to a stop on the threshold.

Sean and the others kept moving, faster now. They knew the reports from the gunfire would have alerted Brock to trouble, which would have only made him run faster.

No one bothered to check as the three sprinted past the body in the doorway and charged ahead around the long curve.

They were near the apex of the bend when another shot rang out from up ahead. Sean jumped to the right and pressed against a door. Tommy and Adriana nudged close to him. The shooter wasn't in sight.

Sean waited, knowing the other guy was doing the same. He would hide like a snake until he thought the enemy was making their move. It was the ultimate game of poker, guessing what the other person's play was going to be and what they actually had for a hand.

Sean remembered the flash-bang disc in his pocket, but that wouldn't do much good. The floor was carpeted, so it wouldn't slide very far. The enemy was more than thirty feet away, and Sean doubted he could throw it with enough accuracy to be effective.

No tricks this time. He'd have to win this standoff the old-fashioned way. He felt the motion of the building slowing. Fear gripped his gut again and wrenched it tight. Then he knew what was coming next. The tower would sway back in the other direction. It was reaching the farthest point in its current trajectory. When that happened, he and his friends would be pushed hard the other way.

"Grab on to me," Sean said quickly over his shoulder.

The others questioned the order with their eyes, but their hands obeyed, reaching out and grabbing Sean's shoulders. He held on to the door latch next to his waist and held it tight.

The building stopped for a second and then started moving again in the other direction. The movement wasn't so strong that it would have flung Sean and his friends across the hall, but it certainly made the world around them spin for a moment. Tommy could feel seasickness kicking in, and his legs weakened yet again. He held firm, though, and was rewarded a second later when two armed men stumbled out of cover in the turn ahead and crashed into the far wall.

"Now," Sean said.

He and the others stepped forward once more, albeit in a diagonal direction. Their legs wobbled, but their arms and hands remained steady as they squeezed the triggers of their weapons and ended the two henchmen with rounds of metal piercing their flesh and vital organs.

The two men fell dead against the wall, one collapsing on top of the other in an awkward pile.

Sean pressed the magazine release on his pistol and saw he still had some rounds left, plus one spare magazine on his belt. He knew Adriana and Tommy had a similar quantity of ammunition left. That might or might not be enough depending on how many more thugs Carson had covering his behind.

They kept going, past the two dead men this time and around the curve. When they reached a point where they could see all the way to the end of the hall, there was no one in sight.

Sean slowed his pace, holding his weapon out to the side but in a ready position that would take him no more than half a second to raise and fire. He stopped at a door to a room and waited for a moment to make sure no one else had the bright idea of popping out to surprise them, then left the opening and pushed forward. They reached the end of the hall, where a set of elevators faced out. Behind them were two doors. One was a closet. The other said Maintenance.

"Cover me," Sean said.

He pulled the latch to the maintenance door and found it opened easily. He'd initially expected to find an enclosed hallway surrounded by concrete blocks, tires, pipes, and all manner of things that were hidden away from the public eye in any major building. He recalled walking down the tunnels underneath Mercedes-Benz Stadium in Atlanta just before a Falcons game and figured this "underground" area would look the same.

He couldn't have been more wrong.

A gust of air smacked him in the face as he stepped through, his weapon in the lead.

To his right, a metal façade rose up to a catwalk that was easily sixty feet above him. To his left was the more unnerving sight. The glass wall of the Shanghai Tower ran around the curved exterior of the building, plunging Sean directly into the face of one of his greatest fears.

His abdomen tightened.

He saw Carson running up a ramp, carrying a golden trident. He'd ditched his helmet on the floor, and it rolled toward the glass wall as the building tipped once more in that direction.

Sean noticed the figure immediately to his right and dove forward before the mercenary fired his weapon. The gun discharged, and the merc turned to finish the job with Sean sprawling on the floor and trying to steady his own gun.

Before the guy could get off a second shot, Adriana barged through the opening and ended the man with one shot through the side of his head. He dropped to his knees and slumped against the wall.

Adriana sensed another danger and spun to her left.

She had only seen the initial threat with the first mercenary and didn't realize there was another. This man, with a thick reddish-blond beard, neck tattoo, and a sinister look in his eye, was about to fire his weapon.

Sean, still on the ground, twisted his wrist and squeezed the trigger. The round grazed the bearded guy on his side, tearing through the flesh under his armpit. He flinched, grimaced, and then sensing the more immediate threat, turned to shoot at Sean.

Tommy burst through the door and opened fire, emptying his magazine at the bearded mercenary, planting every single round into the man's torso.

The guy staggered backward and then fell on to his back.

Adriana sprinted forward. She saw Brock running up the gangway to what he thought was a possible escape. She knew what it truly was.

Sean sprang up from the floor and ran hard toward the ramp, but slowed when he realized what it was. He immediately regretted easing his pace. Something hard hit his right shoulder and then wrapped around him, driving him to the ground in what an American football defensive coordinator would have called a perfect form tackle.

His left shoulder pounded into the ground with an additional 130 pounds piled on top. Sean caught a strand of the woman's hair across his face a second before she popped up and raised a fist to pound him with a hammer blow.

Her legs squeezed his torso like a boa constrictor.

Tommy started to run to lend assistance, but he caught movement out of the corner of his eye. The bearded guy was getting up and raising his weapon again.

How was that possible?

Tommy spun and pulled the trigger on his weapon while he simultaneously lined up the sights with the mercenary's head.

The weapon clicked.

His magazine was empty.

He dove forward, pumping his legs as fast as he could while drawing a hunting knife from a sheath at his side. There was another magazine, sure, but he knew by the time the first one fell to the floor, the gunman would have cut him down.

Tommy leaped into the air and fell onto the shooter, the tip of his blade driving hard toward the base of the man's neck.

Adriana charged ahead toward the ramp. She reached the base of it just in time for Carson to fire from the doorway to the observation deck.

The deck was a metal frame. The design made it look like the observation box was teetering over the edge of the building's exterior. Half of it protruded out over the city below and featured a glass floor.

Carson fired his pistol at Adriana and she barely managed to dive clear of the shots, taking cover under the grated metal plank.

Carson's weapon clicked amid the sound of alarms. He looked at the gun in frustration and then ran back into the observation room.

Adriana rolled out and emptied her magazine, reloaded a new one, and fired again. The bullets pinged off metal. More than a few punctured the thick glass surrounding the observation box. Thick spiderweb cracks spread out through the clear surface, but none of the rounds found their mark.

Carson reloaded and popped out again, firing once more at Adriana's position.

Sean twisted his body hard to the left, jerking with every muscle he could. The move was too much for the woman atop him, and she tumbled onto the floor. He scrambled for his pistol, but she was too quick. Like a nimble forest animal, she sprang up and swung a boot at his face, driving the top of her foot across his cheek.

The room blurred instantly, and Sean felt a terrible, sharp pain shoot through his face.

He rolled back onto his side for a second, unable to collect his thoughts.

He saw a blurry figure step over to him. She loomed above like an angel of death, waiting to take another soul.

"I never cared much for boys like you," she spat.

She reached to her side and withdrew a knife. "But I'm not going to kill you with a gun. I'm going to enjoy this."

Sean's head spun, but he collected himself enough to press his palms to the floor and push back as she dove at him. Instead of plunging the knife into his chest, she missed and caught his knee squarely in the nose.

The blood faucet turned on and poured dark crimson liquid from her nostrils. She howled in agony, grasping at the appendage out of pure instinct. Sean struggled to his feet and took a big step over to her. She was on her knees, her head waist high. He took no pleasure in killing a woman. Call it the Southern gentleman in him. He had to knock her out, though, at the very least. He took a hard step with his left foot and raised the right. The right leg whipped around hard. His target was her left temple, but she let go of her bloody nose with one hand and tried to swing the knife wildly at him.

Sean's kick was strong and true, but the woman's movement had changed her position. The tip of his boot struck the base of her hand and she missed everything with the reckless knife swing. His boot drove the blade hard at her neck until the tip plunged into her skin and deep into the tissue beyond.

Her body shuddered. Coughing followed. Then gurgling. She twitched even as she fell to the floor, unable to swallow or breathe. The hand holding the knife fell limp to her side as the last fleeting moments of consciousness escaped her body.

Tommy straddled the big mercenary, doing his best to drive the knife point into the guy's right eye socket. The merc was stronger than him, but Tommy had converted most of his body mass to muscle over the years and found that he could almost match the killer in strength.

It took every ounce of the merc's strength to push the knife up from his face. It had been close, but now Tommy was losing the battle. Suddenly, the man made a quick flicking motion with his hands. Tommy's wrists snapped, almost to the point of breaking, and he grimaced in pain. The knife fell to the floor, narrowly missing the mercenary's left eye. It clanked on the floor, rattled a second, and then lay still.

Meanwhile, the killer was spreading Tommy's hands apart, pulling with all his strength as if he might tear them from their sockets. Tommy couldn't let him win this battle. If he did, the war would be lost, too. He had only one option and he didn't like it, but there was no choice. Tommy reared his head back and thrust it forward. He felt the man's nose crunch against his forehead, his hands suddenly weakening. Tommy pulled back and did it again, plowing his forehead painfully against the man's nose. It hurt to do it, but Tommy knew it was hurting the other guy far more. The guy's hands almost went completely limp. His head rolled back and forth. Tommy managed to stand up, gasping for air. He pulled back his right foot and, as the mercenary rolled his head the other way, Tommy swung the tip of his boot at the guy's temple.

The boot tip struck hard and snapped the man's head to the side. His hands fell to the floor, and he stopped moving, now in the deep sleep that unconsciousness had to offer.

Brock watched it all transpire with a horrified glaze over his eyes. He'd seen Heather killed right in front of him. His heart rent in half. He'd loved her. She'd been the only woman who ever truly understood him, knew him for who he was, and not once judged him.

He watched as Tre was defeated. It was impossible to tell if he was dead, but Brock feared the worst.

Now he was the only one left, the last bastion of righteousness against a world that had torn itself apart in the name of progress, industry, and convenience.

He raised his weapon to fire at the woman as she approached, her brown hair trailing over her shoulders in a breeze that was coming from the holes in the glass façade of the observation deck.

His gun clicked. He'd forgotten he had just spent all its contents a moment before; such was his devastation.

He tossed the gun aside with a clank and backed up against the wall. There was a cracking sound, and he risked a look over his shoulder at the splintered glass.

In his left hand was the only thing he had to fight with. The Trishula, trident of Shiva. He shifted the weapon and held it with both hands, and took a sideways stance.

Adriana slowed her approach and kept her eyes locked on the weapon.

He lunged forward with it.

She twisted sideways.

He withdrew and lunged again.

She repeated her movement to dodge the attack.

He stabbed out a third time.

This time, Adriana ducked to the opposite side, slapped her hands down on the golden shaft, and squeezed it hard. She yanked it toward her, which also caused Carson to stumble her way.

Adriana kicked out her left foot, extending it straight as her heel struck him in the gut and sent him reeling back toward the glass wall.

His back hit it, and he heard more cracking on the surface. Panicked, he pushed himself away from the edge and back toward Adriana. He screamed, flashing his hands in a variety of martial arts moves.

She tossed the trident backward.

The golden object hit the glass and slid toward the ramp.

Carson swung first with his left, a chop that would have landed on her cheek, but she deflected with her left, countered with a right to his chest. He stumbled back but regained composure and charged again. This time, he swung his legs and his hands in a tornado of furious attacks.

She knocked down one kick, then the other, ignoring the pain the blocks sent through her forearms. He punched at her face, but she twisted her head, wrapped the wrist, and twisted it with incredible force until she heard and felt the snap of the bone within.

He shrieked in pain and tried to withdraw the injured arm, but it was too late. He'd stepped into the spider's web now.

His other arm attempted another feeble punch, but she grabbed that one, too, brought it to the other fist, and punched through until the bone broke. He howled in agony, staggering back with both arms dangling uselessly at his side.

Brock stared beyond her, to the trident lying on the floor. There was no way he could reach it. No way he could defeat this woman. He'd lost everything. His head twisted to the right, and once more he saw the bodies of his loyal soldiers, one a bodyguard, the other a woman he cared so deeply for.

He'd lost everything now. His defeat was complete. His father and mother were gone. He had no relatives who cared about him, other than to ask for money. And now this. His plans had all gone awry.

Sean appeared behind Adriana at the other end of the walkway. He'd forgotten, for the moment, that they were thousands of feet up in the air inside one of the world's tallest buildings. The only thing he was thinking about was Adriana.

She'd barely broken a sweat.

"You!" Brock shouted. "You ruined everything!"

Adriana nodded.

"You wanted to kill millions of innocent people, Brock," Sean said. "You need to get help."

Brock laughed a sickly, evil laugh. His head turned side to side as Tommy appeared at the top of the ramp behind his friends.

"It's over," Sean said. "You're going to jail for a very long time. You can think about what you've done then."

"Jail?" Brock laughed. "I tried to save this planet. I tried to make it new again, to give it a fighting chance! Now, because of you, this planet is going to die because humanity doesn't care enough to save it. And you know what happens when the planet dies? We all die, too! Don't you see? We're all dead!"

Sean shook his head. "Humanity has a funny way of figuring things out right when we need to most. It's not too late to save the world, Brock."

The actor's face trembled. There was a crazy look in his eyes. He glanced back over his shoulder at the cracked glass wall, then back to the others.

"Not the answer," Sean warned. "Don't."

"Wouldn't dream of it," Brock said.

Then his legs pushed hard, thighs flexing as he drove himself toward the glass. His shoulder struck it first, just as Sean reached out his hand.

He yelled at the actor not to jump, but it was too late.

Brock's weight plowed into the glass weakened by the bullets that had pierced it and shattered it into hundreds of jagged pieces.

He fell through it and tumbled into the air, his body toppling head over heels as it plunged through the morning light.

Sean averted his gaze as the man disappeared from sight. He didn't want to see it.

Adriana watched until she was sure Carson was gone and then spun around to face Sean and Tommy. She stepped close and put her hands on Sean's cheeks, and then hugged him.

"It's okay," she said. "It's all over."

Sean nodded. "Can we please go back down to the ground floor?"

She let an awkward laugh escape her lips and nodded. "Yeah."

EPILOGUE

CHATTANOOGA, TENNESSEE

The sun had disappeared in the west, over the top of Lookout Mountain. Brilliant orange and pink hues streaked the sky with a hint of lavender in a few spots where thin cirrus clouds raced through the heavens.

Oak, maple, and poplar trees did their best to match the colors with their own reds, yellows, oranges, and browns. The cool air seemed to remind them that fall was here and that the time was coming for a long winter's nap. A gentle breeze blew through the tree-tops and shook some of the early turners free, blowing them through the canopy above.

Amid the dapple and frost of the southern Tennessee autumn, the cellist's solo sounded almost out of place, save for the occasion and the decorations.

The perfectly manicured grass was surrounded by old mountain stone that matched the Grandview's exterior wall. The old hotel and restaurant were a couple of the more popular places in the region to host a wedding. The panoramas of both the so-called Scenic City and the valley below were unmatched for hundreds of miles. The Tennessee River snaked its way by the famous Tennessee Aquarium, between downtown and the trendy North

Shore, until it disappeared around Moccasin Bend and circled toward Signal Mountain.

The cellist's song changed as the bride appeared at the far end of the aisle. It wasn't a long walk, but it might have been a hundred miles, at least for the anxious groom who stood next to the altar and the minister conducting the ceremony.

"You ready for this?" Sean asked. He stood in his tuxedo, a firmly pressed black jacket and pants with a gray-and-black-striped tie. His hands were behind his back, as ordered by the wedding coordinator, who, Sean was fairly certain, had been in the Gestapo in a past life.

Tommy cleared his throat nervously. "Are you really ever ready?"

Sean's smirk never faded. "No, I don't think so."

The bride's wedding gown trailed behind her, dragging across the white velvet carpet that had been laid down. Behind the veil, her teeth gleamed. She couldn't wipe the smile off her face.

"Not too late to turn back," Sean muttered. "I can make a break for my bike. We'll be out of the city in no time."

"Stop it," Tommy hissed.

Alex shifted anxiously next to Tommy, not saying a word.

The song ended when the bride arrived at the altar. She pulled back the veil as the minister asked who was giving her to be married.

"Her mother and I do," said Tara's father, an older man with gray-peppered black hair and a tanned, weathered face that revealed his many hours at the beach and on the golf course. A tear streaked down his cheek, and he wiped it with one hand. Then he kissed his daughter on the cheek, whispered "I love you," and then went back to his seat next to her mother.

Tara stepped forward and took Alex by the hand. Tears welled in both their eyes. Their lips quivered as they smiled at each other.

Sean had a difficult time fending off his own tears.

He resorted to his usual humor to push them back, at least for a few more minutes. Leaning close to Tommy, he whispered in his friend's ear, "I told you something was going on between them."

Tommy snorted and shook his head.

The minister glared at them, clearly annoyed.

Then he began to recite a passage from the Bible, and the ceremony began in earnest. He talked about how Tara and Alex met, both graduate students at the same university. They'd become friends and both applied for openings with the International Archaeological Agency as research assistants. That job had pulled the two together into an intimacy that transcended most relationships. They loved each other, enjoyed the same things in life, and had a bond that could never be broken.

When the minister was finished with his homily, the vows were given. Then came the kiss. Tara and Alex locked lips for a long moment as he dipped her down just slightly. Those in attendance roared their approval. Even Sean clapped fervently at the display.

After the service, the crowd stood and ushered out the bride and groom, showering them with applause and laughter. There would be a reception in the meeting hall, a place that was a throwback to the glory days of the city's tourist boom following the end of Prohibition. There were dark wooden beams that rose to the rafters. Enormous black chandeliers hung from the ceilings. Matching sconces lined the walls. Bookshelves stood sentry in places that had once been sitting rooms. And there was a bar downstairs, on the ground floor, where the less temperate guests could imbibe their favorite beverages.

Sean followed the procession out, winking at Adriana as he hooked his arm through hers and marched toward the building where a lavish buffet had been laid out for the reception.

She winked back at him, the diamond on her finger glittering in the waning twilight.

They reached the reception hall and took their places at the wedding party table. Sean sat next to Tommy, who was sitting by June. There was a brief announcement about how the lines should proceed table by table, with the wedding party going first.

Toasts would follow. Then there would be dancing and revelry late into the night.

Sean cut into a piece of quiche and popped it into his mouth.

Tommy leaned close, trying to get out of earshot of June. "Aren't you glad we eloped?"

Sean nodded as he chewed. "Yes. Yes, I am. Although when you say it that way, someone who didn't know better would think you and I got married."

"What? No. You know what I meant."

"Remember our first date under the stars?" Sean gazed up at the sky as if fondly recalling that fateful night. "It was an evening much like this one." He stole a sidelong glance at an older woman standing nearby, her ears prickling at the sound of potential gossip, eyes wide with disbelief.

Tommy looked instantly disheveled. He was in the middle of taking a drink and Sean's comment caused him to choke a little. He couldn't correct the situation fast enough.

"Shut up. What is wrong with you?"

"You ashamed of me? Why are you always like this?"

Tommy stumbled through a sentence, full of words that were both nonsensical and hilarious. The woman listening in on the conversation turned and walked away, probably eager to share the "news" with her friends and family.

Sean started laughing. He slapped his friend on the back.

"Thanks for that," Tommy said.

"Happy to," Sean said with a wink.

Sean winked at him and chuckled.

Tommy shook his head and went back to eating the remaining cheese cubes on his plate.

Tommy had just learned the truth about what June had been up to. The conversation had been difficult at first, but once he'd accepted the reality about who she was and what she did he kind of felt like the luckiest guy on the planet. Sure, his girlfriend could beat him up, but in a strange way, he appreciated that.

The four had gotten married together at a small ceremony in a neighboring town, just over the Tennessee border. Ringgold had been famous for its little wedding chapel for decades. One of the more well-known marriages that had taken place there was Dolly Parton's, which the little chapel was more than happy to advertise 24/7.

Sean sipped his sweet tea and smiled at the happy couple seated in the center of the long table.

It had been a month since the incident in Shanghai. He'd reflected on much since then. And had made some decisions. One was that he never intended to let Adriana go again. Not that he could keep her from being her own woman, but that they wouldn't keep secrets from each other, that they'd always be honest, and that they'd always try to be there for one another.

It was difficult, the time he'd spent without her while she was away working with June. Tommy'd felt her absence in his life as if the very air had been sucked out of Earth's atmosphere. Fortunately, both of the women had felt the same way about their men.

Sean had joked with him about how lucky they were to have met women who lowered their standards to their level. The truth was, all of them were lucky. And there was no reason to put off vows any longer.

Not in a million years would they have found a better match for each other. Much like Tara and Alex. Sean and Adriana chose to elope in Fiji, while Tommy and June had picked a beautiful farm in the small town of Ooltewah, Tennessee, just north of Chattanooga. Now, it seemed, the circle was closed.

Ming Lao had been extremely gracious with her thanks to Sean and the others for what they'd done to stop Brock Carson and his crazy scheme.

She'd invited the three of them—Tommy, Adriana, and Sean—to her home for dinner before they left the country.

They'd been treated to an amazing array of food: rice, vegetable dumplings with a savory brown sauce taught to her by her grand-mother, fried tofu with an orange glaze, and a sweetened fruit drink that haunted their dreams.

Ming and her husband had a three-year-old daughter, and the little family lived there in Shanghai. It was no wonder she'd been so fearful of an attack on the city.

Scientists had confiscated the Gada and the Trishula and spent weeks conducting a number of tests that even NASA would envy. The

Gada, it seemed, was the balancer, as was the deity who was purported to have wielded it. The mace was designed to absorb the pulse of the Trishula, thus preventing the global destruction the mythical Shiva desired.

Research was still ongoing as to how the two weapons worked, but Sean wasn't worried about that. The relics were in the proper hands now, and at least for a while, the world was safe.

Tommy had set up a secondary foundation that split off from his International Archaeological Agency. This new organization was dedicated to clearing the waters off the coast of Hawaii and establishing a new awareness of the pollution affecting the world's water supply, the deforestation of the rain forests, and to promote renewable energy sources to ease the strain on air pollution.

With the meal over, the music began, and Tara stepped out onto the dance floor to share the first dance with her father. The gruff-looking gentleman had tears flowing down his cheeks now, his skin red with emotion.

Sean put his arm around Adriana and kissed her on the cheek. "I love you, Mrs. Wyatt," he said in a whisper.

She grinned and put her hand on his thigh. "I love you too, Mr. Villa."

He snorted a laugh at her joke. It caught him off guard. "You know," he said, "I think you and I should take a vacation."

"You mean a honeymoon? Because we haven't done that yet."

"Yeah, I know. I know. Sure, a honeymoon."

"Anywhere, in particular, you'd like to go?"

He glanced at Tommy, who was watching the dance as Alex took over. "As far away from him as possible."

Tommy caught the tail end of the comment and looked his way. "What's that?"

Sean shook his head, laughing. "Nothing, buddy. Nothing."

He turned back to Adriana. "Maybe we should go look for some art."

She grinned at the suggestion. "Yeah?"

He nodded. "Yeah, sure. Why not?"

AUTHOR'S NOTES

Well, it's that time again, my friends—the time where we distill what's real and what was a product of my overactive imagination.

This story required an exhaustive amount of research, more than any I've ever done on a book to date. I honestly have no idea how many hundreds of hours I spent studying and learning. Along the way, though, I enjoyed it thoroughly.

I hope you will, too, because you, dear reader, are worth it.

My resources for all the historical facts, religious customs, and beliefs come from a variety of sources.

The first and most important source is the people who've lived there. I spoke to dozens of experts and Indian nationals regarding Indian history, the Hindu religion, and the overall national culture. I have several friends I leaned on in this portion of the research because of all the religions I've studied, Hinduism was the one I knew the least about. It was a fascinating project that allowed me new insights into a belief system that was somewhat foreign to me before. I'd love to say thanks to my former students, Vinamra and Shailee for the great conversations we had while I was their high school counselor. Some of those talks really gave me some great insights into Indian culture and the memories of those discussions has stood the test of time. I believe they always will. I'd also like to thank John Dyer and his mum for helping me out along the way to make sure I kept all of the cultural and geographical references accurate.

Another resource I used was a variety of books. *A Brief History of India* by Judith Walsh was a terrific resource during the research phase of this story.

Of course, one resource everyone has readily available is the internet, but you have to be careful there. It's important to cross-reference what you learn from multiple online sources so that you get a clear and correct picture of things. One great example of this is in learning about the various deities in Hinduism. Depending on your search, you could end up with conflicting information about their godhead. So, whenever you're conducting your own online research into history, always double-check it with another source. And always dig beyond the first page of results.

Now, on to the story: what's real and what isn't.

In the prologue, the people were entirely fictional, as were the events regarding the snakes that attacked the men who were unlawfully trying to gain entrance into Vault B. To my knowledge, that incident did not happen.

Sree Padmanabhaswamy Temple and Vault B—the golden temple from the story—are real. You can visit this complex in Kerala. Vault B is also real and is the only vault out of the six in the temple that remains unopened. The estimated value of what might lie within has been tabbed at nearly one trillion American dollars, and the Indian government has already removed twenty-two billion dollars' worth of gold and jewels from the other vaults, an act that required the approval of the Supreme Court of India.

The curse regarding Vault B is also real, at least in concept. Whether the curse would actually come to fruition is something I leave to your imagination and musings. While there is no physical evidence regarding this warning, the oral tradition of it has survived for centuries.

As I mentioned in the story, the vault really is sealed from the inside, and engineers aren't sure what would be the best way to open it if that decision were permitted.

The Gada and the Trishula—these mystical weapons truly are part of Hindu lore and mythology. Vishnu and Shiva are often depicted with these objects, along with the others mentioned in the story. The legends surrounding the two weapons are as accurate as I could get them, along with a few additions from my imagination, of course.

The function of the weapons was entirely from my imagination. There is simply no way to know what they did or how they worked. These relics have never been found, to my knowledge.

In regard to the way the Trishula worked in the story—again, from my imagination—this actually comes with a peppering of fact. This is where my degree in psychology finally paid off. While the Trishula—real or not—has never been found, it is possible that a weapon could be designed to disrupt brain waves within a human. If the right frequencies were altered, the result truly would be any number of mental disorders taking shape in a short period of time. Consult the Defense Advanced Research Projects Agency for any real-world applications of human brain-wave disruption...or don't. I leave that to you.

It was a lot of fun to go back and read through some of my old books, get new information from the internet, and just relearn things about the human mind. I even dusted off the old *DSM-IV* (which has been replaced at least twice to my knowledge). For those who don't know, that's the *Diagnostic and Statistical Manual of Mental Disorders*, a very large book we referenced often in the mental health field.

Thankfully, a weapon that creates such a brain-wave disruption doesn't exist commercially, and hopefully it never will.

As for locations in the book, the fortress ruins in Bhangarh are real and can be visited today. The dig site I mentioned in the story was placed there by me and, as far as I know, there aren't any excavations being conducted at this time.

The village ruins of Kuldhara are very real as is the mystery concerning why the once-thriving population seemed to vanish, though many historians believe it was due to drought and climate change that occurred hundreds of years ago. The hauntings and ghost stories are also very real. I mean, I don't believe in ghosts, but they do conduct ghost tours and promote it as a haunted location. As far as there being paranormal activities in the area, I leave that to your own fancy.

The Hampi ruins are an extraordinary place. If you ever take a journey to India, that is one location I highly suggest giving a visit. The temple complexes are extensive and take up most of the valley. The cave temples, too, are real, and the one atop the mountain that is mentioned in the story is also a place you could visit—if you're not afraid of heights. The secondary room in this mountaintop temple is an actual location, though the ancient tomb in the middle of the floor is not, at least not as I described.

Mount Kailash and the Kailasa Temple are real places. While the mountain is situated along the border of Tibet and Nepal, the temple that honors the mountain is deep within Indian borders and exists as described. The engineering know-how and planning required to create such a temple, carved directly from the mountain itself, is absolutely staggering. The fact that anyone could have done that so long ago will remain one of the great mysteries, perhaps for all time.

The metal door and the tunnel leading to the Gada, as well as the statue of Vishnu within, were products of my imagination, though there actually are hundreds of tunnels and caves in and around the temple complex. Most of them have been closed off to the public, but there are three dozen or so that visitors can explore if so inclined.

The MSS—this really is the Chinese version of the American CIA and the British MI5.

So there you have it, the truth and fiction that came from my mind to create this story. There are, of course, several other little details that could be true or false. And it's important to understand that when dealing with any belief system, do your own research and come to your own conclusions. The last thing I would ever want to do is portray someone's religious beliefs in a bad light or relay incorrect information and suggest it's 100 percent true. I recommend talking to someone, reading, and learning on your own.

As a writer, my job is to entertain, so I make my own interpretations about some things from history and am always happy to jump to—sometimes far-fetched—conclusions. But those are the ones that are the most fun!

The last thing I'll say is that Sean's visit to a Hindu temple in Chattanooga during the festival of Diwali was based on my own experience. I went with a few Hindu friends to learn more about their beliefs and the religion in general.

It was a fascinating experience, and I'm grateful they took us in and treated us like family. The people were so gracious and welcoming, not to mention the phenomenal food they had for us after the services and rituals. Growing up in a Seventh-day Adventist school system, I visited many other churches, synagogues, and temples as part of experiential learning about other beliefs. The one I didn't get to visit was a Hindu temple, so I was glad I did it later on in life.

I hope you've enjoyed this glimpse into the mind of a madman with a laptop.

And don't worry, Sean and company will be back again soon to take on another adventure.

THANK YOU

As always, I want to say thank you for reading this story. I love creating stories that entertain people. It's truly the best job in the world for me. So, thank you again for spending your time with one of my stories. I appreciate it.

For more great stuff, exclusive content, and updates, visit ernestdempsey.net.

Ernest

OTHER BOOKS BY ERNEST DEMPSEY

Sean Wyatt Adventures:

The Secret of the Stones

The Cleric's Vault

The Last Chamber

The Grecian Manifesto

The Norse Directive

Game of Shadows

The Jerusalem Creed

The Samurai Cipher

The Cairo Vendetta

The Uluru Code

The Excalibur Key

The Denali Deception

The Sahara Legacy

The Fourth Prophecy

The Templar Curse

Adriana Villa Adventures:

War of Thieves Box Set

When Shadows Call

Shadows Rising

Shadow Hour

BONUS MATERIALS

One of the things I love about stories is feeling immersed in the settings. That can be a tricky thing to pull off with black words on a white background.

I got to thinking about it, though, and came up with the idea of sharing some authentic and delicious recipes from the regions mentioned in this book so that you, the reader, could dive a little deeper into the story. So, I've included links to some of the recipes I used during the production of this story. Just click on them and you'll find everything you need to reproduce some of the food from this adventure.

Maybe you can host a book club and serve some of these dishes as you discuss the story. Or perhaps you just want to try something new.

I hope you enjoy these meals as much as I have and that they enhance your experience of this story.

Dal Kachori: https://food.ndtv.com/recipe-dal-kachori-597178

Daal Makhani (One of my wife's favorites) https://www.purplecarrot.com/plant-based-recipes/indian-daal-makhani

Chana   Masala: https://www.purplecarrot.com/plant-based-recipes/chana-masala

Pumpkin   Matar: https://www.purplecarrot.com/plant-based-recipes/pumpkin-matar-with-coconut-yogurt-brown-basmati-rice

Sweet Potato Curry: https://www.purplecarrot.com/plant-based-recipes/sweet-potato-curry-with-spinach-and-wax-beans-naan-bread

Tikka   Masala: https://yupitsvegan.com/slow-cooker-tofu-tikka-masala/

For Mark Dawson, James Blatch, and John Dyer. Thanks for everything,
guys.

ACKNOWLEDGMENTS

As always, I would like to thank my terrific editors for their hard work. What they do makes my stories so much better for readers all over the world. Anne Storer and Jason Whited are the best editorial team a writer could hope for and I appreciate everything they do.

I also want to thank Elena at Li Graphics for her tremendous work on my book covers and for always overdelivering. Elena definitely rocks.

Another huge thank you goes out to John Dyer and his mum for helping me with this project. John's mother is from Kerala, where much of this story took place, and the two of them were integral in making sure I got the cultural and geographical references correct.

Last but not least, I need to thank all my wonderful fans and especially the advance reader team. Their feedback and reviews are always so helpful and I can't say enough good things about all of them.